DEAD
RECKONING

Craig Johnson

Jared Chaney

Jeff Chaney

DEAD RECKONING

JEFFERY L CHENEY
CRAIG J CHENEY
JARED L CHENEY

Tate Publishing & Enterprises

Dead Reckoning
Copyright © 2008 by Jeffery L. Cheney, Craig J. Cheney, and Jared L. Cheney. All rights reserved.

Published by Tate Publishing & Enterprises, LLC
127 E. Trade Center Terrace | Mustang, Oklahoma 73064 USA
1.888.361.9473 | www.tatepublishing.com

Tate Publishing is committed to excellence in the publishing industry. The company reflects the philosophy established by the founders, based on Psalms 68:11,
"The Lord gave the word and great was the company of those who published it."

Book design copyright © 2008 by Tate Publishing, LLC. All rights reserved.
Illustration and cover design by Mark McCormick
Interior design by Janae J. Glass

Published in the United States of America

ISBN: 978-1-60462-250-8
1. Action/Adventure   2. Science Fiction
08.02.15

To our mother, for a love of reading, and
to our father, for a love of learning.

TABLE OF CONTENTS

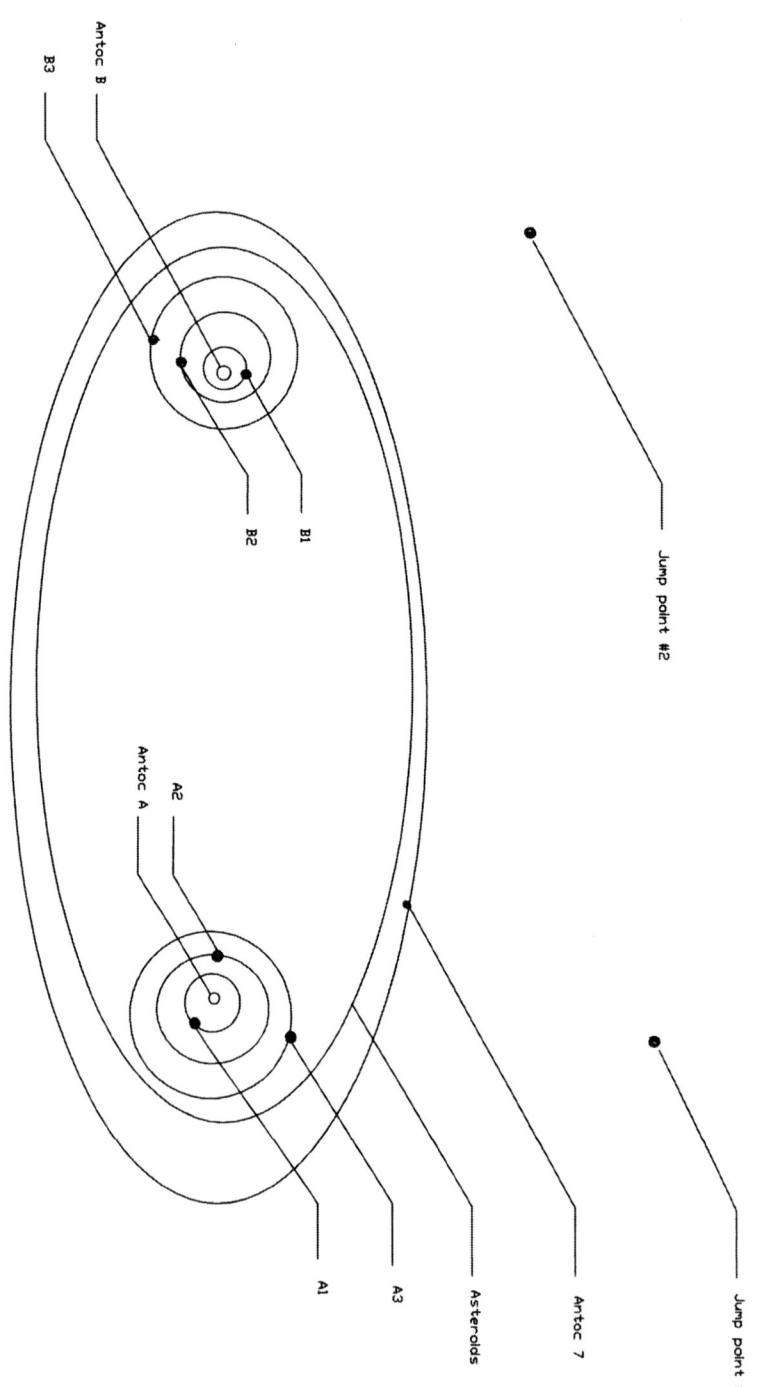

ANTOC SYSTEM

Jump point #2

Jump point #1

Antoc B

B3

B1

B2

Antoc A

A2

A1

A3

Asteroids

Antoc 7

PREFACE

Many historians are wont to point out Gerald Warner's dramatic address to the Families Ruling Council on 22 October, 2787 as the beginning of the Second Interstellar War. History texts never fail to quote him as saying, "I hereby declare that a state of war exists between the Warner Family and all other Families which will not support it in maintaining its guaranteed rights of life, liberty, and property. The Forrest and DaGama Families have violated those rights without provocation, and I will see them punished, so help me, God!"

Lost to most observers were the smaller actions that eventually triggered the grander themes we are all familiar with.

This work is the story of where things actually began, told in the words of those who were there. Admiral Brighton and Doctor Ward have both published their memoirs, and the author has drawn from them extensively, but not exclusively. Other witnesses have also left behind journals, media interviews, and official reports to further document what transpired. Some editing has been done to allow for a narrative flow, but this has been kept to a minimum and no actual facts have been distorted thereby.

The opposite viewpoint in this tale was not so well documented, and much of what is included in these sections are the extrapolation of known facts to cover what was not known, and cannot now be discovered. These items are told in a neutral voice to distinguish them from the accounts of the participants.

Without further delay, then, this is what happened.

PROLOGUE

Warner Family Head Office, Earth orbit

22 August, 2786

"Captain Vanderjagt is dead."

Admiral Conrad Cosina slapped a data folder down on the mahogany desk to punctuate the momentous statement. The tall, broad-shouldered admiral continued past the desk to stand before the floor-to-ceiling windows. He clasped his hands behind his back and stared out at the sharp points of light visible only from space. *Stars on Earth are fuzzy*, Cosina thought incongruously.

Of the four Families which claimed ownership of all extraterrestrial properties, only the Warner Family had made the move to locate their head offices away from the planet surface. The other three, along with the thirteen Families that owned nothing beyond Earth, worked from a position far below them.

The man behind the desk looked up sharply at the intrusion, but did not respond immediately. Gerald Warner headed the fourth largest corporate government on Earth, or off it, as the case was. He presided over more than seven billion citizens, negotiated trade agreements in the trillions on a weekly basis, and had organized the expansion of humanity to fifteen other worlds. It was his habit not to speak without thinking, and so he remained silent. His weathered hands opened the folio and he began absorbing the information within.

"Was it an accident?" he finally asked, his eyes never leaving the report.

"I don't know for certain yet," came the heated response, "but I doubt it. If I can find evidence it wasn't, someone is going to wish they had never been born."

"If it wasn't an accident, then we have bigger problems than avenging a murdered friend." The words were cold, but the look he gave the admiral when he turned was anything but. There was pain written in the CEO's face, pain and loss both. They could not overpower who and what he was, though. He was a Warner, and the Family came first, always.

"There's only one reason Chris would have become a target. If someone did arrange his accident, then the secret has gotten out somehow."

"I realize that, Gerry, but there's more." Cosina strode across the plush carpeting to the desk and lowered himself into one of the carved wooden chairs that sat facing it. "Chris and his security officer, Lt. Sepulveda, were coming to have a face-to-face meeting with me over a recent security issue. He wouldn't be more specific in his message. I think that someone on the project is feeding information to one of the other Families. That's the most likely conclusion given what has happened, anyway. If the leak figured out that someone was onto him, he could have gotten word out to his contact and arranged the 'accident.' Chris' shuttle was on final approach when there was a problem. The shuttle lost altitude too quickly, and crashed on the landing strip."

Warner took his eyes off the report finally and transferred them to his head of military research and development. "Vanderjagt's team has been sealed since the beginning, correct?"

"Yes. We have quietly shut down all requests to transfer out, and no one knew of Project Argo to ask to be transferred in. The information couldn't have gotten out that way. Outgoing communications from the team are all monitored. There's no traffic in the Minoa system. We've been careful, but obviously not careful enough."

Anger and self-recrimination filled Cosina for a moment. He quickly rejected the latter as illogical and unhelpful, while harnessing the former to drive him forward.

Cosina was a military officer, and he had seen more than his share of deaths. That this death hit very close to him personally did not keep him from being focused on his duty, and the objectives he was ordered to seek. This was not the first time that someone under his command had died, and he had learned that mourning could be postponed until immediate threats had been handled.

"What do you want me to do, Gerry?"

"I'll have Thom and his team investigate these deaths. I want you to let him work without looking over his shoulder. Agreed?"

"Yes, sir," he agreed with a casualness that implied to Gerry that he was still going to monitor the investigation, just not allow himself to be caught at it. That was enough for Warner, so he did not comment on what he knew he couldn't change. If the admiral was circumspect, he wouldn't be interfering, now would he?

"As for Project Argo, what would be the most logical response?"

"Turn the project over to Commander Teach, Chris' XO," he ticked items off on his fingers, obviously having outlined a proposal ahead of time. "Turn security over to Sgt. Aichele and add to his team. Shut Argo down until the leak can be found. Move operations to the back-up location."

"Conrad, this is your project and you can run it any way you want. I will not tell you what to do, but I will tell you that I don't want you to do any of those four things."

Cosina stiffened in his chair. "Why not, if I might ask?"

"Don't get your feathers ruffled, Conrad. I am not telling you that this was poor thinking on your part, because it wasn't. You are absolutely right, that is the most reasonable response to our current situation. That's why I want you to find a different response.

"There are several reasons that Chris might have been killed, if the secret is out. Because of his earlier message, covering up someone's identity or activities is the most likely. Still, it might have been done to try to set up a situation desirable to whoever is responsible. Our best response is going to be the one the other side didn't anticipate."

Cosina frowned, shuffling ideas around, testing their potential effectiveness in his mind. "All right," he finally said. "I'll have a new proposal for you tomorrow morning."

He rose and left quickly, his mind already forging a new list of things to do. He barely noticed Warner calling Thom Marshall to arrange a meeting.

CAPTAIN WILLIAM BRIGHTON

From his memoirs, "A Renewed Hope"

13–18 September

I stopped at the door and mentally went through my personal checklist. I straightened my grey uniform jacket and was caught momentarily off guard by the color. Even after ten months in command of the heavy cruiser CFS *Redoubt*, I would have been much more comfortable wearing my WSN uniform. In spite of the black and crimson piping that designated a Warner Space Navy officer posted to a ship within the Earth Forces Combined Fleet, the grey cloth seemed incongruous to me as I prepared to enter the office of Admiral Conrad Cosina, head of Research and Development for the Warner Space Navy. When my mental list was complete and everything was in order, I tucked my soft uniform cap under my belt and knocked twice, sharply, on the wooden doorframe.

"Come."

I quickly strode into the office and came to attention before the center of the desk and saluted. "Captain Brighton, reporting as ordered, sir."

Admiral Cosina looked up from the report he had been studying and crisply returned the salute. "Have a seat," he said indicating the chair to the left of the large desk. I sat rigidly on the front edge of the chair and waited for the man I had served with twice, and who had three years ago recommended me to the Board for promotion to captain.

"Thanks for coming in so quickly, William," Cosina said. "We need to pull you off *Redoubt*," he continued without any preamble. "A situation has arisen that will need your special talents. I need you to take command of *Pathfinder*. She is a prototype exploration/survey ship that is nearly ready to begin final testing. You will be taking over command from Edward Teach, who will stay on board as your executive officer. He has been Acting CO since the death of Captain Vanderjagt, three weeks ago."

I was astonished at this unexpected news. I had never heard of the Warner Navy pulling an officer out of the mandatory Combined Fleet duty for reassignment. "Admiral, I'm sure you realize that I have fourteen months left on my commitment to Combined Fleet. We will have a stiff penalty if you pull me out early," the statement came out before I could stop myself.

"Yes, the two officers have already received their orders," he said, as if complying with the 'two for one' provision of the Combined Fleet Charter was an inconsequential afterthought.

"I certainly would not want to second guess the Board, sir, but isn't this a lot of effort for something that could be accomplished much more simply? What about Commander Teach? Wasn't he in line for the command?" I asked. "He certainly has the seniority for it."

Cosina studied me a moment before answering. "Normally, yes," he said finally, "he would be in line for the slot, but there are some very special security conditions that call for us to stay away from 'normal' solutions. Therefore, we went completely outside the project for the new CO. Will there be a problem working with Teach?" he asked after a slight pause. "I would prefer not to move anyone out of the project until its completion, for security reasons again, but if leaving him in place after he has been in command will cause problems…"

"No sir, absolutely not. I have worked closely with him in the past, and I will have no problems working with Commander Teach."

"Good. Now let me outline Project Argo for you," he began. "The project is designed to create a ship that is capable of creating its own jump gate independent of any external jump gate generators. The implications are obvious to you, I'm sure. This is the first step in developing a true Jumpship, capable of jumping from any point to any other. Also, as a side benefit, any ship with this technology will be able to bypass the normal tariffs that are imposed at jump points. As near as we have been able to determine, no other Families have been able to duplicate our power system and the balancing needed to make the system work. That said, it appears that we may have a leak feeding this information to one of the other Families." He continued on that topic for some time, outlining what was known, along with his fears and suspicions.

"What we need from you are two things. First, we need you to carry the prototype through to production. Finish the testing, work out all the bugs. Second, we need you to plug the leak and make sure that it stays plugged. Can you do that, Captain?"

"Can I assume that I can count on whatever support I need?" I asked.

"Absolutely."

"Then I feel confident that I can accomplish both goals. I would like to request Major Sheli Chowdhury be assigned to replace the security commander that was lost. I understand that she is fairly senior to head up a security detachment that small, but there is no one better and certainly no one whom I would trust more."

"That can be arranged," Cosina replied after only a slight hesitation. "I should have thought of her myself after that Humboldt mess. You two have a fairly tight bond there. Anything else?"

"Not that comes immediately to mind, sir, but I'll notify you if that changes."

"Very well, I'll cut Major Chowdhury's orders this afternoon and the two of you can meet up with our courier at Hugo Station and head out to *Pathfinder*.

I could tell a dismissal when I heard one, so I rose to my feet and saluted.

Cosina returned the salute and I departed through the door and out into the corridor. Cosina could have selected any captain in the fleet for this assignment, yet he had singled me out. He had gone to great lengths to do so, and I determined then and there to prove that he had chosen the right man for the job.

I straightened at the knock on the door of the office I had appropriated for my use since arriving at Hugo Station in the Betre System. I had been engrossed in the schematics of the power system of my new command. This was my fifth command and I had developed a routine that I followed with any new vessel. I was working on the third step of that routine, which called for the memorization of all of the systems and sub-systems. This was done in the same way that all tasks should be done, thoroughly and methodically. Nothing was left out. Before I step on board a new command it is my duty to know more about the ship than any other single individual serving there.

I knew who must be at the door, and the proper appearance would be expected of me. I stood and crossed to the coat rack in the corner of the room and took my uniform tunic from the hanger, smiling to myself as the black tunic with crimson front and back panels now startled me as much as the CF gray had done earlier. I donned the jacket and finished buttoning the second row of buttons all the way to the shoulder before calling, "Enter."

The door opened quickly and a tall, muscular, dark-haired Marine officer entered crisply. She took two graceful steps to the front of my desk and gave a salute that would have been appropriate on any parade ground in the fleet academy. It struck me again that she always seemed to prowl rather than walk. "Major Chowdhury reporting for duty, sir."

"At ease, Major. Please sit," I said, motioning to the chair in front of the desk. This was the opening volley in an ongoing game that had developed in the seven years that we had known each other. I had purposely put her into a situation that she disliked, seating her with her back to the only door. I watched as she settled into a waiting game with me. Earlier that day, I had set her chair carefully so that it was a few centimeters from giving her a view of the door in the reflection from the glass of a picture behind my desk no matter how she moved. As she sat, I resumed my own seat and moved the printouts and data disks from the center of the desk into a stack at the left edge. As I looked across the now pristine desk at the officer in her Marine Dress Blacks, I realized that this had been a tactical error. I began the briefing, making no comment on the fact that the chair had somehow moved those few centimeters without the slightest sound while my head was turned. *She wins another round*, I thought. *But then, she always does.* Eight minutes had been my best effort, but that had been years ago, early in the game.

As was our custom, I made no mention of the game. "Welcome to Project Argo, Major. I know that you have had very little information on what you are stepping into, so I will give you a rough outline. *Pathfinder* is the prototype ship designed as a testbed to prove that ships can create their own jump gates without the massive fixed generators that are currently necessary. As you can imagine, with any project this important, the security has been very tight. Up until a few weeks ago, it was believed that the security was unbroken, but Captain Vanderjagt was on his way to Earth with his security chief to discuss something that he had found when his shuttle was destroyed and they were killed. Security has almost certainly been compromised. I would like you to take over the remaining security detachment and unearth our mole. We have a shuttle set to depart at 0800 tomorrow morning. Here is everything that I have on the security arrangements and possible threats," I said, handing her the appropriate data folio. "Collect anything that you think you may need and meet me at docking bay six at 0745."

"Yes, sir," she said, collecting the folio. "And, by the way, sir, it's good to see you again." She gave me a mocking bow and a slight grin lit her dusky face as she turned to go.

"And you as well," I murmured. I was certain *I* had the right woman for the job.

The three day trip out to *Pathfinder* was uneventful. Sheli had ample time to study the folio I had given her. The lack of any windows or viewports in the courier shuttle gave her little opportunity for anything else. She recognized my need to concentrate as I studied datafolios. She knew from past experience that I would be useless until I had completed these self-imposed tasks, and did not seek to interrupt. We spent some time at meals discussing possible scenarios and strategies we might employ. The courier crew left us completely to ourselves.

"Docking in thirty minutes," the annunciator called. These were the first words we had heard from the crew in two days. The courier crew handled the connection with the ease of a crew long used to ship-to-ship docking. Within minutes of the appointed time, the hatch opened and Major Chowdhury and I made our way through the hard passageway and into *Pathfinder*.

Considering the welcome I had anticipated, the scene before me was far from ideal. The crew was not lined up at attention with shining faces showing eager anticipation of their first glimpse of their new commanding officer. In fact, Commander Teach and Lt. Commander Leung would have been the sum total of the greeting party, if the shocked looks on their faces did not make it clear that they were not there to welcome anyone.

Anger boiled inside me at this unprofessionalism. "Attention to orders," I bellowed. Those crewmen who were just beginning to relax came immediately back to attention. "By order of the Department of Human Resources for the Warner Board of Directors, I, William Brighton, do hereby assume command of the Armed Survey Ship *Pathfinder*, hull number WNC-628."

In the silence, I surveyed the assembled crew. *Pathfinder* was designed for a crew of eighty. Presently, there were only forty-six on board, apart from the two of us just arriving. Of those, there were only about fifteen in the boat bay. All of the faces showed various levels of surprise. Most were glancing toward Teach, as if waiting to follow his lead. Teach now had a look of consternation on his face.

"We were not expecting a new commanding officer, sir," he said with only the slightest hint of emotion in his voice. "Am I to be relieved, then?"

"No, of course not, you will continue to serve as the Executive Officer," I said with pleasure, then, lowering my voice, I added, "It is great to see you again, Edward."

"And you as well," Teach mumbled.

"Would you care for a tour of the ship?" Commander Leung said into the ensuing silence.

"Not just yet," I replied, and moved toward the aft bulkhead. I felt the slight lurch that signaled the courier boat disengaging and moving off. When I reached the control panel mounted on the aft bulkhead, I reached up and pushed two buttons in quick succession. The second button started a strident, undulating, atonal siren. Chowdhury jumped slightly as if she had not expected the noise, a point for me in our game, but she immediately glanced at her chrono. Leung and Teach both stood rooted to the spot where they had stood. Leung seemed to recover first.

"What are you doing, Captain? That is the evacuation alarm," she shouted over the noise.

I said nothing, merely noting the time on my own chrono and settled in to wait. The assembled crewmen looked uncertainly from me to the engineer and then the XO. They were torn between the ingrained need to enter the lifeboats and their knowledge that I had manually set off the alarm and was making no move to evacuate the ship. Training won out in the end and they headed for the lifeboats at a run.

Thirty-five minutes later, I addressed the assembled officers and crew. "Twenty-seven minutes from alarm to completion is absolutely not acceptable. There is nowhere on this ship that is more than four minutes from this boat bay. That is the acceptable limit of time that I will allow you.

"There are many issues on this ship. All will benefit from proper discipline and training. I understand that many of you are new to your jobs and in some cases creating those jobs from scratch. That is no excuse for laxity. Laxity in space can get you and your shipmates killed. That is not an option!"

Turning to the communications officer in the front rank, I said, "Lt. Rex Jhonsruud, how often do you download message traffic from the beacon?"

"Every twelve hours, sir."

"And how long does it take you to decode and get that information to your commanding officer?"

"Well, sir, normally that can be accomplished in two hours but we have been running a heavy load, so the times vary."

"Tell me, if you can, what is the decode time limit on a Fleet Priority message?"

"Sir, by regulation a Fleet Priority message must be decoded and in the hands of the commander within fifteen minutes of receipt. All other traffic is bumped to the bottom of the queue and all available personnel are to be assigned to the decode," he answered as if reading from the pertinent regulation.

"Given those numbers, Lieutenant, can you explain why a Fleet Priority message that was sent to this ship thirty-four hours ago has still not been seen by her commander?"

"Sir, I have not seen any FPM's in our traffic."

"Then I suspect that one of three things has occurred. Either you are incompetent and did not recognize the priority when you saw it, you purposely deleted it from the queue when it arrived, or you were too lazy to check the downloads as they came in. Which is it, Lieutenant?"

The lieutenant wisely avoided the question which had no correct answer and simply said, "I have not found any FPM's in our traffic. If I had, I would certainly have alerted Capt...er...Commander Teach."

"We shall see, Lieutenant," I said in a quiet voice, then raising the volume called, "Sergeant Aichele," turning to address the Marine in his jet black class B uniform. "Why was there no security team in the boat bay while the courier boat was unloading passengers?" The Marine turned red under the scrutiny. "This is a flagrant violation of SOP. Major Chowdhury, I am extremely disappointed in the readiness of your section." Aichele turned his attention to his new superior and any flush on his cheeks was replaced by a ghostly pallor as he took in her expression.

"No excuse, sir. It won't happen again, sir," she responded, never taking her eyes from her team.

"Very well." I knew without doubt that it would not.

"I expect nothing short of perfection from this crew. Don't disappoint me."

I waited several seconds for these words to sink in. "Dismissed," I called finally and strode out of the boat bay amid the silence.

From his personal journal

19 September

The orders I had received from my direct superior were explicit in requiring me to be inventive in reaching the company's objectives. That left me with a great deal of latitude in how I went about it. Most times it is much easier meeting stringent guidelines than finding a solution without any boundaries. Still, it was what it was, and I was determined that I would not only succeed, but do so in a way that no one could anticipate. Well, no one was likely to expect me to move ahead with phase three while phase two was less than halfway to completion.

That was the reason that I was walking down the metallic corridors of the Warner Naval Academy at 0015 hours. It had been a short jump to the school in high Earth orbit, and no one but the duty officer knew of my arrival. That was about to change.

I knocked solidly on the door marked, 'VAdm Franks, C. W., Commandant,' and waited for a response.

"Well, I'll be…" she said, abruptly changing gears from the scolding she had prepared for the cadet that didn't know better than to wake the old lady.

"Not exactly the response I was going for, Commandant, but I guess it will do," I rejoined.

"I apologize, Admiral, I meant no offense, I just didn't expect…" Charlotte said, trying to adjust her mind to where this might be headed. She had never worked directly with me, though of course we had met a number of times.

"Actually, Commandant, that is exactly why I am here. Do you mind if we speak inside?" I asked. I could see that she had not yet retired for the evening, as I had expected.

"Certainly, Admiral. Please come in."

Once we were seated, I got right to the point. "There are two things that I need to ask of you, both quite possibly are equally important to the future of the Warner Family," I said quickly.

"You will have my full support with anything I can be of help with, of course," Charlotte replied. Again, I had expected this response. I don't like dealing with unknown quantities, and I had scrutinized her record before deciding to proceed.

"First, there is a project we have been working on for quite some time. We are going to require some talented junior officers soon. What I want to do is screen for your five top graduates both from this semester and the next. Obviously, GPA and duty fitness exams will account for a lot of our evaluation, but I want you to interview each one on three separate occasions, with different officers in attendance each time, to make sure this is someone we want involved in a critical project. You may allow the students to know that there is a special posting to which the five best will go if you think it will help you," I allowed, "but no other information about the project may be given."

"That shouldn't be too hard, Admiral, we have a pretty fine crop of graduates this year," she said while taking some quick notes, "I will need some of the specifics sent to me on any special talents or criteria we are looking for, though."

"No," I said flatly. She stopped writing and stared at me. "When I said no information that was exactly what I meant. I want the ten graduating ensigns most fit for any type of duty from the next two classes, based on your assessment. I cannot allow any information about this project to become known, even that which might be inferred from my requirements."

"I understand, Admiral," she said courteously, though she clearly didn't.

"Thank you, Commandant. I also have another mission for you personally. I would like you to be my contact officer for another special project. It would mean you would be in communication exclusively with me and Gerry Warner about it, and no one else. I trust you will have a lot of questions, but I have to ask you to hold them until I have made security arrangements. Can I count on your absolute discretion?" I raised my eyebrow to indicate the question needed to be answered.

"Of course, Admiral. If almost twenty years of combat operations taught me anything, it taught me patience. I can wait until you are ready to ask the hundreds of questions on my mind," she responded with a small smile.

"Thank you, Commandant. I'll let you get some sleep now," I said, rising. I had a calm feeling as the interview concluded that I had selected the right person for this job.

The next morning, I entered the familiar office of Gerry Warner. He motioned me to take a seat as he finished a vocom call. I chose my accustomed wooden chair in the center of the semicircle of chairs facing the large antique desk.

"Okay, so what's your plan, Conrad," he said simply, standing and stretching. I didn't take it as a sign of unconcern, but a sign of comfort in working with me that he could be less formal than he was with other subordinates.

"Gerry, I think it's time we hedge our bets," I answered simply.

Warner gave me a patient look, waiting for the rest of the explanation. When I remained silent he asked, "Is there more to this plan, or is that all I get?"

"For now, Gerry, I'd like to keep the details where I know they can't be leaked." I tapped my temple to indicate my secure data storage arrangements. "I want to have complete autonomy to make it work. I don't want anyone to know what I am up to, so I will be working this from the front, if that is all right with you."

"All right," he agreed much more readily than I expected. "I assume that your idea is sufficiently outside the proverbial box that no one else would think of it?" Warner asked.

"I don't know, but I don't think so. I am going to go on a goodwill tour of some facilities and ships. I will be out of the Sol system for most of the next eighteen months," I said, smiling.

Gerry Warner looked at me for a while before responding. "You got me. I don't think that I expected that. If you can turn that into hedging our bet on the Argo project, I am all for it. We have too much tied up in this not to take every chance at success. If this project fails, we will have ten, maybe fifteen years before the Family is taken over by one of our competitors. Make it happen, and let me know personally if there is anything else you need. How are you handling communications, by the way?"

"I don't want anything coming directly here. I will be in contact with an officer in this system that no one would expect, and you will be receiving an increased number of personal letters from your niece containing a datachip. Standard Cosina encryption, your eyes only," I said, smiling at our private joke about 'your eyes only,' since standard Cosina encryption had an ocular biometric algorithm that would only decrypt for Gerry Warner's or my retinal eye scan. "I will leave in the morning."

"Good luck Conrad, and good hunting," Gerry said as I stood.

MAJOR SHELI CHOWDHURY

From her journal

5 October

It has been said that a Marine's life is composed of long hours of boredom followed immediately by moments of sheer terror. Lately my life had taken on too much of the boredom and not nearly enough of the terror. I knew myself well enough to know that I lived for the excitement. I had hoped that this assignment would have some stimulating elements involved. I knew that there was a leak on the ship or in the program support staff and I suspected that they had already killed once. I was intrigued by Captain's offer to find the mole. There wasn't much that would make me give up my position as commander of Gamma Company of the Elite Corps Marines. EC command had been my goal since early in my career. It had not been easy to walk away with the drop commandos halfway through their incursion training, but a personal request from Captain William Brighton had drawn me back into Fleet Security. Any request from Brighton would always receive the same response from me. I owe that man.

When I met Captain at the transfer station he had briefed me on the situation and his suspicions. Currently, there seemed to be more suspicions than hard facts. I had been aboard for two weeks now, and was pretty sure that I had isolated the leak, information-wise at least. Having set up over a dozen different information screens and computer algorithms monitoring all traffic, as well as intra-ship communication. One of the privileges afforded to a Marine Elite Corps Major, who happened to be the security officer of a top secret project ship, was that I had access to just about every byte of data that moved around on *Pathfinder*. Now, it was time to track it back to a person. I continued to review logs and visual sensor data when there was a knock on the door. I grabbed my uniform tunic from the hook behind my desk and slid it on.

The WSMC uniform was a thing of beauty that emanated the deadly violence Marines were known for. Jet black with slashes of crimson across the chest and back and the blood stripes down the left leg to remind an officer that their blood was for the Corps to spend if need be. Rank insignias on both sides of the collar in gold or silver, depending on the rank.

Usually, in a combat unit, the right shoulder would have the tabs of the unit insignia in the same crimson red. This tab was to remind the Marine that the unit came before self, that your blood was your unit's blood, and that the units' collective blood was the Corps'. A Marine in fleet security had no insignia, to remind them that everyone else came first in every situation. Marines take security very seriously, as there is no other security on any Warner Space Naval vessel. It was a uniform designed to impress and intimidate. As a member of the WSM Elite Corp, my right shoulder tab held a gold sunburst with crimson chasing. The Elite Corps was the best of the best. The regular corps had a standing joke about the EC. The joke went that the sunburst chased with crimson was a warning to those around an EC. Mess with this Marine, and the middle of a supernova was a better place to hang out. From the EC's perspective the best part was that it wasn't a joke.

I straightened my tunic and added my best 'security officer' scowl and opened the door ready to intimidate. Lt. Commander Leung recoiled slightly as the door slid open so either the uniform or the scowl was working. She looked slightly nervous.

"Er, … I found this while going through some logs," Leung said handing a datachip to me. I sat down in my desk chair.

I said nothing as I loaded the chip and pulled the diagnostic up on my vid screen. I never took my eyes off of Leung, but Leung was focused on what was coming up on the screen, for all outward appearances agitated and probably a little afraid. It must be the scowl, I decided.

"See, here, this string, that is non-Warner encryption. I ran it against my engineering database to see if it recognized the family string of the algorithm base. It didn't. That means it isn't one of the friendly Families either, meaning there is no single commissioned piece of equipment on *Pathfinder* that should be capable of producing it."

"I am aware of the significance of this, Lt. Commander. You were right to bring this to me," I said absently as I looked more closely at it and focused a little less on Leung. What I didn't say was that I had just seen this encryption pattern. This was a different message than the others, though, and maybe there would be more clues as to the identity of the leak. "Who else have you spoken with about this," I asked curtly. *No sense in relying too heavily on the scowl*, I thought.

"No one. When I saw it, I backed out of the diagnostic and sealed it off so that no one else who came across it would see any trace of its discovery, and I came straight to you. I had my standard security training about a year ago at the beginning of this project, and that was as close to protocol as I could remember," Leung responded absently as she stared intently at the vid screen data load. Leung was now following multiple strands of code on the screen.

"There!" Leung yelled pointing to a small section of log string. "That's an emanation code from a relay switch. That encrypted message must have gone from there."

"Indeed," I said as I saw the case about to break. Leung had turned quickly to look at me. I was busy pulling up vid files and calling up other sub-routines to search security footage around the access areas at an interval around the timestamp.

Got you, I thought. Leung jumped. Maybe I said it out loud. I stood and grabbed her arm.

"You will wait right here. Do not attempt to com anyone or to leave. I will be back presently. If all goes well, I will make sure that Captain Brighton knows that it was you who helped me find a leak in *Pathfinder*'s security. Sit down, get comfortable, have a drink, I don't care, but don't leave this room. Is that clear, Lt. Commander Leung?"

"Well…yes Major, but I don't think it is necessary to—"

"I do," I cut her off quietly but firmly.

"Yes, Major. I will be here waiting for you," Leung said, sitting down in the chair at the vid screen.

"Good," I said as I quickly keyed in codes that blanked the screen, activated the security monitoring of the office and dumped everything to the datachip that Leung had brought with her. I pulled the chip and went out the door.

———————————

"You rang, Major?" Aichele said quietly as he and Jill Burton came around the corner to meet me in the hallway outside the bridge. I nodded at them and was happy to see both already had weapons drawn and formed up on the door.

"Yeah, Gunny, I did. There's an LT sitting at Com in here that has been leaking info to one of the other Families," I said, jerking my thumb over my shoulder to indicate the bridge door. "I talked to the captain to tell him we were arresting one of his officers. Captain just went on the bridge, so he's keeping an eye on him for us. Let's move."

We went through the door quickly and smoothly. Training took over and I noticed every single person on the bridge as I quickly inventoried, threat-assessed, and dismissed them all. Eric Aichele moved around the far left side of the bridge while Burton moved quickly down the right side. Both of them swept the bridge with weapons as they moved into position. I had my sidearm out, but not raised. "Lt. Rex Jhonsruud," I said loud enough that the noise of the bridge evaporated, "you are under arrest for suspicion of treason to the Warner Family Space Navy. Stand and place your hands behind your head. Everyone else, sit down at your duty stations until we finish here."

Lt. Jhonsruud went white in his seat and he started to stammer that he was outraged. He looked to the captain and to Commander Teach, where he saw no sympathy. Teach did sound upset, though, but I couldn't spare him a glance. He had stood when we entered the bridge and was apparently angry at our presence. I motioned with my weapon that Rex had better stand up. He did, slowly bringing his hands up behind his head. I moved in to place wrist locks on him, holstering my sidearm as I went behind him while pulling the wrist locks out.

All of the sudden, Jhonsruud spun and lashed out at me. Rex was a big man, young and strong. However, he was far from the fastest man that I had ever dealt with. As quickly as he had spun on me, it wasn't quickly enough. I grabbed his leading hand and twisted it as I pulled him to the ground. He found himself on the floor with a dislocated shoulder for his efforts. His scream of pain was chilling to those on the bridge.

Burton and I escorted him out, an arm locked under each shoulder as his wrists were bound behind his back. His left shoulder, the side I chose, was out of its socket and looked grotesque as Aichele followed us off the bridge.

"Captain, was this necessary?" Teach hissed under his breath to Brighton as the doors closed behind us.

LIEUTENANT COMMANDER
KATHERINE LEUNG

From her personal journal

2 November

I was pleased with how my luck was running lately.

I knew that Brighton was trying to find someone disloyal as soon as he arrived. Why else would you bring an Elite Corps major to head such a small security force? Nervous did not begin to cover my feelings. Major Chowdhury could intimidate granite.

I immediately set to work triple-checking logs to be sure my own activities would remain a secret. Imagine how lucky I felt when I discovered proof that there was *another* leak on board. Now Brighton and Chowdhury trusted me completely.

I sat and pretended to listen to Commander Teach vent about Captain Brighton and his Marines taking over the ship. The time since the arrest of Lt. Jhonsruud had been tense. Captain Brighton had ordered all crew and officers to either be in one of three places until further notice: their quarters, their duty station or the commissary. This had been understandable to most, but the restriction had gone on almost a month now, and it was starting to grate on a lot of nerves. This was my second bit of good fortune.

Teach was down in Engineering, supposedly looking over schematics and test data. This was the third time in as many days that he had complained to me on the same subject. I had spent much time and effort to have him see me as an understanding commiserate. He was frustrated and felt betrayed by Captain Brighton. The time was right, I judged.

"Commander, what if there was a way to take the ship back? Would you want to know about it?" Leung asked quietly.

"What do you mean?" Teach said quickly, looking alarmed.

"I was just saying, hypothetically, if there were a way out from under their improper regime, would you want to know about it," I answered quickly, hoping I had not miscalculated.

Teach sat there looking distantly at the wall for a long while before turning back to me. "Yes, Katie, I would. Tell me what you were thinking."

I carefully laid out a version of my current plan, one that made it appear that Teach would be in charge, and claimed that I knew of a way to contact someone, not that I already had. No need to alarm him too much.

Teach took the bait. He wanted me to make sure there would be no trace, but make contact and find out what our options were.

"We will need Lamont," I said quickly when he made to stand up.

"Why?" Teach asked with suspicion in his face.

"We would need three bridge officers to override systems, if needed. Him specifically, because he is in agreement that this ship has gone beyond normal WSN protocol and is untenable in its current situation," I said quietly.

"You have thought a lot about this haven't you?" Teach queried.

"I think about a lot of things. I think we are in the right, though, and the rest of humanity, if maybe not the WSN, will agree with us in time," I responded, playing to his twisted sense of moral virtue. "I trust you, Edward, and will follow your lead, but I think we really should consider this option."

"All right. Let's wait until you have made contact, to see if it is possible, and then bring him in. No need to endanger ourselves needlessly if we can't make it happen," Teach said.

"Sounds like we have a plan, and Commander," I paused to emphasize my point, waiting until Teach had turned back to face me, "please, let's be very careful. Say what we will about Brighton and Chowdhury, they are still very astute." He grunted noncommittally and left the Engineering area. He had been right, though. I had thought a lot about this topic.

I really wished that it hadn't had to go this way. Captain Vanderjagt had been a good man to work for, easy-going and genial. If anyone was to blame for his death, it was the powers-that-were at Warner who had trapped me at my current grade. I pulled the well-worn letter from my tunic pocket and folded it open.

10 April, 2786

To: Lieutenant Commander Katherine Tyler Leung

From: Warner Human Resources-Naval Division

RE: Application For Command

Commander:

We appreciate your interest in the command positions that are currently available within the Warner Space Navy. Your efforts to advance yourself are commendable and an example to all of your fellow officers.

In response to your last request to the Board, it is with deepest regrets that I must inform you that we were unable to approve your request at this time.

It is our hope that you will continue to work for the good of the Navy as you strive for excellence in all that you do.

With regards,
William S. Remarr, Senior Resource VP
Warner / Gateways International

The letter itself was not so bad. The bad part was that it was exactly, word for word, the same as the last two times I had applied for open command slots. Nothing else could have made it so impersonally clear that Lt. Commander Katherine Tyler Leung had climbed as many corporate rungs as I was going to be allowed. So if I was going to advance now, it was not going to be by playing by the rules.

I had already been stationed here, and I knew the Argo Project was "not to be mentioned to anyone outside of the project." So if Warner would not promote me and give me a raise, I could find another way to make Warner pay.

A few discrete feelers while on liberty at Hugo Station had brought an enthusiastic response from the Forrest Family. They were willing to meet my price, but not for the engineering specs. They wanted the ship itself. Warner was already too near completion, they had argued. It would do them no good to come in second. I was willing to argue that point, but Forrest was the one willing to pay for my retirement, so I hadn't.

Stealing a ship is infinitely more complicated than stealing data, though. To be successful, I had to have accomplices. I had been able to pick my own engineering crew, and most were long time acquaintances. Those I had already carefully approached were willing to give me their loyalty in exchange for a piece of the very large pie. I thought that would be the case with all those of my department, with only a few I was not sure of.

The problem before had been co-opting officers. Now, luck had again intervened in my favor. It looked like that would no longer be a problem.

28 June, 2787

Something didn't feel right, but I couldn't put my finger on what it was. I had been lost in thought and something had jerked me back to the present. It was more of an impression than knowledge at that point, but I had learned to trust those feelings when they came. I ran the conversations back in my head.

Yes, that was it.

Loud voices continued to call out data on all sides as I re-ran the suspect calculations through my head. The information was flowing around the bridge in a seemingly random confusion. This was not the case. Each voice had its place. Raw data flowed to officers and technicians. Refined calculations flowing back to those who needed them. The bridge of an exploration ship has been described as orderly and frenetic at the same time. This is an apt description. Gravity readings, position reports, the locations of all the surrounding bodies and ships, all of this information needed to get quickly to those who required it. You soon learned to hear the things for which you were responsible and ignore the rest. I, however, as captain, needed to hear it all and file it away for future use or need. This was a talent that some were never able to master and they became buried in the inundation of data, or else relied on their officers to be correct every time.

This blind trust was not in my nature.

"Position report, Ms. Johnson," I said sharply, to cut through the general volume.

Fyonna Johnson snapped her head back to her console and away from the calculations that she had been running on a side panel. Her long black hair swung as her head spun. Johnson had been with me briefly on CFS *Redoubt* prior to my assignment to *Pathfinder* and I had been pleased to see her as my helm officer on Pathfinder when I arrived. She showed promise, and a posting to *Pathfinder* would look good when she next faced a promotion review board. She was calm and steady, qualities which were always essential on shakedown cruises.

"106.31, 88.067, 214.71, sir. Twenty minutes to jump point," she replied quickly and returned her attention to the helm controls.

"Astrogation, we received a course update from Fleet, did we not? What should our present position be?"

Lt. Neil Lamont jumped as if shocked, then whipped his head in my direction and rapidly began inputting the data into the console to recheck the calculations that he had just sent to helm control. He was the direct opposite of Lt. Johnson in most respects. Where she was calm and steady, he was mercurial and hot-tempered. His short, blond hair was as bristly as his personality. After a few moments, his head came up and he turned to report. "Our present position should be 106.31, 88.067, 214.746 relative to Betre, sir. We are coming in too shallow for our JP. New course coming to helm now, sir."

"Bring her back up, Ms. Johnson."

"Aye-aye, sir."

After she finished inputting the course change that Lt. Lamont had forwarded to her I said, "Please step over here with me, Mr. Lamont. You have the conn, Mr. Teach," I said to my first officer.

"Aye-aye, sir. I have the conn."

I wanted Lt. Lamont to come out into the corridor with me because, while everyone would know he was being reprimanded, it shouldn't take place for all to hear. Under normal circumstances, I would try to have this conversation in my office during non-watch hours but we would not be leaving the bridge for several hours and I did not want to leave this hanging for that long.

Tension crackled around the bridge. Watchfulness was evident on every face. Amid the bustle and hurry of the crew as they went about their various duties, there was an underlying current of unease. Of the twelve people stationed on the bridge during these special operations, all were intently studying their consoles or moving quickly about their duties. They were studiously avoiding eye contact with the astrogation officer as he moved out the bridge door with me.

"Explain yourself," I said quietly. I have found that officers tend to be much harder on themselves than I have ever had the heart to be. Short, terse commands often bring out self recriminations more quickly than reprimands. Chastisement tends to bring out defensiveness instead.

While that was true, the scolding could not be omitted. I still had a duty to the ship and to the crew to ensure that they were protected from harm.

"I am sorry, sir. The data in the astrogation computer was never updated with the recent download information. It could be a computer error, or the astrogation tech might have mis-keyed the data. I should have double checked everyone's data but I took for granted that they knew their job," he responded. He stood precisely stiff and formal with just a hint of defiance in his face and tone. His hands were clenched and there was anger evident on his face. Clearly, he was defensive about any possible blemish on his professional standing. I stood looking at him for several moments, trying to decide how much further to push this issue. As Captain, I could not allow his insolence towards me and still maintain the respect of the remainder of the crew. However, at some point, the correction would no longer have a positive effect. I finally concluded that he was too near a breaking point and would not tolerate much more. Further correction would bring out comments that his career would not survive. As Captain, it was equally my obligation to protect him from himself, and not put him in a position where those comments were likely to come out of his mouth.

My largest dilemma was that I also had a responsibility to the ship and to the crew to ensure that they were protected from harm. My accountability to the ship as a whole outweighed my responsibility to any one individual.

"That is not acceptable. I know that you are capable of much better. This course update was your responsibility, no one else's. You spend too much time finding blame in others and not nearly enough time ensuring that your own work is up to standards," I said sharply. "You will review all course corrections and changes planned for the next six weeks of this test to ensure that the information has been updated correctly. And you will report your findings back to me by the end of your watch."

"Aye-aye, sir," he replied stiffly.

"Dismissed."

Reprimands are sometimes necessary. I know that intellectually, and it has been proven to me many times by my experiences. Exactness and precision are required in ship movements, and in crew interactions. Everyone must know their job and their role in the crew. These were the thoughts that were going through my mind as I watched Neil Lamont, move quickly back to his station. His anger and embarrassment were evident in the tension and rigidity of his back. The rest of the bridge crew maintained their watchfulness, and pointedly did not look at him. They were embarrassed because of the lecture that they knew he had just received. I felt sorry for him, but I also knew that he would not allow *Pathfinder* to drift off course again. Corrections must be delivered with sharpness and sternness to impress on the receiver's mind the need for exactness.

Nothing else would let a ship like *Pathfinder* return home safely. Every crew member must know their job perfectly, and perform that job flawlessly.

There was no room for error.

It was the principle duty of all WSN captains to ensure that none of their crew would die from preventable errors. There was enough risk involved on this particular trip without introducing carelessness into the mix. Mr. Lamont would make sure that *Pathfinder* was where it was supposed to be from now on. Hopefully, this event would focus his energies on honing his skills in astrogation, so there would be no need to repeat it. Astrogation required effort and concentration.

My marks in astrogation at the Academy and a strong recommendation from my instructor had gotten me aboard *Courser* as then-Captain Cosina's astrogation officer. That single assignment really was the one that changed my career and put me on the track for my own command. That same experience working with the admiral also led to my command of *Pathfinder*. Admiral Cosina, himself, had pulled me from my command of a heavy cruiser in the Combined Fleet and assigned this ship to me following the death of her captain. He was very firm in the assertion that *Pathfinder* would need a skilled astrogator in command of her. I was pleased that he trusted my skills enough to select me. I was especially pleased once I became familiar with the nature of my new command.

Revolutionary steps forward in shipbuilding are not seen in every generation. The prototype that became *Pathfinder* was a true design revolution in many ways. Warner Gateways Inc. had made its early fortunes from proving and developing the previously theoretical links between star systems. These linked "jump points" had made colonization and exploitation of the stars possible and very profitable. These jump points were foci of gravitational anomalies, at which gates could be created.

Gates can be opened by powerful energy field generators located at the jump points. These jump gate generators, when linked with other gates in the network, allowed ships to move instantaneously from any one jump point to another which shared a gate-link, though not all jump points are linked to every other.

Pathfinder was the next logical step in the progression from static to dynamic access to those jump points. It would tap into the jump gate system without needing to be physically present at one of the jump points. It could create its own link from wherever it happened to be. Or, at least, that was the theory. The ship would use its own hull to create a powerful bubble of energy and thus become a jump point in its own right, as well as serving as the gate generator.

That step, however, was for the future. For today, our mission was to create a jump gate from the known coordinates of the Betre JP and jump to the Antoc JP. From there, we would perform additional surveying of the Antoc system and then jump back to Betre from the same JP. The other JP in the system did not have a link to Betre. While the Betre system jump points were long established and much used, the Antoc system had no jump gate generators installed.

Although a ship could enter a system that did not contain the massive generators to power the jump, they could not jump back out without constructing such a gate generator. These structures focus the energy to create the 'bubble' needed to twist space and propel the ship on to its destination. Each JP was physically linked to only a few exit JP's. The frequency of the 'bubble' was adjusted to match your desired exit point. If anything went wrong with our tests, we would be forced to either re-energize and activate the old single use gate that *Courser* had used to exit the system sixteen years ago, or else create a new gate generator from the prefabricated units in our storage hold.

This voyage would prove that a full-sized survey ship could routinely create a jump gate by using the new technology. Earlier testing had successfully proven the technology on smaller manned and unmanned ships, but *Pathfinder* was the culmination of the nine-year project.

The secondary objective of our mission would be to survey the Antoc system. *Pathfinder* was designed from the core out as a survey and exploration vessel. The Antoc system had been discovered and partially explored by then-Captain Cosina's expedition sixteen years previous, but had never had a follow-on expedition to do a more thorough exploration.

What no one else knew was that I had received orders for a tertiary mission. I was to investigate a terraforming crew working in the Antoc system that had been out of contact for the last year.

Having been a part of Admiral Cosina's earlier exploration, I knew many things about this area of space. This was probably an additional reason for selecting this particular system out of the many available choices. However, its selection also limited our options in many ways. Antoc JP1, which we would use to enter the system, only had three possible destinations. It linked to the Betre system, which was our starting point for this test, it linked to the Reston System, which was equally unexplored, and it linked to the Antoc JP2 at the far side of the system. While it was common for jump points within a system to be linked, it was not always the case.

JP1 did not have a full gate generator, but did have a small communications gate generator which would create a gate just large enough to send communications pods through. This gate had been added by the terraforming crew when they had arrived in Antoc space to begin their work.

I had been a junior officer with Captain Cosina aboard *Courser* during his now famous exploration cruise. I had learned more about astrogation and command in those two years than in my whole four years at the Academy. We had discovered nine new systems, documented eighteen jump points, and found sixteen planets and moons suitable for human life with very slight terraforming. Now, I would be given the opportunity to revisit at least one of those systems and complete the survey that we had started.

"Steady on course 39.699 by 57.469, sir. Speed 81.87 km/s. Two minutes to JP," Lt. Johnson said in crisp tones that hid her excitement.

"Power the jump cells, Ms. Leung."

"Aye-aye, sir," she replied, already busy sending the commands that would build a charge in the capacitors sufficient to power the jump engine.

The normal noise levels felt subdued as crew and officers alike seemed to hold their collective breath. This was not a controlled simulation under strict engineering oversight. This was a real-life test under very real conditions. The only other ship to attempt this self-powered jump had been *Pathfinder*'s own launch, *Vanguard*, sixteen months ago. While that had worked out successfully, *Pathfinder* was a much larger and much more complicated ship. There were so many more things that could go wrong. Plus, the energy required expanded geometrically with the size of the ship.

"Charge nominal in the capacitors, sir."

"JP in 30 seconds," intoned Helm, "20 seconds … 10 seconds … "

"Verify jump by computer control, Ms. Leung," I ordered.

"Confirmed. Jump tied to automatic clock." Lt. Johnson continued, "5, 4, 3, 2, 1. Jump point, sir."

The flash of light that was the normal accompaniment to any jump was the same for this self-powered transition, but nothing else was quite the same. There was nothing that I could point to and say, "That wasn't right," but there was a subtly different "feel" to the process.

"Astrogation, position report," I snapped. I sat waiting tensely with all of the rest of the officers and crew. If we were on target this should just be a matter of checking reference stars to verify position. If we were not on target, the process could take much, much longer.

"Antoc system, 815.5, 7514, on the plane, sir. Right on the numbers."

"First watch to stations. All others stand relieved," I said several hours later. "Set up a normal watch routine, Mr. Teach."

"Aye-aye, Captain."

"You have the watch," I said, officially turning over control of the ship to him. He acknowledged receipt.

The routine survey of the outer system near the jump point was really only beginning. We had days of tedious readings to keep us busy and everyone would need to keep their attention focused on the tasks that they were given. That was why we were divided into four watch sections for survey operations and each section stood a six hour watch. During maneuvering and other "action stations" we could expect all officers and crew to be at their stations, but those times were not the norm on a survey vessel. I had placed Lt. Lamont in first watch under Commander Teach to allow Eddie a better opportunity to keep an eye on him. The young officer had potential, but I was uneasy about his emotional make up. Eddie seemed to have a much better rapport with the astrogator, so I had assigned him to oversee his training and development. I had far too little patience to deal with him most of the time. I had assigned Tim O'Neill, the burley systems tech, to handle all astrogation duties that were necessary during my own third watch, to allow Lamont to be reassigned. I could trust Teach to handle any training issues that might arise, and to loyally represent me to his watch.

Loyalty is not something that comes along every day. That is what makes it so special. When it is accompanied by friendship that is developed over years of association, then it is doubly precious. Commander Edward Teach had been with me in different capacities for almost eighteen years. We started out as ensigns together on the *Hermes* in the Sol system, right after graduation from the WSN Academy. The *Hermes* was a rusting hulk of a system picket that rarely moved outside of Jupiter's orbit, but to us she had been a magnificent warship. Though we hadn't hit it off initially, we soon became fast friends. Captain Mallory had called us "Coal and Flame," like the characters on the holoprogram, because we were always together. I was tall with fiery red hair and Eddie was shorter with striking black hair, black eyes and was just starting his trademark bushy black beard. In the holodrama, Flame was the star and drove the duo in their adventures, but in our friendship, Eddie was always the adventurous one. I was always more intense, more driven. That time of my life was the stuff of dreams. I was finally out in space. I was an officer in the WSN. These had always been my aspirations, the focus of my life. These were the adventures that we had both awaited all of our lives.

Years later, after several separate postings, we were reunited in the Combined Fleet ship *Resolute*, which truly was the magnificent warship that we had believed *Hermes* to have been. Our friendship and camaraderie grew and developed, and Edward Teach became my best friend inside or out of the service. I was saddened two years later, when he was posted to *Invincible*, and we were separated again.

When I was directed to leave Combined Fleet and take this command, it was an added bonus to find that he was here already as Executive Officer.

As I looked at him sitting hunched over his console where he was backing up the young astrogation officer, I was pulled out of my reverie and back to the important events in the here and now. I was struck again by the feeling that there was something not quite right with our new AO. His academy transcript showed great potential, but also several incidents where he had let his temper get away from him. This was a character flaw that I happened to share with the lieutenant. So far, everything had checked out, but something was off with him. I had alerted Major Chowdhury, our security officer, to my suspicions. I was sure that if there was anything solid to these misgivings, either Eddie or Sheli could be trusted to bring it to my attention.

Apart from Lamont, busy with his penance, excitement was evident everywhere on the bridge. Officers who had been relieved of duty were remaining at their stations. They all seemed to want to share this moment and were not anxious to let it end. I started to make a comment to bring the people into line and push the stragglers out of the bridge area but I stopped myself. I had turned the watch over to Teach. He had control of the bridge. I would not usurp his authority.

It had been much the same when we had entered this system with Captain Cosina for the first time. We had all wanted to share the experience by being together as much as possible. We didn't want to miss out on any single event. He had roared and chased us off of the bridge, but had never made a further issue of the fact that most had returned on one errand or another and simply stayed in the background.

I would leave it up to Edward. If he could stand to have them looking over his shoulder, I would not make an issue of it.

Teach watched me out of the corner of his eye, as I had not moved to leave with the other members of the bridge crew who were not part of first watch. I started to let him know that I would just be a few minutes longer, but I stopped myself. Captains should not get in the habit of explaining themselves to their officers or crew, or the crew began to believe that they had the right to receive that explanation, even when there was not time to give it.

The truth was, I wasn't sure that I knew what explanation I could give. I was more uneasy than I had ever been while in command of any vessel. Just as with the erroneous astrogation data earlier, I felt that something was wrong. In this instance, I could not review the data flow and isolate the problem. Yet it was still my duty to understand the nature of the quandary and find a solution.

Duty weighs heavily on the captain of any ship that is operating on its own, away from easy contact with higher authority. I had always dreamed of my own command, but I remember clearly that terrifying moment when I had realized that I was responsible for everything. Not only for everything that I did, but everything that anyone else did on my ship. It was now my duty to protect my crew from external threats and also to protect them from themselves. It could become a crushing weight if you didn't learn how to cope with it.

Each captain had to develop their own method of dealing with these stresses. This was my method. I stayed on the bridge when not on watch, and reviewed data. Whether that was done by mentally reviewing the events of the day or physically going through records didn't matter. Either method allowed me to relax and let my subconscious bring out the things that were bothering me. On this particular occasion, I decided that I needed to physically go through some records. I didn't know it at the time, but this was one of the most fateful decisions of my entire life.

I turned my attention to the astrogation logs that I had selected to review. They showed the astrogation data for the last ninety-six hours, since we had cruised out of Hugo station in the Betre system for this final phase of testing. They also contained the planned courses and adjustments for the next six weeks of our scheduled deployment. These were the same logs, in fact, that I had assigned Lt. Lamont to review and apprise me of his calculations. I could see him sitting at the AO console dutifully rerunning all of the assigned calculations. With a sigh, I began my own calculations to verify his work. As was my custom, when I was trying to take my mind off of other things, I did the calculations in my head.

Math always cleared my mind. There is a calming beauty to having only one correct answer instead of the myriad permutations available to any command decision.

Discrepancies were, of course, impossible in any course projection. The planned route was set up to enable us to use our available time optimally. The program had been reviewed and adjusted constantly up until our departure from Hugo, the final update was received only a few hours before our jump. I had reviewed that course in minute detail so often that I knew the numbers by heart. The program in front of me in the logs, however, was no longer the same. It did not include the information from the last three updates. It was a glaring omission. The route would appear the same to a cursory viewing, unless you knew those updates were supposed to be there.

I began to run back the entry codes. According to the codes, there had been no changes in the logs. I had personally reviewed these numbers as we moved away from our construction base twenty-three days ago, and I had monitored every update. Yet they were different now. They showed no evidence of having received those three previous downloads.

The communications logs showed the same gap, covering the same period of time. The very fact that two separate logs had missing data, indicated that the omission was intentional. Someone had tampered with our logs in the last fifteen hours and had managed to erase or bypass the code tags that would have shown that changes had been made. Our leak apparently had not been plugged after all.

There were only six people on the ship who had the knowledge and expertise to accomplish this. The first two were myself and Commander Teach. I knew that I had not done it and I trusted Eddie with my life. We had been together too long for him to be capable of such treachery. That left Commander Leung, Lts. Lamont and Johnson, and Major Chowdhury, the security officer. I had to trust Chowdhury. She was brought in after the fact in order to catch the informant. Lt. Johnson had helm and astrogation duties on her fourth watch, and while she was quite capable of the astrogation, I wasn't sure she had the requisite computer skills. It was best to include her until I could prove otherwise. Tim O'Neill held the astrogation duties on my third watch but while he was an expert with computer systems I did not think he had the mathematical expertise to make the adjustments.

As I contemplated these facts, I noticed that I had been so absorbed in the computations that I had missed the watch change. Eddie was gone from the bridge as well as his watch standers. In fact, it was now my own third watch. I had completely missed *two* watch changes. I was more engrossed in solving this mystery than I had realized.

Despite my lingering doubts about Lamont, there was no one in that group that I had found to be unreliable. Regardless of who the culprit turned out to be, it appeared to me that someone I trusted was not worthy of that trust. I could not account for the current state of the logs, and I again had that realization that, ultimately, I was responsible.

ANTOC SYSTEM
DAGAMA BASE

28 June

"Jump detected!" the shout rang out across the command center. Commander Palmira Agostinho practically flew through her office door into the room. She had mostly become accustomed to the very light gravity here, but excitement had gotten the better of her. "Report, Salomão," she called, weaving around workstations to approach the sensor station. The detection was not unanticipated, but given a nineteen-week window of when to expect this arrival, the waiting wore on the nerves. Especially when no one was sure they had guessed right about the system where this test would be made. Their source had stopped providing information before the shakedown location had been determined, but there was a short list of systems that could be used, and this one was the most isolated.

It was nice when the brains in the head office got one right.

"Nominal post-jump speed, about 81 kps. Exit angle matches a jump from Betre System. I think we've got our fish."

Agostinho grinned. "Well, let's see about reeling it in, then."

Lieutenant Vasconcellos came running in from the hangar, out of breath but still in respectable form. "Did I hear right? Fish on?"

"Fish on, Stephen," the commander confirmed. "Get your teams loaded up. Departure in twenty. Follow the plan, and bring us home a big prize!"

He gave his superior a slanted grin along with a lackadaisical salute. "Aye-aye, ma'am!" He didn't wait for the salute to be returned, too anxious to remember courtesy. His shouts to the boarding party could be heard diminishing as he headed back the way he had come. "All right, you apes! Time to earn our pay..."

"Tina," the commander said, turning to her operations officer, "scramble the on-deck teams and transfer our tactical data to the shuttles."

"Aye-aye, ma'am." The response was much sharper than the laid-back Marine lieutenant had managed. The sound of the claxon announced the completion of the instructions.

Agostinho seated herself calmly in the center of the flurry of activity *Pathfinder*'s arrival had created. It was an odd sensation that after so much time spent planning and waiting that when the moment arrived everyone was frantically busy except her. The only thing that she was directly responsible for now was more waiting, hopefully waiting for the success of her and Lt. Vasconcellos' planning.

The plan itself was simple in its design, as all good plans are. Always, the devil is in the details. The DaGama Family had known about Project Argo almost from the beginning. One of their corporate plants, Agostinho didn't know the man's name, had managed to get himself assigned to the secret venture early on. A high priority had been given to any information that would allow DaGama to take their first steps toward building an extraterrestrial presence. The four remaining Families who had first discovered the secrets of jump points: Warner, Sterling, Fermi, and Portales, had monopolized the opportunities these presented. DaGama, and a few others, were no longer content to pay the high tariffs to ship to these other markets. With the new technology they wouldn't have to; technology that had just come swimming into Agostinho's net.

The information the undercover agent had provided had been sufficient for DaGama Aerospacial to start their own development effort, but insufficient in technical details for any measurable accomplishment.

Eventually those in charge had decided that they needed more expertise in some areas than they had available in house. A joint venture was proposed, and accepted, with the Forrest Family, who had similar ambitions of expanding their influence. Among Forrest's diverse holdings was a very advanced jumpnet research and development team. Advanced, but still a decade behind where Warner had managed to progress.

So DaGama provided information gathered from Project Argo, and Forrest provided the experts to make use of that knowledge. The results? Not what either Family had hoped for. One test, forty-three deaths and the loss of the test ship.

It was at that point that clues crept into the working relationship which indicated that Forrest, now aware of Argo, had made their own contacts there. And worse, their contact was able to supply them with more technical detail than they were getting from DaGama. With their own source of information and most of the experts in that field of study, outside of Warner Gateways, the DaGama Family was smoothly moved out of the loop, evicted from the partnership they had created.

Well, no self-respecting DaGaman was going to let that stand unchallenged!

Before their source had stopped providing intel, they had learned that Warner had made a successful test of their system on a limited scale, and that they were approaching readiness for a full-scale test. It seemed, from subtle clues that Forrest had somehow arranged to take possession of the full-scale test ship after the system was proven. The general consensus on the DaGama board was that Forrest had co-opted the captain of the ship.

The operation that Agostinho was leading had been designed to cut themselves back into the picture. DaGama may or may not be able to reverse engineer a self-jump system, but if they were the ones with ownership of said system there was no way that Forrest could leave them out in the cold.

"*Oeiras* to Control, request clearance to depart," the annunciator broke into Agostinho's reverie.

"Clearance granted, *Oeiras*. Go scoop us up a fish."

28 June

"We can't do it that way, Neil. We've gone over this a hundred times. We can't kill anyone," Commander Teach said to the young astrogation officer. "We have to maintain the moral high ground."

As usual, I let Teach take the lead. He always seemed to have a better handle on the kid than I could ever hope for. Usually, I just wanted to beat the kid senseless and leave him in an alley somewhere, but we were far too committed to indulge myself that way.

It sure would be nice, though.

"We need to be sure that *he* can't stop us. Some of the crew will follow him. You've seen how some of them are with him. And Chowdhury scares me," Lamont said with a shiver. "If she thinks there is a chance to 'save' him she will move heaven and earth to do it. He needs to be beyond saving. All we need to do is make it look like an accident."

I shook my head. They had been having this same argument every day for the last three weeks. "Neil, we have made our plan. It is already in motion. We will have control of the ship the day after tomorrow. We set him down on A3 and that is the end of it. Most won't even know anything has happened."

"You don't really believe that, do you? He hardly ever leaves the bridge now, so the bridge crew will know. They won't keep it quiet unless they are all gone, too," he said with that condescending sneer that colored all of his interactions with others, officer or crew. *Sometimes, I really hate this snot*, I thought to myself.

I looked around Teach's quarters again as I silently counted to ten. I was struck once more by how empty it always looked. When I reached ten, I moved on to twenty. It didn't help. I still wanted to kill them both. Okay, maybe just hurt them some.

Teach and Lamont had just come off duty on the bridge and Lamont was all worked up about some imagined slight that he had gotten from the captain. "Just tell me that you got the communication logs cleared of those incoming transmissions," I said, trying to head off another tirade. "If Brighton or Chowdhury see those, we're done for."

Teach cut in, "I don't know why they had to risk another communication at this late date. They didn't actually change our meeting, or give us anything new."

I responded, "They just wanted reassurance that we were still on schedule, I think."

"Yeah, they're clear," Lamont said, answering the original question, then seemed to hesitate. He peered up with his face turned half away. "I'm not sure that they're completely clean, though," he added in a near mumble.

"What does that mean?" Teach exploded.

"He caught me with a course correction while I was trying to clean the log, and I had to dump the whole thing. It's gone but I don't know whether there are other traces." He sounded like a little kid trying to get his explanation out in a rush so that he could get it over with.

"For crying out loud, Neil, you said that you could pull this off without a trace."

"I sure didn't get any help from you up there, did I?" Lamont said, standing and leaning into Teach's glare. "You could have at least pulled his attention off of me for a few minutes. You know that those files can only be accessed from the bridge, so you also knew I had to be busy with them when *he* started shouting. This is just as much your fault as mine."

"*That is enough!*" I yelled, to head off the testosterone buildup I could see developing. "The walls aren't that thick here. Keep it down. Do you want Chowdhury down here to see what's going on?"

They both stopped in mid-yell and turned to look at me. They were both emotional and volatile. This was the reason that they had each been amenable to my plan. It also made them each a royal pain to work with. If I had my preference, I would have shoved them both out the airlock and moved on without a second thought, but I truly had no choice. I needed both of them to make this work.

It was fairly easy to motivate Teach with the promise of finally getting out from under Brighton's shadow, and the kid didn't need any extra motivation once he thought Brighton had demeaned him.

"That is enough," I repeated in a quieter tone. "Sit down, both of you, and let's figure out where to go from here. It doesn't matter how we got here, let's deal with it."

"We can't kill anyone. Nobody," Teach repeated, as if the last few minutes of conversation and confrontation had never taken place.

"That is a given," I said. "But Neil is right, too. We need to find a way to neutralize him."

"And we already know the best way to do that," Lamont said with determination as he stood and left the compartment.

I followed him to the door and turned back to Teach. "It looks like we're not going to get anything decided right now. I've got to check Engineering. Get some rest. We still have two days to figure things out. I'll see if I can talk to Neil after he cools off." With that, I turned and left also.

Once in my office in Engineering, I started checking logs. At least, that is what I intended to do. While Lamont was right, the logs could only be edited from the bridge, I had access to view them from my office. When I went to do that, the computer would not let me in. No denial, no message, just—no logs.

Brighton was on to us. He had to be. There was no other explanation for him locking me out of the system. I could probably expect a visit from Chowdhury any minute.

I knew what we had to do. I grabbed some of my engineering mates and headed back to Teach's compartment. My engineering crew was all in on our plan. They knew the score. That was one advantage of being the head of the department and able to screen and select my own crew.

I sent McIntire, Green, Trendle, and Morales to grab Sheli Chowdhury. Chowdhury was our security officer and she was extremely good at her job. Lamont was right to be scared of her. Truthfully, so was I. While not physically impressive at a slim 180 cm, she had a dominating, confident presence that radiated a lightly leashed menace. If anyone could disrupt our plan, she would. I began to wonder if four crewmen would be enough.

After warning Teach and leaving him two crewmen, we split up again. Teach headed to the bridge to take control there. I already had engineering under control so it was time to start rounding up those who were out of the loop. I sent Biltcliffe and Giannini to secure the aft weapons locker. Then I detailed Chin, Danis, Bezates and De Saumserez to start bringing all off-watch crew to the boat bay. Teach had said that he would take care of the forward weapons locker. Martin Terry I instructed to find Lamont and ask him to meet me in Engineering.

It wasn't supposed to go this way. The plan had been to neutralize Brighton quietly and then operate from a position of authority. Teach was second in command. If Brighton could not be found, the ship fell to Teach. But now we were scrambling. Brighton had the bridge. Teach would have to take control there by force. The cat would truly be out of the bag.

As I went, I was passed by three more of my engineering crew running by with pistols.

"Where are you going?" I yelled to Chandler.

"Chowdhury," was all she said, and she never stopped running. Neither did Young or Goesch. I wondered if she was running to help or running away. With Chowdhury involved, it could be either one.

What a mess, I thought.

Then it got worse.

I walked into Engineering, but Terry and Lamont were nowhere to be seen. *The ship is not that large*, I thought. It shouldn't have taken more than a few minutes to locate the wayward lieutenant and direct him here.

Then the floor shook, and I was thrown against the bulkhead. I shook away the cobwebs and instantly regretted my action. Pain flashed through my head and my hand came away bloody when I probed the source of the pain.

What a sorry mess.

That felt like the lifeboats launching. If Brighton was that far ahead of us, we were in serious trouble.

I went to Lamont's quarters to find him. No luck there. I kept moving forward along the starboard corridor until it branched back toward the central corridor to the bridge. I could hear a large party moving aft and Teach's voice could be heard shouting orders to all and sundry. I turned to follow the port corridor down the other side of the ship. Still no luck.

When he wasn't in Engineering, I had expected to see him in the middle of the action that he had been eagerly anticipating for so long, but the action had quieted and he still had not surfaced.

At the corridor junction, I ran into Terry, who admitted that he had not seen any trace of our missing lieutenant, either.

What a stinking, sorry mess.

As neither of us had checked the boat bay, we continued aft.

We entered to a strange scene. Teach was pacing back and forth in front of a large group that included all of the officers who were not a part of our cabal, except that skinny ensign, what's his name. Our five ensigns had only recently joined the ship's complement, and I still couldn't keep them straight. Teach was screaming and cursing and waving his pistol at everyone. Great.

I moved over behind him and tried to get his attention. He ignored everyone around him and, if anything, got more agitated. Finally, I told Terry and Danis to grab him and get the gun away from him. They did so and he immediately went back to his tirade as if he hadn't even noticed.

I took the gun and pocketed it. I detailed Terry and Chandler to watch him and I resumed my search for Lamont.

What a filthy, stinking, sorry mess.

I kept moving forward to the bridge. Lamont could be there inputting our new course. If Teach had Brighton under control, there was no sense continuing to move in the wrong direction.

The bridge was locked. I input my code and the doors opened. I re-locked it behind me and changed the codes. I didn't trust Teach to hold onto Brighton or any of the others, and for all I knew, Chowdhury could get loose and come for me.

I sat down at the helm amid flashing red lights. All of the panels were dead. I got up and went to the captain's chair and began to input the over-rides. Nothing changed. I was still locked out, even from here.

Another jolt to the ship caused me to stumble as I moved over to the communications console. A side screen came alive, showing *Vanguard* launching. *At least we still had some way to get him off of the ship*, I thought to myself.

Maybe Teach's codes would still work. Perhaps Brighton had still trusted him enough to leave his codes alone. Not likely, the way our luck was running. If not, we would need codes from Teach, Lamont, and me to be able to get past the lockout.

What a bloody, filthy, stinking, sorry mess.

28 June

When I realized that it was my watch, I took a careful survey of my surroundings. Elle Williams had the helm under the somewhat dubious guidance of Ensign Monica Samuels. While Ms. Samuels was technically "Officer of the Deck," I retained all control and was the only rated bridge officer on this watch. Ms. Samuels was learning quickly and would likely receive a favorable review at the conclusion of this deployment. While her conduct was not exemplary, it certainly was above standard. Seeing that everything was operating smoothly, I returned to my investigation.

I had concluded that there were only six people on the ship who had the knowledge and expertise to have modified the logs. Disabling the command privileges of the officers concerned only took a few moments. I moved to the astrogation console to take care of that task, and to continue my investigation. While I would never have suspected Edward Teach of any complicity in the falsifying of records, I was forced, by regulations, to disable his privileges also. Any other action would have been unthinkable. I would not circumvent regulations for friendship and Eddie would not expect me to do so.

With their codes locked out, those officers could still move freely through the ship and operate any equipment and have access to all areas, but the computer would no longer accept any changes from them, nor give them access to any programs or logs. This function was completely separate from the so called piracy protocols designed to protect the ship from outsiders. The code lockouts could only be put into place by the captain or the first officer by inputting the proper codes, while the piracy protocols could be executed by any officer from any of the bridge stations by pushing a single "capped" button after the system was activated. As I moved to the astrogation console, I uncapped that button and began to activate the system, just in case.

I doubted that I would need it, but with the evidence I was uncovering, it paid to give myself that option. I did not know who the guilty party or parties might be, or what their intentions were. Who knew what information the conspirators had been trying to hide? If they, whoever "they" were, had something planned, then it could hit at any time now that we had jumped into the Antoc system. And the most obvious thing that they would be planning was to help themselves to a now proven prototype ship. The potential rewards could be staggering. Any of the other spacegoing Families would pay handsomely for such a coup. It was even possible that one of the other Families would use the ship to begin their own reach into space. This was the eventuality that Admiral Cosina had warned me about when he gave me command of this ship. Major Chowdhury and I had tried to cover all of the possibilities that we could envision, but with the completion of the jump, most scenarios had changed.

The Families were something of a recent development in the history of the world. Wealth has always gone hand in hand with control in most political states. Sometimes the control is open and overt, as in most monarchies, and sometimes it is less evident but no less real. The history of the current Families Government has elements of both. Although they no longer operate from behind the scenes, that is how they began. The term 'Families' was something of a misnomer in that they were in fact corporations with little or no familial relationship to each other or to the other Family groups. The seventeen current Families control nearly 95 percent of the world's wealth, but they began as small, self-contained enclaves within the confines of established nations. After a century of competing with their mother countries, they organized a loose confederation called the Family Ruling Council. Dieter Rial, the first Chairman of the Family Ruling Council had been ruthless and tolerated no compromise with the other governments. Within a century, they were the de facto rulers of the world, accomplishing with money what no dictator had been able to accomplish by force of arms. Many territorial nations still existed, but they held only a shadow of their former prominence.

While the Warner Family is one of the four wealthiest families, it has exerted very little in the way of governing power within the Ruling Council, preferring to concentrate on economic and scientific expansion instead. The Warner, Portales, Sterling, and Fermi Families, in truth, controlled all of the planets outside of the Sol system. The Forrest, Norcross, DaGama and Seligman Families were making some headway into space but were forced to play catch up to those who were already established. If some of these Families could gain access to any JP without having to control the gateway system, they would be able to colonize at will and support those rogue colonies with ease.

If another Family was trying to jumpstart their own expansion capabilities, the addition of *Pathfinder* would be a monumental advancement to those ends.

Major Chowdhury and I had discussed the possibility of someone attempting to take *Pathfinder*. We had evaluated the existing protocols for their effectiveness in defending against emergencies such as this particular scenario.

It is also true that emergencies could happen on ships in space at any time. That is why there are plans in place to help us work through those situations and not be required to make all decisions cold. It is also why the piracy protocols were put into place. The Warner Family wanted to protect its shipping from pirates by making sure that there were fail-safes in place to disable the ship and thus deny the pirates of their prize. While they don't always work as planned, at least there is a plan in place.

For *Pathfinder*, the protocols were much more involved than they were on other ships. They disabled the astrogation computer, cut contact to engineering, severed power to the engines, and locked out all computer access to anyone without bridge officer's codes.

The purpose was to make the ship unmanageable to the pirates. They were supposed to move on to easier prey. This was sometimes hard on the crews who received the brunt of the frustrated pirates' attention, but the pirates soon learned to avoid Warner ships.

While viciousness had never really been a part of my nature, I felt that I needed to do something extra to protect my ship. The thought of criminals in control of *Pathfinder* nearly sent me into a rage. The conspirators, if they were indeed crew, might find a way to disable the piracy protocols and a backup would be necessary. The protocols could be disabled either by me or any combination of three bridge officers working together. I accessed the astrogation controls and added a personal lockout. This was keyed to my personal codes and only I could disable it. To that lockout, I added other measures.

First, I set the lifeboats to be ejected if the protocols were activated. These would be the only method that the conspirators would have to move large groups off of the ship. Next, I set the astrogation computer to overload and burn out if someone managed to regain computer control and tried to alter the course settings that were established in the memory lockout file. I slaved all of these precautions to the protocol button so that they would be activated automatically with the standard protocols. I could not do as good a job of disabling the ship as the protocols, but it would certainly fry the astrogation computer and sever all command functions.

I had barely finished double-checking my work when the bridge doors swung open and two crewmen jumped through holding pistols. I did not hesitate. I slapped the protocol button to my right and began the sequence that would set in motion the extra precautions. The Navy-designed piracy protocols performed as intended and the system went dead at my command. The bridge watch came out of their seats at the sudden intrusion. Then, my best friend came in behind Kasdorf and Morrison, holding a pistol and directing the actions of the crewmen.

Disbelief warred with fury and betrayal inside me and I fought to keep all three from my face. I stood by the chair I had just been occupying and his eyes turned to me. There was no friendship in them now. There was only anger and intensity.

"Everyone sit back down," he said, just as the ship was rocked by the small explosions that indicated that the lifeboats had ejected on schedule.

He stood there and looked at me. Indecision showed plainly on his face. He had not expected the explosions and was unsure both of their importance and what his response should be.

"I said to sit down, Captain," he repeated finally, and waved his gun at my watch crew. They all resumed their seats, but I could not bring myself to respond in any way to his orders. I just folded my arms across my chest and continued to try to figure a way out of this for myself and my crew. At this point, there was no way out of this for my friend.

"What was that noise?" he asked me as he moved over to stand in front of me. The intensity in his eyes was more pronounced up close. Equally noticeable was the smell of fear and desperation that surrounded him. My anger kept me from answering him. If I said the things that were in my mind at this point, it would provoke him into actions that could not be taken back. He was clearly on the edge.

Having received no answer from me, he turned to my bridge crew. "I am taking command of this ship. All officers and crew who wish to stay on the ship will be welcomed and receive the respect and treatment that they deserve. I will no longer allow the kind of abuse and harassment that has been the norm under the previous command," he said.

Anger welled up inside me at his words. Who was this person standing in front of me? It was evident that this was not my friend. Our friendship had been a sham, a charade. I saw the thrill in his face as he realized that he had wounded me deeply, and my hand struck out and attempted to remove the smugness from his face. He staggered back a step and I realized what I had done. I was risking the lives of all my crew for momentary satisfaction. I stepped back to the AO console. Maybe I could protect my crew by drawing the attention more fully to myself. Once I reached the chair I turned to the others on the bridge.

"Take no immediate action. Do as you're instructed. Loyal members of the crew will no doubt be here soon to collect these misguided lunatics," I said to the three watch standers at their controls. They seemed to relax as they received their instructions, but Teach seemed to swell with rage as I took an active role against him for the second time. I had pulled the command back from him and, as I had planned, refocused his attention on me. His next words clearly indicated that he had guessed my intentions.

"You are no longer in a position to give any orders on my bridge, Willy," he said, using the nickname that my mother had used.

"Ms. Williams, you will set a course to Antoc-A3," he said to the helmswoman. She never made any response. I had tried to shield her and the others, and she was bringing that attention back onto herself. Surely she could see how truly close to the edge he was. She was putting her life in danger for no reason. The controls were now locked and she would be unable to follow his order. The show of defiance was completely unnecessary.

"Did you hear the order, Ms. Williams?"

"I heard some noise come out of your mouth, but I haven't heard any orders. Orders come from the captain," she said, with more emotion than I would have guessed at.

I was watching Teach closely, so I saw him begin to swing his pistol around. I moved to grab him before he could fire. I hadn't realized that one of the crewmen with Teach had moved around behind me until I felt the butt of his pistol explode into the back of my head. It hadn't been hard enough to knock me down, but he immediately followed it up by grabbing and holding me. To my ultimate regret, I was disoriented enough that I never even thought to make a grab for his gun. I was more concerned with Ms. Williams and I forever missed my best opportunity to halt this takeover before it really got started. I turned to find that she had thrown herself out of her chair and away from the trajectory of the darts. Edward had not fired again, even though she lay on the deck beside her chair staring daggers at him.

Teach turned to the crewman holding me and said, "Take them down to the shuttle bay. Put the captain on one of the lifeboats and don't let him talk to anyone."

"Aye-aye, sir."

Major Sheli Chowdhury had been with me off and on for a number of years, and I knew her to be a competent and thorough security officer as well as a highly dangerous physical opponent.

The crew clearly shared my opinion of the physical danger that she represented to them. As I exited the bridge, I watched as she was marched out of the port corridor and down the central passageway in front of me. She had both hands manacled behind her back. Trendle and Green were behind her with drawn pistols trained on her head. As she went by me, I could see that her uniform was covered in blood. Her only injury seemed to be a small cut on her forehead that was bleeding. As neither of her guards was marked in any way, I assumed that they were not her original captors. I had yet to see the day when Sheli got the worst of any confrontation that she was involved in.

They were followed by Young and Chandler carrying the unconscious form of Jill Burton. I could see that she had been shot, but I could not tell if she was living or dead from the brief look I had. Beacham and Jenkins followed them with weapons drawn. Both were covered in blood. These five continued across the main walkway toward sickbay.

Similar scenes were repeated as far as I could see along the corridor, as crew and officers were being herded down to the boat bay.

Tense, angry crewmen were very much in evidence as we entered the boat bay. I was pushed in first, followed by Morrison, who had become my personal guard. I was moved over to the extreme right near lifeboat nine in the aft section of the bay. Morrison tried to undog the seal on the access hatch, intending to stow me inside, but found that it would not unseal. It was only then that he noticed the red light on the side panel indicating that the pod was no longer there.

The bay was noisy and all the rest of the crewmen and officers were moved to starboard, near the closed hatchway to lifeboat ten. They were being kept completely away from me. It seemed to be three separate groups arrayed for battle, one group at each point of a triangle. I stood in my corner, rebellious crew were close to the main corridor door blocking all three exits, and the rest of the crew in the opposite corner. I was surprised to see how small the group was near lifeboat ten. As I watched, Elle Williams moved from that group toward me. There were murmurs among the pirates, but no one moved to block her way. Drew Le Vesconte followed her after a slight hesitation. Both moved to stand next to me and glared at their captors.

As the doors opened again to admit Teach, the room quieted slightly in anticipation. He surveyed the bay and singled out Dr. Ward from the other group. Ward looked disoriented and stunned as he moved hesitantly to stand near Teach. Eddie said something to him that I could not hear. They stood and looked at each other and Ward clearly answered. Teach looked stunned, and barked some orders to Simon Chin and Ward was escorted out into the starboard corridor.

As the assistant medical officer was accompanied out of the bay, Teach seemed to collect himself and turned to address the larger group. As he did so, more crewmen and officers were pushed into the bay to join the huddled group, nearly doubling its size.

"Respect is a hard thing to earn," he said in a voice that barely reached to where I stood. "It is also impossible to live without. For the last nine months we have been working as slaves to the ambition of a heartless captain without any proper respect, recognition, or acknowledgement. That ends now!" He stood and surveyed the group as if waiting for applause. None arrived. Many of the members of the large group were looking at the three of us across the bay from them.

"Soon you will be called upon to make one of the most important decisions of your lives. Brighton will soon be sent down to a nearby planet. He will have food and water enough to support life. Those who will not acknowledge me as rightful captain of the *Pathfinder* are welcome to join him there. You can stay here and be free of the tyrant or you are welcome to share his meager existence. You must choose now. Those of you foolish enough to reject my generosity, please join him now. If you wish to take part in this venture as free men, stay where you are."

The officers and crew seemed unsure what to do. I found the officers within the crowd and watched them. They had obviously been caught off guard by the events of the morning and I would once have been confident in their decisions, but I still felt thrown off balance by the defection of my best friend. To hear the words that he had spoken to the group was even more stunning than the sight of him striding onto the bridge with a pistol. The vehemence and spite evident in every word was totally out of character with the man I thought I knew.

I was watching Lt. Johnson as her face went through the emotions from shock to determination. She seemed about to make a move when she was pre-empted by the bosun, Master Chief Derrick Mackey, who took two steps toward Teach and spat on the deck plates at his feet. He continued to stare at the traitor as he moved purposefully to join me. He stood in front of me and snapped a parade ground salute. Nearly two thirds of the remaining people, led by Lt. Fyonna Johnson and Major Chowdhury, quickly followed him to join us. Only nine people were left in front of Teach.

Ensign Stuart Omundson's face was a mask of indecision. He should have known where his duty lay, but he seemed unable to see it. I was disappointed.

Ensign Samuels looked pleadingly at me. She did not move. It seemed that she wanted to join us but she could not consciously choose to sentence herself to our fate. I knew that she would not have the strength to survive the ordeal to come. I looked into her eyes and nodded my agreement with her decision. She seemed to collapse into herself and cried. Amber Sullivan was sitting near her on the deck with her wide eyes darting back and forth, but she also made no move to join our group. Then, just as suddenly, Samuels was moving toward us. She grabbed Sullivan and pulled her to her feet. They had quick words and both moved to our group.

The seven who remained behind were Ensign Omundson, CWO2 Brooke Fields, WO Hilary Calvi, Asst. Quartermaster Timothy Crowson, Electronics Technician Mark Goodwin, and Crewmen Sheila Semrad and Nick McGough.

Teach sent those seven to their quarters, under guard. He then approached our group. "Each of you crewmen will be allowed to return to your quarters to grab clothing and whatever personal items that you cannot live without. You will be guarded at all times. If you come to regret your rash decision, simply inform your guards that you wish to stay and you will be allowed to remain in your quarters. All officers, security and bridge crew will remain in the boat bay."

My nine loyal technicians and crewmen departed, guarded by Trendle and Green.

Loyalty was something that I had always taken for granted among the crew. It was one of the things that I liked best about both the WSN and Combined Fleet. You always knew that you were a team that depended on each other to survive. Some were more worthy than others, but you could count on all to be loyal and follow the orders that they were given. That belief had been one of many to suffer abuse during the course of the last few hours. Honor was not the universal attribute that I had believed it to be.

I thought of the officers and crew who would follow me into exile, those who would put their lives on the line for their honor. In addition to myself there were Leonard Ward, the assistant medical officer who had just returned to the boat bay and joined our group with carry sacks and medical boxes hanging all over his body; Lt. Johnson, the tall, slim helm officer who had looked positively regal as she had led the group in joining me against the pirates; solid Derrick Mackey, the bosun, who never wavered in the performance of his duty and who now bore many marks and scrapes that showed that he had not come willingly to the boat bay; Elle Williams, who had risked her life to obstruct the traitor Teach, even though there had been no need to do so; Jens Fujinami, the exobotanist, whose small frame and endless curiosity obviously hid a brave and determined man; four of our five ensigns: Jordan Hayes, Jherri Roberts, Josiah Mitchell, and Monica Samuels, who had overcome her fear to do what she knew was right; Eric Aichele, one of the Marines assigned to *Pathfinder's* security force; Amber Sullivan, an electronics tech who seemed to have been led like a puppy into our group; Drew Le Vesconte, our quartermaster; Steve Long, an engineering Warrant Officer; Claire Paul, a survey specialist; Kara George, assistant quartermaster; Tim O'Neill, the control systems tech from my watch; Clémence Queneau, our cartographer; Kieran Delacoeur and Ricardo Smith, ship's cooks; and finally Roberto Alcaraz, crewman 1c completed the assembled group. These were the men and women who were willing to trust me with their lives.

Of the personnel that had come in and out of the boat bay, four were still unaccounted for: Glenn Morales, Lt. Lamont, Crewman Brandon and Dr. Johnson, whom I assumed had remained in the sickbay tending to Burton.

When everyone had returned to the boat bay, Teach began the unlock sequence on the nearest lifeboat. The hatch stayed closed, and the indicator stayed red. The lifeboat was gone. Not believing the evidence of his eyes, he had his toadies check each of the other lifeboats. All of the lifeboats in the bay were gone. This was one of the first items on my modified protocol menu.

His reaction was very surprising. He stood there and ranted and raved at his crew, at my group, and at me, specifically. At one point, he had to be physically restrained by the crewmen standing next to him. Katie Lueng had a haunted look on her face as she pocketed the pistol that her engineering crewmen had taken away from him before he could do further damage. I knew that I should feel sorry for her but I could not bring myself to. She was stuck on a ship with an unstable commander by her own choice, but my loyal crew and I were about to die, either by the hand of that madman or consigned to a slow starving death later on, through no choice of our own.

Teach finally seemed to regain some control and sent crewmen to the remaining lifeboats fore and aft to check their status. Surely he knew what they would find. He stood as still as a statue lost in his own thoughts. It should be obvious to him that the only way off of the ship would be to put us on *Vanguard*. I had personally disabled the eject command on the survey craft. I hadn't known that it would come down to this, but it seemed a wise precaution to not sever all chance of getting people off the ship in an emergency. *Vanguard* was capable of jumping home on its own and would be our only chance at salvation. It would give us options beyond Antoc.

Finally he started issuing orders.

"Bezates, Danis," he called. "Get into *Vanguard* and disable the long range transmitter. Jettison the communication pods and pull enough batteries to disable the jump engines."

Anger was still my overwhelming emotion, but for the first time I began to see hope. I tried to remain quiet and stoic to keep from provoking any other irrational responses from the crew. Teach was mumbling to himself and pacing back and forth near the doorway. I didn't let the fact that he had been disarmed lead me to a false sense of security. He was still just as dangerous to us as he was before. A single word from him could still send us out the airlock to our deaths. The crew would follow his commands and only later think things out and understand the enormity of their mistake. I did not think we would be in a position to appreciate their remorse at that point.

The crewmen assigned to disable *Vanguard* returned quickly. They did not carry any batteries or equipment, so I assumed that they had simply sent it all out the launch's starboard airlock. The crew was marched at gunpoint to the deck hatch and down the ladder that led to *Vanguard*'s port airlock. The gunmen soon returned for the officers and we were all secured behind the inner airlock door. Major Chowdhury spoke a few words to Aichele who was standing behind her and I saw the handcuff come loose on one wrist.

Teach stepped forward and offered one last time for anyone else to save themselves from the fate that awaited us.

"I need you to stay aboard. I'll be back for you," I said quietly to Samuels. Samuels stood and pulled Sullivan back out of the hatch without ever acknowledging my remark or looking back at her abandoned fellows. Aichele stood from his seat next to Chowdhury, and moved out of the hatch with his head down, as if in shame. I didn't know if sending Samuels out would be of any help in the long run, but at least I had saved two people from the ordeal to come. I vowed to come back for them if it took me the rest of my life to track them down.

Johnson yelled out derisively that Teach might as well shoot us now, if he was not going to provide some supplies. He rejected her entreaty.

Chowdhury complained that there was no protection from animals and no way to hunt without weapons. I could see her mind working, and I knew that she simply wanted a weapon to try to retake the ship. I was surprised when Teach had pistols brought. The gleam in Sheli's eyes had to be visible to all. I prepared to move to support her quickly if she were truly able to make an attempt. Teach took the pistols and turned to remove the power packs from the butts of each gun as he walked back down the corridor and then threw the pistols at the feet of the security officer where she stood just inside *Vanguard*'s inner hatch. Not having seen him remove the power packs, she made the attempt that I had been expecting only to realize that they were dead as Teach laughed uproariously in her face.

The hatch slid shut on all of us. He took the power packs from his tunic pocket where he had put them and tossed them on the floor near the inner hatch and closed the outer hatch.

We were truly exiled from our ship. It was barely morning, 28 June, 2787. It was the worst day of my life.

I had lost my best friend and I had lost my ship.

LIEUTENANT LEONARD WARD, M. D.

From his memoirs, "There and Back Again"

28–29 June

I was awakened from a deep sleep, after a long rotation in the medical bay, rather abruptly. I was not very lucid at the time, and it took me a moment to register that there were two men standing over me who were trying to rouse me. Apparently, my continued slumber caused them some consternation, for one of them proceeded to fling me bodily out of bed. In fact, I believe he threw the whole bed with me in it, for when I came to myself I could see that it too was upside down and out of place.

I certainly was not used to being handled in this fashion, and came immediately to my feet to demand what they thought they were doing, treating me in this manner. I could see that my protestations caused them some degree of amusement, which was not at all the reaction I had expected or desired.

I recognized both of the men, obviously; our ship's complement was not all that large. De Saumserez and Danis were their names. The latter I had treated the week previous for a minor burn. Clearly he was an ungrateful sort at heart, because he was the one which had overturned my bed, and then grabbed me by the arm and marched me out into the passageway.

At this time, I must admit, I began to fear for my own safety. I had no inkling of events in other parts of the ship, and my trepidations were completely for myself at this point. Both of the men who were frog-marching me aft outmassed me by 40 or 50 kilos, myself being of a relatively slighter stature. My fears were generally ungrounded, as I arrived in the launch bay with nothing worse than a slight bruise on my left arm.

Ours was not the first such party to arrive, nor the last. Several officers and a few of the crew, apparently the bridge watch, since Captain Brighton and two others were secluded in one corner, and they were being watched by armed men. I was taken to a different group containing about a dozen people. All of them were silent and had a look of astonishment on their faces, to one degree or another.

As quietly as I could, I asked Fujinami, the exobotonist of our excursion and a close friend, what was transpiring. He responded that the executive officer, along with others, had conspired to steal *Pathfinder*.

A thousand questions flooded my mind, but I had no time to ask them. Teach, the executive officer, had entered the bay. He looked over at our group and then sent one of the crewmen to fetch me to him.

"Ward," he said, "this ship is now under my command. You no longer have to fear severe treatment from Brighton. It is my intention to put everyone off of this ship who will not follow me. There is a planet near here that is capable of supporting life, where they will have a good chance of surviving indefinitely. Will you join me, or will you take your chances with them?"

The bluntness of his proposition caught me off guard, and his steely gaze did not make it any easier to think just then. I was tempted to stay on the ship; it seemed the easier course of action. Life on a maiden planet was hard, and we scarcely had the numbers and diversity of skills needed to begin a new colony.

However, I realized, Teach was committing an act of piracy, even if it was an "inside job," as the media like to call it. The penalty for that crime, if caught, was death. Once the ship was reported missing, the Warner fleet would begin searching for it. It was almost certain that the stranded crew on the nearby planet would be rescued, and equally sure that the thieves would be caught, eventually. With that in mind, I thought my chances better with the party to be stranded, even if that hadn't been my natural inclination.

Perhaps ten seconds had passed while I considered, then I replied that I would take my chances with the others. He inhaled sharply, as if I had offered him some offense, then turned his back on me and addressed Crewman Chin.

"Take him back to the medical bay. Let him take the portable medkit, and any other small items Dr. Johnson says we can spare. Then let him gather some of his belongings from his quarters. No more than he can carry himself. And let him change clothes. I am not putting anyone off this ship in their pajamas."

Chin did not say a word to me all the way back to the med bay, simply following behind me as I made my way there. Meghan was not at her duty station, as I had expected her to be, since I had not passed her going aft on my way forward. After a moment's confusion, though, I saw her through the window in the operating room.

She glanced up as I approached, but went straight back to her work. I could see that the patient was Jill Burton, and that she had taken a blaster pulse to the right side of her torso. The breast and much of the skin on that side were gone, and it would be a miracle if she retained the use of that arm. As I watched, Meghan was struggling to bypass the melted and charred portions of the brachial artery and anterior humeral circumflex artery with a synthetic replacement. Without the replacements to restore blood flow, and quickly, the entire arm would be irrecoverable.

I vacillated as to what to do, but only for a moment. There was a patient who needed help, and that was my first and foremost responsibility, even if it meant numbering myself amongst the mutineers. Chin looked into the room for a second and went straight to the sink to vomit.

I punched the button to call into the sealed room. "Meghan, hit the unlock tab and let me come scrub in."

She didn't look up, didn't stop her feverish efforts to repair the mangled body on the table before her. "What's going on out there, Leon?" she asked instead.

I ran my fingers through my hair and tried to organize my thoughts into a coherent summary for her. "Commander Teach and some of the officers and crew are taking over the ship. I don't know how many he has with him, but he plans to put everyone else off the ship."

"I thought that's how it was," she responded wearily, all the while moving quickly and skillfully about her task. "You'd best not come in, Leon. I can handle Jill's injuries as well as both of us could, for the most part. If you scrub in, you'll be stuck on *Pathfinder* with the rest of the traitors."

Simon Chin had put himself back together enough to find a seat, but he had deliberately not come back over to the window. He was close enough to hear, though, and he flinched at the word 'traitor.' I didn't much care if his sensibilities were offended.

"Besides," she continued, head still down over her work, "we're responsible for the entire crew. Wherever the others wind up, they're also going to need a medical officer."

She was right about all of it, except for her not needing help with Burton's operation. I could see that the Marine's vitals were stabilized, so she was going to live, but saving her arm was a matter of minutes, and four hands would speed the time to completion.

Dr. Johnson looked up then, for a moment, as she sensed my hesitation. "Go, Leon. I'll make it an order if I need to."

"You might have to," I said stubbornly. "You might not save her arm without help."

"Yes I will!" she said fiercely. She softened her tone immediately. "Now go, and stop distracting me. This is not the easiest thing I have ever done."

She was right again. This was not the easiest thing she had ever done, but she was showing as much surgical skill as I had ever witnessed. While I had stood there, she had restored the blood supply to the arm and was beginning to work on repairing the tissue damage. Rather than the speed necessary for the former, she now needed accuracy and patience. And no distractions.

"Goodbye, Meghan. I hope I see you again sometime."

"I hope so, too, Leon. Godspeed."

I turned then, and went to collect the medical kit I had been promised. I kept myself turned away from Chin, so that he wouldn't see the tears in my eyes.

Since Chin was not about to go ask Meghan for what could be spared, as he had been instructed, I decided that I would simply load up what I could carry until he tried to stop me. He never did. I walked out with more of our medical stores than I had thought I would. The medkit Teach had specifically allowed me contained a wide variety of instruments and supplies.

In addition to the medkit, I carried a considerable amount of medicines; antiradiation, antibiotic, pain, quickmend, etc. I was also foresighted enough to gather items to aid in assisting us in surviving on an unknown planet until help could arrive. Two large sealable containers were loaded with sheets and blankets, plus air splints, monotubing, and bandages. I finally decided that I had everything that might be useful within my ability to carry.

At that point, I nodded to Chin and left, the two containers strapped over my shoulders and my arms full of the other things. I never said anything to Meghan, not trusting my voice to remain steady if I made the attempt. I would see to it that Brighton was aware of the sacrifice she had made to do her duty.

My quarters were just around a bend from the med bay, which had been convenient in going on and off duty. Meghan and I shared the space therein, which had worked out amicably thus far in the voyage, as one of the two of us was always on duty, so we had all the privacy we needed; always crossing paths, but never really together except to relieve each other at our station.

In gathering up things there, I was tempted to take everything I owned, but realized immediately that was not practical. I spent a few minutes gathering my personal effects and locking them all in my foot locker, and then tried to forget about them, trusting to fate to bring them back into my possession someday. Meghan would look after them for me, I was sure.

To my bundle, I added only two pairs of pants, my extra shoes, socks, briefs, and my two readers—one with all of my medical reference texts, and the other with recent medical journals and other light reading I had planned to catch up during the lengthy exploration. When I changed out of my sleepwear and into my uniform, I took four scrub shirts and put them all on. I collected my load and made to leave, then returned and kicked the bed back onto its legs and threw the blanket over my shoulder.

Chin had remained silent throughout, and I did not even spare him a glance as I left and headed back to the launch bay, though I could hear him following right behind me. Just before we reentered the launch bay, where I would have to rejoin the rest, Chin stopped me by finally addressing me.

"Ward…" I paused, and turned to look at him, but he continued to say nothing for a few seconds, as if he had used up his allotment of words. Or perhaps it was the glare I bestowed upon him that caused him to be unable to continue. Just as I was about to turn back to the hatch, he said, "Good luck, Ward."

My estimation of Simon Chin changed drastically then. Previously, I had thought of him as I would a bully forcing his will upon me which I had no power to overcome. He had been a hated enemy, and a symbol of the betrayal of trust to which I had been subjected. As I looked upward into his eyes, though, I saw that he was almost as trapped by circumstances as I was. He had chosen to support the opposite party in this situation, but he clearly was not happy about the consequences of his choice, or what he was forced to do because of it.

All hostility toward him drained out of me, and I said simply, "Thank you, Simon." I looked at him for a moment more, then went through the hatch.

When I entered the launch bay, my detained shipmates were not in the same corner they once were. The group had been moved next to the launch's access hatch, and they were in the process of climbing down into the access corridor.

Captain Brighton was now among them, and he seemed tensed and ready to spring into action, should there be the slightest opportunity. His eyes scanned from side to side, taking in all about him. The crewmen who were aiding Teach in his treachery kept a close eye on all of us, though, especially the captain, Lieutenant Johnson, the helm officer, and Major Chowdhury, the head security officer.

Several of the men also derided and shouted epithets at us, particularly the captain. For his part, Captain Brighton remained silent and aloof, though it was clear to all that he was exerting every effort to control his mounting rage.

The survey launch into which they were loading us had two seats in the forward area, intended for the pilot and copilot, and seats for ten others in the main area. It was into this area that we were sent, one after another, until nearly two dozen of us were stuffed inside. I had to quickly stow the supplies I had brought aboard to make room for more shipmates to be packed in.

Sheli Chowdhury approached me while I was about this task. Her hands were cuffed behind her back. "Have you seen Burton, Ward?"

"Yes, Major. She's going to pull through, and I think she will be able to keep the arm. Dr. Johnson was confident that she would."

She thanked me, and moved off to convey the news to Sgt. Aichele, the other member of her security team.

When all were aboard, Teach appeared at the airlock hatch. He repeated his earlier offer to all of us, asking if any would prefer to stay aboard *Pathfinder* rather than be exiled to Antoc-A3. I presumed at the time that he was referring to the habitable planet on which he planned to strand us, though I had not heard the name before. To my great surprise, three individuals arose and exited the craft, including Eric Aichele. He seemed ashamed of himself, and well he should, I thought. Fujinami told me later that six others of the crew had accepted Teach's generosity while they were held in the launch bay.

Before Teach could disappear and seal the hatch, Lt. Johnson asked about getting some food to take with us. Teach answered that the galley had not been stocked, but the emergency rations were still aboard, and that we would have to make do with those.

Chowdhury, perhaps emboldened by Johnson's request, asked about getting weapons to defend ourselves on the planet. How had she gotten out of those handcuffs? I wondered. Teach considered for a moment, then nodded and disappeared from my view. When he returned, he tossed four handguns into the launch. Chowdhury grabbed one immediately, but just as quickly discovered that the power cell had been removed. Teach laughed, then sealed the inner airlock hatch and, I learned later, left the cells in the lock before sealing the outer hatch.

No more than thirty seconds passed from the time Teach sealed the outer door before I felt the launch being pushed out of the bay. Captain

Brighton stood behind the two pilot's seats and watched as the ship which had, until a short time ago, been his to command slowly receded from our view.

Mackey, who was in the copilot's seat, made contact with *Pathfinder* via the short-ranged vocom, but his entreaties produced no positive response; quite the opposite, in fact. Whoever was manning the vocom equipment, and I did not recognize the voice, seemed to be happy to threaten, yell, upbraid, and deride us in response to Mackey's pleas. Long, Johnson, and Smith all became very angry and yelled right back. Ultimately, the shouts we sent had no effect on them, and *Pathfinder*, our home for the past fourteen months, powered itself away like a mother abandoning an unwanted child.

Captain Brighton remained motionless the entire time *Pathfinder* was still discernible. He stood behind the pilot's seats with his hands clasped behind him and stared at the diminishing shine of her engines. This was perhaps a total of ten minutes, though it seemed far longer. Within a minute, all conversation on the little launch had ceased. Everyone waited expectantly for the captain to direct us, to tell us what to do or what to expect. For his part, he seemed to be unaware of the heightened attention we were giving him, as if the firefly glow of *Pathfinder*'s running lights had him mesmerized and oblivious to all else.

It was easy for me to understand the captain becoming melancholy over the loss of his ship. Clearly, being put out of the ship was a great shock to me, but it must have been many times worse for the captain. He not only found himself in the same dire straits as the rest of us, but he must surely be blaming himself, undeservedly of course, for it as well. It was no wonder that he should find himself emotionally cast adrift in exact parallel to our physical circumstances.

Much as I felt I should offer the captain some comfort at that time, I could not bring myself to do so. Firstly, I felt myself to be just as needful of comforting; I do not mind admitting that I was quite anxious, and more than a little frightened at our current state. Secondly, if I had tried to commiserate or bolster the captain's spirits, it would have diminished him in the eyes of the others. The morale of our group was a very fragile thing indeed just then, and the only thing, I felt, that could hold us together would be to keep confidence in the captain's ability to guide us and direct our efforts. Lastly, I did not have a relationship with the captain that would have allowed such intimacy. Though he and I had dined at the same table perhaps a hundred times, still there was an invisible barrier between him and everyone around him. The only ones I believe that were close enough to him to have attempted such would have been Teach, Chowdhury, and Johnson; of which one had just betrayed him.

I cannot, to this day, imagine how Captain Brighton must have felt. Just that day, he had accomplished a singularly notable feat: successfully guiding the first full-sized ship to make use of a jump gate powered only by the ship itself. Yet within twenty hours of that great achievement, he had lost his ship, the majority of his command, and one of his best friends, or so he had thought. To be brought to such abysmal depths after such soaring heights would be enough to crush a lesser man's spirits.

It was not a dejected or discouraged man which turned away from the viewport, however. As he turned, his eyes displayed the fire of anger and determination for all to see.

"Ms. Johnson," he said crisply.

"Yes, sir?"

"They haven't taken to a new heading yet, and I don't expect they will. Just in case, though, set up a scan to follow *Pathfinder* for as long as we can range her. Make sure all our data gets dumped to the log."

"Aye, sir."

"Mr. Le Vesconte?" The captain addressed himself now to the quartermaster.

"Yes, sir."

"I need an accurate inventory of everything aboard this launch, especially food and fuel. Have the ensigns assist you."

"Aye-aye, sir."

"Ms. Williams," he said, turning next to the attractive young helmswoman, barely older than the ensigns herself. "As your captain, I would appreciate it if you could see your way clear to set course for Antoc-A3, bearing 267.11, same plane, from our current location. We have a lot of velocity to counter, so we will need to pile on the acceleration for several hours."

"Aye-aye, *Captain*. Course laid in," she replied with the undercurrent of some private joke.

"Mr. Long, I want you to take O'Neill and Alcaraz and see what access we have to the internal power lines from within the cabin. I already know what lines are accessible from various panels, but I need to know what else we can make accessible given the resources we have available to us."

"Aye, sir. I'll get right on it."

The Captain then looked around the cabin at the remnants of his staff and crew. "The rest of you are going to need to be accommodating to those with assignments. I know we are crowded in here, but do your best to stay out of their way.

"Dr. Ward." I started at being addressed, as I thought he had concluded handing out duties to be performed.

"Yes, sir?"

"I see that you were able to bring a fair amount of supplies with you. Could you itemize them for Mr. Le Vesconte? I'm sure that will help him complete his assignment."

"Certainly, Captain," I replied.

I moved to obey, and Le Vesconte directed me to provide the information to Ensign Roberts, who was collating all the information the other two ensigns and Drew himself read off to her. It took me no more than a few minutes to provide Jherri the requested information. I had long ago committed to memory the items in the medkit, and the other things I had collected were still fresh in my mind. Since I was not required to physically go through the items in question in order to list them, I completed my portion without interruption while the others waited for their turns to add what they had found in various compartments and bins.

I returned then to my seat, which was not actually a seat, as those available were already occupied before I was put aboard, but was a section of the floor that I considered "mine" by the expedient of having sat there prior to getting up. My assignment having been completed, I took a look around the cabin and realized that the feeling of anxiety and gloom which had hung over our party had dispelled to a large degree, to be replaced with energy and determination.

The reason for this change was not hard to understand. Previously, all of us had felt cast adrift, no pun intended, by the events of that day. All of our regular duties and routines were taken from us, and replaced with unknown and unknowable dangers and difficulties. When Captain Brighton began directing us it acted as an emotional anchor. We could again feel that someone had control of the situation. By trusting in the captain, we could convince ourselves that he would take care of us and see us safely through whatever came. Perhaps logically that does not make a lot of sense, but emotionally it did not need to make any sense at all. The results were what mattered.

Drew Le Vesconte did not take long to make his report to the captain. They were near the front of the cabin while I was at the rear, so I did not hear everything the report contained. Captain Brighton listened attentively to the complete list. At one point he asked, "That's all? You're sure?" which

I do not believe he meant to say loud enough for all to hear, but otherwise he remained silent. When Le Vesconte concluded, the captain said something to him which I did not hear, then dismissed him.

He turned then to Ms. Williams, and gave her some order that was below my hearing.

Drew's "seat," or perhaps "spot" would be more accurate, was next to mine. As he seated himself, I asked him what had caused the captain such consternation. He responded that it was not, as he expected, the food supply which had caused his response, but the amount of battery power.

"Look," he said to me, "the launch has an emergency supply of arbars, (by which he meant the ration bars that would provide everything needed for one meal of a 2000 Kcalorie/day diet) enough for four weeks. But the supply is calculated on an eight-man crew, which is all a survey shuttle this size is supposed to carry. It won't last the nineteen of us near that long."

"And the batteries?" I prompted.

"Well, if the emergency rations are just as they ought to be, the batteries are not. It's clear they intended us to go to the nearest planet and nowhere else, because there's not power to go any farther than that. It looks like they pulled most of the battery packs out of their connections before they even loaded us onboard. Once we get to A3, I doubt we'll have any way to get back off of it on our own."

At the time, I did not know why this information should distress the captain, but I quickly put it out of my mind. I, like Le Vesconte, was more concerned with our ability to feed ourselves until help arrived. I knew nothing whatsoever about our destined exile planet, save the name only, with which I had become acquainted a scant half hour previous. Teach had said that those stranded would have "a good chance of surviving indefinitely," but I was less than inclined to accept his opinion on anything just then. I would likely have disputed that water was wet, had he made the claim.

I stewed about the problem for some time, then realized that there really was nothing I could do about it until we reached our destination and saw what was available for food. This, of course, lead me to the further realization that there was precious little I could do about it one way or another even then; either there would be food available in some form, or there would not. I would just have to trust the captain to deal with whatever problems were to arise.

I just as quickly ignored my own sage advice and went back to worrying about the food situation.

I next went through the calculations in my head which indicated that we had less than twelve days' rations for all of us on which to survive. I was about to go forward to ask the captain if he knew anything about the planet to which we were headed, and if we would be able to find anything edible there. When I looked up at him, though, I decided to stay in my place. Captain Brighton was deep in thought; he always tapped his jaw with one finger that way when he was trying to analyze something. Every now and then he would pull out his notepad and search for some datum, then return to his previous percussive rhythm.

After perhaps a half hour of this, the captain stood from the seat he was in and walked to the front of the main cabin, turning to face everyone except Williams and Johnson in the two pilot's positions. Instantly, the muffled conversations going on about the ship ceased and all eyes turned to Captain Brighton.

It seemed that he was about to ask everyone for their attention when he saw that he already had it, and he paused for a moment before continuing. After running his fingers through his red hair, he started again.

"I am sure that all of you are aware of our general situation. Teach expected to leave us no options but to go to Antoc-A3 by leaving us in proximity to that planet, and restricting the amount of food and battery power available to us. I do not mean to do as Teach expects, now or ever again. To that end, I am rationing our food and our use of the batteries, effective immediately. I have already instructed Warrant Williams to replot our course toward the planet, taking more time, but using less power. I have not discussed it yet with Lieutenant Johnson, but it is in my mind that we can land on the planet without using our gravitic engines at all, and thus conserve even more power.

"I do not have a complete plan yet, but Ms. Johnson and I will discuss the particulars and make you aware of them when it is finalized. In the meantime, we must take every opportunity to conserve four things: food, water, fuel, and power. Water is not normally a problem, because the launch is equipped to recycle it with only minimal loss. However, the recyclers use power from the batteries, and the batteries cannot be recharged with the means currently available.

"What I am asking each of you to do is to submit yourselves to my authority in rationing our resources, and that you will do so without complaint or dissent."

He again paused while the import of his words sank into our minds and souls. Clearly, he already had the authority to issue whatever orders he chose. In fact, given what I had previously heard others saying about him, that is precisely what I would have expected him to do. Perhaps the betrayal, both personal and professional, that he had suffered caused him to be reticent in exercising his authority. Whatever the reason, I think that the very fact that he asked all of us to follow him, to trust him, unified our group to a single purpose as a dictatorial commandment could not have.

There seemed to be no dissent among us, but that was not sufficient for the tall captain. He stood before us and called each of us by name, starting with Ms. Chowdhury and proceeding from most senior to most junior. He asked each of us if we would submit to his authority, and in each case the response was a quick and ready, "yes, sir!" Ensign Hayes even stood and saluted when he was called on, and everyone thereafter did as well.

"Thank you all for the confidence you have placed in me," he said then. "If you will follow my instructions, if you will bear up under the struggles we will certainly face, I promise you that I will do everything in my power to see you all safely home again." His eyes burned and he held a clenched fist before him as he continued. "And I will find Ed Teach and the rest of those traitors and I will see justice done upon them, if I have to move the universe itself to see it done!"

I can attest, without the slightest fear of equivocation, that no one among us doubted the captain's word. I heard Derrick Mackey, the ship's bosun, say "Amen," as if to add both his agreement and prayer to Captain Brighton's oath with a single word.

That discussion ended, Brighton took over Williams' seat and sent her back to the main cabin. I could see that Johnson and the captain were discussing what he had in mind. Captain Brighton was doing most of the talking, though they were speaking softly enough I don't believe that anyone could overhear them; I certainly couldn't from my spot against the aft bulkhead. I did see the lieutenant give him one or two looks of disbelief, however.

The journey to Antoc-A3, from the time our launch left the *Pathfinder* to the time we could see the planet unaided, took over 28 hours. Apart from dividing three ration bars nineteen ways for three meals, Brighton and Johnson were deep in discussions the entire time.

Orbit was achieved by means of the reaction mass thrusters, without engaging the gravitic engines. Brighton began immediately to scan the planet for a suitable location to land. He seemed to be having some difficulty in getting readings, and I wondered if he was trying to keep from using battery power with the scanners also. I must have said something aloud without intending to, for Clémence Queneau, the survey cartographer, explained that the sensor package on the launch was very powerful and accurate, but only for the things for which it was intended to be used. It was designed to be extremely sensitive to fluctuations in gravity fields, and detecting mass in the vast emptiness that comprised almost the entirety of space. Being able to "see" through the interference of atmosphere to get a clear picture of the ground was not one of its primary tasks, and so the system's designers had given it a low priority. With the result being a delay to us to make sure we could see where we were going to land.

After the breakfast "meal" was distributed, around 0830, Captain Brighton ordered us all to get some rest. He and Johnson would spend the next few hours finding our landing site and calculating our landing course. I pulled out the blankets and sheets that I had packed and distributed them. There were not enough to go around, so I settled down without one. I didn't seem cold in the least, even though the ambient air was not being heated in order to conserve power, and I had to chuckle to myself.

With all the anxiety and tension I had been through since our forced exile, it was the first time I had noticed that I was still wearing four shirts.

28–29 June

The two assault shuttles under Vasconcellos' command, *Oeiras* and *Caxias*, lifted cleanly from the small base tucked away in the system's asteroid belt and settled on an appropriate vector for their intercept of *Pathfinder*'s current track. Acceleration was kept low, less than 50 g, in order to keep their target from knowing they were there for as long as could be managed. Once they approached too closely and were spotted there would be no disengaging. Their best hope of success could be found in delaying that moment for as long as possible.

Vasconcellos settled himself into the proper mental track as easily as he had directed the ships. This was yet another example of the military's "hurry up and wait." It was so familiar by now that he couldn't imagine life being any other way. As always, he used the wait time to prepare himself for all of the things that might or might not happen during those hectic hurry up moments. At this velocity, he would have plenty of opportunity to prepare.

He ran through the status of all of the shuttles' systems, marking each green light off his mental checklist. He called his noncoms for each squad's readiness. He ran a passive scan of *Pathfinder* and found that it had not altered course.

Those items cleared from his task list, he went through the plan of attack step by step, looking for potential problems, as he had many dozens of times already. The two shuttles he commanded were headed, not for a direct rendezvous with their objective, but for a point well behind it. There was no possibility of getting within striking distance while approaching broadside. Instead, phase one of the plan would have them limit their emissions while moving behind *Pathfinder* and then use the interference of the larger vessel's engines to mask their attack run.

Once in position, phase two was to disarm the ship. The first difficulty to overcome would be the two chase missile tubes. Each of the shuttles would target one of them, and hold fire until either it was clear they had been spotted or they were within 10,000 km, whichever came first. The same distortion which would mask their presence would create problems with accurately targeting their tubes, but the benefit of using high-powered lasers was that you could hit whatever you could see.

Vasconcellos hoped to close with their wounded prey quickly at that point. He was not expecting to make it without any return fire coming his way, of course. Only a fool expects his enemy to make his life easy for him, or that every break will fall his way in an engagement. The best you could do was to prepare for the worst and hope to be pleasantly surprised.

The worst that could happen was for *Pathfinder* to react immediately to the attack, turn to face them and open up with their three remaining missile tubes and single laser mount. Even then, it would be close to a fair fight. The two shuttles had two lasers and four tubes a bit smaller than the enemy's between them. Still, evading a counterattack would be difficult at such short range.

They would have surprise on their side, as long as they could successfully sneak into position without being spotted. The shock of the unexpected attack should be sufficient to slow their response by as much as a minute or more. That much time would allow them to destroy the remainder of the target's offensive weapons before they could be brought to bear.

Once the external defenses were dispatched, phase three was to board and take the ship. *Caxias'* Marines would board through the boat bay, with ready access to Engineering, while Vasconcellos and *Oeiras* would enter directly behind and above *Pathfinder's* bridge. The assault shuttles were designed for just this kind of boarding. Each would seal itself to the outer hull of the target, then use controlled plasma bursts to create a sizeable entrance.

Once inside, the four squads of Marines in battle armor should find little resistance. Data from their source claimed there were only three security personnel aboard *Pathfinder*. It took fifteen minutes for a top-notch and motivated soldier to don protective gear. Vasconellos didn't plan to allow them that much time. That left the crew of swabbies, which would be no threat at all.

His mind at rest, the lieutenant decided to work on the second most important preparation for the coming conflict. He went to sleep.

"Lieutenant, you'd best take a look at this." The words were not spoken loudly, but it immediately brought his mind back into focus. A quick glance at the chrono showed that he had at least managed a few hours of sack time.

"What is it, Mark?"

"Passives are returning two signals now. Looks like *Pathfinder* sent *Vanguard* out to survey on its own." Second Lieutenant Cinquini, First

Platoon's leader, did not look the least bit pleased. Vasconcellos felt much the same.

This was not an eventuality that had been considered in their planning or training. They could not capture either of the ships and leave the other active to raise the alarm, and they did not have the ships and men to take them both at the same time. He was going to have to contact the base for new orders. He hated to do that, especially when the smart money said Agostinho was going to scrub the whole op. He had no choice, though. This scenario was not covered in the current plan, and his orders did not allow for this much discretion in forming a new plan on his own.

"Fire up the directional comms, Mark. We need to take this up with the Old Lady."

"Yes, sir." He still didn't sound happy.

When he got the commander on the horn, she didn't either.

"Well, there goes six weeks of planning straight down the toilet!" was probably the mildest thing she had to say on the subject. After the initial venting, though, she was quiet for some time. Vasconcellos could tell she was percolating a new idea, so he also said nothing and waited.

"Where is *Vanguard* headed, Lieutenant?"

Vasconcellos checked the plot on the tactical display and saw that the ship in question was currently decelerating hard to approach the third planet on this side of the system. He passed that information on.

"Perfect!" Vasconcellos could hear the grin in her voice.

"How so, m'am?"

"One of the big worries about our plan was that it might backfire on us. Instead of making sure we guaranteed our share of the prize, we could have made Forrest so pissed off that we went to war over it.

"Opportunity may be knocking, Steve. With the two ships separated, we can take *Vanguard*, and leave *Pathfinder* for Forrest to scoop up. We get our hands on the new technology without the need for conflict with Forrest. In fact, if we do it right, Forrest doesn't even have to know."

Vasconcellos could see the truth in that, once it was pointed out. He liked the new objective better for selfish reasons as well. With a smaller ship, fewer crew, and no armaments, taking *Vanguard* would involve much less risk for him and his team.

"All right, what is the right way to do it?" he asked.

"Can you make it to the planet before they get there?"

"No, ma'am. Not without being spotted. If we alter course now and keep our accel under the detection threshold, we're still…thirty-eight hours from planetfall," he said, reading off the numbers the comm sergeant held up for him. Onboard a ship was not his natural environment, and the complex physics involved in calculating trajectories was not in his line of work. He was the proverbial ground-pounder, and proud of it.

"Okay, I think your best bet would be to pose as the terraforming team we cleaned out of the system. Get them to let their guard down and then make your move. You may not be able to be believable if they get to the terraformer's encampment before you do, in which case, make the best tactical assault you can, given the circumstances."

"Understood, ma'am. Vasconcellos clear." He keyed the system off, then headed out to the main cabin.

"All right, you apes, listen hard. As is usual, the other side is not acting like we told them to, so there's been a change of plan…"

ENSIGN JORDAN HAYES

From his personal journal

29 June - 1 July

Captain Brighton had asked all of the officers, including those of us who were mere ensigns, to keep a journal for the purpose of having several records of these events. I'm not really good at this, but here it is. A journal is different than a diary, right?

Anyway, Captain wanted to make sure the rest of the crew got some sleep, while we finalized plans for landing on Antoc-A3. It didn't take a lot of convincing for the crew. They slept noiselessly as we listened to the captain and Johnson instructing us on what to expect in entry and landing. We didn't like to think about it too much, especially since we weren't sure how well we could land while trying to conserve the power cells as Captain Brighton desired.

Lt. Johnson did her level best to assure us that all would be well. The confidence Captain showed in her helped ease many of our fears about the impending landing. It was more than that, though, for me. I wanted off of this boat, at least to stretch my legs a little and get away from the cramped quarters. I felt a desire to be outside in the sunshine and fresh air, to see if the stench of the betrayal we all felt could air out a little.

Exhaustion was starting to overtake me and make my eyes droop a little, when Captain Brighton ended our briefing and instructed us to try and rest while we made a final approach before landing. He intimated that while it was likely we could rest on the planet, there would be work to do and would not be any slack time to be found.

If there was one thing I had learned in my posting aboard *Pathfinder* with Captain Brighton, it was that whatever he suggested, you should take as an order. So I did. I found a nice piece of mostly unoccupied cushion and fell asleep as soon as I hit the floor.

"Strap in!" yelled someone, most likely Captain I thought, as I came suddenly awake. "Prepare for turbulence." The lack of room made for uncomfortable sleeping conditions, which was why I had to put my neck back into good order before I sat in the chair that I had marked as my own. I was more than a little groggy.

I grimaced as my stomach growled, and caught a lopsided smile that Ward threw my way as his stomach seemed to echo mine. As everyone was getting into straps, for those in seats, and cargo harnesses for the rest, I couldn't help but see the hope and concern of the group. I would have to say that I was feeling it, too. I made small-talk with Mitchell as we both tried to keep each other in a positive mood through some unspoken agreement.

Our landing site was selected due to its perceived likelihood of having food and water available. Our long-range scans, such as our planetary sensors were, indicated that there was a river running through the valley here that supported life and a heck of a lot of vegetation.

"Ladies and gentlemen, here we go!" Johnson said from the pilot's seat, as she brought us down, breaking atmosphere none too gently. I could see that Captain Brighton was at the command console next to her, and was busy checking everything on the three displays, as he watched *Vanguard's* attitude, velocity, and trajectory carefully.

Boy, it seemed like we came in hot. I was used to the lazy, slow descents that came with the Gravitas drives. When space travel had begun centuries ago, it became obvious that for any lengthy duration of spatial voyage, artificial gravity as well as inertial dampening were going to be necessary. Sterling and Warner had co-founded the Gravitas organization which developed the first inertial dampening fields and artificial gravity generators to be used in space vessels. Since the initial founding, a few other Families had joined the organization. The next goal of the organization was an improvement on the basic, and costly, chemical drive engines that were being utilized.

About 300 years ago, the first Gravitas drive had been born. It utilized much of the basic technology developed in the artificial gravity projects to create a drive engine capable of producing a gravity disparity to the surrounding space allowing the vessel to be propelled at a much higher rate of acceleration without the expensive fuels required for the large chemical drives. Generally, a vessel landing on a planet had the ability, with a Gravitas drive, to float down to the surface. That said, all Warner ships had backup chemical drives in place for emergencies, and that was what *Vanguard* was relying on to conserve the massive amounts of power required for the Gravitas engines.

Johnson was pretty good, and Captain had plotted a perfect trajectory. Together they placed us within a few yards of the point they had decided on the night before.

Captain had allowed us to wait to make planetfall in the daylight, which was why we had a glorious vision as the hatch cracked open and the sunlight streamed in. The fresh air smelled verdant and rich. I was looking forward to walking out into that sunlight.

"It's beautiful," Roberts said as she exited the craft, just ahead of me.

"It sure is," I replied, as I stepped out into the warm morning sunshine. I couldn't help but smile. It seemed to be catching. I think that at that time I didn't realize how it affected me, but as I looked back on it, that moment was the one that saw me through so many others. In that radiant morning sun on Antoc-A3, the bitterness I felt was melting away, to be replaced by thankfulness and determination.

Of course, maybe the determination was a little because of the way the captain smiled and said, "All right ladies and gentlemen, we didn't come down here to stare. Listen up." He was hard, but he oozed competence and determination.

Landing Site Prime lacked any edible food, and showed no trace of the river we knew was nearby, hidden in the vegetation. Captain Brighton split us into an exploratory group, and a defensive group.

Captain Brighton left Lt. Johnson and Mackey with Mitchell, O'Neill, Smith and Alcaraz to watch the craft and the landing site. I knew all of them pretty well except Alcaraz, but figured that the group of them would be more than competent at guarding the ship.

Since we were not overly trained in planetary exploration, by which I mean that the closest I had come to *actual* training was running on the Academy cross-country team, we just followed Captain Brighton into the forest.

Now, I wouldn't say I knew nothing of the outdoors; it's just that my experience was limited in many ways. Growing up on Earth, in the part of North America known as New England, and being a very outdoor-oriented boy, I had a fair knowledge of trees. This forest, however, was nothing like anything I had ever seen. While a verdant green, the trees appeared to me to be neither conifers nor deciduous. They might have been one or the other, but I wouldn't be the one to tell you about it. As Jherri Roberts looked over at me, with an eyebrow quirked, I guessed that I probably should be more alert for a river or animals, than in staring up at the vegetation.

Since we had only the four guns that Teach had let us take, Captain Brighton had left two of them with the *Vanguard*, and had one of them himself. That left one other which Chowdhury had out. She clearly knew how to handle one, and seemed to be completely comfortable walking along next to the captain, her eyes and head more scanning the area than looking for anything. Apparently, being a security officer on a survey ship involved more training than I had thought. I guess Marines get different training at the academy than regular fleet officers. Or maybe it was just her. That made a better explanation for the way she moved on planet. I was trying to figure out what animal she most resembled, maybe a hunting cat like a panther, when we heard somebody shout behind us.

Delacoeur was yelling, by which I mean screaming like a little girl, when we got back to him. His hands were over his ankle, and we feared he had broken his leg. Ward quickly attended him and, forcing him to lay back, he examined the ankle. After a few moments, he announced that no bones were broken, but that he had possibly torn some ligaments, and was going to be "uncomfortable" for a while. The doctor suggested that we could splint it enough that he could move around. Ward gave his patient a couple of melting tablets after glancing up at the captain, who shook his head when he proffered the intramuscular injection. Ward nodded to himself and continued.

Captain gathered us together as Delacoeur slowly calmed down. He squatted next to Delacoeur and asked if he was going to be okay. He nodded, and the captain said, "Good. Now if you, or any of you," as he turned to face the rest of us, "ever harm yourselves due to your own carelessness or recklessness, I will be forced to do something none of you will like. Each one of you has a role in this venture, and each one of you is important. We are all going to be pushed beyond what we are physically used to, and it will take every ounce of your muster to keep going at that point. Moreover, it is not acceptable for any of you to expect someone else to carry your weight. You will all take care to make sure your physical condition is not hindered by stupidity, *period. Am I clear on this*?"

We all acquiesced with nods and quiet "yessirs" as Delacoeur colored and looked down while forcing his eyes to close to blink away the tears that had formed while he was howling with pain. We then all set down our gear and looked around while we waited for Ward to set the splint. No one said another word, not even a whisper, while we watched the doctor work.

When he finished, Captain Brighton walked back over to Delacoeur and turned to speak to him, but I could tell he meant for all of us to hear him.

"That said, Kieran, I will help you carry your weight today," he said while squatting down next to Delacoeur. "I will not be making a habit of it, though." He helped him up to a standing position with Ward's help, leaning heavily on the captain.

I came forward and said, "Captain, if you would, let me. You are more needed in leading us, and I think it fair for me to say that nobody else really knows how to handle a weapon as well as you or Major Chowdhury."

Captain Brighton looked intently at me for a moment. Steve Long stepped up right then and said, "Captain, I can help. That way it won't be too hard on Hayes, either." I was glad that he had spoken up. I wasn't sure how the captain was going to react, but I was glad in that heart-pounding moment that anyone was willing to stand with me. I seem to have a problem with speaking before I think the situation through.

"All right. But if you start to lag, I will be taking over with no arguments," Captain Brighton said.

Just like that, he passed Delacoeur to Long and me and we helped him move down the trail.

"Thanks guys," Kieran said in a low tone, as Captain Brighton moved back up to the front with Chowdhury.

"No problem," I said, as my heart began to return to a normal pace.

"Yeah, I am sure Hayes at least would have done the same for me!" Long said as he lightly slugged Delacoeur who laughed a little in response. Delacoeur was really heavy, but since calling him fat was an understatement, that was to be expected.

We continued onward, until we heard some excitement up ahead and realized that they had encountered the river. As we came up, sweating a river of our own helping Delacoeur, we found a group had gathered near Captain Brighton at the river. The captain looked back and, as we came into view, he locked eyes with me and gave me a slight nod. I think that is when I realized that he was proud of me for stepping forward back in the clearing to help Kieran. Well, that, or at least he wasn't annoyed with me. I smiled at that thought.

Water flowed clean and fast across the rocks in the small rapids formed by a shoal in the river. It was a beautiful sight, and we moved Kieran over to a small boulder so he could sit. Long and I moved down to the water with the others and drank from it, as we saw the others doing. Ward was filling his water bottles, so we both assumed the water was safe enough.

I filled my water bottle after a couple of drinks and took it up to Delacoeur. He smiled a little as I handed it to him. He hadn't been talking much since the meds that Ward had given him had taken effect. He had been smiling a little though.

We waited together until the captain got us all moving again. Long and

I got Kieran back on his good foot and acted as his crutches for him as we followed. We decided to try not to be in the back of the group, so we stepped up our pace to put us a couple of people ahead of the back.

I let my thoughts drift a little as I was contemplating our situation while we walked. I was thinking that in all my "vast" twenty-two years of life experience, I never imagined that graduating the Warner Naval Academy, and getting signed on for my initial posting with *Pathfinder* (for which there had been some pretty extreme competition) would find me out on a planet in the back-water of space, helping an overweight injured cook walk down a slope through the forest, looking for a cave. I did not particularly like the idea I had of what lay ahead, but I was truly hopeful that Captain Brighton really had a plan that would eventually get us home. This place was nice and all, but there was no way that I wanted to spend "indefinitely" here.

While I was musing, I overheard Delacoeur mumbling something softly to himself. I realized though, as I focused on him a little more, that he was asking us a question.

"What do you suppose is going on back on *Pathfinder*?" he repeated at my prompting.

"I dunno," Long said back at him. "They probably are a lot less burdened than we are." I could tell he was a little angry, but I supposed it to be more about the thought of *Pathfinder* being taken out from under us all.

"Sorry about that," Kieran said softly.

"Don't worry about it, I think Steve's just a little miffed at Teach and his thieves," I said, looking over at Long, who looked away. "They are probably making a run for wherever they had planned to go with her. It seemed pretty obvious that they had planned it out pretty well."

I realized that I was pretty angry too. I know I had been really mad when they had stuffed us all in the *Vanguard*, but I was fuming ever since they had marched us all down to the boat bay and told us what was going on. I hadn't even considered their offer about staying aboard *Pathfinder* with them. There was no way I was going to associate myself with criminals just to spare myself some struggles in life. That just wasn't me, nor could I have lived with myself had I done it. I knew I was young, and that there would be dangers, but I knew myself well enough to know I wasn't going to be able to stay aboard if they were mutinying.

"I am flaming mad," Long had said then. "If I had it to do over again, I would have tried for a weapon and killed as many of the rats as I could. I thought they were going to put us in the brig, and drop us off somewhere, not put us off in the *Vanguard* without enough food or power…They are cowards who wanted us all dead, but didn't want to fancy themselves as murderers, most likely."

"Where could they be taking her?" Kieran asked.

"Oh, who cares!" Long answered before I could express an opinion. "They have a buyer for the new tech or for the whole ship. One thing's certain, they will be long gone and none of us will ever get a chance for a speck of revenge on them."

"I don't know either, but one of the other Families, especially a competitor, would likely pay pretty heavy for the tech she carried aboard. That's why they gave her to Captain Brighton and his picked crew of officers," I replied, trying to keep my own disgust for the whole situation out of my voice.

"For all the good that did the captain, or any of us," Long quickly replied.

"Yeah, I have to agree with you there," I said, resignedly.

"Well, regardless of what happened, or what they are doing back on *Pathfinder*, Eddie and his crew aren't going to get away with it, if the captain can get us back somewhere where there is some civilization," I pointed out.

"Eddie?" Long asked. "Were you on a nickname basis with that snake, Teach?" His lifted eyebrows caught me off guard, as I saw Delacoeur also look at me askance.

"No," I stated. "I was just being a little petty and vindictive. I don't think he deserves to be called by anything resembling a polite term. Eddie was the name of that donkey in that old holoshow," I said sighing.

"Sort of degrades the donkey a bit, don't you think?" Steve said, laughing a little.

Even Delacoeur smiled at that, and I couldn't help but let out a little chuckle.

With that, we dismissed the subject and didn't broach it again while we walked toward the cave the captain had described. We walked for about another hour along the bank of the river, and the captain allowed us a couple of short breaks, during which we made sure to top off our water bottles. We then turned away from the bank, and up a gentle slope toward some low hills. We walked perhaps another hour or so before we got to where we were going.

Frustration appeared to ooze from Captain Brighton as he was stepping out of the cave when we managed to get up there with Kieran in between us.

"It's not the right one," he said simply to those of us who had assembled there.

There was nothing in the cave, I saw for myself on my quick look after Kieran had been settled on another rock. The cave wasn't even that big, really. It was possibly a little larger than the space aboard *Vanguard*. I didn't know what Captain thought would be in the cave, but it seemed as if he had been very disappointed to find it empty.

I exited the cave and looked back at the captain as he was looking at the sky. He watched the top of the foliage for a bit, then looked back down at the small prints taken from the cartography machine (which apparently could make an 'okay' print of terrain, but it was made to print astral anomalies and space scans), then back over to the cave.

Captain cleared his throat and we all turned toward him. "All right, folks, this isn't the right one. We saw what appeared to be four caves with a river nearby from the scans we did in orbit. I had hoped to guess right on the first try, but I suppose that perhaps we shouldn't count on getting too lucky based on everything else lately," he said.

"We are heading back to *Vanguard*, and we will try another of the cave areas. Follow me." With that, he turned and started back the way we had come. I heard him saying to Major Chowdhury as they passed me, "It has to be one of them … I'm sure of it."

I was getting pretty tired, especially helping Delacoeur, and I could tell that Long was pretty winded too. We had to push pretty hard to keep up with the captain's pace, and with the lighter food rations, I was really starting to feel weak. I was not sure we were going to make it without having to take a break by ourselves when we came around the last bend and saw the captain and *Vanguard* in the clearing. Everyone had beaten us back except Fujinami, who was pretending to be busy taking plant samples, but I was pretty sure he was staying just behind us so that we weren't the last ones back. I suppose it's possible that he really was that distracted, but I didn't think so. Either way, I appreciated the fact that he was behind us as we closed in on the craft and the rest of the crew.

Ward helped us get Delacoeur into *Vanguard*, and he thanked us all. The doctor was giving him a couple more melt-tabs for the pain. I stepped outside to get the last few gulps of clean air before getting back onboard to go to the other landing point. The daylight was starting to wane a little, as it was approaching late afternoon, when the captain finished with Lt. Johnson and told us to load up.

A few minutes later we were airborne on the chemical drives again, and Lt. Johnson took a ballistic course just slightly breaking the atmosphere and then bringing us back down. *Vanguard* screamed in on our new landing site. We all held on for the flight.

Ms. Johnson, true to form, set us down safely and smoothly, without too much backlash for us riders. I was happy about that. I realized I was still tired and more than a little sore as I got back up and began exiting the cargo/crew space. As I stepped out, I saw that Captain Brighton and Ms. Johnson had found us a nice landing site in view of another river. Unpleasantly, however, I noticed that the sun was showing midmorning. I had a feeling that meant no real break as we went in search of cave number two.

Sure enough, Captain Brighton quickly organized us again, and sectioned off six people to stay with the craft while the rest of us went in search of the cave. He changed out a couple of people from the previous group, leaving Ms. Johnson, and Mackey again, but substituting Delacoeur (for obvious reasons), Long (to my astonishment), Le Vesconte, and George. The Captain looked at me as he finished his grouping, and I nodded my acknowledgment to him. He felt I could do it fine, and so I would.

Unfortunately for us, the hike to the cave and back was long and unfruitful. We didn't like the fact that we had done it again for no apparent reason, but nobody was about to say anything to the captain. He was obviously disappointed, but within moments of the discovery he had regained his composure and we were "cheerfully" hiking back to the *Vanguard*.

The second trip, all things considered, went much more smoothly for me, and I actually felt better when we got back to the *Vanguard* than when we left it, my muscles felt stretched and well-worked. Captain allowed us to take a food break when we got back. Not that we had much in the way of food, but it tasted good, and made my stomach quit whining. Captain was pretty strict about making sure that everyone was getting enough water, so at least no one was getting dehydrated.

We quickly loaded up onto *Vanguard* and Captain and Ms. Johnson got us underway once again. As soon as we began disembarking from *Vanguard* at the third site, I heard Captain tell Ms. Johnson, "I think this is the one."

I hoped so, as I was once again included in the exploration party. We were obviously moving planetary west, as it was again midmorning. I was beginning to think that my first happy thoughts about being outside the ship were a little presumptuous. Oh well, I supposed the fresh air and sunshine were nice, I was just a little tired of hiking.

I was actually hoping that Captain Brighton would call a rest break when I saw the mouth of a cave. Since I was walking in the lead group, more to prove something to myself than to the captain, I was among the first few to enter it.

"Right, this is it," the captain said as we walked in. "Follow me back here and let's get those packs."

I was ecstatic when I saw what he had discovered, or I guess rediscovered would be more accurate. There was a bundle of power cells, and some bundles of food and some other supplies. Captain clapped Chowdhury lightly on the shoulder and she nodded back to him.

We all gladly accepted the extra weight of the gear as we loaded up for the trip back to *Vanguard*. It appeared that a lot of the food package seals had broken and a lot of it had spoiled. Not all of it, though, and we were glad of that. We couldn't figure out how we were going to get it all back in one trip, so we made sure to get all of the power cells, and what food we could, leaving the rest for a promised return trip.

We made good time getting back to *Vanguard*, all things considered. Everyone was pretty happy about getting the food, small amount that it was, but Captain was happier about the power cells. I was beginning to think that this might all work out okay after all.

I actually volunteered (what was I thinking?) to be in the smaller group to go back for the rest of the supplies. Another group was sent to explore the surrounding forest for food, or anything else useful.

We had a smaller group this time, but we were a little more jovial, knowing that we had found what we expected. Captain was smiling, which was a rarity in itself, and we made very good time. I actually got up the courage to ask the question we were all dying to ask, and the one which all of the older, 'wiser' group members had left unsaid, I queried the captain as to how he had known about the cache in the cave.

He smiled a little, and looked at me a little closer.

"History, Ensign Hayes. Do they still teach that at the Academy these days?"

"Yes, sir," I nodded while I said it, knowing that I was obviously missing something.

"Ah, well, Mr. Hayes, I think that maybe you never heard about what was one of my earliest space journeys. The fact that I was there ensures that I know about it, but few others have heard the details of Captain Cosina's exploratory adventures. I thought perhaps more would have, but then again, perhaps it is good that most haven't. I happened to be on this very planet when I was a bit older than you are, when we were staging supplies for a terraforming team which was to be coming through along with initial supplies to start a colony here. We delivered three caches like these. The initial terraforming was accomplished, here at least, but the follow-on colony was never approved. The caches weren't recovered, since the cost of recovering them far outweighed their value. I knew there was one here. There are two more in this system. Anyway, I am glad we found this one and that it was fairly intact, especially the power packs."

With that information to digest, I moved back a little. There were two more. There were two more! I started to grin and couldn't help but let it spread into a full smile.

When we returned to our camp, Captain asked us to build a fire, then moved off a ways with Major Chowdhury for a private discussion. It turned out that this order was not as easily accomplished as one might expect. Apparently, matches, lighters, flares, heaters, and anything of that sort were not considered essential for a standard emergency kit. Finally, after about twenty minutes of futility, Chowdhury returned, took over, and we had a fire in two minutes. "Ensigns," she muttered as she walked away.

We ate better than usual with two animals that Jherri had caught, and enjoyed the fruit that she and her group had found as well. I was seated on a small log we had carried nearer to the fire, and Captain Brighton sat next to me. He leaned over and asked me what I was thinking.

I paused, startled at the familiarity implied in the remark, but quickly replied, "Sir, I was just thinking this has been the longest day of my life."

He smiled. "Just wait, Ensign."

Later, Captain Brighton had called us all together to outline for everyone the full version of what he had told me earlier.

Captain let the information soak in, and then continued, "What we found in the cave here on Antoc-A3 demonstrates what I was hoping for. The supplies are all likely still out there and the power cells are functional," he said as he looked to each of us, drawing us in with his eyes. "Ladies and gentlemen, I intend to take us to each of those caches and recover enough of the power cells to take *Vanguard* out of this system on her jump drive. I intend to take us home."

I was smiling. We were going to be headed home soon. The general air, though, seemed subdued. It was a big change from what most had been expecting, which was more along the lines of Robinson Crusoe, waiting for rescue. Not for me. If I remembered my Literature class correctly, Crusoe waited twenty-eight years for rescue.

The planetary dawn was maybe an hour or two off at the most, based on the slight lightening of the horizon when we settled back to try to get some rest. I was amazed when I looked over and saw that the captain was already asleep. He had probably fallen asleep as soon as he lay down, since he couldn't have gotten to his spot more than a few moments ahead of me.

Mackey was charged to lead the guard duty for the remainder of the night. I saw him talking with the other four who would be staying up, as I began to settle myself in for some much-needed shut-eye. While I couldn't quite make out who was with him, I was confident that they were up to the task. I knew that I sure wasn't, at this point. If my mental calculations were correct, which I was unsure of due to that selfsame lack of sleep, I had been awake, moving, and quite frankly, working hard, for about forty-two standard hours. Those with Mackey had gotten at least a full four hours of sleep by rotating watches while I had been cave hunting. I was hoping to get at least that much.

Sleep came quickly for me as well, but I was still baffled by how quickly it seemed to have come for the captain.

30 June-1 July

Speed and stealth are mutually exclusive goals; you have to trade one to get the other. Vasconcellos knew that, had known it for years, and still hated it. In this case, the nearer they approached this planet the more easily they could be detected and therefore the more they had to reduce their engine output in order to maintain their deception. Most of his Marines were showing visible signs of frustration and impatience well before they were able to touch down in *Oeiras*. *Caxias* remained in orbit as a spotter. Their two platoons of Marines would not be needed to round up the ten or so Navy pukes that would fit in *Vanguard*.

Luck was with them so far. *Vanguard* had landed on the far side of the planet from the location of the base that had housed the scientists who were once terraforming the planets of this system. Apparently, *Vanguard* did not know where this camp was, but they were looking for it. The recon tech on *Caxias*, PFC Apellido, was certain he had picked up returns that indicated two suborbital hops that had brought them closer. The delay while the Warners looked had been enough that Vasconcellos' team had been able to land, conceal their ship, and begin setting things up to look like they belonged.

Rummaging through the supplies that had been left here produced clothing that nine of his soldiers could wear; the rest would need to conceal themselves out of sight somewhere, at least until they made their move.

"Energy readings, LT," Apellido sang out over the comm. "Ship approaching, bearing 261.4 from your position. About six minutes out."

"All right, you apes, you heard the man. Let's get our happy scientist faces on and play out our scene. Second platoon, keep out of sight until you get the signal," Vasconcellos ordered. There was a brief rush of activity in response, but most everything had already been set up to the lieutenant's satisfaction. Everyone pretended to be busy with something and waited out the remaining three minutes.

Then they waited five more hours.

Eventually, after repeated checking by Vasconcellos, Apellido reported that the ship had set down in a clearing two clicks away, a fact he was only able to determine because they had built a fire for the night.

"All right, apes, let's bunk down for the night. Tomorrow, we'll go meet the new neighbors."

1 July

Mama said there would be days like this, but she never said that it was possible to string so many of them together. Of course, she said that I would come to a bad end one day, so what did she know.

At first, I wasn't sure what Captain was up to when the ragged terraforming group came into our clearing.

"Stand easy, Major," he called. "These are the friends that Colonel Truman told us about."

I perked up at the name and made a show of relaxing. Truman was the name of the CO of the commandos that sold me out and led me into a trap nine years earlier. I wasn't aware that Captain knew about that particular episode of my career. Stand easy? Not likely.

That name told me something. He wanted me on watch. Captain and I had been together long enough that I could usually tell where his thoughts were headed. He was one of the most devious men that I had ever met. I loved that about him. He always left himself a way out of any situation. Preferably three or four ways out so he could choose the best one.

Several things were immediately obvious. These men were lying through their teeth and they had guns on us from somewhere. They claimed to be the terraforming crew that had been sent out by Warner Command but for some reason, Captain wasn't buying it. They probably had covering fire somewhere. You could bet on it.

When Captain tasked me to gather a group to go to their camp, I felt the loss of Aichele once again. I wished, sometimes, that I hadn't sent him back onto *Pathfinder*. Like I said, Captain likes to give himself lots of options, and maybe I'm finally learning. But I could really use someone here that I could trust.

Even after nine months together on *Pathfinder* and now our short time on *Vanguard*, most of the crew was still unknown to me. Johnson was a known entity, as she had been together on *Resolute* with Captain for a short time and I had served with her on *Fearless* when she was an ensign, but she was still young and developing as an officer. Mackey, I had known for years.

He was steady and solid but he only dealt with threats as they came. He never anticipated trouble. The ensigns were green and raw. They could probably only be trusted to do the wrong thing at the wrong time. That is what ensigns do best. Mackey was the best choice but he didn't have the rank.

"Johnson," I called, when I was away from the strangers far enough for them to be unable to overhear, "I am going to leave you in charge of security here at the ship. Have Mackey post guards and maintain a constant watch. Captain feels there is something wrong with this group. They aren't what they seem. Keep everyone under cover as much as possible and protect the ship at all costs. Without the ship, we're dead." Her eyes got big for a moment, but I don't think anyone saw.

I selected our party and we went off to the terraformer's encampment, leaving Johnson and Mackey with two guns to cover the group that stayed behind. While we walked with them to their camp, it became obvious that whatever these men claimed to be, they were military. There are always little clues in the way they work with each other. I would bet my next paycheck that they were either a Raider Strike Unit or Drop Marines. This made our survival much less likely.

On arriving at our destination, I could tell right away that this was either a secondary camp or they had been here a very short time. There was no evidence of occupancy. Those little bits of ourselves that we leave all around without thinking. There were no families and very little clutter. I whispered to Captain of my suspicions, but he just nodded. He knew already. That's what I love about him. He sees things. After we finished our meal and Captain told them some more lies we prepared to head back to camp.

"Well, the food was excellent," Captain said as he stood casually. Now was the critical moment. If they wanted to take us, now would be their best opportunity. "We enjoyed this meal and we greatly appreciate you sharing your meager stores with us."

I stood and casually separated myself from the group. Drew began gathering the supplies that we had received. He was also being very wary of our hosts.

We had secured the ship as much as was possible before we left, but I felt that they would make an attempt on us before we got back to *Vanguard*. It made sense to attack the groups while they were split. 'Defeat in detail' they call it. I had picked out six of the troopers that were paralleling us in the jungle on the way in. I figured that I could get three before they could cover the ground necessary to get to us unless they had armor, but I didn't know what kind of weapons they had. They might be able to keep their distance, but I didn't believe that they had any stand-off weapons, and I had seen no evidence of energy weapons at all. Of course, that could all be part of the ruse. It was best to assume that they were armored and had the normal weapons load out of a Raider unit. That put at least eight troopers in the woods in addition to the six that were pretending to be terraformers.

Just as I thought we were going to get out of the open clearing and into the cover of the trees, a bright flash and thunderous noise rocked the clearing. Heavy assault rifles by the sound. I squinted against the flash to preserve as much of my sight as possible and drew my pistol as I leapt into the woods to my right while everyone else was shielding their faces from the blast.

Everyone was scattering at the sound of weapon's fire and the 'terraformers' were pulling pistols from under the mounds of foodstuffs. I picked my targets and fired as quickly as I could. The troopers in the woods were a priority target but those in the clearing were easier to get to and would soon be just as great a threat. Two troopers went down with my first two shots but the second was still moving. They did have armor, then. That had been a clean heart shot.

"Captain, get them back to the ship, I'll cover your back," I called and let off two more shots at the terraformers. One connected and the large trooper went down. The second connected also, but the raider had managed to roll at just the wrong time and had taken the shot in the back. He was stunned but still struggling for cover. I shot him in the head and he lay still. I scanned for the captain but they were all moving up the trail. Captain looked over to my position and motioned to those still in the clearing. Shots were impacting all around them. Roberts was down but had managed to get under cover. Le Vesconte lay face down in the clearing where he had fallen after taking that first shot from ambush. Captain pointed to me and I waved. Got it, they were my responsibility. Many would dither and risk the group to rescue those still trapped. Not Captain Brighton. Command decisions are very difficult and the mark of a good captain is the ability to make the tough decisions quickly. If I had not been available, Captain probably would have stayed behind to get Roberts out but instead he moved off with the others towards the dubious safety of the ship. The remaining raiders in the clearing were all under cover and I could hear movement behind me coming down the hill. Time to move.

I found cover near the bole of a large tree about thirty meters to my right. The raiders in the clearing had gotten daring and were trying to move on Robert's position. One went down as Roberts let loose with a large rock that connected with the side of his head. The other kept going without firing. He obviously wanted a hostage. I got a clear shot just as he was about to reach down to grab the Ensign. My shot took him in the back of the head and he fell forward on top of her. She took his pistol and let loose a wild volley that forced everyone else back into cover. Good girl. All six of the terraformers were down, though two were obviously still alive and firing back.

I could hear movement behind me so I went up the tree. People get very used to looking at everything two dimensionally. A good trooper will be aware of what is above him but most aren't. I holstered my pistol as I saw my target. My pistol would be totally ineffective against the heavy armor that he was wearing. His helmet made it less likely that he would see me above him as well. He was moving slowly and cautiously through the trail. His weapon and helmet were both tracking from side to side slowly and methodically. He was doing everything by the book, slow and easy. When he reached a point on the trail that was directly below me, I swung off of my branch and dropped fifteen feet to land with both boots on his upturned faceplate. His weapon was swinging up towards me but my feet got there first. The weapon went off as I hit, burning the outside of my left leg and we went down in a heap with me on top of him. His heavy armor was not much of a cushion. Luckily for me, the helmet coupling of his armor was not strong enough to take an impact at that angle and it had come apart and broken his neck in the process. Grabbing his rifle, I rolled off to my right, favoring my burn as blasts came in from three directions. They were firing blind at any noise or shot without regard for their comrade. We must have gotten lucky and taken out their officers.

I decided that it was time to bug out. I slowly moved off of the trail and cut quietly through the light brush. I stopped every few seconds to listen. It sounded like they were trying to get around behind me. I kept moving until I reached a position near the trail back to the ship. I could see Roberts as she randomly took shots at one of the fake terraformers. She had pulled Le Vesconte into the shelter of the woodpile with her. How had she managed that? The other terraformer was nowhere to be seen.

"Roberts," I yelled as I opened fire with my heavy blast rifle, "run for it." She looked at me and with a quick glance at the scene she sprinted to my position and continued on to a large tree behind me. She jumped behind it and I followed her as the treeline erupted with return fire.

"Le Vesconte is dead," she said without preamble.

The fire abruptly stopped and I could hear movement to both sides. They were moving around to cut us off from the ship.

"Let's get moving then. Stay behind me and watch our backs."

We ran as quickly as possible down the trail.

We moved out, but we had not gone ten minutes before I heard weapon fire from in front of us. One of the sounds was from a large assault rifle like the one that had killed Le Vesconte, but the others were the sounds of our blast pistols from the vicinity of *Vanguard*. We could also see occasional flashes from that direction. It appeared that I had been right in deducing that they had been headed for the ship.

I slowed down and waved Roberts into the jungle. I scouted ahead a little and came back to her. "Wait here for ten minutes," I began, looking directly at Jheri and motioning to her wristwatch, "then follow up the trail slowly. If there are any issues, I'll try to come back and stop you before you run into them. You watch our backs." I handed her the rifle. "Be careful." She nodded and moved back into the brush.

I slowed again just short of the clearing, then moved up behind the men trying to take the ship. By my best count, there had been fourteen raiders between those in the clearing and those that had been covering us. We had accounted for five in the clearing, counting the one that I had landed on. I wasn't very impressed with their coordination. If I had fourteen Marines, no one would have gotten out of the clearing unless I wanted them to.

The one that I had landed on had been wearing heavy armor but the two that I could see from my perch were only wearing light assault armor. It was not top of the line equipment and the one directly to my left and five meters in front of me was totally oblivious to her surroundings. As I watched, I could see the reason. Her right shoulder bore a shield that was half red and half yellow divided diagonally by a narrow black stripe. That was the shoulder flash of the DaGama Family. They were not the last group that I would expect to see here, but pretty close. The DaGama family was very small and had no space interests outside of the Sol system. What were they doing here? As far as I knew, they had never conducted an actual, live, planetary assault. No wonder they were screwing up by the numbers. Of course, they would have to do a lot of screwing up for us to be able to slip through them and back to the ship.

I saw Roberts moving slowly up the trail with her captured pistol in her belt and the rifle sweeping jerkily back and forth as she tried to watch in every direction at once. I slipped quietly down from the tree and moved back towards her.

"We need to hold here for the moment," I said as I pulled her into the heavy brush along the side of the trail. She looked very young and scared. She also looked very relieved to see me. Once again, I missed Aichele and Burton or any of the other personnel that I had trained with over the years. I was going to need reliable backup if we were going to pull this off.

"You are doing great," I told her. "I want you to wait here until you hear my distraction. When you hear it, run for all you are worth. Run straight down the trail and shoot at anything you see. Don't worry about hitting me, you won't. Try not to shoot towards the ship. Once you get there tell Captain to raise ship. You are going to need to yell your name as you cross the clearing so that they know who is coming."

"What about you? We can't leave without you."

"If I'm not right behind you, I'm not coming. Don't wait for me."

"But—"

"That is an order, Ensign."

"Yes, ma'am"

I moved back up to my tree and continued to watch.

It appeared that they only had the one heavy gun. The others were armed with light carbines and pistols. In the time that I had been away, they had consolidated into two groups. I couldn't figure out why they weren't rushing the ship. As if answering my thought, two members of the far group tried just that. They had only gotten about ten meters before a heavy rifle opened up from the treeline to our right, firing into their midst. No one was hit but they broke off their attack. The heavy rifle in front of me opened up immediately to suppress his fire. Whoever was up there quit firing but there was no evidence that he had been hit. It looked like it had been a feint to draw fire so they could locate and eliminate the sniper. More important to me were the questions, "Who was up there and where had they gotten a heavy rifle? Normal load out for a light assault unit was two heavy rifles, ten light carbines, one demolitions pack and two pistols for the CO and sergeant. I had taken one heavy and the other was right in front of me, where had the third come from? A CO that liked to carry firepower? Wherever it had come from, and whoever was firing it, they were using it to good effect. A couple of quick shots before moving to a new location.

My musings were cut short by the sound of *Vanguard* warming up her engines. Captain knew that he couldn't hold for long as darkness was beginning to fall so he was getting ready to go whether we got back or not. He would hold out for as long as possible, but he would not risk the entire crew for two or three individuals.

Time for my distraction.

I slid back down from my perch as quietly as I could. Moving with as much stealth as I could manage I moved up behind the last heavy rifle. She had a good field of fire and she would be able to pick us off as we ran across the clearing if I didn't take her out first. My pistol would be almost useless against her armor which was designed to absorb energy and disperse it without allowing it to penetrate. The same went for high velocity projectiles such as bullets and flechettes. The reactive armor would feel the impact and harden itself to prevent penetration. Oddly enough, the best weapon against the armor was a knife. The slower entry speed did not activate the reactive armor and a knife blade would penetrate. Of course, bringing a knife to a gunfight had its own problems. I regretted the loss of my favorite knife, but I had left it in Morales when he and Brandon had jumped me outside my cabin. Captain had almost smiled when I reported the loss of those two crewmen. It was almost as if he had won a bet with someone.

Luckily for me, the raider was a newbie and had developed a terminal case of target fixation. I came up out of my crouch and had my second best knife in her kidney before she began to spin to face me. Her spin pulled the knife out of her back and I plunged it back in just below her ribs. I pulled her rifle away as she fell and began to target the group that stood in the path between Roberts and the ship. I got one in the shoulder and the group scattered quickly. The rifle in the treeline opened up at the same time and Captain came out of the ship with Hayes and Mitchell. Each had a pistol and they began to fire indiscriminately at the raiders from behind as they turned to face me.

They scattered into the brush even though the pistols could have no effect through the armor. Roberts came screaming down the path firing wildly in all directions. She drew some return fire but much less than I would have expected.

I started moving towards the ship as well, firing as I went. Roberts passed the three defenders as the raiders finally started a charge towards the ship. Mackey came out of the brush to the right of the ship and let off a volley with his rifle that caused the raiders to hit the dirt. He stopped at the captain's side and continued his rapid fire to keep the raiders pinned down.

The captain yelled something and Hayes ran back into the open airlock. I quit firing and ran for all that I was worth.

The clearing was only about 300 meters long and the ship was near the far end, but it didn't seem to be getting any closer.

Suddenly, the landing lights came on and I did stumble as I tried to shield my eyes from the sudden, dazzling brightness. I continued the roll and came back up running. The pursuers were well back, and I finally made it inside the perimeter. Both doors were open on the airlock and the crew was aboard already. Captain, Mackey and Mitchell were standing at the hatch, holding their ground against the charge. They opened fire as I went past to further discourage my pursuers.

As I slowed to enter the hatch, I could hear the sounds of the thrusters firing up. The defenders followed me in and the outer hatch closed behind us.

"Where is Le Vesconte?" Captain yelled over the noise.

"Dead."

"Are you sure?"

"Yes, sir. No doubt whatsoever."

Captain yelled forward, "Lift ship, Lieutenant."

ANTOC-A3, OEIRAS

1 July

It was clear now, in hindsight, that Brighton had not been fooled for an instant. It had appeared that they bought the story, but perhaps Vasconcellos had simply seen what he wanted to see rather than what was. It would not happen a second time, that was certain.

He had planned to divide the enemy into as many groups as possible, and then take them prisoner a piece at a time. While his orders allowed him to execute them if need be, when he saw how poorly armed they were he hadn't thought that would be necessary.

Instead of catching the Warners off-guard, the DaGamans had instead been caught unaware in a pincer move that pinned them down while the ship made good its escape. Now he had seven dead and five wounded in exchange for only one confirmed kill on the other side.

And a two click run to reach their own assault shuttle to pursue. *Our luck didn't hold for long*, thought Lt. Vasconcellos. But there was no sense whining about it. Just deal with the situation.

"Cinquini, Morisse, go get the shuttle and bring it here. Ogeia, Riordan, when you are done patching those two up, pull out the bags and seal up the bodies. Apellido," he keyed his comm to contact the orbiting shuttle, "do you have a track on *Vanguard*?"

"We got faint energy readings on their way out, but we lost them right after. They should have been plain as day on our scanners, but they're not. I think maybe the new technology includes something to mask their engine output. Lt. Harris has the ship headed toward a moon that's on the last known heading. Once we're in range, we'll scan again with our active emitters."

"Very well, keep me informed."

Oeiras arrived to retrieve them after twenty minutes that seemed much longer to Vasconcellos. Every minute they lost here was another minute's distance between Vasconcellos and his target. Sensing his mood, the troops loaded up in record time and they were breaking atmosphere twenty-four minutes after the last shot was fired.

Once they were out in the void, Vasconcellos asked, "Where are they, Apellido?"

He didn't receive an answer right away, which did not improve the lieutenant's mood. Finally Apellido said over the comm channel, "I'm getting nothing, sir. No energy readings at all. This makes no sense. If their engines were putting out anything at all, I should be picking them up. They can't be far enough away that we'd miss them."

"Cinquini."

"Sir?"

"Let's scan the planet. Harris, you check out the back sides of the three moons."

"Yes, sir," echoed from both platoon leaders.

It took less than an hour to circle around each of the moons, at which point *Caxias* joined the scan of the planet itself.

Nothing.

It was as if *Vanguard* had made itself invisible. Finally, Vasconcellos had to admit that he had lost the trail. It was a hard acknowledgment, but it was the truth. He had wounded that ought to be back at the base.

He would be back to pick up the trail as quickly as he could, though. He had a score to settle with Brighton and that Marine that had dismantled his north flank.

He would find them, and the next time they met, it would be them footing the butcher's bill.

1–3 July

The engines roared and I felt as if an elephant, or maybe a pregnant water buffalo, was sitting on my chest. I hadn't expected this level of pressure. Lt. Johnson had mentioned that we would lift off with our reaction drive instead of our gravitic engine and that would cause our artificial gravity plates to function erratically until we were clear of the planet's influence. She forgot to mention the water buffalo.

After the force of lift-off relented and we were able to talk somewhat, Ensign Roberts was overwhelmed with requests for information.

Major Chowdhury just laid her head back and closed her eyes and the other girl gave short, terse answers interspersed with glances at the quiet Chowdhury. No one attempted asking their questions of her, especially after seeing her clean blood off a knife before resheathing it.

Things quieted down soon after and remained silent for a considerable time. Everyone was left with their own thoughts. Despite the excitement of our departure, eventually calm contemplation was the order of the day. We soon settled into the unvaried routine of our shipboard existence.

"Unvaried" was also how I described the food on our boat. Our supplies in that area were both meager and limited in type. The vast, though I hate to use that word to describe it, majority of our foodstuffs consisted of ration bars. These were uniformly dense, tough to chew, and bland, nearly lacking in flavor altogether.

Apart from that, we had a small supply of food which had been brought aboard by members of our party prior to our narrow escape, and turned over to Brighton for mutual use. Also, we had a small amount which we had found usable from the stores in the cave, which included four or five kilos of jerked meat and dried fruit of a nondescript variety.

Fujinami had identified a kind of fruit on the planet that was edible, though not to be enjoyed very much. It was about the size of a cantaloupe, shaped like a pear, and deep purple in color. The fruit was bland and soft, but the skin was very spicy, and burned lips and tongue if eaten. Kara

George began calling them fireplums, and the name came to be generally used by all of us.

Most of the food and water gathered while we were on the planet were consumed while we were there. That took care of our needs at the time, but as I said, it did not add much to our supplies.

Provisions were the first topic which Brighton addressed when he began to go over with us his plan to get us all home. He shared few of the details, but did cover the salient points. First, we would need to make our food last us for some weeks. Second, we would need to have more power, enough to use the jump gate engines of *Vanguard* to get us back home, or at least back to civilization where we could expect help in returning there. Third, we needed to take ourselves out of this system before those on *Pathfinder* realized what we were about. Should we be discovered, they would no doubt take action to keep witnesses from escaping to report their activities. The people we had encountered on the planet were another source of potential trouble. Clearly they meant us ill, and it was possible that they would follow us and attack again.

While the overall plan seemed simple, I was sure that the devil would be in the details. How much power would we need? Where were we to obtain it? How would we keep from starving to death? How much time did we have before we were in danger from *Pathfinder* or the others?

I was not the only one contemplating such questions; though I appeared to be the only one contemplating them in silence. Everyone seemed to want to try to ask them of the captain at the same time, and the cacophony which ensued was terrible. Our cramped quarters were not fit to contain so many voices. It didn't last for more than a handful of seconds, though, before Captain Brighton roared for silence.

He was instantly obeyed.

"Now, we will continue the same rationing schedule we have been using. Three meals per day, three ration bars per day split eighteen ways." A dark cloud seemed to pass over us all at the reminder that Le Vesconte was no longer among us. Brighton, too, seemed to feel it, but continued on after a moment.

"Jumping out of this system will require more energy cells than we currently have. Teach felt confident that we would be confined in this system for at least the near term because he had removed most of the energy cells *Vanguard* normally carries. Therefore, in order to escape this system, we must reach a secondary jump point I have identified with more cells than we now have, and all of the cells will need to be fully charged.

"The Warner Family once expected that permanent bases would be set up here within short order, and the caches we discussed on A3 were to be used in that effort. A terraforming team was thereafter sent to work on the three usable planets in this system, and they had, at last report, made excellent progress on two of them.

"The evidence would seem to point to that team having been eliminated or captured by the group we encountered on A3.

"The cells we've added to our stores were left for the use of Warner citizens assigned to this system, which at the moment means us. The other two caches are located on Antoc-B2 and Antoc-B3, the other two planets undergoing terraforming. Added to what we already have, the power cells in these two locations should give us enough energy to transit the jump point on the far side of Antoc-B. The biggest problem we face is that the amount of energy *Vanguard* will require to transit is only a little short of the sum of all the caches together, plus what we started with.

"Starting now, we are going to have to stop using every joule of energy we can possibly avoid, and we are going to have to find some other way to power the things we cannot do without.

"Long, O'Neill, and Alcaraz, I want you to find a way to make that happen. We must have the oxygen scrubbers, water reclamation, heat, and we must be able to use the scanners from time to time."

"Aye-aye, sir," Long answered for all of them. "What about our astrogation and control systems?"

"Yes, Mr. Long, I've thought of that, too. I think we can disconnect the astrogation computer. First, it is an energy sink, and second, it doesn't do anything that a human brain can't duplicate, if not nearly as quickly. Since we will be using reaction thrusters instead of gravitic propulsion, we should have plenty of extra time to make sure we have the correct calculations.

"We will need to have our control systems active, but see what you can do to minimize the power budget. Hopefully, you can connect everything to a single control station and cut power to the other three. That may not be possible, or perhaps something better will occur to you."

"Sir?" Clémence Queneau asked. "Why are you planning to use the secondary JP? It doesn't connect to a Warner-controlled system. Shouldn't we jump back through the primary JP?" She was in a much better position than anyone else to know to where each of the jump points in this system connected, being our survey cartographer.

"I would if I thought we could, Ms. Queneau. By using reaction thrusters, we're going to be slow, which affects our food rations. Basically, once we have collected the power cells from the other two caches in this system, our food supply will not last much longer, certainly not long enough to traverse the entire system back to the primary JP.

"Once we have the power to leave the system, we're going to have to take whatever opportunity is the closest. Fortunately, the nearest jump point connects to a Portales-controlled outpost. The Portales Family is as close to a friendly ally as you could hope for out here, and as the old adage goes, 'Any port in a storm.'

"Are there any other questions?" The Captain's eyes swept over each of us in turn, but no one had anything else to ask.

Mackey surveyed those around him briefly, and seeing that no one was looking to take the floor, said, "Captain, I wonder if you would be so kind as to offer a prayer to ask God to prosper our endeavor?"

Captain Brighton seemed stunned by the request. It was clearly not something he had thought about, and he took several seconds before he answered.

"Mr. Mackey, I am not a very religious man, and I would normally have no idea what to say. However, I do remember a sailor's prayer that I read in a very old story. I believe that those words would be appropriate now."

The Captain clasped his hand before him, bowed his head and closed his eyes. He stood for several seconds before saying anything.

"Almighty God, Thou seest our afflictions. Thou knowest our need. Grant that we may quit ourselves like men and women in the trials and dangers that lie before us. Watch over us. Strengthen our hearts; and in Thy divine mercy and compassion, bring us all in safety to the haven toward which we now direct our course. Amen."

The Captain nodded to Derrick Mackey. There was a respectful silence for a short time, of which I believe many availed themselves to add their own silent plea in their own traditions. Eventually, Captain Brighton broke the silence by handing out more assignments.

"Three duty watches will need to be manned in rotation. I will command first watch, consisting of Mackey, Hayes, Smith, George, and O'Neill. Second watch will be under the orders of Ms. Johnson, and is comprised of

Long, Queneau, Delacoeur, Mitchell, and Paul. Ms. Roberts will take third watch, with Chowdhury, Fujinami, Ward, Alcaraz, and Williams.

"Any duties will be discharged by those on watch. Everyone not on watch should rest as much as possible to conserve energy.

"I see that we are currently two hours and twelve minutes into second watch. Ms. Johnson will take the helm. The only other assignment is for Long, O'Neill, and Alcaraz to work on a means of conserving our battery power. The rest of you may consider yourselves off duty."

Conservation of energy was paramount in their minds as Long, O'Neill, and Alcaraz huddled together to discuss their assignment. By this I mean that they were busy discussing what they could trade for power to operate the necessary systems on our little ship. "Energy don't come free," Steve Long said at one point. Between the three of them, they seemed to possess all of the needed skills and training for the task Brighton had given them.

I was not on watch, so I should have been trying to sleep. I found it difficult to do so, however. As tired as my body was, my mind just would not shut down. So instead of sleeping, I sat awake listening to the three men discussing and rejecting various ideas.

They started by making a list of the systems for which they would need to have power, and estimating the amount that would be required for each. Tim O'Neill was most familiar with the control systems, and he said that connecting everything to one station, as Captain Brighton had suggested, would be quite feasible, and that it would result in a marked reduction in power used by the system. He warned the others that the whole system was really very efficient in its use of power, and that it would not result in major savings from a quantitative point of view.

Alcaraz knew the oxygen scrubbers inside and out, and warned that they would use a large part of the final energy budget. He went into great detail about how the ceramic wafers (which were apparently the main components) generate oxygen via the direct electroreduction of CO_2. He explained more about the system, but I'm afraid I don't remember much of it, and I didn't understand the majority of it at the time. The exchanging of atoms from one gas to another with a carbon byproduct, which he described, was basic organic chemistry, but his description of how the electricity was employed and controlled was simply outside my experience. I do know that the summary was that the scrubbers would require about 60 watts, at least, to keep up with the carbon dioxide we were creating.

Long countered that an estimate was not going to be good enough; that we needed to account for every erg, and use as few as we could. To that end, Long accessed a multimeter from the service kit, and the three of them went through the boat from back to front and measured what power was being drawn from the batteries, and to which systems it was going.

I don't recall what their total list turned out to be, but I remember that the O_2 scrubbers were using much more than Alcaraz' estimates. Long pointed this out to him, rather tactlessly, in my opinion. Alcaraz countered that his estimate was the minimum required to keep up with the production of carbon dioxide, and not what was currently being used. The total wound up being in excess of 10 kilowatts, which Long was certain would be well outside of anything we could produce.

Several items went straight to the "would be nice to have, but not essential" list, lowering the energy budget by 80% immediately. The largest of these items was the artificial gravity field. The loss of that item would mean a lot of changes affecting our comfort, but it was clear that we could not provide the power to operate it without drawing it from the batteries. A few other items were added to the same list after a bit of discussion among the three of them.

Further reductions were proposed by one or another through making the essential systems more efficient. Alcaraz noted that the scrubbers, being such a vital system, were greatly overengineered. Some savings could be gained by narrowing the safety margin to 10%, or even 20%. O'Neill suggested that the control systems did not need to be powered at all times, only when orders needed to be input to *Vanguard*'s systems. He believed it would be possible to reduce power consumption by more than 95% by merely adding a switch to power down to a standby level, instead of moving everything to one console.

O'Neill was also the one to propose a design for an electrical generator. He claimed that he had built one while at school for his senior year project, though that was clearly many years past. Still, it made him the closest thing to an expert we had.

Long proposed making changes to existing systems first, then checking the energy usage before beginning on the generator. All seemed to be in agreement. Alcaraz went to work on the scrubbers, and O'Neill started with the nearest control station. Long went to discuss their plan with the captain and what would be required of all of us once the gravity plates were disconnected. The captain listened intently to the whole plan outline, and asked several questions regarding other options they might have considered. Long gave clipped answers, and it was clear to me from the other side of the compartment that Long resented the interrogation. Captain Brighton seemed not to notice, but eventually approved the plan without amending anything.

Unneeded items were the first things that Long gathered together for raw materials, but he certainly did not stop there. There were four control stations. The first two were in the pilot's compartment, one each for pilot and copilot. The other two were to the back of the partition that divided the pilot's compartment from the rest of the ship. These were the engineer's and auxiliary controls. Once O'Neill had disconnected power to the auxiliary control station, Long harvested all of the wiring. He left the datacords where they were, not simply because O'Neill needed to reconnect some of them. Being fiber optic, they would not provide suitable materials for the generator that was planned. O'Neill then used some of the pieces to make a switch for the copilot's and engineer's panels.

The seats were next. There was no grumbling from anyone who was evicted. They had all heard the decision to disconnect the gravity which would make their seats useless. Plates from the walls, plumbing fixtures, and vent gratings, anything not absolutely essential was gathered by the big technician and set in an ever-expanding pile.

Several hours went by like this, and I became so tired that I could hardly keep my eyes open. I tried to sleep then, but it was still very difficult.

Worry about our situation was only one of the reasons sleep eluded me, as it was also eluding most of the others. Our space had become even more cramped to accommodate both Long's pile and allowing the three men to move about the cabin. Add to that the noise of prying, dragging, banging, and occasionally Long's vociferous swearing, and the sum total equated to enforced insomnia.

I tried changing to several positions, and I must have dozed off now and then. When I again opened my eyes, the pile had grown considerably, and all three of the assigned techs were working together on the generator.

Alcaraz was working on a frame of some sort. He was cutting pieces of wall paneling with what I eventually found out was one of my laser scalpels, and using a quick-drying glue to form them together into a large box. Long was working to create a crank for the generator out of support bars from the partially disassembled seats. O'Neill was carefully winding a long wire around and around a plastic cylinder.

As the three of them worked, it seemed as if each of them was paying more attention to the work of the other two than his own. O'Neill commented to Alcaraz that the cover was going to be too small. Alcaraz looked at the ceiling, as if seeking patience from above. Long thought the frame would be big enough, but thought that the cylinder was too small for the magnetized bar. O'Neill demonstrated that it would indeed fit. Then Alcaraz wondered how the crank Long was making would connect to his frame.

At each of these interruptions, the actual building process had to stop while one of them explained what he was thinking, while the other two listened and nodded sagely. It was a wonder the generator was ever completed at all. Oddly, none of the three men seemed the least bit offended by the kibitzing of the others. If anything, they seemed to be drawn closer together as a team, as if by continually putting their two cents in, they were adding their stamp of approval.

Morale, in my opinion, continued to be relatively high. The loss of Le Vesconte was still in the back of everyone's mind, but the activity kept it from moving to the forefront of our thoughts. Even though not all of us were busy, it was easier to stay positive knowing that, as a group, we were working to get ourselves home. The bustle we could see going on around us acted as a focus for our thoughts and energies. And by concentrating on what we were doing, we didn't have time to worry or bemoan our lot in life.

I must admit that I was a bit startled to realize that this was the case. As the only medical officer aboard *Vanguard*, I had been keeping a concerned eye on all of the crew. I knew a long list of problems: mental, physical, and emotional; that could arise from the stresses and deficiencies we had all been undergoing. I had more than half expected to begin seeing the early signs of such, but to my amazement there were none.

All of the crew seemed to bear up remarkably well under the circumstances. All were generally amiable in their conversations with each other, at least insofar as that was in their natures.

Part of the reason for our amiable conversations was likely the fact that we avoided speaking of the events immediately preceding our departure from *Pathfinder*. Claire Paul and Elle Williams had broached the subject once, as it was perfectly natural that they should. However, they did so within the hearing of Captain Brighton, who lashed out at them with a towering fury. I do not think that I have ever seen the captain so angry, either before or since. He informed the two young ladies that it was no fit topic of idle conversation and that he did not wish to hear of it again.

Uncomfortable silence lasted for the next ten minutes or so, until

Johnson started a conversation with Mackey on an unrelated subject. Since then, no one had dared to bring it up again.

Eventually, O'Neill pronounced that the generator was completed. The multimeter was again brought out, and the three of them began testing the output with various test loads attached. They measured amperes, volts, watts, and whatever else it was they needed to know about the production capacity of the generator that they had spent so many hours working on.

What they found was that it was not sufficient. They revisited the list they had compiled, but, after a few halfhearted suggestions, decided that there was nothing left to trim from it. Instead, they wound up taking the generator apart and winding more wire around it.

The second test concluded much improved. They were able to generate enough power to cover every item on the "can't do without" list, though it required maintaining a fairly rapid speed on the crank. I think O'Neill would have taken it apart to add more wire, but he had used the last of it already. As a final step, the entire unit was welded to the rear wall for stability.

Brighton had been watching the whole proceeding, and gave the three men profuse praise for their work. He asked Long if he was satisfied that the system would work well enough to meet our needs. Long straightened to his full height and responded that he was.

Brighton nodded once and ordered them to immediately connect the generator to the required systems, and to disconnect the batteries from everything. The three assigned men did as they were ordered. It required a relatively short amount of time to complete, since all of the power connections had been left accessible.

Before the gravity plates were disconnected, we moved the remainder of Long's pile into the unused galley. Everyone then had to move to the aft bulkhead and stand there with our backs to what would soon be our floor. Johnson and Brighton were strapped into the two pilot's seats. Long made a last search of the cabin to be sure there were no loose items on the floor. He informed the captain that he was ready to cut the artificial gravity, and the captain reduced power down to one g of thrust.

When Long cut the power, I knew in my mind what to expect, but it still made me a little bit dizzy. The physical feel of it was that the ship had suddenly accelerated forward, and was continuing to barrel ahead unchecked. In reality, the artificial field, which had cancelled out the feeling of thrust, was erased in an instant and replaced with Newton's reaction to the action of our thrusters.

It took more than a minute for my brain to accept the sudden change, during which time I was experiencing a bit of nausea. Once I had gotten over that, I realized that we were going to be in for a long, uncomfortable trip.

If I had thought that things were crowded before, it was nothing compared to all of us being confined to one wall of the cabin. The aft bulkhead was a little over six meters wide, and less than two and a half tall. With two people in the cockpit, that left sixteen of us to fit in that limited space.

The generator was situated near the port side of our craft, at about the right distance that one could sit with one's back against what used to be the floor and use legs to "pedal" the crank. This was how it had been designed from the start.

Teams had already been assigned by Brighton with this duty in mind. After we had all reset our equilibrium, and were comfortable again, he addressed us. We were currently in the latter half of first watch, and so Mackey, Hayes, Smith, George, and O'Neill would take turns operating the generator. I had eleven hours before it would be my turn.

I couldn't see how I would be able to rest in that time.

LIEUTENANT FYONNA JOHNSON

3–7 July

Eleven years, I thought to myself. It had been eleven years since I started dieting regularly and working out, with aerobics and weight training, all to keep my weight down. Eleven years since I was a freshman in high school and a visiting naval officer addressed our school and forever changed the course of my life. Now look where all that weight control and conditioning was getting me. I weighed in at about seventy kilos solid, or at least I had been when we left *Pathfinder*. *This diet is a little stiff, even for me*, I was thinking. Right then I was wishing I still had access to the pounds of fat that I had been avoiding for so long. My muscle tone didn't seem to be maintaining either.

Of course, with the lower weight, my caloric needs were a little less than most of the crew, and I was getting the same ration as the rest. I also fit into a somewhat smaller space than many of the others, which was definitely an advantage when stretching out to rest. The men were trying to be polite and not complain, but it was obvious that the larger ones were suffering from the tight quarters. I watched as Kieran dealt with a cramp that he was trying to work out without kicking Mitchell and waking him up. I was also feeling cold. Too cold to fall asleep, so I decided to speak to the captain about it.

"Fourteen degrees," the captain said as I climbed up to the pilot's compartment, as though he could read my thoughts. "It's been dropping for the past half hour, ever since we switched the enviro systems over. The O_2 levels are dropping as well. The men have been working the generator constantly, but we're just not keeping up."

He looked a bit discouraged. He was keeping his voice low. I looked around. Most everyone in the ship was asleep, and no one had overheard.

"Are you asking for suggestions, sir?" I asked.

He actually smiled at that. "No, there is only one thing we can do: return to the planet. There's another reason for going back. We never had a chance to restock our fuel before our hasty departure, and we won't have enough if we don't go back for more mass to burn. I know that it's not your shift yet, but I've already turned us around. I'll be asking you to pilot us into atmosphere, of course."

"If you could take a seat, Lieutenant, I'd like to consult with you," he said. It may have sounded like an invitation, but I took it as an order. Captain Brighton was not the sort to ask for someone to keep him company for social reasons.

I finished climbing up and took the seat at the copilot's station. I could see that we were facing the small third moon and that we were slowly moving away from it. "You slingshot us, sir?" I asked. Of course I already knew the answer, but it provided an opening to the conversation to gain the information I was really after.

"Yes," he answered.

"That moon doesn't mass very much," I commented.

"No," he responded.

"How close were we?"

"53.685 meters, from our center of gravity, of course."

"Of course," I replied, trying to keep emotion out of my voice. Our autocrat of a captain had done a close approach on this moon, only 50 some-odd meters from the surface, and he calls me to consult only after it was all over. I don't know if he didn't trust my driving, or was just selfish. *No, that's not him,* I thought. *He just didn't think about coming and getting me for something he could do himself.*

"It's our braking that concerns me. How much can this hull take on re-entry?" he asked.

I looked over the numbers. "Not this much," I replied. "We'll have to up the acceleration. I'd recommend 1.4 standard gravities, sir. Do we have enough fuel mass for that?" I asked.

"Yes. I'll warn the crew first, then go ahead and do it. You have the ship," he said. He went down the ladder and I heard him talking to the crew, explaining why they were about to become even more uncomfortable. He didn't show any emotion in his voice. It was just an announcement. He then came back up the ladder and climbed into the other seat.

"Proceed," was his only word.

I had already set the controls. I pushed the button and put on almost half again my normal weight.

"Well," I said, "if we can't gain weight with extra rations, we always have this option to keep us from blowing away."

"Are we steady on?" he asked, not noting my feeble attempt at humor.

"Yes, sir, sixty-seven minutes till re-entry. We'll be pulling about four and a half gravities when we hit the air."

"4.46332," he said. "Don't exaggerate, Lieutenant."

"Aye, sir." I couldn't tell if that was an order or his own feeble attempt at humor.

"We need to land far away from where we saw the soldiers," he said. "Please plot your course and make adjustments as needed."

"We want to be near a water source, of course," I said.

"Yes. Besides fuel, where there is water we'll have our best chance of finding food. You still have the scans we made the first time?"

"Yes, sir. I know just where to put us down. We'll be a quarter of the planet away from that settlement."

"That will be satisfactory," he replied. "You have the watch, Lieutenant." Then he climbed down the ladder and went to sleep with the men.

It was the first sleep he'd had in a long while. I was going to let him sleep until just before re-entry. He wouldn't thank me if he woke when the weight hit. Nevertheless, he didn't sleep the whole time, but climbed back up the ladder after forty minutes. He didn't comment on the difficulty, nor did he seem to notice it. He didn't relieve me, nor did he make any comment at all. It was a very interesting half hour. I tried to make conversation a couple of times but received one-word answers, so I quit trying.

Before very long, I had too much to do to worry about Captain Brighton. Bringing the ship down safely, with the unfamiliar propulsion system, took all my attention. I managed a passable landing, not the best, but it earned no condemnation from the captain.

The first order of business upon piling out of the ship was to lighten her. The captain ordered a thorough search to be made of every compartment and bin, and anything that was not essential to our survival was to be left behind. I think this was a wise decision on the captain's part. The more mass we had to push around, the more fuel we had to expend, and we couldn't refill our tank if we ran out somewhere out in interplanetary space.

Still, this one action seemed particularly difficult for some of our number to understand, or at least to comply with. Fujinami, George, Queneau, Paul, Smith and Alcaraz had all taken several items of a personal nature when we had been evicted from our previous home. Many of these had been collected because their owners could not bear to lose them. It was not any easier to give them up now than it had been earlier. The crew tried to hide the pain it brought when Captain Brighton gave the order that they must be left, and I had expected him not to notice, but he surprised me. He had Dr. Ward empty one of the portable storage bins and used this to contain and seal all of the keepsakes. This bin was then secured from a high tree branch. The captain made a solemn promise to each of them that if he could arrange to be in this system again, as he intended to, that he would see to retrieving the items for them. This really was more compassion than I had ever seen Captain Brighton exhibit.

It was while we were removing extraneous items that Alcaraz discovered a solution to our previous problem. We were not going to be able to leave the planet without producing more energy for our environmental systems. The oxygen scrubbers and heaters could not be operated as they were if we expected to live for long. Since we had disconnected the ship's systems from the batteries, we now had all of those power lines available to construct a second generator. Captain Brighton was very pleased and put Alcaraz, Long, and O'Neill to work on it at once.

Ward and Williams were assigned to complete the task of removing everything we could do without, making sure that we retained the means to reattach the batteries to the jump engines. Ensign Roberts and I were given responsibility to resupply the water tanks, both for reaction fuel and for potable water. The rest of the crew was asked to see if they could gather food to add to our supplies. They organized themselves into groups of two or three for safety's sake (no one had forgotten how our last visit to this planet ended) and went their separate ways.

My task did not take that long to complete, since I had purposely landed near a clear flowing river. The item I had failed to remember was that we would be required to operate our generator to provide power to run the pump. Roberts and I connected the lines and I went inside to pedal the generator. It was very cramped, since our three "engineers" were trying to put together a second generator next to the first that I was operating. Rank has its privileges, though, and the others tended to defer and make room for me.

Maybe twenty minutes passed before I was able to stop, but this was still much less than a normal workout length. Easily finished. Perhaps those eleven years had paid more dividends than I had thought.

Once that was done, I debated whether I should assist Ward and Williams or go out looking for food. Long and the others certainly didn't want me kibitzing. I finally decided on foraging, after checking on the other task. They would be done cleaning out the ship well ahead of the other generator, and would be heading out to find food themselves. The seat parts had been the bulkiest items, and those had already been removed.

That decided, I gathered Roberts in tow and picked a course at random. We did not have a great deal of time to search before the time Captain Brighton had specified that we were all to be back, and so we came back empty-handed. I saw that we were not the only group to do so. The most common item collected was what the group had been calling fireplums. I didn't like them, but I found the old adage true that hunger made excellent sauce.

The amount of food was so slight that the captain decided to simply add it to our 0000 meal. Besides my cube of ration bar, my meal consisted of one and a half fireplums, and a long, green, juicy, tasteless something that no one bothered to find a name for.

Our corps of engineers completed building and testing the second generator at 0215, 4 July, and we all loaded back into *Vanguard* for our second departure from Antoc-A3.

Third shift should have put Williams in the pilot's seat, but she had been preempted so many times by the captain or myself, that I doubt she expected to take the helm during liftoff. She probably could have handled the job just fine, but every time I looked at her all I could see was how young she was. She had one of those babyish faces that look ten years younger than they should. Since she had only turned 21 since reporting aboard *Pathfinder*, ten years younger did not even come close to that look of maturity that inspires confidence. Unlike me. Right. Like I looked old enough to be an executive officer.

Anyway, I decided to compromise. Captain Brighton had stepped in to take the first shift on the new generator, which was a little more difficult to operate. I asked Williams to take the copilot's seat during lift off and had her read off the checklist for me, just to give her practice. The controls at the copilot's station were unpowered at the time, so there was no way that I could turn the controls over to her, and then take them back if necessary, without finding a rational reason to expend the extra power. I guess I was just looking for one more reassurance that she could handle the assignment before I put all of our lives in her hands.

Once we were out of atmosphere, I turned the controls over to her, and instructed her to follow the plotted course to slingshot off this planet's primary moon. She had a momentary look of panic before she acknowledged the order. I had planned to take over for her before the actual slingshot, but I changed my mind. She might never again have an opportunity to perform one. They are tricky, precision maneuvers that have become obsolete with the massive accelerations possible while using a gravitic drive.

The captain completed his turn at the power generator, but did not come up to take one of the two seats in the cockpit. Instead he lied down below and fell asleep at once. He must have been near exhaustion, with only two short naps during the last two days to keep him going.

I watched everything Williams did for the next several hours, ready to jump in with corrections or advice as needed. I was silent the entire time. At some point, I would think, *she ought to check*—and then not complete the thought as she did just that. If I hadn't known better, I would think she was a mind-reader. We completed the maneuver that added the moon's orbital velocity to our own, and I could not find one instance of fault or even anything needing improvement.

"Very smartly done, Ms. Williams," I said, and put my mind completely at ease concerning her abilities. She flashed me her child-like smile and said, "Thank you, Lieutenant." Child-like perhaps, but she was certainly no tyro.

At 0800, the captain was still sleeping. He was scheduled to be on duty, but he had left no instructions as to whether he wished to be awakened or not. I was also not sure about taking it upon myself to see to the distribution of our morning ration. This was what finally decided me, and I gently nudged him. His eyes popped open at once, and they moved immediately to the time/date display on the forward bulkhead.

"First Watch, Captain," I said lightly. "Permission to distribute rations?"

"Yes, Ms. Johnson. Please see to it."

"Aye-aye, sir," I said, and climbed up to the galley. Captain Brighton climbed the ladder right behind me and continued past me to relieve Williams at the helm.

After I fed the troops, I found an unoccupied spot on the aft wall and curled up to sleep. I did not wake until nearly 1600. It seemed I had just performed these actions, but I climbed up the ladder and addressed Captain Brighton.

"Second Watch, Captain," I said. "Permission to distribute rations?"

"Lieutenant, you do not need to ask at every mealtime. Consider it your assignment to make sure the food is passed out as set forth on our rationing schedule. However, if you would take over the helm, I will see to this meal."

"Aye-aye, sir. I relieve you."

"I stand relieved."

There was not much to do for this watch. Our next stop was planned for Antoc-B2, but we could not take a direct course there. Such a course would have put us through the middle of Antoc's primary star. Our course was instead an elliptical one which took us out toward galactic north of the star. At least that had been the plan before the navigational sensors picked up something out of the ordinary just after 1830.

"Captain," I called out. "Sensors show a contact, bearing 64.05 relative, on the plane. Signal indicates a WSN lifeboat."

That sent a buzz through the crew and brought the captain up the ladder. He queried the system for all the available information, which wasn't much. Our sensors had been scaled down to what was barely safe to aid in astrogating through the system. A five minute wait allowed us to triangulate the distance, and thus the position of the signal source.

The captain closed his eyes for a few seconds and then said, "New course: true 51.52019403 by zero, one standard g acceleration."

"Coming to new heading 51.52019403 true, same plane, at one standard gravity, aye, sir." And that was that. We had altered our course enough to rendezvous with the lifeboat, presumably to add to our supply of both food and power, but it would still be more nearly three days before we reached it.

The excitement wore off gradually. When Williams relieved me at watch change, and I was back among the crew below, I heard several talking about the benefit the additional stores would give us. I had to agree. I knew exactly what each lifeboat contained, and the rations aboard it would almost double our current supply of food. It also contained a battery and valuable electronic components that we could use to repair the long-range transmitter which had been destroyed before we boarded *Vanguard*.

Still, seventy hours is a long time to anticipate, and it ceased to be the main topic of conversation until we were beginning our final approach, to match course and speed.

Second watch rolled around on the seventh, and I was again at the helm, making subtle corrections to ease us into position. I had asked to increase the sensitivity of the sensors for this stage of the project, and Tim O'Neill had obliged me. I had the data screen set to full display mode, and that was how I happened to notice a bit of information which I had not previously seen.

"Captain," I yelled below, to be sure he heard me over the hum of the generators in operation. "The lifeboat is broadcasting a code one. There's someone on it!"

And that was when it exploded.

7–9 July

Dejection was written on the face of everyone in our little ship. We had all been hoping so much to gain access to the extra food and power available in the lifeboat. Our morale diminished sharply in that instant, and it seemed as if our hunger was increased after the anticipation of more food was taken away from us.

Not two minutes ago, we had been cataloguing all the things we would be able to add to our supplies. Now the loss of the lifeboat left the taste of ashes in our mouths.

I was physically ill when I thought of Johnson's report that there was a person aboard the pod. Who could it have been? An unknowing crewman in the wrong place at the wrong time? One of the traitors caught off guard? One of the loyal crew bound and placed there awaiting the taking of the ship? I had no way of knowing, and no way that I could find out.

The more puzzling question was why the lifeboat should explode like it had. There was no reason for it that I could imagine. The whole episode was an enigma, and the irrationality of it added to the shock we all felt.

What could we do to prevent the same kind of sudden, catastrophic destruction to our launch? The answer, of course, was not a thing. It clearly had been a freak occurrence, infinitesimally unlikely to happen again. My mind may have realized that, even at the time, but the gut-wrenching emotional shock outweighed everything else.

To calm myself, I willfully thought of all the positive attributes *Vanguard* had. She was our protector, our provider, our mother; carrying us all in her womb to a place of safety.

I took a deep breath and raised my head. Fujinami was seated closely to my right and Ensign Williams to my immediate left. Jens seemed to be in control of himself, though he was staring straight ahead with unfocussed eyes. Elle, though, held her face in her hands and her shoulder-length, strawberry blonde hair shook with sobs she was doing her best to control.

I wasn't sure whether she was crying because of the death, or because of the loss of the much-needed supplies. She likely didn't know herself, and it was simply a combination of everything we had all been through. I didn't know what I could say to her, and so at first I said nothing, just gripped her near shoulder with one hand to offer her support and encouragement.

She turned and buried her face between my neck and shoulder, and I had no choice but to put my arm around her and offer what soothing words I could think of.

Mitchell called out at that moment from his awkward perch above us. A temporary seat had been rigged to have someone on watch manning the low-powered sensor array. Whatever the ensign had been feeling, he had not forgotten his duty.

He reported picking up another contact, matching size and speed for another of the lifeboats. Everyone's ears perked up at that news. The emotional see-saw we were all riding kicked us upward then, and the previous dejection was put in abeyance.

Elle Williams lifted her head from my shoulder and dried her eyes. She gave me a game smile that was at once thanks and apology.

A minute had not passed when Mitchell again reported another new contact. Three of the twelve lifeboats from *Pathfinder* had now been accounted for. Hope and expectation blossomed in all of us, with one exception.

It being second watch, the tall, slender frame of Lt. Johnson occupied the pilot's station. She eagerly turned to Captain Brighton and asked permission to shape our course to rendezvous with the two lifeboats. Rather than answer her directly, he turned to Mitchell and asked to know the bearing and distance to the pods.

Mitchell dutifully read the numbers off his screen, then, anticipating the captain's next request, began calculating the necessary course change to enter in. This was not really his responsibility, but Captain Brighton had been taking every opportunity to drill the junior officers in the skills and knowledge they would one day need. Astrogating without the aid of a computer, as we were, had given him a unique situation, of which he was taking full advantage.

Brighton never called for the results, however. Mitchell had barely started setting up the complex equations, when the captain grimaced and ordered Johnson to maintain course and speed.

"Maintain course, Lieutenant," he ordered, with no further explanation forthcoming.

The disappointment this time was not nearly so acute as that which we had experienced a handful of minutes previous. Perhaps we had not let our hopes be raised very high in anticipation of such bad news. For my part, it was trust in the captain's decision. If he had weighed the options and not pursuing the lifeboats was the most favorable course of action, then that was sufficient.

"Sir," Queneau asked, "I'm not disputing the decision you've made, but how do you know no one else is aboard either of the two life pods that might need rescue?"

He was silent for such a long time, that I believed Clémence's question would never receive an answer.

Eventually, Captain Brighton responded to the specialist's question. "I do not care to explain myself, Ms. Queneau. Suffice it to say that I know for a fact that no other lifeboat could be occupied."

As if to emphasize that the conversation was over, the captain arose and climbed up to the cockpit. He exchanged a few words with Johnson, then she climbed down and settled into Brighton's vacated position.

We sat in silence except for the whirring hum of the generators. Finally, Long said, just loudly enough to be made out over the generators, "So, how does he know?"

"How could he know?" George rejoined.

"I don't know," Johnson said, settling in, "but one thing I can tell you for sure, the captain wouldn't say he knows unless he is sure."

All of us wanted to discuss this a little further, or so it seemed to me, but we knew that Captain Brighton did not want it discussed, and either duty to or fear of the captain held our tongues.

When I speak of fear of the captain, I do not want you to think that Captain Brighton was a bully, for he was not. I meant simply to imply that we did not want the captain to single us out for added scrutiny. Though the captain was 38 cm taller than me, and had nearly twice my mass (I remember clearly from his medical records), the most intimidating thing about him were those piercing blue eyes that could look through a man and take the measure of his soul.

Many stories in the media have played upon Captain Brighton's temper, which matched his fiery red hair. He certainly had a temper, but anger was not his normal state, and I do not believe he ever acted without thinking. My memories of him are of an intelligent, detached man, who took his responsibility and duty to those in his charge with utmost seriousness.

Conversation turned to other matters after a time, generally matters of no importance. To lighten the mood, Long told a story of a practical joke he had engineered during his last tour, on a ship called *Halcyon*. His supervisor had been inspecting his repairs on a cargo shuttle when the fire alarm had triggered and he had been halfway immersed in suppressant foam. Long, of course, was never suspected because the control systems were not accessible to him, or so they believed, and the whole thing had been written off as "faulty sensors."

Several others shared humorous stories from their past. I told about the incident in medical school where we had embedded some radio-controlled robotics in the arm of a cadaver and nearly caused an apoplectic fit in poor Doctor Steenen. We were fortunate that she never learned who had caused it, though I think she had her suspicions.

Activity was kept to a minimum, of necessity. Today was the seventh day of drastically reduced rations, not including the days spent on Antoc-A3. Signs of weakening had begun to appear in several of our crew, including myself.

Still, smiles could be seen on every face as we sat and shared our happier memories with each other. It pleased me to see that our emotional seesaw came to rest after an upswing. Our situation was desperate and difficult enough to manage as it was. Anger, bitterness, lethargy, or depression, any of which would be expected responses, would certainly cause the situation to worsen still further.

Asteroids began entering our detection range toward the end of second watch. Captain Brighton was still manning the pilot station, and reduced our acceleration to almost none at all. We still had considerable velocity built up, and he made no effort to slow us. Still, by not adding to our velocity, we would have a bit more time to make corrections to our vector, if necessary.

This seemed prudent to me, since our sensor range had been limited by the reduced power we had available. The benefit to us was that there was just enough thrust to keep us all on the floor, but the reduced apparent weight was a relief to each of us.

O'Neill called up to the captain, who answered without taking his eyes off the sensor display before him. After some discussion between them, Captain Brighton gave him permission to see if he could find a way to harvest some of the material to be found among the asteroids for additional fuel mass. The captain seemed quite pleased that he had asked about it, and eagerly set him to the task.

For his part, O'Neill began his work just as eagerly and climbed up our improvised ladder to the storage area and closed the door behind him.

Eventually, we went back to our previous conversations and I silently hoped he would be successful.

Fujinami asked Chowdhury if she would mind trading places with him. She agreed easily enough, though she looked at him oddly, wondering why he had asked. When they had both moved to their new positions, Fujinami stood rather than sitting. From his new location, next to the secondary airlock, he could look out the small viewport in each of the two hatches.

Fujinami had an inquisitive nature, and the newness of passing through an asteroid field prompted him to do what he could to gain new knowledge. I'm not sure that he was able to see much of anything, though.

Unlike my friend, this was not the first field of asteroids through which I had passed. I had the same desire to see what it was like the first time, and I was utterly disappointed. While an asteroid field does have big rocks of all shapes and sizes, they are dispersed to such a great extent that they must be either very large indeed or else passing by very closely to be spotted with the unaided human eye. Not at all what one would expect from watching popular holovid programs, which, unfortunately, was once the source of most of my knowledge of space work.

It was still a bit more than an hour before third watch would begin, and I was scheduled to take the first shift on one of the generators, so I decided to try to rest a little. I leaned my head back against the wall and shut my eyes, willing myself to relax. My body was its normal obedient self, but my brain just would not stop processing information.

One thought that I had, almost against my will, was to realize the sum total of the food I had consumed in the seven days since our first departure from A3. When I totaled up the calories I had ingested, it did not even reach the amount one would see a hungry man eat at one meal.

This realization startled me to such a degree that my eyes opened and my head snapped upright. Elle, sitting next to me, noticed me jump and asked what it was. I told her it was nothing, but neither of us believed it.

I knew that we had been on short rations; how could I not? But the extent to which we were withholding sustenance from our bodies had not hit me intellectually. I certainly could not settle down to rest now. My mind filled with the myriad problems we would be subjected to as our bodies began to shut themselves down. I wanted to go discuss my predictions with the captain, to see if there was any way we could relax our rationing somewhat.

I thought better of the idea and kept my seat.

The captain had not asked my opinion when he set the rations forth. He had looked only at two things: how much food do we have, and how long must it last. Both of these were things over which I had no control, nor, for that matter, did the captain. 'What cannot be changed, must be endured,' had been the favorite phrase of my roommate during third year at medical school. It seemed very appropriate now.

I would simply have to prove the words true and endure what was necessary until it was over, one way or another.

O'Neill climbed out the hatch of the storage room at watch change to receive his dinner ration. Brighton remained in the pilot's couch and allowed Johnson to see to distributing the food to the crew. Elle Williams normally took over piloting during third watch, but the captain waved her back down to her seat.

I took my ration from Johnson and went to relieve Delacoeur at the left generator. Alcaraz was due to take over the right, but O'Neill asked if he could switch with someone and help him, and asked Long if he would also join them. Fujinami was working the sensor station, so Elle said that she would take Alcaraz' slot, if that would be all right with the captain. He merely nodded ascent.

The size of my portion of food reminded me of my earlier thoughts, but Elle's smile as she sat down brightened my mood again.

I had been scheduled to be the "odd man out" this watch, catching 4 one-hour shifts at the generator, while the other four had three. Brighton's decision to remain at the helm had added Williams into the rotation, and Alcaraz was still pulling his shifts, though out of order, which meant I had only three shifts instead. I managed a nap in between my first and second turns, which the captain not only allowed, but encouraged, even though I was technically on duty.

I had finished my second round of near-endless pedaling twenty minutes past, when O'Neill came out and said he would be ready to try to gather in additional fuel when material could be detected within a limited range. *Vanguard* had matter collectors located at the front which pulled in any material located in its path. The collectors were not designed or intended to collect fuel for the reaction thruster, which are usually used only for maneuvering and station keeping. The gravitic engines are much more powerful and efficient, and so, under normal circumstance, she would not use much of her reaction fuel.

The purpose of the matter collectors is actually to protect the ship from colliding with said particulate matter lying in its path. The fact that the matter is added to the fuel stores is incidental to this primary undertaking.

Since fuel was a limited resource for us, as was most everything, O'Neill thought to take advantage of this incidental task. His plan was to try to use a narrow, controlled tractor field to pull additional material into our path, where the collector would then add it to our fuel supply. In this plan, he had two difficulties which had to be overcome.

First, and most difficult, would be timing. We didn't have the power to spare to operate a continuous gravity field, and the field's strength would lessen with increased distance from *Vanguard*. So the tractor would have to be engaged a number of times to pull an item to a point that would intersect our path exactly at the moment we passed.

Second would be locating and selecting appropriate asteroids to pull in. If they were too small, it probably would not be worth the energy we would expend to collect it. Too big and it would destroy the collectors instead of being collected.

I was back to pedaling for the last time that day when Ensign Roberts, manning the sensors at the engineering console, reported a suitable candidate. O'Neill climbed up to replace her. He had connected the tractor controls at that station, since it was the only remaining radar display still powered.

Tim made several adjustments before activating the tractors for two or three seconds. He watched the radar display intently, and ran his fingers over the data feed on the sidebar. He pulled out his datapad and started entering figures. After a few seconds he stopped.

"Ms. Roberts?"

"Yes?"

"I'm not going to be fast enough at this. Can you calculate a delta-v for me as I read off the position?"

Jherri pulled out her own pad and indicated that she was ready.

"Mass reads as 34.42 kg. Position one, bearing is 315.2 by 70.15 relative at 5251.2 km. Fifteen second spread, position two, bearing 314.16 by 70.13 relative at 5191.8 km."

Roberts was entering the given data quickly when Captain Brighton answered from the cockpit.

"Eighty second delay. Mark. Four seconds at 87.4 gravities."

O'Neill began setting up the tractor to activate automatically on the given schedule. There were 24 seconds remaining when Roberts sang out, "Confirm acceleration, time, and duration."

I was amazed! Chowdhury, pedaling away to my right, nearly had to remind me to keep my generator going. The captain had solved the entire complex equation in a matter of seconds with no computational assistance whatsoever!

The tractor activated on the zero tick, and deactivated four seconds later. O'Neill eagerly collected data off the display and calculated the new course of the chunk of rock we had pulled toward us. After a minute, he let out a sulfurous curse.

"Captain, could you check my math?"

"Go ahead, O'Neill."

O'Neill provided the captain with two bearings, and the time between the readings. I would swear on a stack of Bibles that Captain Brighton had the answer in two seconds!

"We must have gotten bad mass readings, Tim, because we didn't pull it in enough. From the vector change, it must be 328 kg; too big for us to collect."

"That matches my numbers exactly, Captain," O'Neill said dejectedly.

Captain Brighton called back to him, "Don't get down on yourself, young man. You showed exactly the kind of initiative and problem-solving we will need to get home. I think our initial attempt was encouraging, and you've earned a reward for your efforts. Johnson, I want O'Neill to have a slice of the dried fruit with his next ration."

"Aye-aye, sir," the second in command acknowledged.

"Thank you, sir," the suddenly beaming warrant officer said.

"Well deserved, Tim, well deserved. Now find out why the mass reading was off, so we can make it work next time."

"Aye-aye, sir."

O'Neill turned the radar station back over to Roberts while he went back to the storage room to retrieve a diagnostic kit. Alcaraz climbed up to collect a second kit and set about assisting. Long likely would have done the same, but at that moment he was curled up in a corner, asleep. He had missed the entire event.

It was not long before I had completed my assigned hour of converting calories into electricity. Williams came and took my place before I had a chance to call out to Alcaraz, who should have been my successor. I was glad of it, as the work he was already doing might turn out to be just as important to our survival.

I made my way carefully to the open spot Elle had just vacated. I was surprised to find that my legs trembled all the way there, and did not cease when I sat down. My leg muscles continued to quiver for an additional ten minutes or so before finally settling down.

My body's exertions had finally overcome my brain's distractions, and I fell at once into a restful sleep.

Cheerful eyes greeted me upon awakening, and Elle handed me my "breakfast," which I had slept through. I checked the clock on the forward bulkhead, now the ceiling, and saw that I had been unconscious for almost nine hours and it was now approaching "lunch."

Jens filled me in on some of the events of this watch that I had missed. The three designated engineers for our ship had twice gone over the entire system which measured the mass of objects within our scanner range and could find no defect.

O'Neill had attempted another grab at the next suitable rock that turned up, hoping to refine the mass calculation as had been done before, by detecting the vector change from the applied acceleration and solving for m. Two iterations of this process had produced widely variant values in the solutions.

O'Neill threw his hands up in frustration, but Long went back to the diagnostic board and found the culprit. The mass readings had been accurate all along, but the directed gravity was not the amount programmed in. Since the tractor was no longer drawing power from the main batteries, it could not produce more output than it had power available as input.

Long and Alcaraz calculated that the maximum output available would be between sixteen and seventeen g. O'Neill tested again, and asked both generators to be pedaled as fast as possible and was able to see almost twenty gravities output.

Using this new information, the captain was able to create vector changes with longer pulls at lower accelerations. As I had slept, O'Neill was able to gather in five portions of detritus of varying sizes. The captain said that would represent an additional fifteen hours of thrust for *Vanguard*.

Unfortunately, that was all that there was to be had, since we had left the asteroid field a few dozen minutes before I had awakened.

Johnson brought up a subject that I hadn't considered. She commented that she was relieved they had not picked up any trace of other ships in the asteroid field. I had completely forgotten about the soldiers on A3, being focused on life inside our ship, and said so to her.

"Well, those people got to A3 somehow, which means they have a ship. If they attacked us once, what's to keep them from attacking again?"

"I guess I can't dispute your logic. It just never occurred to me," I told her.

"Well, that's why they pay us command officers so handsomely; to make sure that we worry about everything," she rejoined with a smile at the long-standing joke. She even managed to get a chuckle from Brighton, which I was pleased to hear.

At watch change, Johnson again retrieved, divided, and distributed our food allotment. That task completed, she climbed up to the cockpit to take over the controls from Brighton.

"Second watch, sir. I relieve you."

"I can man this station another watch, Ms. Johnson."

"Aye, sir," she said, and started down the ladder. Halfway down she stopped and climbed back up. "Mind if I join you, sir?"

I thought he would send her away, but instead he smiled and invited her to sit in the copilot's seat.

She certainly was earning her princely salary now, worrying about the captain. When I thought back on it, I realized that aside from the first few hours of second watch yesterday, Captain Brighton had been manning the helm for the last 32 hours, and certainly had not slept in at least that long. If the captain would not allow himself to be relieved, at least some conversation would help him to stay awake.

I tried to listen in on their discussion, but it was difficult with the level of noise around me. I heard only fragments, but they seemed to be talking over how they would have gone about surveying the asteroids, and what they possibly might have discovered thereby. Unlike the last reminder of our change in situation, there seemed to be no anger or defensiveness in the captain's manner.

It seemed a good sign to me, and I hoped that Captain Brighton had used the self-enforced isolation to work through his issues. If so, perhaps I could stop worrying about him. I smiled to myself at the thought that I might be collecting my pay without earning it, if I did stop worrying.

Emptiness slid past us just beyond *Vanguard*'s metal skin, and time crept onward. The rocks we had had for occasional company a few hours before were now in the distance behind us. Star-dotted blackness was all that was to be seen from the upward view. There was nothing to be gained or learned there.

Nothing of import was to be gained by staying awake at all, and most of my crewmates were asleep during the last hours of second watch. The human body tries to impose its own circadian rhythm to the world around it, and for most everyone, this was the late evening part of that cycle. My own body had become accustomed to being awake all night, so third watch was no inconvenience to me. Being the junior medical officer, I had the 2000 to 0800 "graveyard" shift while on *Pathfinder*.

At two minutes to watch change, Elle climbed up the ladder to take over the piloting duties. Captain Brighton accepted her relief with no additional comment and climbed down to the main floor.

He went straight to the storage locker containing the food bars and began dividing them for the third daily meal. I accepted my portion on my way back to the generators for another round of exertions. Brighton continued handing out cubes of concentrated sustenance to those who were awake, and noting those who were not to see that they received their equal share.

Delacoeur was last to receive his portion, after he was replaced at the other generator by Alcaraz. He popped the whole piece into his mouth and chewed it heartily. When he was done with that, he turned to the captain and asked if there wasn't any more to be had.

Brighton was so startled by the question that he said nothing for a few moments. "No, Delacoeur, there is no more to be had. We will not have enough to see us through if we do not maintain the schedule."

"But, Captain," the cook sounded plaintive, "I'm so hungry. Couldn't I just have a little extra?"

"Impossible." The statement was firm, but not the angry roar I had expected. "Don't you think all the others are just as hungry as you?"

"But that's not fair, sir. I'm twice the size of some of the others, like Ward."

"And with a significantly greater amount of stored reserve, too!" He was approaching that roar now. "You are not bigger than me, man, and I will not take one ounce more than my share. Nor will I allow you to do so. This will be the last I hear of such a preposterous request, or I will *reduce* your ration. Is that clear, Delacoeur?"

The big cook looked like he was going to press the issue further when he noticed an armed Chowdhury standing at his right shoulder. Johnson was standing just out of arm's reach to his left and the eyes of every crewman were fixed on him.

He deflated to the deck. "Clear, Captain."

9–17 July

Exhilaration and fear were both present the next morning as I awoke. Despite my best efforts, I had collapsed into slumber soon after my confrontation with Delacoeur. I could not believe that he was actually complaining about his portion. I knew that we would have some grumbling before our ordeal was over, but I had been sure that everyone would endure rather than looking weak to their fellows. I had been wrong in that. Although, despite the cramped quarters, no one was sitting next to Delacoeur. Most were avoiding looking at him and those that did direct their attention to him had looks that ranged from pity to anger. No one was looking at the cook with apathy. All had an opinion, one way or another.

If I had been wrong about the actions and attitudes of the crew, I wondered what else I had been wrong about. No, I must not dwell on the negatives. That was the way to indecision. I must make the best decisions possible and then go forward with all my energy.

This morning, I had awakened to hear sounds of revelry by most of the crew. This was accented by the somber silence of the others. I looked at the chronometer which was located on what was once the front wall of the cabin, but which was now the ceiling above us. 0540, 9 July, it displayed in bright red numbers. If I hadn't known that there was no alcohol on board, I would have thought them all drunk. I soon learned from their shouted conversations that they were indeed drunk, but with a completely different substance. They had just received the ZFlash beacon call from *Pathfinder*.

The ZFlash beacon is only jettisoned as a last resort, to download all of the logs of a dying ship. Similar to the "black boxes" still used in atmospheric craft and personal transports, the beacons made it possible to track the fates of those who could no longer answer questions for themselves. Considering the treatment that our little band had received at the hands of the traitors, it was no surprise that many felt happy to see them receive their just desserts, as it were. My response fell closer into line with the silent minority. *Pathfinder* had been my ship. Her loss struck me again as a personal blow.

I was being forced to relive her loss all over again. Therefore, I hope that I can be excused for not realizing the obvious for several moments.

The beacon must be a deception. It had to be. What better way to hide the theft? With us safely tucked away on Antoc-A3 with no method of communication, and with a functioning ZFlash beacon, time would be lost searching for the debris to ascertain what had happened, time which Teach would then use to make good his escape.

This spurred me on to action. If Teach wanted time, then we needed to deprive him of it. The sense of urgency again pushed at me as much for this reason as for the DaGaman pursuit. What if all of our sufferings and trials were in vain because we had delayed too long? If they regained full control of *Pathfinder* before we could jump clear of the system, they would see our movements and add their efforts to the DaGama ship in an effort to hunt us down and destroy us.

Time, then, was our enemy as much as the DaGamans and certainly more than those who had remained behind on *Pathfinder*. We needed to have a plan. We certainly needed the batteries from the beacon but we needed the transmitter that it contained even more. The beacon transmitter was long-ranged, and, while not intended for continuous use, it was better than the mangled wreck of our long-range transmitter, or the very short-ranged vocom gear. Our receiver was a separate unit and had escaped most of the destruction that had been heaped on the transmitter. We had been able to repair the receiver in a matter of less than an hour from our launch from *Pathfinder*. Thus we could hear everyone and talk to no one.

But was my growing plan even possible? I closed my eyes to concentrate better and pictured the geometry of the system. Antoc was a binary star system with seven planets. Antoc A was the larger of the paired stars and held three planets in orbit around it. It was to the third planet circling this star that the thieves had intended to maroon us. JP1 in this system was outside the orbit of all of the planets in the system but it was much nearer to the star Antoc A than to the secondary component of the system. *Pathfinder* was on a course to skirt the edge of the system which would have taken it inside the orbit of the asteroid belt and the planet Antoc 7. Antoc 7 was not orbiting either sun, but rather the gravitational center of the system between the twin suns. Its orbit was well outside the asteroid belt which in turn was outside of any planets but it was currently on 'our' side of the system. The secondary sun, Antoc B, also had three planets orbiting it, and we needed to make planetfall on two planets circling this secondary sun.

On thruster power alone we would take many days to collect the various items that we would need in order to make our return possible. The ZFlash beacon would be one more item that we would now need to retrieve in order to get home. It would also be necessary to retrieve it before we left this half of the system. It would take almost five days to reach the beacon from here. Once we moved to the other side of the system the time and distance would make it nearly impossible to reach.

I knew that we did not have the fuel necessary to get to the beacon and then do a direct course change back to our current destination, at least not in a reasonable amount of time. That would entail a burn to kill our outbound momentum and then begin to build velocity back to B2. I rapidly began the calculations in my head. I would need to double check them by hand later to be absolutely sure, but I should be able to determine whether such a thing would even be possible. I was careful to keep my features blank. I didn't want to cause excitement before I was sure. I felt a strong desire to protect my little group from any unnecessary disappointments. They would have many challenges during our voyage and I didn't want to contribute in any way to causing them to give up hope.

Hope is a powerful motivator, and it might be all that we would have left before we were done. Here in the few moments since learning of *Pathfinder*'s supposed destruction, the crew looked more revived and energetic than they had at any time during the last eighteen hours.

The realization of the enormity of our undertaking was beginning to wear down the energy of the crew. The return to A3 to repair the ship had been like a dash of cold water in the face. Everyone was becoming more and more aware of how small our ship was and how vast was the space of the system.

I knew that we would find the beacon in the vicinity of Antoc 7 because of the general bearing of the signal. ZFlash beacons are programmed to head toward, and orbit around, the nearest planet-sized gravitational signature that it could identify after it was launched. Seven was the only body on the right bearing so I knew that recovery would take us near the planet and we could use that to turn ourselves around.

"Ms. Williams," I said after looking up to the pilot's couch to see who was on duty. "Set a course to the beacon."

A number of heads came up at my orders. The celebration seemed to die like a toy whose power pack had run down. Soon, silence had again filled the small compartment. Faces looked at me eagerly, as if waiting for me to tell them that all of their troubles were over. They should have known better, but hope overrides common sense sometimes.

When it became obvious that I was not going to illuminate them further, debate started almost immediately amongst them. Voices called out from all sides. Some wanted to save the power and continue on our most direct path, others wanted to search for the wreckage and see what could be salvaged. Pandemonium descended and the resulting chaos made it impossible to think.

"Quiet," I roared when I could take no more. "This is not an election and the Fleet has no place for democracies," I continued. "Ms. Williams, you have your orders."

"Aye, aye, Captain," she replied from the cockpit above us.

Silence greeted my pronouncement.

"There are two Turin batteries on that beacon," I continued in a more normal tone. "If we can capture the beacon and strip out the batteries, it will add to our power supply. By my calculations, we will expend far less in fuel mass to make the attempt than we will gain by adding those power cells to our supplies, and the net gain will bring us closer to our goal. More importantly, however, there is a transmitter on that beacon. We will increase our chances of survival exponentially if we can recover that transmitter, and any other salvageable electronics, from that beacon. We will add about six days to our trip, however, and that will necessitate further rationing of our food and water supplies."

The chronometer read 0810, 13 July, as *Vanguard* finally moved into position to snag the beacon. As it was still under power, headed for Antoc-7, we were able to nearly match its trajectory. At over 1000 km/s we were moving faster than the beacon, so we would need to snag it as we went by. It would be difficult, but not nearly as challenging as it would have been if the beacon were stationary.

Ms. Williams, and then Ms. Johnson, had piloted the craft nearer to the beacon with ever-increasing delicacy on the controls, and Long and O'Neill worked with the tractor controls to secure the transmission platform.

Finally, the beacon had been secured. The celebrations were oddly subdued. O'Neill simply collapsed onto the deck and rolled into the corner shaking. Long was sweating, despite the slight chill in the cabin. The others left them alone, other than the occasional pat on the back. It was as if the crew felt that any celebration was out of place and premature until we were safely home in Warner space. Or, possibly, they were simply remembering the last time that we had tried to secure an object and were waiting for it to explode and kill us all.

Whatever the reason for it, I broke the awkward moment by starting to hand out assignments.

"Long," I called to get his attention. "Take what supplies you need and remove the batteries and the transmitter from that beacon. Will you need any assistance?"

"No sir, I should be able to do that on my own. The components are fairly easy to remove, even suited."

"Very well, then. Make it happen, please."

"Ensign Hayes, suit up and accompany him to the outer hatch. You will observe from there and maintain a safety line on him at all times."

"Aye, aye, sir."

With those assignments made, I watched them move to the suit locker which was currently one of our 'steps' in the ladder up to the pilot's compartment. It took quite a bit of maneuvering to get into suits and into the airlock. They finally gave up and crawled into the airlock, pulling the undonned suit pieces after them. They closed the inner hatch door and then laid on the side of the hatch and finished dressing in their suits.

I sat back to think of anything else that needed to be done. I awoke as Long returned through the airlock with his first load of batteries and equipment. I could not believe that I had fallen asleep. My body had betrayed me just as surely as any pirate. I looked around to see if anyone had noticed. I felt sure that the EVA work would have taken Long at least two hours. It was not realistic that I had sat in my chair asleep for that long without anyone noticing, but I could not see the condemning looks that should have been on every face. The crew should have been able to put their trust in me to see them through, but instead, I was sleeping. I would have to take pains to keep that from happening again.

Long remained in the hatch and passed the batteries down to O'Neill who began stowing them into the battery compartment while Long went out after another load. The inner hatch slid closed again and I heard the lock begin to cycle.

With the transmitter and the batteries from the beacon in our possession, options were now available to us. We had used up a portion of our reactor mass to match trajectories with the beacon, but we had added the power of two Turin cells to our growing cache. As important as those cells were, however, they were not the reason for our detour. In addition, we had gained a horde of electronics that would enable us to repair the transmitter and put us one step closer to our ultimate goal. This had been a hole in my designs up until now.

I had a plan to move us out of this system and to an occupied planet, but our inability to repair the transmitter would keep us from contacting anyone at the other end, and would subject us to the possibility, however slight, of friendly fire at the completion of our journey. That would be an ignominious end after all of our struggles. Now we had the means to correct that lack.

The most unfortunate part of the recovery was that we now were going in the wrong direction for our next stop. While we had slowed considerably to pick up the beacon, we would need to expend more fuel to come to a complete stop and then accelerate in the opposite direction. We were currently out beyond the orbit of the asteroids circling Antoc A and B. We would need to go back through the asteroids and to the inner orbits to get to our next planetfall. While we would be able to replenish some of our mass from the asteroids themselves, we had seen the difficulty of that endeavor. It was doubtful that we would be able to make up for all of our usage.

"Ms. Williams, please set course 205.24, inclination 20.012. Maintain 9.8 kps² acceleration until we are 15,000 km from the planet and then reduce to 45% power. I will take over the piloting duties at that time. We will refine that course on the other side of Antoc 7 but that will get us into the proper area for planetfall on Antoc B2."

"Aye-aye, sir."

I turned and addressed the crew who were watching the byplay with anxious faces. I decided that I needed to provide information to reassure them. I said, "It will take us nearly six hours to reach Antoc 7. Seven is a wandering rogue planet that fell into the gravitational pull of this system at some time in the past. It doesn't orbit either star but, rather, orbits the system gravitational center outside the orbits of all of the other planets. We will be able to use its orbital velocity to accelerate and change our course back to the inner system. We can now resume our approach to Antoc B2. This will take quite some time, however. During that time we need to conserve our energy and our resources as much as possible. I would encourage all of you to sleep if you can manage it and to move as little as possible if sleep escapes you. You will need all of your energy when we reach the planet."

With those pronouncements, I went to sit with Ms. Williams at the helm. While it was not time for my watch, I could no longer bear to see the expectant faces in front of me. They were so desperate for me to make this attempt work that they looked at me with a hope in their eyes that was heart-wrenching to have to face. I needed a reprieve from those expectations, but there would be none forthcoming.

I began to spend more and more time in the copilot's seat. I was not successful in mixing with the crew, and they seemed uncomfortable with me in their presence. I lost track of how many changes of shifts we went through, but finally we entered the gravitational pull of 7. Our plan was that we would use the gravitational pull of the planet to point ourselves in the right direction to make our planetfall on B2. This was the only way that it had been possible for us to make the trip out to pick up the beacon.

Gravitational Trajectory Adjustment was the term that they had taught us in the academy for the procedure that we were attempting. I don't think that I had heard that term since. The common term, which I could hear repeated in many conversations coming up from the crew compartment, was slingshot. The common view of a slingshot is some form of a Y with an elastic band that stretches and fires a projectile at the target. With this in mind, I can understand why there is some confusion about why we use this term. The truth is that the slingshot in its original form was a pocket on a leather thong that was spun, and the missile was launched using the centrifugal force that was built up by the spin. This was closer to what we do with a ship. The momentum that the ship carries is combined with the orbital velocity of the planet, by means of the centripetal force of the planet's gravity, to speed up or decelerate the ship and the centrifugal force of the ship's journey around the planet is recovered at a precise time to adjust the direction of travel. This involves a very complicated calculation and should not be attempted lightly.

We were about to make the attempt without computer support. I had run all of the calculations and I knew timing and course corrections throughout the maneuver. Without the computer, we would have to make all of these adjustments by hand.

We had already been through two slingshots, but those were much easier than the one before us. First, we had built up a great deal of velocity. We had been under constant acceleration for days, ever since leaving A3. In the two others we had only a few hours worth of accumulated speed. Our two course changes had minimized that, to some extent, as well as slowing to capture the beacon. Still, we would begin the maneuver with a velocity of almost 860 km/s, and exit the maneuver with over 930 less than a minute later. All of the careful adjustments would take place as we moved toward the planet. If we had precisely balanced our speed with the distance from the center of mass, the planet's gravity would provide our centripetal force, and bend our vector around the planet.

Second, Antoc 7 had many times the mass of either of the two moons we had used previously. The greater the mass, the more effective your acceleration is, but also the narrower the margin of error. So we would have to be very precise in this maneuver.

I gave the list of time checks to Lt. Johnson. "These will be your responsibility. I will have all that I can do to monitor the course changes and keep us on our flight path. I need you to call out the times. Give me a five second warning and a countdown to each change."

"I understand, sir," she replied as she took the list and began to attach it to the control panel just above the chronometer. There was no hint in her actions or voice that she felt herself better suited to handle the controls.

While in many ways she may have been correct, this was not one of them. This operation would have very little to do with the 'feel' of the ship, but rather quick calculations and adjustments. While she was one of the best in the fleet in the first category, she was not my equal in the second.

"Good, here we go," I said simply, without addressing those issues.

The following two hours were a blur of activity. I had to balance the pull of the planet against our course and make rapid, minute adjustments almost constantly. I knew the sequence of our course changes and Johnson faithfully called out the time markers.

Finally, I leaned back into the seat back for the first time since the maneuver had begun. My tunic was soaked through and all of the muscles in my shoulders and back seemed to be on fire.

I took a deep breath and let it out slowly. "Very well done, Lieutenant. I wouldn't care to attempt that very often."

"No, sir. Neither would I. Luckily, we won't have to do it again."

"That is true. We will maintain this course for three and a half hours and then we will kill the engines. From that point on we will be ballistic until we do our final adjustments at Antoc B2. I have the watch. Why don't you try to get some sleep. Have Williams relieve me in about four hours."

"Aye-aye, sir," she said as she headed back down the ladder.

I tried to relax as I began my monotonous study of the gauges in front of my chair.

17–18 July

Lieutenant Vasconcellos was not happy. He was still nursing a massive headache from the large rock that had connected with his head in the midst of the battle on Antoc A3. In so many ways, that rock had been symbolic of everything else on this whole mission. Totally unanticipated and painful.

Everything had gone downhill after that. *Whoever that Marine was, I owe her,* he thought. Seven dead and Keilly would probably never recover from the knife wounds.

It had seemed like a perfect setup. They appeared to be totally taken in by the terraforming ruse. Their quick reaction to the ambush showed that they hadn't been nearly as fooled as they had appeared. Things had gone from bad to worse thereafter. The blocking force on the trail had rushed in at the sounds of the ambush coming apart and had allowed Brighton to get most of his group out. That same group had allowed the Warners at the ship to surprise them and execute an ambush of their own, losing one of the heavy rifles in the process. That rifle had allowed the targets to hold them pinned down until the critical time when Brighton and then the Marine had been able to break through the perimeter and rejoin the main group.

Seven dead and five injured in return for one Warner dead and few if any injuries. Painful and unexpected.

None of the exercises Vasconcellos had participated in had ever gone this far wrong. It did not occur to him that exercises were all the experience any of the DaGamans had. The Family had always been limited to duty on Earth, which was by and large uneventful. This was their first foray into the wider universe, but that same inexperience kept him from seeing the difference between exercises and real combat.

"Coming up on the coordinates of the beacon," Laertes called from the scan console breaking into his reverie. "Nothing detected."

"Stay on it. They are here somewhere and we need to find them."

"So far, we have been totally unable to crack their stealth systems, sir. They could be right in front of us and we wouldn't see them. I don't know how they are able to mask their energy emissions," he added in frustration.

"Keep trying. Standard search grid. We'll figure it out," the lieutenant added with more confidence than he felt.

"Yes, sir."

Six hours later they had still made little progress. They knew where *Vanguard wasn't* but had no clue where it *was*. Vasconcellos' temper was deteriorating with each passing hour.

"Message from base, sir," Apellido called from the comm console. "They have a track on a bogie that they believe to be *Vanguard*."

"Coordinates," Vasconcellos snapped as he rushed to stand behind the young commo tech.

"124.8 by 229.71 by 0.6, sir. Inside the asteroid belt. Moving fast. Radar contact, still nothing on the scanners."

"Get us moving," he snapped to the helm. "Signal *Caxius*. MOVE! They are not going to get away this time."

18–21 July

Missiles were the last thing that I expected as we passed a large planetoid near the outer edge of the asteroid field. However, that was exactly what we got as two launches were detected and two missiles were accelerating to pursue us through the field.

We were not under power, having shut down the engines to conserve fuel for our deceleration burn.

Our velocity was a constant 1,057 km/s. We had intended to collect fuel as we moved through the debris field and try to snare as much as we possibly could. The course change we had made to capture the ZFlash beacon had used up a high percentage of our total reaction mass, and so it had been necessary to change our planned approach to our next planetfall. Rather than being able to make the journey under continuous power, we were forced to cut our engines three and a half hours after slingshotting around Antoc 7.

The pursuit behind us was again forcing me to adjust our plans.

I was at the controls, so I immediately added thrusters to increase our velocity. There had not been time to warn the officers and crew below, other than a shouted, "Grab hold!" I could hear the muffled impacts and cries of dismay as we suddenly sprinted forward. Long's sulfurous swearing summed up my feelings, as well.

The only chance that we had was to accelerate away before they could close the distance on us. If we were free to use *Vanguard*'s primary engines, we could rapidly leave these chemical rockets behind, given our relatively high velocity when they launched. We were not free to do so, however. Operating on thrusters alone, we were barely staying ahead of them, and their velocity was climbing much more rapidly than ours was. It would be about fifteen minutes before they matched our initial velocity and began to overtake us, but our fuel reserves were very low and I had no idea what their powered range would be.

I should have considered the possibility of a DaGaman base in the system. The logical place to locate that base would have been on one of the planets, unless you were trying to hide your presence. I should have prepared for this eventuality. These missiles had to be from base defenses or else a larger defensive screen that was put into place when the base was established. While depositing raiders on a claimed planet might cause some ruffled feathers in the Ruling Council, placing a weapons platform in the system of one of the other Families was an act of war. All of this was irrelevant to our present crisis, however. I didn't know the reasoning behind the attack but the entirety of my energy and attention were focused on escape. I knew that we would have to be lucky in order to get away from them. I despise having to depend on luck.

Concern gripped my conscious thoughts as I studied the readouts in the pilot's compartment. That was truly all that was left to me. I could not second guess my decisions because we had taken the only options available. We must keep going. In essence, we were running for our lives. But there was a cost to that decision. We had been running at 22.7 m/s^2 acceleration for the past 47 minutes. That meant that our mass converters had been operating at maximum for the same period. Our mass conversion had barely been able to keep up with our usage. They were not meant to operate for that long at those levels. Soon, damage would begin to occur, and we did not have the equipment or the parts to make any repairs to the unit. The pursuing missiles were still gaining slowly on our position.

Finally, the moment came that I had been waiting for. The first missile and then the second lost their propulsion. I assumed that they were out of fuel. When the missiles were overtaking us we could do nothing but flee directly away from them. Any attempt to turn or evade would allow the missiles to cut inside our turn and shorten the distance more quickly. Now the fuel had run out on the missiles and they could no longer make any adjustments to cut us off.

Vanguard was not easily maneuverable with the thrusters alone, but we did not need to move far off of our path to generate a miss when the missiles could make no adjustments. I pushed the nose down and gradually moved *Vanguard* off of its course, then aimed her nose toward Antoc B. The lack of fuel we had been forced to expend now meant that we could no longer slow down enough to rendezvous with B2. I had left us with only one option; a dangerous slingshot around the sun itself to use its gravity to help slow us. I cursed my own shortsightedness that had led to this.

Once I was certain the missiles would avoid us and the new vector was set, I again cut the engines, this time with plenty of warning for those below. While the crew scrambled for handholds or straps and discussed our escape from the missiles, fuel was still my primary concern. We had not been able to replenish our supplies fast enough to match our usage in order to stay ahead of this new threat, but perhaps there was still a chance to collect enough fuel to be able to brake enough to make planetfall. The only way that we could collect more fuel was to strengthen the pull of our tractor. As it was, we would still have to spend the remainder of the trip back into the inner system on a ballistic course without any thrusters. That would increase the misery for all of the officers and crew.

Life in zero g was exciting when someone else was telling about it in a story, but the reality was far less exciting. I suppose that you would adjust over time, but it is exhausting to try to stay somewhere that you want to be without holding on constantly or tying yourself in place. *Vanguard* was designed for a different technology, so it had no convenient handholds or stays to keep things and people where they belonged.

Still, our fuel levels were the more immediate problem.

"Long," I said, addressing the tech. "Get what you need to put the second generator into the tractor circuit and make it happen."

"Sir," he said, looking at me incredulously, "that will take out our life support and heat."

"It can't be helped," I replied, fighting the need to bite his head off for questioning orders again. "We can live off of the oxygen in the cabin for about seven hours before the CO_2 levels get dangerous. If we keep our activity to a minimum, that is. Much longer with one generator still tied into the scrubbers."

"Aye-aye, sir," he said, still looking dubious and rebellious.

Sooner or later, he's going to push back too hard and I would have no choice but to yank him up short, I thought.

My thoughts returned to our escape from the missiles. My plan had always had a safety margin built in, however small it might be. "Things happen," Captain Cosina used to say. "Plan for those unexpected events." I would have to suppose that this would be one of those events. Hopefully, there would not be many more.

"Long, O'Neill," I called. They both looked up expectantly. "When you are done with the generator, I need you to reattach our weakest Turin cell to the drive system. I don't want any other systems attached. Not even navigation or helm. And I don't want any other batteries connected."

They moved off and began to work without any further grumbling. Well, no grumbling from them, anyway. I could hear several disgruntled comments as they later moved those who were off watch into new positions away from the battery access covers. The job would require one of the two techs to climb inside the battery area and worm their way back to the connections to the selected cell. There was very little room to the side of the batteries, so the job would not be pleasant in zero g.

I would not use the battery if I had any choice. Our near brush with annihilation, however, had reminded me that we always needed options.

My watch ended, and I began calculating our new course. The burst of acceleration would necessitate a longer braking burn, which we did not have the fuel to perform. The new plan would require the addition of another slingshot around the massive Antoc B in order to spill enough velocity to rendezvous with B2. We did not have enough fuel for any other option. I would not have considered such a dangerous course, otherwise. The slight drop that I made to move out of the path of the missiles was easily corrected, and would make little or no difference in the end.

Some time later, I sat in the copilot seat and watched Fyonna Johnson as she piloted the craft. Not that the pilot had much to do at the moment, as we were now shooting back in toward B2 on a ballistic course. Lt. Johnson still was taking her responsibility very seriously, as she kept a constant running watch on all of the readouts. I had remained in the forward area because my presence seemed to dampen the mood of the crew and, also, I didn't want to expend the energy to climb back "down" even with the zero gravity that we were dealing with currently.

I was strapped into the seat and leaning my head back, trying to relax as much as possible. Confidence seemed to infuse the crew. I listened to them as they interacted. Fujinami and Ward, especially, were trying to make everyone feel comfortable and relaxed, as much as conditions allowed. I was very appreciative of their efforts. There are a good many things that I am good at, but playing cheerleader has never been one of them.

While radiating confidence and reliability are truly a command function, it has never been in my nature to 'rally the troops.' Ward and, even more so, Fujinami were able to do this with a facility that I truly envied. Their genial manner put everyone else at their ease. I glanced at Fujinami as he made his way carefully through the pack of bodies from one end to the other. Everyone was taking advantage of the weightlessness to gain a little more personal space than had been possible while seated together on the deck. His smile never left his face and he always had a word or a pat on the shoulder for all of his fellow sufferers. It was almost comical to watch the spinning bodies left in his wake from those companionable pats.

As the steadily diminishing diet took its toll on his energy reserve, he did not move as quickly or say as much, but the smile never changed. This low-key, hopeful attitude was contagious. You could not be around Jens Fujinami long before your own face shared his smile.

The good-natured attitude did not seem to carry over into the discussion of food, however. This subject seemed to be off limits by mutual consent.

In order to make the food last until we had a legitimate chance of escape, we were allowed only one ration bar for each meal.

We also had a small supply of jerky and fruit, obtained on Antoc-A3. These I had decided to reserve for emergencies and as a reward for special events. Morale and attitude would be just as important, if not more crucial, than physical strength in the coming days.

"Have you noticed how everyone has their own way of dealing with the shortage of food?" Lt. Johnson asked, without ever taking her eyes off the readouts.

"Yes, I had," I answered warily, not sure where she was going with the question.

"I think it's interesting that everyone finds some way to take comfort, or create some ritual to take their mind off of how little they have."

"Are you referring to the way that Mackey always says Grace before he consumes his morsel?" I asked.

"That's one example, yes. Queneau saves her breakfast and lunch portions and eats them all when the dinner ration is served. And Ward sits and watches until all have eaten and he is satisfied that they are done. Everyone has their way of coping, I guess," she said.

"And what is your preferred method, Lieutenant?"

She got very quiet for a moment, and I wasn't sure that I was going to receive an answer, but after a few moments her response came out in a voice barely more than a whisper. "I do my duty, sir. It's all that I know how to do."

She looked over at me and her large brown eyes held more words than she had been able to utter. I could clearly hear what she couldn't bring herself to say. "Are we going to live?" "What more can I do?" "Am I adequate to the task?" These were the questions that she really wanted answers to, but would never allow herself to ask. I decided that I would not shame her by answering them directly, either.

"Duty is all any of us truly have. You are a good officer already, and have the potential to be a great leader, because you care enough to do your duty always. Do you know why I take our position every day at noon?"

She seemed to be caught off guard by my question, but she recovered quickly and said, "To be able to accurately plot our progress, I presume."

"Partly, that is correct, Lieutenant. I could do the same thing mathematically, however. It is not as if we were adrift on an ocean where we would have to correct for wind and tides and other variables. We are on a fixed trajectory and will not deviate from it until we reach the point I have marked on our projected course where we will begin final corrections for the slingshot." I shook my head. "No, Lieutenant, the real reason that I take the position check at exactly 1200 noon, ship's time, is that the crew needs to see me take that position check and verify that we are where we planned to be. That is truly my duty now. To give the crew hope. To let them know that there is no way I will allow them to give up."

Hearing a commotion in the lower cabin, I turned and looked over my left shoulder. I could see Crewman Ricardo Smith moving from the head back to his 'seat' on the opposite side of the compartment. The other crewmen were jeering and making comments or playfully pushing at him as he made his way through their midst. This caused him to bounce into others as nudges changed his trajectory.

"I had better check in on them down there," I said. I made no mention of her previous doubts other than to say, "Keep doing your duty. It will be enough." And with that, I levered myself out of my chair and swung over to the seat brackets along the wall that we used as a ladder to access the pilot's area.

As I floated closer to the gathering, I saw the cause of the disturbance. Crewman Smith was clean-shaven. My hand ran through my own three-week growth before I thought about it. Our beards had become another manifestation of our status as outcasts. It was simply another thing to be tolerated. Smith, however, had decided that it was not something that he wished to endure. Starting with a small utility knife from the emergency kit, he had spent his off hours honing and reshaping the blade into a straight razor. That morning, he had finally been ready to make the attempt. It had clearly not gone as well as intended. He continually dabbed at a spot on his chin with the tail of his shirt. The single miss told me that this was not his first attempt with a straight razor, however.

"Was it worth the effort, Smith?" I asked, to transfer the crew's attention back to him after my interruption of their teasing.

"Yes, sir!" he said emphatically, as he reclaimed his spot between Long and O'Neill against the left wall. "It reminds me of home, sir." He added much more quietly, "My papa loved straight razors, sir."

Everyone quieted at that, no doubt lost in thoughts of home and the things that they missed the most.

"Well, Smith, when we get home you will have plenty of razors to choose from," I said to reengage the crew before they were lost in their melancholy thoughts. "You can show me your favorite when you come for the hanging."

"Hanging, sir?"

"Surely you don't think this can end any other way for Teach and his cutthroats, no pun intended," I said pointing to the bloody spot on the under side of his chin.

This got a few chuckles, but everyone was watching me intently. It was O'Neill who finally got up enough nerve to say, "Do you really think they will be caught, sir?"

"I not only think so, but I will not rest until it is so."

"I heard Leung and Danis talking about their plan to sell the ship while we were gathered in the launch bay. It sounded like they had everything planned out. They were supposed to rendezvous with a ship and collect their profits. Most were very confident. I don't kn—- er, it will be very difficult to catch them, I think," O'Neill said, correcting himself so as not to contradict my statement.

"I think, Mr. O'Neill, that they will find it very difficult to carry out their plans," I said firmly. "It is not wise for us to discuss this much among ourselves, however." I knew that we would need to give evidence in a Warner Court and that the more we discussed the events, the more each person's individual recollections would be shaped by those of the group. It was our duty to protect that evidence by remaining circumspect and not discussing the case.

"Commander Teach would have it well planned, sir."

"Mr. O'Neill—" I started, struggling to rein in my surging anger. "What you do on your own time and what you think are, of course, your own business, but you will not refer to that traitor, Teach, with any previous military courtesies or rank in my presence. He has lost any right he may once have had to receive them. Am I clear?" I swept my gaze over all of the assembled crew until I had affirmation from each of them. "That being said, you are correct. If given the option, he will not remain where he can be found. He may not have that option." I gave everyone another stern look. "This subject is now closed, and we shall not open it again."

Having again shown that mixing with the crew was disastrous for me, I climbed up and reclaimed my seat in the cockpit, envying Ward and Fujinami.

ENSIGN JOSIAH MITCHELL

From his written account

21–22 July

It was late in second watch on the 21st when Captain Brighton called me up to speak to him. Normally, I would have been very nervous to be called in to face the old man, but he had already made the same request to Lt. Johnson and Major Chowdhury, as well as Jherri and Jordan. Being the fifth to be called up at least let me know that I wasn't being singled out for something I had done, either good or bad.

"Sit down, Ensign," he told me, indicating the copilot's seat. The cockpit was really the only place to have a private conversation, or close to private anyway. The head was doubling as a storage locker, so there was no longer room to fit two people in it. I sat down as directed.

"Ensign, I have some information to give you, and I want you to remember as much of it as you can."

"Yes, sir. Understood, sir," I responded. I know that sounds more stiff and formal of me than the captain's statement would indicate was necessary. But I was speaking to The Captain, who is second in authority only to God Above. Captains just are not addressed informally by mere ensigns. Not ever. And especially not this captain.

"Earlier today," Captain Brighton continued, "I finished making a record of all that I remember of this system, including a rough chart and most of the mass and gravity readings that we will require. I want to make sure that all of the officers have access to this information.

"The terraforming units have obviously done some work on these planets, and I was surprised by the amount of flora on A3, but I don't believe, from previous reports, that they were able to do much on B2. I'm hoping that the supplies will be more intact on that planet. However, that planet was also much less hospitable in many ways."

He took a deep breath and focused his attention back on me again.

"This pad," he handed me a standard datapad, before returning his attention to piloting, though there was little need while we were following an unpowered ballistic trajectory, "will be kept at the pilot's station from now on. The data encryption key is not active, and the power-on key is 'Vanguard.' Go ahead and activate it."

I did as he instructed. The security key worked as he said, and the last data on the system was displayed unencrypted.

As I pulled up the files he indicated, I realized that the captain had a much different definition of "rough chart" than I did. The detailed and annotated chart that I was looking at would have earned an A in my Cartography course at the Academy. That class still haunted my memory because I had received a B+ and lost the 4.0 average I had carried up to that point. Because of that class, I was now junior to both of the other two ensigns on *Vanguard*. I did not know what the status of the other two ensigns still on *Pathfinder* was, but I had also been junior to them until our separation. Competition to get assigned to *Pathfinder* was stiff, even though, or perhaps because of the fact that everything about it was shrouded in mystery prior to its departure.

The chart, as I said, was very detailed. In addition to the two suns, seven planets, and asteroid belt, our course, both traveled and projected, was overlaid. Each course change was noted, with acceleration, bearing, and initial velocity cited for each. I saw at once that the next major milestone on our cross-system trek would be a braking slingshot around the smaller of Antoc's two suns. Several notes had been appended to the course at that point.

"If you don't mind my asking, sir, don't we need to have computer nav control for this slingshot coming up? That much gravity leaves a slim margin for error."

He seemed pleased that I had noted the difficulty ahead, and he smiled as he responded. "That would be nice, Ensign Mitchell, but it is a luxury we cannot afford. I have done as much as I can to prepare, but I will just have to make corrections fast enough to be sure we stay on the bubble.

"Now, you'll see that there is some information missing from my calculation. What should be our insertion angle and distance from the surface, given our current velocity?" At which point, I was required to perform, by hand no less, and with the old man himself eyeing me, the complex calculations required to set the initial course for the maneuver.

It took a long time. I had done similar calculations by hand many times while studying at the Academy, but I had grown used to the speed and precision available from simply feeding the raw data into the navicomp. I read off my results to the captain, a bit hesitantly, I'm sure.

Captain Brighton frowned, and I cannot describe the effect to anyone who has not met the captain. I'm sure I gulped.

"How sure are you?" he said, and it was as if the bottom had fallen out of my world. Five seconds before, I had been pretty sure; now I knew I had made some hideous mistake that would have killed us all if I had been astrogating. I began to set up the problem again, but Captain Brighton's bass rumble cut me short.

"I expect an answer when I ask you a question, Mister." If I was flustered before, now I was terrified.

"Uh, yes, sir. Um, not very sure," I managed to stammer.

"Why did you give me an answer of which you were 'not very sure'?" I was sweating heavily, and it looked like I had compounded my math error, digging myself an even deeper hole. I decided my only hope was to answer truthfully and hope for mercy. Looking at the captain's stern scowl, it was a fool's hope.

"Sir, when I gave the answer to you, I was very sure it was correct. Your response made me think that you had detected some error that I missed, and I was much less sure. Sir." That last was added to fill the painful silence as Captain Brighton continued to scowl at me.

"Ensign Mitchell, apparently several lessons which were drilled into me at the Academy have been dropped from their curriculum these days. First, I want you to know that there was nothing wrong with your calculation. In fact, I was impressed with the speed at which you were able to arrive at the answer. However, having the right answer is not enough.

"An officer must lead. In order to lead, your subordinates must have confidence in your commands. Take time to think things through, and make sure you consider everything that should be considered, but don't dither. Come to a decision, and then stick to it. You won't always be right, but hesitating or vacillating will always be the wrong answer.

"Sir Winston Churchill once said, 'Never worry about action, only inaction.'"

"Yes, sir. Understood, sir," I said. I sat still, hoping my grilling was over, but not able to escape until I was dismissed. Who was Churchill, anyway?

"Now, then," he began the grilling again, "what other problems do you see coming up along our course?"

Problems? Where to start? Just the simple fact that we were astrogating on dead reckoning was a problem. We didn't have enough food or power. The crew was living in cramped quarters with no privacy. But I knew that these things were givens in our current equation, and not what the captain was asking about. I returned my attention to the pad in my hand and continued tracking our projected course past the upcoming slingshot.

I brought up the notes for our next planetfall. We would be braking all the way from the slingshot to B2, but we would still have some velocity left over when we arrived. Not much; easily dispersed with atmospheric braking. I didn't see anything to worry about, so I immediately assumed I had missed something. A second check revealed nothing, and I was about to start in with triple checking when I realized what I was doing. I had to consciously will myself to move on to the next planet, B3, conveniently close in its orbit to the position of B2.

The planet was near enough that we would not exhaust our fuel, so long as we refilled our tanks with reaction mass while on B2. So, a quick boost, turnover, brake; nothing to worry about there, either. I looked at the notes on the planet itself then, and that's when I saw it.

"Are these readings for the magnetic field of B3 accurate?" I asked, and my voice must have conveyed my disbelief. The captain laughed. Really, I am not making it up.

"Indeed they are, Ensign Mitchell, indeed they are. And what do we do to compensate?"

"First, we should move the turnover point up. We can't plan to use atmospheric braking to slow us down. The ship would not stand up to that kind of shear."

"Good. What else?"

What else? I wracked my brain for the answer. Was there any other way to slow down? No, if we turn over at the exact midpoint, we would arrive with a zero net velocity, but we would still have to fight against the gravitational pull of the planet. We wouldn't have the fuel remaining at that point to gently ease our way down.

Maybe we could coast with no thrust for part of our trip between planets, even as we were doing now. That would save fuel that we could use to reenter the atmosphere more gently. We could do that, it was true, but the trade off would be adding time to our journey. I was sure that the captain would not find any additional delay to be acceptable. No, I decided, the time added would not be worth it.

"Some straps would be helpful. Something the crew could use as restraints. Planetfall is bound to be very turbulent."

"Nothing else?" he prodded again.

Rather than run through the same analysis again, I answered at once.

"I can't think of anything helpful, unless you want to slow down the transit from one planet to the next," I said with as much confidence as I could manage.

"Much better, Ensign," the captain said.

"Thank you, sir," I responded.

"Do you have any other questions about the information there?"

"I see that your plans call for only a four to six hour stop on B2. Won't we need to stay longer than that, maybe see if we can gather food?" I asked him.

"No. There is nothing usable on the planet except the Turin cells we need to recover, and fuel to power the reaction thrusters. As quickly as we can collect those two things and get off-planet, we will do so. My estimate might be a little optimistic, but hopefully not. Anything else?"

If I had more questions, they were not worth the price of another of Captain Brighton's scowls, so I gave a simple, "No, sir."

"Then I have one more thing to discuss," he pronounced, and the scowl was back anyway, full force. His focus came off the controls in front of him, and landed instead on me. His eyes were like twin lasers boring into me. "I want your word of honor, that if command devolves to you, you will use the information I have given you, and you will get these people home."

I was sweating again, despite the fact that our generators were keeping the ambient temperature at about 14 or 15 degrees. I couldn't think straight, but years of Academy training took over. When receiving a direct command from your superior officer, there is only one appropriate response.

"Aye-aye, sir," snapped out of me, followed by a salute. I couldn't help it, it just came out. Captain Brighton did not think the salute inappropriate or ingratiating, thankfully, but returned it immediately.

"Carry on, Ensign," he said, and with that I was finally dismissed.

As I was heading 'down' the ladder, Tim O'Neill, at the engineering station, asked for the captain's attention. I slowed my progress a little, to hear what was on his mind. He was asking for permission to use some of the power we were generating to increase the size of our collection field.

That reminded me of my neglected duties, and I hurried, as carefully as I could in the absence of any gravity, to the generators to take my shift. It was 2312, but Queneau did not complain that I had not relieved her on time. She was aware of the reason for my delay; it would have been impossible to hide anything that happened on a ship this small.

A few minutes after I had settled into a comfortable rhythm, O'Neill asked Lt. Johnson and me for our "best maintainable speed" on the generators, while he took some measurements. I was thankful for fresh legs. My best maintainable speed turned out not to be maintainable for more than five minutes, which still allowed his measurements to be taken.

Being stationed on generator duty was actually not too bad just then. The exertion was not so difficult in zero g, and sitting against the wall while pedaling allowed me to easily hold my body in one place. This was a big problem for me when not at the generator. Sleeping was almost impossible without something to anchor to. The small repositioning motions common to sleeping would send me gently floating away, at which point I would bump into someone or something and come awake.

Dr. Ward was in the process of looking for a way to keep people from floating around at the same time that O'Neill was trying to gather more fuel. I thought Dr. Ward more likely to find success. I doubted that there was much of anything to collect, even with a wider field, out away from the asteroid field. Our high velocity helped in that regard. By moving more material in range of the collectors we were gathering more fuel. Still, the material in question was too sparse to make a larger field worth the extra effort at the generator. At least that was my opinion, until Jherri pointed out to me that there was less complaining while people were busy with little projects to try to improve things.

She had a good point, and after the comment I began noticing for myself that it was generally true. Generally, but not universally. The exceptions to the rule were Delacoeur and Long. Neither of them seemed happy about being asked to participate in any project, but not for the same reasons.

Delacoeur was a lazy pig. A fat, lazy, selfish pig. No, that still is not strong enough, but hopefully it conveys my opinion of him clearly. Delacoeur was never interested in doing anything that benefited anyone but himself. He could occasionally be persuaded to help in some task that would profit all of us, so long as his personal gain was clearly spelled out to him.

I thought Ward had it right, though he wasn't being serious. Kieran Delacoeur would have been most useful carved into little pieces and fed to the matter converters. Smith said that he had been the same in the kitchen on *Pathfinder*. Since he was head cook, he didn't actually cook, only 'supervised.'

Long was a different story. He was neither lazy nor selfish. His problem was that he chafed at being under someone else's authority. He was usually fine with being given a task to perform by the officers, but if one of the crew wanted his assistance it had better come as a polite request, or they could forget it. And heaven help the man, crew or officer, who told him how to do something.

He and Captain Brighton had once had a conflict, back on *Pathfinder*. I didn't see the event, but I know that he was assigned extra duties for a week.

I had half expected some problem of that type to have hit us already. As I mentioned, most of us were living with a short fuse from all the stress, and Long's shorter than most. Thankfully, though, there had been no problems from Steve Long.

Long had been given an assignment, but it was one of his own devising, as O'Neill's was. Earlier that morning, he had asked the captain if he could look into the fuel converters to see if he could raise their efficiency. Captain Brighton had given his blessing, and Long had been working on it since, with his only 'breaks' coming when he was working one of the generators during my own second watch.

At midnight, my turn on the generator ended. Ward came to relieve me, moving very cautiously. For him and the other specialists, and some of the newer crew, microgravity was still a very new thing. I think several of them would have lost their lunches if there had been much there to lose. All in all, they were handling things okay, but it was clear from their movements that they still had to think about what they were doing. Those of us who had had a little experience had already picked up the habits required before, and it was just a matter of remembering them. It was sort of like shifting mental gears to fit new surroundings.

Major Chowdhury was completely comfortable maneuvering while weightless. The security officer moved like a water snake. She clearly had had much more experience than me in this environment.

Ward had finished rigging up tether lines from some kind of rubber tubing, and I was looking forward to trying one out. Unfortunately, there was only the spot Ward had just left available, and it was claimed as soon as he left it by Lt. Johnson. Chowdhury had relieved her early, so that she could distribute our evening meal, or as some called it, the midnight snack.

Johnson had completed her duties and was settling in before Ward had inched his way over to me. I doubt she even noticed I was disappointed at the loss.

Ward noticed, however, and pointed out that there were two more tethers not in use. I had not even seen them previously, because they were well forward in the compartment, almost to the cockpit. Usually, everyone stayed toward the back, as if Captain Brighton had marked off the forward area as his personal retreat, and no one wanted to try invading it.

I didn't want to invade it, that was for sure, but since Ward had pointed it out, there was no socially acceptable reason not to use one of the two spots. So I pushed off the back wall to the fore and glided all the way there, absorbing my momentum with bent elbows and catching the tether to avoid any rebound. Once there, I attached the tubing around my center of mass, folded my arms, closed my eyes, and prepared to drop off immediately to the sleep my body desperately needed.

Sleep which wasn't about to come.

Since it was watch change, Williams had come forward to relieve the captain. He passed the station over with a formal, "I stand relieved," and moved into the tether next to mine. How was I supposed to sleep then? What if I floated into him and woke him up? With the short tempers everyone had, coupled with his famous volatility, I was likely to lose some teeth! There was no way I could go to sleep like that.

Captain Brighton didn't have any difficulty falling asleep. He was motionless and breathing in a slow, steady rhythm almost at once.

And just as quickly, he was awake again, as Long swam up and called out to him.

"Captain?"

"Yes, Long, what is it?"

"I've finished working on the engines and I wondered if you wanted to inspect them," he said.

"I'm sure that won't be necessary. How were your results?"

"I added about 3% to the conversion output, is all."

"Excellent work, Mr. Long, excellent."

"No, sir, it's not. Not by a big margin. But it is the best I could manage with the tools and material we have available."

"Perhaps so, Long, but it is better than we were yesterday. And sometimes the difference between success and failure is an even thinner margin than that."

"Yeah, I suppose so, sir." He didn't sound very convinced to me. "With permission, I'm going to turn in."

"By all means, yes, Long. Here, take this tether. I'm not really ready to sleep yet." I knew that wasn't true, but I don't think Long did. He accepted the proffered line and strapped himself in, to the relief of both of us.

I thought the captain would go back to the cockpit, where there was an unoccupied seat, but instead he went to the sensor station to check in with O'Neill. He had had exactly zero success in gaining more fuel than we had been before. The captain reassured him that this was not his fault, and that it had been worth a try. O'Neill let out a sigh and told the captain that he would go and route the power back to its previous configuration. The captain agreed, and off he went, with the captain sliding into the harness to man that station.

I still wasn't quite comfortable enough to allow myself to go to sleep. The idea of accidentally bumping into Long was only marginally better than bumping into the old man. At 0200, I offered my spot to Fujinami, who was just coming off a generator shift.

He accepted gratefully, and then made the oddest sort of comment.

"You know," he said, "the sun is still so far away that it doesn't seem to be getting any bigger, like we're not moving at all. It makes things seem, I don't know, sort of timeless. Unreal. Like we're not connected to the universe anymore, you know what I mean?"

"I know you're a fruitcake," I managed not to say. I nodded my head instead.

Captain Brighton said, "This is real enough for me, Mr. Fujinami. A deck beneath my feet and a star to steer by, that's been real enough to sailors for centuries now."

"Exactly my point, Captain," he said, warming up to the topic now. Didn't he know others were trying to sleep? Not me, of course. "That sense that things are the same now as they have been for centuries!"

He was losing his grip on reality, I could see. Not my department, though. Let Captain Brighton and Doctor Ward worry about it.

"Well, there is some truth to the idea that history repeats itself," the captain agreed, "at least in the general sense. The particular details are always changing. I suppose it's possible that some group in the past has faced challenges like these before."

"Hmm, yes, I suppose so." Fujinami was in a thoughtful mood then, which had the benefit of making him quiet. I thought the captain's last comment a little odd also. If there ever was such a group, I wondered if they made it.

Probably not, I thought. *And if they didn't, how would anyone ever know?*

11 July

Sergeant Carmo was reviewing logs and data screens when Lieutenant Heliodoro entered the command room of the DaGama base. The base had gotten a lock on *Vanguard*, and some over-zealous weapons tech had launched missiles targeted at them. He had hoped to disable *Vanguard*, and allow the base to easily go and pluck her from adrift in space. He had been reprimanded for firing at the wrong time, and so had his tac officer.

Carmo, though, thought there were some positives to the situation. It appeared that *Vanguard* had stumbled into the wrong area. Whatever technology they were cloaking their emissions with, it did not deflect the radio waves of the radar that was being used to keep a look out for asteroids that might threaten the base. In fact, that's what the weapons tech had thought they were, and had simply attempted to get in some target practice. It wasn't until the rock dodged, that he had realized the truth.

They had slightly changed course to a new heading, and given their base velocity, they were able to stay a safe distance from the missiles. Even if the base had self-destructed the missiles in the hopes of the blast affecting *Vanguard*, it would have been no use. The missiles never got close enough for that. What they had done though, was to allow the DaGama base to track their vector and acceleration.

"Sir, we had them for just long enough. We were able to get a velocity and vector, and they didn't change direction at all after the initial changes. I don't think they want to change it sir, their reaction bespoke a minimal consumption of resources to avoid the missiles. Moreover, it appears that we know where they are going," Sgt. Bonifacio Carmo said.

"Where to? A onde?" Lieutenant Adão Heliodoro of the DaGama Aerospacial Naval Armada exclaimed and repeated in Portuguese.

"Straight towards the sun … Sir, it appears they are headed straight for Antoc-B," Sgt. Carmo said not understanding his own answer.

"Será que ele vai?" Lt. Heliodoro slipped into the native Brazilian form of Portuguese as he posed the question which was loosely translated, 'will he?' The DaGama Family had a base of 31 enclaves, the original 22 of which were in old Brazil. The newer ones had been taught Portuguese (the Family language) regardless of their geographical location, as well as the Family Council's standard English.

"Pode, Lieutenant," Carmo replied, beginning to think like his commander and instinctively responding in the same form of Portuguese, 'he can.' "It is possible that something is wrong with *Vanguard*, or they are now for whatever reason sure they cannot escape us for long."

If their instincts were correct, there was likely only one reason that this Captain Brighton would be taking his very special ship towards Antoc-B. He meant to scuttle her in the sun before the DaGamans could get hold of her. They would have to bring this to Agostinho.

"Sergeant, bring the data from the logs, and come with me. We need to talk to the Commander," Heliodoro said.

They both gathered the things they thought they needed, and went out of the command room with data in tow. They headed down the short corridor and into the outer base ring. They moved quickly, Heliodoro barely pausing to return salutes of those who stopped to salute him.

Almost to their destination, they passed the main tactical room, seeing the bustle of people as they were processing some of this very same data. Soon they came to a door guarded by two Marines. The Marines came to attention as they approached.

"Lieutenant Heliodoro, Sergeant Carmo," the Marine sergeant on the left said, "Commander Agostinho said to disturb her only if it was important, can I assume by your pace and faces that it is?"

"Yes, Sergeant Graça, it is definitely urgent," Adão Heliodoro replied while slowing to come to a stop in front of the two Marines.

"Wait one moment then, sir," Graça replied as he reached for his com and quietly spoke into it.

The small group stood in silence and Graça waited for a response from his com. Shortly the com chirped and the two Marines moved out of the way as Graça motioned them through the door he was opening.

Carmo and Heliodoro stepped into the office of Commander Agostinho as she looked up from a series of data screens and nodded to them.

"Come over here, Adão and Bonifacio. I assume it is important news, and I hope it is good," she said, motioning them over.

"Yes ma'am, we think that our sensors have tracked them, and that we know their heading and destination," Heliodoro began once she had motioned them to give her the data chip.

"Where are they headed? Are they moving back around to rendezvous with *Pathfinder* or something that we didn't expect?" she asked as she loaded the data.

"No ma'am, we don't think so at all, we think that somehow they must know we are trying to get the ship from them. Ma'am, they are heading right toward Antoc B. The only reason we can come up with for that is that they mean to scuttle her in the sun," Heliodoro said showing the intense worry he was feeling that he was right.

"You really believe he would?" she asked as she began reviewing the data scrolling up on her screen now.

"We do, ma'am. It's what we would both do if we thought we couldn't get away and were afraid of losing the technology to a competing Family," Sergeant Carmo replied, standing at the end of the desk with his hands clasped behind his back. "We have already established that for whatever reason, *Vanguard* is not capable of jumping anymore, or she would have headed straight for the jump point to Warner Space. They appear not to be involved with *Pathfinder* since they were expelled, probably for not being in on the sell out. Those still on *Pathfinder* are probably the same reason that *Vanguard* can no longer jump. We thought maybe they were trying to come up with a way to get back to *Pathfinder* to take her back or something; honestly, we aren't really sure why they are choosing their destinations. Nothing seems to link them as far as we can tell. Perhaps Captain Brighton thought that there might be some way to find a planet to wait it out on, but with us chasing them … It seems the only logical explanation we can come up with, ma'am."

Agostinho looked at him more closely. This was probably the most he had said in her presence in this entire mission.

"You concur, Lieutenant?" she asked Heliodoro, turning to him.

"I do, ma'am," he replied simply.

"Then we don't have much time to lose. I think you are right, too. I want them both, Lieutenant, and I think this may be our only chance at them," Agostinho said looking at them firmly.

"Yes ma'am," they both said in unison.

Agostinho reached for her com and called for Vasconcellos.

The Marine lieutenant arrived within 45 seconds of her com, obviously at a flat out run from the tactical room.

"Lieutenant Vasconcellos, we believe that they are taking *Vanguard* into the sun. We need a plan to go and get her, and we need it fast," she said without prompting as he came to a halt in front of her desk.

"Into the sun? Are we sure? I don't know, Brighton's a fighter, and so are some of his people," Vasconcellos responded.

"The data is pretty conclusive; we tracked them long enough to see their vector and their base velocity and accel. They are headed right at Antoc-B," Lt. Heliodoro said to Vasconcellos.

"If you are right, then we have to go after *Vanguard* right now. Let me see those headings and data," Vasconcellos didn't really care if they thought Brighton was headed into the sun or not. Based on these readings, it looked like the DaGama assault shuttles had a much higher acceleration and maximum velocity. In short, he could catch them. That was all that mattered. "It will probably be tricky flying, we better have the best pilots, so that my Marines can get to it and get aboard."

"I will be flying *Oeiras*, and Lt. Heliodoro will be flying *Caxias*, Lieutenant Vasconcellos. This is the best shot we have got, and we are pulling out all the stops. I want you on *Oeiras* with me. Tell me what else you see, I trust your mind," Agostinho said.

Lt. Vasconcellos looked over at Heliodoro and, struck by something he just realized, he started laughing.

"What's so funny, Lieutenant Vasconcellos?" Adão asked, affronted that he was being laughed at.

"Your name, Lieutenant Heliodoro. It means 'gifts from the sun,'" he said with a wicked grin. "Commander, let's go collect our gift."

22 July

I awoke with a start, quickly looked around to see if anyone had noticed that I had fallen asleep and realized that just about everyone else was sleeping as well. My heart came back to a normal pace as I suddenly remembered where we were and that I was not on duty. My mind got fuzzy on dates still. Actually, to be honest, it was probably worse now than it had ever been. It had to be July 22nd and, just guessing, it was probably morning, ship's time. Somewhere toward the end of third watch by the looks of who was off duty.

I hated how my mind missed details that I used to take for granted. The general lack of food, good sleep, and comfort had driven most of us into a condition of near stupor and at least mild irritableness. Is that a word? I hope it is...

I moved myself with care, trying not to wake anyone as I swam closer to the bridge area. I could see the captain and Ms. Johnson in the chairs, and from the size of the sun in the viewport, I could tell we were approaching time for the slingshot.

Now, granting that I was not the most knowledgeable human being, I was still a fine student of history as far as academic learning had allowed, and I was pretty sure that no one had ever done what we were about to do in a vessel like ours, or even anything remotely close in size to it. I thought I had remembered reading about a couple of vessels that had burned up trying it in the earlier days of space travel, but their names eluded me.

Slingshot maneuvers had been taught to pilots and officers of the Fleet ships from every Family for a long time. Using the gravity of a planet (or moon) to change vector was a task which could be accomplished relatively safely with careful calculation. Traditionally, you wanted to choose the smallest celestial object that you could to minimize the stress on the vessel and maximize your margin of error.

In case no one else has ever clearly defined it for you, a sun is not a small celestial object. It is as big as they come in inhabited systems. It also adds extraneous elements into the calculations like solar radiation, heat, plasma flares, etc. Normally, the larger your vessel the higher the amount of stress you can safely subject it to. As a general rule, slingshot maneuvers were only calculated by astrogation computers, the really complex processing ones that also plot jumps with the jump gate computers.

A few months ago, I would have been really scared to hear of an officer doing that kind of math in his head and announcing that most likely it would be okay to risk all of our lives on it. Now though, after seeing the kind of ability Captain Brighton had with calculations and vector calculus demonstrated time and again, none of us batted an eye. I had always prided myself on my math and quick thinking, but Captain had a different level of ability than any mortal being I had ever heard of. If there was a man anywhere who I did trust to make these calculations, weighing everything, it was Captain.

Perhaps his utter confidence and resolve about it lent us the belief that he could do it, or perhaps his disposition allowed no one the confidence or leverage to argue about the attempt. Either way, we were going to do it, and I felt pretty sure we would pull it off.

Pretty sure.

I saw Captain lean over, to announce the need for safety restraints. I had my grin on as I strapped in next to Jos in two new sets of tubing straps that Ward had assembled on the forward bulkhead.

He looked at me and said, "You really aren't right in the head, are you? I swear I am surrounding myself with fruitcakes!"

To which I replied, "Who else besides me?"

Jos smiled and said, "Just about everyone but me, I think."

I grinned. "What can I say? We can't all be as mild-mannered as you, Ensign Mitchell."

"You could have said you snuck some food, or that you had been hiding a horde of it since A3 or something. I wouldn't call you a nutjob then."

"Sorry, Jos, no such luck. You'll have to settle for my charming self today." I was fully into my straps at this point, looking across the main cabin to the generators mounted on the opposite wall. I said, "No, I am just excited. I haven't ever slingshot around a sun before."

"Yeah, me neither. Of course," Jos replied dryly, while rolling his eyes at me.

I laughed but didn't respond.

"You know, I have been thinking," he said, looking around to make sure who was around us, "with the way things are going for us, I think a few B's in the Academy would have done us good."

I laughed pretty hard for a moment, until I saw Josiah's very straight, almost melancholy face looking back at me, which kind of took away my spark, and silenced me.

"Buzz killer," I said, as his face cracked in to an ear to ear grin, once he realized he had gotten me.

Our positions were pretty uncomfortable for this kind of thing, since we didn't really have two walls here to wedge against, just the one. The other thing was that most folks didn't really like being up next to the bridge. Our straps were mostly secure though. They could take a fair amount of stress; at least . . . we hoped so.

Ms. Johnson called back, "Hold on folks, we are now into the gravity path. This might be a bumpy ride."

"Execute the maneuver, Ms. Johnson," the captain calmly said while Johnson rolled *Vanguard* into her final position. "You have the conn and I will keep us on the glide path."

My thoughts were interrupted by bumping solidly into Jos. *Vanguard* was buffeted by a little solar wind (I assumed) and Ms. Johnson got her tucked nicely into the path that Captain supplied to her. We were probably about halfway through the maneuver, and had really only had some minor shaking and groaning on *Vanguard*'s part to let us know how it was going. I overheard Captain tell Johnson, "I think we have seen the worst of it." This buoyed my spirits a bit, until I realized I was holding onto a support bar (the only thing Jos or I could really reach to keep us from hitting each other often) pretty stiffly with my right arm. I guess I was a little scared after all. I smiled, trying to shake out my nerves.

My amusement was cut short by the very real shaking (by which I mean worse than any planetfall I had ever experienced) that began. We were coming in on a tight turn slingshot that brought us in about as far as the radiation shielding allowed for. The tight turn radius put us square in the heavy gravity shell of Antoc B, and allowed *Vanguard* to transition direction easily while dumping incredible speed.

By the time the shaking and buffeting had slowed, I began to hear muffled cries of alarm from many of the crew. I realized then that I had closed my eyes, and was surprised to see Jherri calmly sitting in her straps watching Jos and me when I opened them. She smiled a little smirk when I made eye contact. I was sure she would give me static for closing my eyes.

The shaking continued for a little while, and I could barely overhear the captain ordering minor course corrections to Johnson throughout the maneuver. I could hear the strain in his voice as he would give correction after correction to her. The course he had plotted was so precise, we couldn't afford to be off even a little bit, or the exit vector would do us no good. Worse even, they would mean we would have to spend invaluable power to slough inertia that was heading the wrong way. The fact that we were at the stress limits of the craft, and the fact that the far side of Antoc B appeared to be far more active at this point than the near side had been, did not bode well for staying on our precise trajectory.

My mind raced through possibilities, all of our deaths figuring in many of them. I prayed silently that *Vanguard* would hold together and that Captain's math and Johnson's quick controls would keep us alive. I was amazed at the clarity of thought I had, how quickly I was able to conjugate possibilities and do probabilities. Apparently, adrenaline was a good brain stimulant.

Suddenly, there was calm. *Vanguard* was no longer shaking and groaning. Captain and Johnson were quiet except for the sound of their checking every instrument panel and gauge, and everyone else was equally silent, waiting to hear if we were through. At least Antoc B was now clearly visible to the captain and Ms. Johnson as we backed away from it. It had to be behind us, or, I mean, we were facing it while we decelerated, but it was behind us.

Whatever.

The captain said, "We're clear, everyone, you can unstrap, and Mackey, you may say prayers of thanks now. We appear to be intact and traveling exactly the bearing we wanted with only a slightly higher velocity than I had hoped."

Cheers went up among those of us aft, and I heard Captain congratulate Ms. Johnson on her fine piloting.

I wasn't cheering, as I realized that there had been a serious lack of planning on my and Jos' parts. We had the straps on the forward bulkhead, which, now that we were decelerating for planetfall, was up in the air about 12 meters, and too far away from the ladder to reach until after we unstrapped. I wasn't too sure these pieced together straps were going to hold us for long, either.

Oops.

It was then that Chowdhury yelled up, "Would someone go reel in those ensigns?" When she said 'ensigns,' it was clear she meant, 'lower life forms.'

Mackey climbed up quickly to give us a hand, literally. He reached out to catch us and swung us over, one at a time, to grab onto the ladder and work our way back down.

Jherri came over to us, and said, "I've heard that some simple animals will close their eyes and think that you can't see them. Is that what you were doing up there?"

I played the only defensive card I had. "I know it sounds crazy, but I was falling asleep I was so bored! I could hardly keep my eyes open."

Jos and Jherri laughed pretty hard at that, and Jos followed it up saying, "The scary part is that YOU probably could sleep anywhere, you louse!"

"No, only if he had a full stomach!" Jherri said, smiling.

I could only smile, though being reminded of my non-full stomach made it short-lived. Still, everyone was congratulating the captain and Ms. Johnson. We were all happy to be alive, well, and moving toward home with a sense of great accomplishment at having sat through one of the most daring special maneuvers ever attempted.

The captain called back at this point to Kara George, as Ms. Johnson came back, to pull out some of the dried meats and fruit and to pass it around. "We need a little celebration," he said.

Celebration followed. Nobody was going to turn down extra food.

While we were thus engaged in drinking water and chewing the tough stuff, everyone was happy. I paused and looked around. Oddly, the contrast was really apparent to me right then. I don't think I had gone a ten minute span where I hadn't seen at least someone bemoaning one thing or another for days, maybe weeks. Not now. We were alive, on a proper heading to intercept the next planet at a high rate of speed, and it was beyond lucky. It was Captain Brighton.

We carried on like this for a long stretch of time. I am not sure how long. While we were celebrating, and congratulating the captain and Lt. Johnson, O'Neill began complaining that we needed to quiet down. He was carrying a sensor pad and was saying something about oxygen. We all began calming down as O'Neill made his way up to the cockpit to Captain and Ms. Johnson.

Obviously, O'Neill had something he needed to bring to their attention, so we all started quieting and soon a low murmur was all that remained of the boisterous celebration of the last half hour.

"There's a whisper breach sir," I managed to hear.

"There's a what?" Captain asked, his voice raising.

"Sir, it's the oxygen. The levels are dropping, and we have lost pressure. There's a leak somewhere aboard *Vanguard*," O'Neill said, handing the sensor pad over to the captain.

It got really quiet.

Captain Brighton looked at O'Neill, then at the rest of us. The calm of his voice was belied by the fire in his eyes as he slowly said, "Find the leak, and be about it quickly."

All of us were suddenly re-energized for a completely different purpose. I suggested to Jherri that we should begin an organized search of *Vanguard*. If we lined up around the floor, where all of us had congregated, and slowly worked our way upward, with each of us responsible for checking a section of wall, floor or roof carefully, we should be able to locate the leak. She was nodding thoughtfully when I heard Chowdhury snort behind me. *Does she enjoy sneaking up on people?* I wondered.

"That would probably work, Ensign, if we had several hours to devote to the project." Once again, the word ensign had not sounded like a compliment.

Then she began handing out orders.

"Dr. Ward, please get me a surgical glove from the first aid kit. Lieutenant Johnson, would you prepare to kill the engines?

"Everyone else, sit down on the floor and don't move." Most dropped to the floor as if they had been shot. Sometimes she could be really scary.

Dr. Ward backed out of the storage area with a handful of the thin gloves that were used for emergency surgeries when a sterile field was not available. He handed them to Chowdhury and sat down next to Williams near the starboard wall.

Chowdhury pulled one from the stack and shoved the rest into her pocket as she began to inflate the glove and tie it off. I almost began to laugh as I suddenly had a picture of her in my head making balloon animals. Luckily for my continued existence, I kept the image to myself.

When she had her balloon inflated, she indicated to Johnson to disable the thrusters and we all held on to stay put. Chowdhury climbed the ladder about halfway and released the inflated hand near the center of the compartment.

At first it didn't appear to do anything, but soon there was perceptible movement. It gradually moved forward and towards the starboard bulkhead. After about five minutes, it came to rest against the bulkhead not two meters from where Jos and I had been strapped in.

Long and O'Neill jumped up and climbed the ladder as soon as it came to rest.

Steve drew a circle on the bulkhead and Tim spread some quik-seal and covered it with a patch.

Chowdhury turned to me and said, "Much quicker, don't you think?"

We all instinctively started to move again, until Captain said, "As you were! There may be other leaks. Hold your positions."

As I pulled myself back to my spot, Ms. Chowdhury stared at me from her spot at the bottom of the ladder with something akin to her 'stupid ensign look.' I comforted myself in the fact that she didn't reserve it just for me. In the time aboard *Pathfinder*, I had heard a lot of stories about her. None of them made me less wary of ever being in her way, or worse, in her sights. All in all, though, I was very glad we had someone of her caliber aboard.

The only other leaks were a set of micropunctures in the seam that O'Neill had come across. Captain, O'Neill and Long had gotten those resealed internally within about five minutes of finding them using the same emergency repair kit from the engineering area. I didn't see much of the work as Major Chowdhury was right next to me and had changed to her 'don't even consider getting in the way' look.

Captain suggested that if that didn't hold, it was likely that we would have to do some EV repairs. Lt. Johnson gave us a quick acceleration warning, and then fired the thrusters once again.

By the time we finished, I had a pretty significant headache. I thought that it must be from straining my eyes and ears, trying to find any potential leaks from where I was sitting. Sometimes I had gotten headaches from focusing too hard on things, so I didn't think too much about it until I realized that just about everyone was having some sort of similar pain, and a few were seemingly dizzy or groggy looking.

Oxygen. Duh.

As I moved to the group that had accumulated in the center of the main area, I heard that they were coming to the same conclusion. We had lost too much air. We were a little oxygen starved now. I could see fear rising on many faces.

Captain, Ms. Chowdhury, and O'Neill were off to one side, quietly talking about the likelihood of EV repair needs. I could overhear only a little of it.

I brought my attention back to the conversation about oxygen, just in time to see Delacoeur pass out. We quickly turned him and straightened him, checking his pulse, and listening for his breathing.

His vital signs appeared OK, but labored breathing suggested that perhaps the lower O_2 levels had taken its first toll. I know this may seem very uncouth, insensitive, and maybe a little spiteful, but I was glad it was him if it was anybody. At least in this state he wasn't likely to be complaining about everything. We all knew that close quarters and stress have a way of making people get on each other's nerves, and certain people grated on certain others'. I think Delacoeur grated on everybody's.

Now that Delacoeur had succumbed, some of the group started to get a little panicky. The way that *Vanguard*'s life support systems worked essentially involved a chemical process on the CO_2, shunting the carbon out and returning the 'clean' O_2 to the system. It also involved small amounts of water to keep the vapor levels good. There are a lot of stages, obviously, and it is far more complex than that, but that is the core of it.

Unfortunately, I wound up taking charge of Delacoeur, and took him slowly back out of the way to where Lt. Ward was already waiting for me. Ward amazed me. Our doctor had been a thin man when we stepped aboard *Vanguard*. Now, though, he was starting to look emaciated. He was still as sharp as ever, if quirky. Despite his obvious physical discomfort, he kept right on taking care of everyone and everything he needed to do, including never failing to take his shift on the generators. I liked him, and I trusted him, in that weird way you can do only with a good doctor. You knew he would never give up on anyone.

My mother had been a ship's doctor, until she met my father during a stopover on Earth. She was picky about who she worked with, saying that a good doctor had that 'feel' about him. She would have approved of Lt. Ward. I was more than happy to leave Delacoeur in his capable hands after helping the doctor get him strapped to the floor.

Dr. Ward said that he would probably be fine, just a lowering of O_2 to his brain.

When I got back up to the group that I had been with, more people had gathered into it. Captain Brighton had come down from the cockpit and was coming over at the urgings of some of the other ratings. Alcaraz was the one doing the talking. He explained, with the help of the sensor readings on the data pad he was holding, that the O_2 levels were low, perhaps dangerously low. Many people were going to be affected by it, as Delacoeur had just demonstrated. He had an idea for replenishing the oxygen supply on *Vanguard*.

Captain listened intently as he presented his case.

"So you see, if we take the extra water supply, and we can setup an electrolysis system, and split the water into H_2 and O_2 molecules, we could pipe the hydrogen over to the H cells, and the oxygen into the living space. We should be able to give us enough O_2 to replenish the supply here, but it will decrease our water supply significantly. What do you think, sir?"

As he was speaking I could see a couple of the more mechanically minded folks, and the three of us ensigns, looking a little dubiously at him. There was a lot of piping and system work involved here that he wasn't really taking into consideration.

"I think, Crewman Alcaraz, that the lack of oxygen is affecting your thought process. Or at least I hope that is the case," Captain said with no mirth. "What we need to do to restore the O_2 levels onboard is very simple. Long, O'Neill, I would like you two to go back to the EV suits, pull out 2 of them, and bleed the O_2 out of their compression pack into the living space. Two suits only. That should be sufficient to return us to about 20–21% oxygen and about 78% nitrogen in the ship. We will save our water supply and spare equipment for when we need it." The Captain looked around the group, polling silently if there were any other silly questions. There were none. O'Neill and Long began moving back toward the EV suits.

I had to smile to myself. Simple solutions. That was what they tried to teach us to look for at the Academy. It appeared that my instructors had been right after all. You just had to actually be thinking.

As they began bleeding the compressed atmosphere into the living space, we all started to breath easier. No pun intended.

We were all glad to know that our air supply was being replenished. As Long and O'Neill finished up, it seemed like most of the anxiety that had been building was dissipated or at least was dissipating. Headaches and lethargy were still pretty prevalent throughout the crew. It was now my turn to head over to the generators again. I could tell that my muscles were sore, most likely from the lower O_2 levels, coupled with my near double shift on it yesterday and the adrenaline ups and downs today.

My brain was still a little fuzzy. I felt sometimes like I was almost not there, that it was somehow not real. Pain, like in my legs as I started in on the generator, reminded me that it was all too real.

As I was bounding along in my own mind while pedaling, the captain came down to talk with Long, who was seated near the generators. When he came into the space with you, you knew he was the captain. He had an aura about him, and his eyes, well, they could pierce your soul, take your measure and let you know what he thought with one brief instant.

As he turned to me, I felt as if he were once again measuring my worth. I nodded and pedaled all the harder as he looked at me, and then he nodded back and exchanged a few words with Long before leaving.

I just hoped that I was never found wanting under that gaze. I realized it was probably the single most motivating force in my life at that moment.

22 July

Lt. Vasconcellos tried to run through his normal pre-op routine while the two shuttles accelerated hard in pursuit of their prize, but he couldn't seem to sort things out in his own mind. He had his own seat forward in the troop bay, which kept the jostling the others were enduring from being a distraction. Eventually, he couldn't remain seated any longer, and prowled forward down the main corridor.

"Apellido," he called when he reached the tactical station on the left side of the command deck. "Do we have a track of where *Vanguard* has been?"

"No, sir. We haven't been able to maintain a position lock on them for any length of time, as the lieutenant is aware."

"Yes, Private," Vasconcellos said, stressing the rank a little as a warning that he was not in the mood for a disrespectful tone, "but have we charted where and when we've spotted them and tried to piece together what they're up to?"

"No, sir. I don't think we really can, though. Too many unknowns."

"Show me as much as you can then," he said and took a seat next to him at the sensor console.

"Yes, sir," the private responded at once, knowing a command when he heard one. He cleared his screen and keyed in a few commands to bring up a representation of the binary system. "Here is the track we have on them when they left *Pathfinder*. They were decelerating pretty hard, over 800 g, for a shallow ellipse to A3." Apellido caused a slightly curved dotted line to appear. "At this point, they drop their accel down to 380 and take a slower parabolic course to the planet." A solid, disjointed curve appeared.

"Why?"

"I don't know, sir. From what we know of *Vanguard*'s specs, 800 g is pretty close to their maximum output. Maybe something broke, or they just decided not to strain the engines too much."

Vasconcellos thought quietly for a few moments, then motioned for Apellido to go on.

"When they left A3," the private continued, wisely avoiding a recap of events there, "their exit angle made it appear that they were making for one of the planet's three moons. *Caxias* made the hop there at our maximum speed, which is almost 200 g less than *Vanguard*'s maximum. If they were flying at top speed, they would have gotten there first. If they kept to the 380 g speed they were last using, we would have beaten them there. There isn't any way for us to tell what speed they were traveling at, nor what course they actually took, since they never showed up at that moon.

"The next location we know they were at would be the ZFlash beacon that they silenced. We have a timestamp for when it went dead, but it was a long time from the last contact, and we don't know where they went or what they did during those twelve days."

"Okay, what about the glimpse we got of them when they went past our base?"

"Again, we don't have enough information to tell what they were doing. Look here, sir." He indicated the line, mostly dotted but with a solid curve in the middle, which sprang to life in the display. "They landed on Antoc-7 for some unknown reason. They boost at an unknown acceleration for an unknown period, reaching a velocity of a little over 1,000 km/s, then cut their engines to try to sneak past us. We detect them, fire missiles, they accelerate away from us, alter course slightly, and then we lose them again. There just is not enough here to really learn anything."

"This doesn't look right, Private. What delta-v does *Vanguard* have after we fired on them?"

Apellido scratched his head. He entered a few commands and the annotated acceleration was shown on the screen as well. "That can't be right," both said at the same time, then looked at each other.

Running for your life at two and a half g? Not even that high! It made no sense at all. Trying to avoid missiles, a sane man would accelerate as hard as his ship would. But even if they had cut engines just before being detected, they had to have added velocity at twenty or thirty times that rate to reach the velocity they displayed. Higher than that if they had gone ballistic before they approached the asteroid belt, which they almost certainly had.

He was missing something. Vasconcellos knew that there had to be a reason for the decisions Brighton had made, but try as he would he could not find one. Did it have something to do with whatever they were using to mask their engines? Not knowing how that worked, it was possible, but he could not imagine how.

He hated not knowing. He especially hated facing a man that he couldn't figure out. How could he plan for eventualities when everything his opponent did seemed illogical and random?

"All right, assuming constant acceleration from the time we lost their track, where would they be now?"

A few keystrokes added a red line terminated in a white dot. "There, sir."

"And where are we?"

The two blue lines which popped into being already extended beyond the red one. They had anticipated *Vanguard* accelerating at a minimum of 50 g, and perhaps that was still the correct value.

Should he order the ships to reverse course? What did he really have to go on? It was not reasonable to assume that they would keep traveling that slowly. At least, not if they had a choice.

"When we detected them flying by, what did their engine output look like, Apellido?"

"Actually, we didn't pick up any energy signature at all. It was the radar system that detected the ship. It identified a fast moving mass that could have been an asteroid. The tech on duty at that station could see right away that it would miss us, but it was the closest approach yet, and she decided to test the missile system on it. It was only when their velocity changed that we knew it was a ship, and not a hunk of rock."

"No engine output, even when we know they were increasing speed and changing vectors?" Vasconcellos knew the answer that was coming, but he needed to be sure.

"None that we could detect, sir, but they've already shown that they can mask it somehow."

"Have they?"

A memory flashed in Vasconcellos' mind, one he had not realized the significance of at the time. *Vanguard* slipping out of his grasp, thrusters firing to lift it away from the planet and give it the space needed to engage their Gravitas engines.

But the fire and thunder of the thrusters never died, only diminished with distance. They never used their gravitic engines at all, that's why they disappeared from our sensors as soon as they left atmosphere, he realized. And it was also why no one had been able to pick up their location. They had been scanning for an energy field that did not exist.

Without another word, he turned and crossed the bridge to share his deductions with Agostinho.

He was not completely successful at convincing her that he was right.

She was only convinced that he *might* be right, but that was enough. *Oeiras* would decelerate to check Vasconcellos' theory, while *Caxias* would continue to push hard to make sure Brighton could not beat them all to the sun and scuttle his ship unopposed. Both ships would be using mass sensors, which technically detected natural gravity, rather than looking for the artificial field that was so much easier to see because of the higher energy level.

It was more than four hours decelerating before Apellido's red line touched *Oeiras'* position. Yet again, they were not where they were supposed to be. Neither had they made an appearance at the sun. Of course not. Vasconcellos was getting tired of being wrong.

He wracked his brain for an explanation, some clue where to find them now. He and Apellido were staring at the incoming streams of data from their continuous scans.

"You said they were traveling ballisticly when they first appeared?" the lieutenant asked suddenly.

"That's right. Probably trying to sneak by us," Apellido answered.

"How would they know where we were? That there was a need for them to hide in that area?"

"I don't know, sir."

"If they *had* known we were there, they wouldn't have come anywhere near. I think they're low on fuel. That's the only thing that makes sense. And if that's the case, I bet they stopped accelerating as soon as they had avoided the missiles. Where would that put them, Private?"

"Right about here," the young man said, indicating a point more distant from the sun, and not on the red track at all.

Another consultation with Agostinho resulted in another partial convincing; perhaps even more dubious than the last. Being only partly in agreement with Vasconcellos, she ordered that this new location be investigated as quickly as possible so that they could return to the more likely station in proximity to Antoc-B.

In the event, it was this choice that contributed to the later disaster.

Agostinho ordered maximum acceleration, but by the time *Oeiras* came to be near enough to *Vanguard* to detect it, they had accumulated a considerable amount of velocity. The closure of the two vehicles as they passed each other was in excess of four million m/s. At that speed, there was no time for anyone aboard the DaGaman ship to take any action before their quarry was again lost in the dark void.

Apellido called out the contact report, but the first word was not out of his mouth before his screen went blank once again. Agostinho was skeptical that the brief contact was in fact their target no matter how much the Marine lieutenant insisted that the location of the sighting made the most sense given what was known, and precious minutes were spent reviewing the recorded data for telltale signs of an unpowered ship.

Once enough evidence was shown to support the picture Vasconcellos had painted, Agostinho immediately ordered a course change to follow them. With so much momentum, though, hours were used up before their velocity spun down and they were even moving in the right direction.

Vanguard was definitely moving fast, but no one can move fast enough to outrun the EM waves of a vocom communication. Word reached *Caxias* well ahead of the Warners, and they positioned themselves to interdict them before they could scuttle their ship.

The contact information that was transmitted was sketchy at best. *Vanguard*'s current velocity was not measured directly, since the contact duration was too brief, but rather inferred from the distance and time separating this contact from the last. *Caxias'* commander, Lt. Heliodoro, was aware of the limitation of his data, but reasoned that it was a close enough approximation to allow him to pick his ambush location. He knew about how fast they were traveling and about how much they might decide to accelerate; that gave him a window of time in which to expect his visitors.

He further knew the location of the last contact, and the fact that they were planning to scuttle their ship meant that they were headed for the middle of the sun. This was sufficient information to choose a spot directly in their path where they could catch them in a tractor field and decelerate them well short of the sun's magnetosphere, which must be avoided at all costs, since magnetic fields tend to destructively interfere with the artificial gravity fields used to drive all ships.

Given the innate errors in what he knew to be true, Heliodoro wound up in the wrong place at the right time, with catastrophic results.

Caxias

Lieutenant Heliodoro stopped the engine's thrust just as the v-indicator dropped to zero. With no further tasks as pilot, he intended to take up his command responsibilities, and made that clear to all when he left the helm station and sat in the center seat. He quickly found that there was nothing needed in that area either.

He was the only officer on the ship; the two other bridge slots, Tactical and Communications/Sensors, were manned by noncoms drawn from the two Marine platoons aboard.

The navy man thought about checking to see that Sergeant Wainwright was ready with the tractor net, but opted not to say anything. Noncoms hate officers looking over their shoulders. Wainwright knew what he was about, and would be ready when the time came. They had at least thirty minutes yet before *Vanguard* could possibly arrive, anyway.

Heliodoro sat more or less patiently for almost half of the allotted time before he was doing exactly what he had tried to avoid: looking over the noncom's shoulders for news. None was forthcoming.

"Where are they?" Heliodoro asked five minutes after the window had closed. "Did they spot us and veer off?"

"Couldn't have, Lieutenant. We were sitting dead, no emissions, and we would have picked up active scanners," Corporal Dyas explained without taking her eyes off the scanners.

"Go to full scan, Corporal. The ambush clearly didn't work, and we need to know where they are before we can do anything else."

"Aye-aye, sir. Got them. Their course is going to take them near, but not into, the sun."

"All right, feed the course to my station and we'll get after them. Notify *Oeiras* of our status," Heliodoro ordered, crossing the bridge and resuming his earlier station at the helm.

Heliodoro plugged the course and speed information into the astrogation computer and sent the results to the ship's engines without thinking about them. The procedure was the same as he had performed a hundred times before. *Caxias* accelerated after *Vanguard*, on a line between where Heliodoro's ship was and where the Warner ship was going to be.

Oeiras was still well behind, but now had overcome their momentum away from the sun and were at least headed the right way. Heliodoro was pleased to see that Vasconcellos was not going to be able to catch them up before Heliodoro had claimed their prize. That was fine with him. He disliked people who made fun of his name, and if Vasconcellos' hunches led them the wrong direction and all the glory came to Adão Heliodoro, that was fine as well.

"Ready tractor," he ordered. Wainwright sat as tense and rigid as the lieutenant, watching the distance indicator creep slowly downward. Almost there...

Heliodoro opened his mouth to give the order, but he never uttered a sound. The ship lurched violently under him and threw him forward out of his seat. Rather than land on the deck in front of him, his trajectory never curved and he flew headlong into the forward viewer. Arms over his head protected that sensitive organ, but he rebounded and continued not to fall in the sudden weightlessness. He flailed madly for some purchase, but every convenient object eluded his immediate grasp.

Dyas and Wainwright also flew forward in the sudden cessation of both gravity and acceleration, but unlike Heliodoro they had consoles before them which arrested their momentum. They slammed into the system controls just as they erupted in a massive electrical discharge, as the full power of *Caxias'* engines fed back into themselves when its drive field collapsed.

The smell of burnt meat indicated to Heliodoro that the two other bridge occupants were dead, while screams and curses from the troop compartment indicated that others were not. Once he finally came in contact with the aft bulkhead he was able to push off and swim to the command chair. Its control panel was unpowered, and a quick visual check showed no power anywhere on the bridge.

Caxias was blind, deaf, dumb, and impotent. She had no way to affect her fate in any meaningful way.

Oeiras

"I've lost contact with *Caxias*!" Apellido shouted into the tense atmosphere of *Oeiras'* command deck. The officers were watching the telemetry feed from their sister ship, to avoid both of them lighting up their target with active scanners. The same information was evidenced by the suddenly blank viewscreen.

"Where are they," Commander Agostinho demanded with sudden dread.

"No energy readings from either ship, ma'am."

"Active scan!"

"Active scan, aye." Apellido was always more formal when he was nervous, and he could hear the near panic in the commander's voice, though he didn't understand the reasons for it. When the active scanner's return signal was processed he put the tactical and navigation information on the screen.

"What was that idiot thinking?" The panic was gone from her voice, transformed into anger. "New course: 46.12 by 0.11, emergency power to engines."

"What happened?" Vasconcellos wanted to know.

"Heliodoro cut too close to the sun in pursuit, and blew out his engines. The gravity field a ship generates is powerful enough to handle a planet's gravity and magnetic field without problems, but a star has fields powerful enough to interfere with the ship's field. The energy bleeds from the more powerful one into the smaller field of the ship and burns out the field generators. It probably fed back into the power systems, too."

"What about *Vanguard*?"

Agostinho's head snapped around and her harsh gaze held Vasconcellos motionless. Having found a convenient target, she cut loose with the anger and frustration boiling at the surface.

"Perhaps you're too feebleminded to appreciate the seriousness of this situation, so let me explain it, and I'll use small words so you'll be sure to understand. If we do not get to *Caxias*, and I mean right now, they are all dead. No energy output means no engines. No engines means there is nothing to keep them from falling into the sun. In case no one has mentioned this to you before, it's not easy to survive that sort of thing.

"And even if we can keep them out of the sun, no power means no shielding to protect them from solar radiation, which is just as lethal. No cooling from the sun's heat. No heating from the cold of space. No air scrubbers to replace the oxygen. Any one of those things can kill them if we're not quick enough. So excuse me if I am more worried about our own people then tracking *Vanguard* just now."

Oppressive silence dominated the command deck for perhaps twenty minutes while *Oeiras* raced sunward. It was Vasconcellos that broke it, and his first words demonstrated that his thoughts had still been centered on *Vanguard* rather than the rescue everyone else was focused on.

"Brighton did this."

Apellido was the one to respond, caught off guard at the change in subject. "Did what?"

"He set this up. He set *us* up."

"You think *Brighton* arranged all this?" the sergeant asked incredulously.

Vasconcellos gave his junior a sharp look, but continued in a normal tone, "I do. Brighton is devious, and he must have had more information on us than we thought he could have. He played along on the planet, let us get cocky, then turned the tables on us. And now this. He flew right past our base. Right past us! Too fast for us to do anything right away, but accelerating at a low enough rate that he knew we'd come after him. He faked the low acceleration to appear weak where he was strong. He's flying an unarmed ship, so he is using the sun to fight his battles for him. Like I said, devious. As Machiavellian a strategist as I've ever seen.

"The next time, we're either going to have to plan to do the unexpected or pounce on him before he knows we are there. We can't let him anticipate our moves anymore."

Apellido turned back to his displays and kept his face neutral as he muttered agreement. Agostinho, who had heard the exchange, simply shook her head in disgust and disbelief. No one was *that* devious. There were simply too many variables for anyone to have manipulated the situation the way Vasconcellos claimed…weren't there? No, no one was that good. It was simply bad luck and inexperience.

Apellido called out suddenly that they were entering the magnetosphere, and all attention was once again on the job at hand.

"Reduce power to 50 percent standard. Stand by tractor." Agostinho unconsciously leaned forward in her seat. Due to their differing vectors, the two ships would only remain in proximity for a short period. They had to be exact on the first try. There would not be time enough for a second attempt.

The seconds ticked away in silence, then, "Engage tractors!"

"Positive lock on tractors," Morisse reported. The ship lurched as the two momentums were linked together. The effect was barely felt before the artificial gravity redistributed to compensate. They had a hold of their drifting comrades, but their struggle was not yet completed. The merged vector was still falling into the sun. They needed more thrust to avoid certain death for all of them.

"Three-quarters power to the engines. Ramp it up slowly, and pull back if we start getting feedback," the ship's commander ordered. The amount of power feeding into the gravity field of the ship gradually increased, though no sound or sensation could be heard or felt on the bridge to indicate its change in levels.

Cinquini, at the helm, kept light fingers on the power settings and watched the field indicators with calm intensity. His readings spiked upward before he had reached the 70% level and he pulled back to the half power mark immediately.

It wasn't fast enough.

The energy surge tore through the internal power circuitry and burned and fused the metal at contact after contact. The greatest current draw was in the tractor emitters, and these burned out first, causing *Oeiras* to shoot away from *Caxias*, and away from the sun.

The engines were the next to go, followed by internal gravity. In that, they were more fortunate than their counterparts; merely floating off the decking rather than slamming into walls. Still, they now had much the same problems that *Caxias* faced, with three notable exceptions.

First, they were farther away from the sun and retained a greater velocity than the other ship. That gave them more time to effect repairs. Second, none of their crew were injured, which gave them more able hands to get some sort of engines running to limp back to base.

And third, the people aboard *Oeiras* were going to live.

Caxias was not.

24–25 July

Immobile against the rear wall's sheeting lay Kieran Delacoeur. Kara George was a meter away, in the same state. Both were pallid and much thinner than when our trials had begun. Kieran had lost a lot of his former mass, not that he was unique in that. The hypoxia we had all been through seemed to have affected these two to the point they still had not recovered fully, and their bodies were not able to function yet.

What singled the two of them out to me was the fact that they could hardly find the energy to move unassisted. On her last watch, Kara had gamely tried to take her shift of pedaling, but found that she couldn't maneuver well enough to cross to the generator. She had to have Queneau hold the waterpouch when she wanted a drink, and had a hard time finding the strength to chew her portion of our tough food.

Delacoeur was much the same, perhaps worse. Though bigger, and still not thin, he seemed to be without any strength. He did not have the same problem consuming food, but was not able to hold his arms steady to receive it. I had discussed their condition with the captain during first watch, and he allowed me to place them on sick list, and exempt them from duty, along with Jens Fujinami.

Indomitable though he had always been, physically Jens was in a matching situation. His body was failing, and his systems were beginning to shut down. He did not concern me as gravely as the other two, however. He was weak and lethargic, but he still retained some of his normal spirit. He would smile, and try to carry on conversations, though I could see these actions weakened him. Mostly, I think, he was determined that he would hold out as long as anyone else did. His positive nature aided him in looking forward to better things, and not giving up.

Healthiest of our crew, I would say, were Steve Long, Derrick Mackey, Sheli Chowdhury, Fyonna Johnson, Claire Paul, Elle Williams, and the three ensigns. I attribute their better state to one of two things. All of these individuals were either younger than most, or else had been long-time participants in a rigorous physical training regimen. In some cases, I could say both applied.

All of these individuals had been remarkably willing to shoulder extra responsibilities or duties when there was need. Mackey had not had a watch in several days where he had not finished out someone else's turn on the generator when they became too depleted to continue. And this service was always given cheerfully, with not the slightest stinginess.

Mackey was a stalwart soul, and kept all our spirits buoyed. Still, small signs indicated to me that he was asking too much of his body to continue at his current pace. Captain Brighton pushed himself far harder than anyone, though.

"Inexhaustible energy" was how I was used to describing Captain Brighton. I had not realized how appropriate those words were. Though he had become gaunt and hollow-eyed, he still had not plumbed the depths of his energy reserve. Brighton was still doing the majority of the piloting, often as much as sixteen hours out of each day. In addition, he was taking one or two rotations on the generator each day. How he managed this feat on the short rations and limited sleep, I did not understand, even after witnessing it myself.

Captain Brighton was physically a large and powerful man. No more so, however, than others I have met, and even others in our party. He should have had no greater internal reservoir to draw from than any of the rest of us. I believe that he kept going because he would not let himself do any less. For the same reason that he continued to wear his uniform tunic and maintain his personal appearance, his personal code would not allow him to show any weakness, nor fail to discharge his duty as he saw it.

Most unexpected of all was the manner in which Clémence Queneau responded to our poor circumstances. She had been raised in the bustling streets of New York City, and her lifestyle and occupation could best have been described as sedentary. I had believed that she would be among the first to show physical problems stemming from our reduced caloric intake, but I must admit that I was wrong in my belief. While I do not number her among those bearing up the best, I have to admit that she was managing better than I was.

Queneau was a very interesting young woman, though not what one would expect among that small percentage of people who work in space. The most notable difference I had seen in her was my impression that she was completely unimaginative. Not unintelligent; for she could hardly perform her duties well enough to have been assigned to *Pathfinder* if she were.

Her mind was quick and full of knowledge, it simply never strayed out of the well-worn tracks it had established.

Her lack of imagination, or apparent lack, if I were to give her the benefit of the doubt, led directly to some of her other qualities. She was always very trusting of others, and loyal to Brighton and the Warner Family without the slightest exception. The case in point being that we had just concluded a very dangerous "slingshot" maneuver about one of this system's binary suns, and she was likely the only one among us to be unconcerned.

Computerless as we were, it was difficult to believe that we could precisely balance our velocity against the immense pull of gravity that we would feel at such close proximity to the star. And using only the power which we ourselves were generating, how could we protect *Vanguard* from the intense heat?

My knowledge and experience were in the field of medicine, so I tried to hold to my faith in Captain Brighton's abilities to see us safely through. Others of our group, though, understood how difficult it would be to accomplish, and they shared their concerns with the rest of us, albeit very quietly. It was enough to cause my imagination to run wild. Clémence seemed to have been unaffected, but she was the only member of the crew for whom I could make that claim.

During the slingshot, our power requirements were a little more than had previously been the case; we did not need a heater, but we desperately needed cooling off. Cooling the cabin actually required more power than heating it had. This kept both generators going at full speed.

During one of my shifts at peddling, Elle was working the other generator, and she explained to me what we had gained by flying so close to the sun. I had made a stray comment that showed how little I knew of such things, something like, "If we gain velocity by letting the sun's gravity pull us in, don't we just lose it all again as we pull away?"

She smiled at me and then explained why this wasn't exactly so without talking down to me. First, she explained, during a slingshot our own engines would be constantly adding to our base velocity, so we would certainly build up a higher speed on the other side. Without that, it would have been as I said, that the gravity would pull us toward the sun equally while heading toward it and while heading away, with no net benefit to our final velocity.

Out in space, the thrust we experienced is a Newtonian reaction to the force being pushed away from us. As such, it is a function of the two masses involved. By continuing to expel our fuel as we executed the slingshot, we were actually gaining more kinetic energy than we would have away from any gravity source.

Again, I let my ignorance of the physics involved show when I asked her how that could be. "I thought that the law of conservation of energy says that you can't get more energy out than you put in." She laughed.

"It does, and you can't," she said. She took a minute to gather her thoughts, and I was just as glad. I was having a hard enough time keeping my legs going, and keeping up my part of the conversation was winding. Fortunately, she knew more on the subject than I did, so most of my responses to her, in general, to that point had been limited to nodding my head.

"Okay," she began, "this is not a perfect analogy, but it should demonstrate the reasons." I nodded. "Let's say that you're floating in space and you have a 5-kilo weight. You push it away from you as hard as you can, and you go the opposite direction." I nodded. "Now let's say that the 5-kilo weight was actually *Vanguard*. What would the difference be?"

I couldn't get away with just nodding, so I said, "I'd be going faster."

"Yes, you would, even though you may have expended the same energy by pushing as hard as you could in both cases. The difference between the two is that you had more to push against, which allowed you to be more efficient in using your muscles to generate kinetic energy." I nodded. "In the same way, the fuel we are pushing behind us as we pass the sun winds up trapped in its gravity well. Essentially, that gives us more to push against."

I nodded.

"Secondly," she went on, "in most cases, the sun is immobile in relation to the rest of the system; it sits in the middle and everything revolves around it. In our case, the sun we're slingshotting around is not motionless, but orbiting with its counterpart star. Depending on the entry and exit angles of the slingshot, you can add up to twice the star's orbital velocity. Our velocity relative to the sun wouldn't change, of course."

I nodded yet again. I really hadn't followed that second point, but I was too out of breath to ask about it. How Elle could carry on so loquaciously while pedaling was more than I could fathom.

"Of course, that's not the case here," she continued. "Since we are using the slingshot to kill velocity instead of build it, everything is reversed. The same physics applies, and the same acceleration is generated, just pointed the opposite direction."

"Of course," I agreed sagely, in one of my few non-nodding responses.

Soon, our turn at the generators ended and I went quickly to sleep. My energy level had dropped to such a depth that I found it difficult to go more than four or five hours without some sleep. Jens woke me after two hours, when it was again my turn on Torquemada's bicycle. We were just about a day past the actual slingshot by then, and the sun was still visible through our overhead viewport. I was groggy and sluggish to begin with, but when I completed my hour, I found that I was not immediately ready to go back to sleep.

I took the opportunity to make my rounds and check on my patients. Jens still seemed cheerful but weak. No change in his condition seemed evident. Kara and Delacoeur also appeared unchanged. I worried about them both, though I was still more than a bit puzzled at Kieran's state. Kara George was quite slender to begin with, and her lost weight made her seem skeletal. She had a high metabolic rate, which made her current plight understandable. Jens was taller, but with the same slender build and the same metabolism. Unfortunately, at least under the present circumstance, I could also be described in that way. Except for the tall part, of course.

Kieran, though, was heavyset. He had lost quite a bit of weight, ten or twenty kilos by my estimation, but I would still consider him overweight, so his suffering being equal to Kara's truly had me stumped. I would not have predicted it, at any rate.

It was while I was trying to puzzle it out that I had an idea to help them. I was worried mostly for Kara, because she was having difficulty eating the tough ration bars, due to her weakness. I was wishing that I had some way to give her a boost that would give her body at least the strength to eat. Normally, the prescription for a temporary boost would be a stimulant of one sort or another. I never even considered that as an option. Even if it allowed her to sit up and eat normally, it would cause her to burn up more energy than she gained.

What she needed was a permanent boost, not a temporary one. Then it hit me. I had something in my med kit that would do exactly that. I had to climb up our makeshift ladder to our lavatory-turned-storage room. In my excitement, I hurried up a bit faster than I should have, and I had to sit back down in the storage compartment while a wave of dizziness passed.

When I was able to stand without shakiness, from one of the large cases I had packed I drew out a large syringe, three needles, and an IV bag. I filled the syringe, and then placed the bag back in the case.

I climbed back down and went first to Kara George. She was using her uniform tunic to lie on and her arms were bare to near the shoulders with her undershirt. I didn't need her to move, so I did not even bother to rouse her. I found a vein inside her left elbow and slowly fed in a third of the glucose mixture I had drawn up. After drawing the needle back out, I used a small amount of wound sealant and held the vein until it had dried. Kara hadn't even stirred during the whole exchange, a sure sign of how badly she needed the extra calories I had just given her. I gave a sad sigh as I turned next to Kieran Delacoeur.

Unlike Kara, Kieran had been watching me during the whole procedure. "What was that you gave her?" he asked, with fear in both his eyes and his voice. He quickly sat up and slid himself up against the wall, as far away from me as he could manage with the crowding we had lived with for so long.

Why was he so frightened? I wondered. And where had this sudden burst of energy come from, when he and Kara had seemed to be equally depleted? At once, I had the answer, and it meshed completely with the questions I had already been worrying over for the last several hours. It was a dark suspicion, which would not have normally occurred to me. I would not have guessed that any of our group would have claimed more fatigue than they had, simply to be able to shirk their share of the work. At this point, though, it was only a suspicion, and I needed to be sure.

"It's something to help you sleep, Kieran. Now be a good patient and roll up your sleeve," I directed.

He tried to pull himself farther away with no result. "I don't need nothin' to help me sleep," he said.

"Yes you do, Kieran. You keep waking up, and every time you wake up, you use more of our resources. You're not contributing anything, and you're using up our food and oxygen, so I think it would be best if you just went to sleep."

"You mean you're *putting* me to sleep?" he shouted, horrified. His were not the only eyes staring at me with the same look, either.

"Do you need me to hold him down for you?" Sheli Chowdhury asked calmly. I wasn't sure if she had guessed what I was doing and was playing along, or if she really was willing to euthanize him because he was not pulling his weight. The hungry smile she gave Kieran spoke to the latter. *That is one scary person*, I thought. As soon as Kieran turned back pleadingly to me, Sheli gave me a wink. I had an equally hard time keeping both a smile and a look of relief off my face.

"If you wouldn't mind," I said pleasantly. "This is pretty fast acting, so you wouldn't need to hold him long."

"Are we going to eat him?" Again that wolf's grin speared Delacoeur, and the shock effect held everyone motionless. No one could believe what was happening around them, their brains too frozen to decide to act.

Truth to tell, it shocked me, and I took a moment before I could answer. "I hadn't thought of that. I was just planning to put him in the waste system for additional fuel. I suppose we'd have to cut him into small chunks to do that anyway. We might as well keep him for food."

Up to that point, Kieran had been marshalling his defenses to fight us off. Now, though, his face was white and he looked like he was about to cry. "There's no need for that. I can still pedal the generator. Please don't put me to sleep, Dr. Ward. I'll work hard, you'll see."

"I don't know, Delacoeur. You seemed to be pretty weak until a few minutes ago. I don't think you have anything to contribute anymore." He'd confirmed my suspicions now, and I was unwilling to let him go unpunished. "I think we need to just put you down. Besides, Sheli is right; we really could use the extra food."

"You can't do that, Ward. That's murder!" He turned to give Sheli his whole attention, deducing that she was the entirety of the threat against him.

I've always been small, which made me an easy target for bullies when I was younger. That's what led me to study martial arts for years; self-defense. I must have been angrier than I knew, because all the years of training came back in an instant, and I viewed the situation through those eyes.

Even before I had really thought about it, I reached out with my left hand and, spinning around him, grabbed his right thumb, pulling it behind his back and driving his arm up. His yelp of pain turned to panic as the syringe in my right hand pricked his neck just over his carotid artery.

"And do you think it's not killing the rest of us to have to do your share of the work for you? Isn't the fact that you are ducking out on your responsibilities to the rest of us just another form of murder? And isn't the punishment for murder death?" I spoke at a normal volume, but my voice held unmistakable venom.

When I moved into action, I had thought that the threat presented by the syringe would keep Kieran from working against me. Or perhaps I acted without thinking much at all. In any event, it didn't hold him motionless. His free left hand came across to grab both my hand and the syringe it held and pulled them forward. At the same time, he twisted his body and threw me across his hip. My shoulder and head hit the ridged decking of what used to be the floor simultaneously, and a bright light flashed inside my skull.

My vision cleared just in time to see Kieran advance on me with his fist drawn back. I hadn't even had time to be frightened when Sheli Chowdhury's spinning foot hit him in the middle of the forehead with a loud crack that echoed off the walls of our narrow enclosure. The speed of her strike was so great that neither he nor I had seen it coming, and it was such an impact that his forward momentum was completely reversed, at least for his head. His legs continued forward, but his head went backward and was the first part of his body to make contact with the deck. He was unconscious before he knew he'd been hit.

Just like that, it was over. I looked up to the pilot's seat, but Captain Brighton's entire attention seemed to be occupied with maneuvering our craft. Incredible as it sounds, I don't think he noticed any part of our confrontation. Instead of bothering him, I turned then to Johnson. "Ms. Johnson, I believe Delacoeur can be returned to active duty now."

"I can see that, Doctor. Now what was it that you gave Kara?"

"Sugar water," I answered with a smile. "I drew some up for her, Kieran, and Jens, before Kieran's paranoia allowed me to see through his deception."

"I see. Carry on then, Dr. Ward."

I noticed then that I had managed to hang onto the syringe, but Delacoeur's grip had ejected some of the precious fluid. The needle was bent, and I doubted it could be salvaged. I traded the needles and moved over to Jens. It wasn't until I looked up to move that I noticed that people were watching me.

Their scrutiny made me uncomfortable, so I focused on what I was about and tried to ignore them. Jens was looking at me admiringly when I got over to him. "Roll up your sleeve, and stop looking at me like that," I told him.

"I don't need any," he said simply. "I'll get by. Save it for those that need it worse."

"I'm the doctor here, now roll up your sleeve."

"Aye-aye, sir! I've seen what happens to people who don't obey doctor's orders." He smiled to take any sting out of the words, and I smiled back while I watched him comply.

Sheli had seated herself nearby, and she added, "That was a good thumb lock, but if you had watched how his weight shifted, you would have seen the throw coming."

I nodded acknowledgement and said, "Thanks for backing my play."

"That's my job. I had already suspected that Delacoeur was faking, and I saw the look in your eyes go from puzzlement to understanding, so I knew you were up to something."

"I could tell you were up to something, too," Jens put in. "I hadn't suspected Delacoeur of anything, but I knew we were nowhere near bad enough off for you to start talking about cannibalism."

"It won't come to that," Sheli said firmly. "The captain will have us out of this system before any of us die of starvation." She spoke with the conviction of one who knew, and not one who was trying to convince herself. I knew she had served as a Marine officer for many years before joining *Pathfinder*, and I wondered briefly about what she might have experienced in the past that led to her conviction. Still, her certainty was infectious, and I felt more confident myself.

I had one more round with the generator before third watch ended, and first watch began. Delacoeur still had not come to, and I checked his pulse and respiration to be sure he was doing okay. Aside from a goose egg in the middle of his forehead, he was fine.

Kara had awakened, and when I asked her how she felt she responded that she was a little hungry, but otherwise felt better than she had in days. This was very encouraging news, and I told her so. I kept my fingers crossed to see if she would be better able to deal with her rations.

Johnson climbed up to the storage room to retrieve our breakfast at watch change. Kara received a double portion since she had been asleep during the last watch change. She seemed to have no difficulty eating, and I was much relieved.

Jens also reported improved energy, and proved it by taking a turn on the generator and completing the full hour. Mackey was the beneficiary of Jens' generosity, which was simply a return favor for Mackey taking an extra turn during third watch. Kara had asked permission to return to duty, and I allowed it, provisionally. I asked her not to take on more than two turns at the generator per day, until I saw how she was able to handle the additional load.

Delacoeur revived a little after mid-watch. Much as I didn't want to speak to him, I knew that others would take their cue from me, and we needed him to feel included in our crew. If he deemed himself ostracized, he would have no reason to participate in our mutual maintenance unless we forced him. We would all benefit if he could be brought to feel like part of the group.

I moved to sit down by him and asked, "How's the head?"

"Hurts like the devil," he responded guardedly. "Why should you care?"

"I could quote you the Hippocratic Oath I took, but my attempt to dislocate your shoulder might make it difficult for you to believe. Mostly it's the fact that we are all in this together, and everyone here is my responsibility, medically speaking." I could see he still didn't believe me, but he didn't stop me from examining his injury. I put some numbstrips on the site of the blow and I could see the tenseness drain out of him as they went to work.

"You could have done that while I was out, you know," he said to me, pointing at his forehead. "I could have woke up without a headache at all, if you're so concerned about me."

"Pain isn't all bad. I have found it to be an excellent teacher, in fact." He stared daggers at me for a bit, but when I refused to be embarrassed or drop my gaze, he submitted and lowered his own.

I could see that he was more willing to listen now, so I said, "Look, Kieran, you did a dumb thing. It probably wasn't the first time or the last time. The problem is that it affected all the rest of us, and not just you. None of us can afford to let that kind of thing happen."

I continued to look at him until he met my eyes and nodded.

"I can't speak for the captain, but I'm willing to let it slide this once, if you promise that it won't happen again."

"All right," he said. Then after a moment or two, "I hope I didn't hurt you with that throw."

I shrugged. "Scraped a knee, is all."

He nodded and I left him.

Two hours before second watch was to begin, Elle offered to take over the controls, and Brighton gladly accepted. He climbed down the rungs of the ladder, stretched himself out and was asleep in less than half a minute. I don't understand how he was able to train his body to do this. It was like his mind and body were issued to him with an on-off switch. When he woke he was instantly alert and active, as well.

The proof of that was almost immediately available. The captain had been asleep less than half an hour when Lieutenant Johnson descended from the storage room and nudged him awake. Instantly, his eyes opened and he sat up.

"What is it, XO?" he asked in a clear voice.

"I regret to inform you, sir, that some of our food is missing. A kilo or so of the jerky has been taken."

Disbelief was written on the faces of everyone who had heard, which was to say all those who were awake minus Elle, who was out of earshot in the pilot's seat above. Anger was to be seen in many sets of eyes, and one by one those suspicious eyes turned to look at Delacoeur.

"How long has it been since the last inventory?" Captain Brighton was asking now.

"I'm sorry, Captain. I have been counting the ration bars each time I go to retrieve one at mealtime, but I haven't been checking the extra stores. It's been four or five days." Johnson had a pained look on her face, which she seemed to be trying to hide behind a stoic mask. I could tell that she felt personally responsible for the loss, and was willing to accept whatever punishment the captain cared to mete her.

"Wake everyone," the captain ordered, and everyone turned to those nearest them and shook them awake. In less than a minute the task was accomplished.

"For those of you who haven't heard, approximately one kilo of dried meat has been removed from our provisions. That removal was not authorized, and I mean to know who is responsible, and see that they are appropriately punished." Captain Brighton's voice was deep and firm, and his eyes were cold as he looked from one to the other of us.

"Lieutenant Johnson, did you take the missing food?"

Fyonna appeared caught off guard by the directness of the question, but she held the captain's gaze without flinching and answered, "No, sir."

"Major Chowdhury, did you take the missing food?"

She, too, looked directly into the Captain's eyes and answered firmly, "I did not, Captain."

He turned next to me, and the ice blue eyes held me in their scrutiny. I felt as if my immortal soul was being weighed and measured for the slightest impurity. "Lieutenant Ward, did you take the missing food?"

I had to clear my throat to be sure I had it under control. "No, sir. I have not taken any food since boarding this ship, except from you or Lt. Johnson." I made sure to look him in the eyes as I said it.

He continued next with the ensigns, and proceeded by rank to ask each of us the exact same question, finishing with Crewman Alcaraz. As far as I could tell, we had all answered with the same firmness and conviction. There had been a tense expectation about us as the captain asked Crewman Delacoeur, but he responded with an unhesitating, "No, Captain."

Captain Brighton must have detected something I had not, for he next addressed three specific individuals.

"Specialist Fujinami, do you know anything about the missing food?"

"No, sir. Your announcement a moment ago was the first I knew of it."

"Crewman Smith, do you know anything about the missing food?"

"No, sir," he answered simply.

"Ensign Roberts, do you know anything about the missing food?"

"No, sir."

I could not detect any more trace of untruth from these three than I had from any of the others. Captain Brighton looked at each of us in turn and I could see him growing angrier and angrier as the seconds ticked by.

He was in a towering rage when he finally spoke. I will not try to recount his words here, for I know I could not accurately portray them. He said that he did not know yet who had taken the food, but that when he did, he would personally see to it that a like amount was carved out of the offending person's backside, with interest. His tirade continued for the better part of a half hour. I would have to say that it was the only time in my life that I felt myself lambasted. I knew myself to be innocent, yet I could not help but feel ashamed, so powerful was the verbal assault and so heavy the scorn which William Brighton expressed that day.

Eventually, the ordeal came to its conclusion. There was no communication among us, not even glances. Silently, Captain Brighton climbed up the ladder and deposited his frame in the copilot's seat. Even without his presence, though, no one was inclined toward conversation. One by one, people lay flat or curled up and tried to rest. I noticed a few sneaking glances at Delacoeur, and I knew that they suspected him of the theft.

I didn't know then, and I still do not know to this day, who took that jerky, but I sincerely hoped that they would have many sleepless nights from the guilt. I couldn't quite go far enough to hope that the captain found out who it was, for I don't think he was exaggerating in the least with his threats of physical retribution.

I slept then for a time; long enough that when I roused myself, it was again mealtime. Johnson distributed our meager portions, and, seeing that the mood was still subdued, I went back to sleep.

Excitement greeted my next waking. The crew of our little craft was abuzz with anticipation, and several chattering conversations assailed me at once. Elle had been relieved by Johnson and she had found a place next to me. I asked her what all the noise was about and she told me that we had detected B2 visually. I hadn't realized that I was anxious about the subject until I felt the relief her words caused.

The renewed energy and conversations around me testified that the same relief was communally felt. The source of the anxiety, of course, was the knowledge of how vast and empty space is, and how small a target we had been aiming for without any astrogation more advanced than the captain's dead reckoning.

A glance at the chrono told me that I had only 20 minutes or so before the watch changed again, and I would have to report to generator duty. Somehow, it didn't fill me with such dread, knowing that we were again close to fresh air and elbow room. Hopefully, we could add to our food stores, as well. Not from native plants or animals, of course, since word had gotten around from conversations that B2 had not been completely terraformed, as the other planets in the liquid water range had been. Still, we might be lucky enough to retrieve stored food from the materials cache we expected to find there. I had just enough time to change the dressing on my right knee before I took over for, of all people, Kieran Delacoeur.

At watch change, Elle had climbed up to the cockpit to take over piloting from Lt. Johnson, but Fyonna remained at the controls and Elle came back down with Captain Brighton. The captain took longer than normal to emerge from the store room, and I knew that he was checking the remaining amount of all our rations. He returned to his accustomed seat in the cockpit after distributing the meal.

After a grueling hour on the fatigue generator, I traded off to Elle and made a brief examination of Jens and Kara. Both seemed to be doing as well as I could have expected. Kara had not had a repeat of her earlier trouble with chewing the ration bars.

Not long after, Fyonna warned us all that we would be entering atmosphere soon, and that it would be a turbulent entry as we bled off the remainder of our speed not already dissipated from the reverse slingshot. We did our best to find things to brace ourselves against, but having cannibalized the actual seats and belts needed to strap in, there simply was no way to immobilize ourselves completely. Reentry did have the benefit of reorienting our craft so that we could spread out on the actual floor. This also allowed us to use what minimal straps we had constructed for zero g. That helped some.

It was disorienting for more than a minute that "down" was now a different direction. My brain and eyes kept trying to insist that it was the old direction, and I found it easier to wait for them to adjust while sitting on the decking of the proper floor.

The actuality of the insertion was less of an ordeal than I had feared. It lasted much longer than I would have thought, and there was considerable bouncing and jerking, but no injuries, even minor ones. When things had calmed down, Captain Brighton announced that he had identified our landing site, and we would make for it on our next orbit. The landing itself was soft and gentle, as was Johnson's habit.

Rocky hills and a broad valley were my first view of this world as the captain exited the main airlock and fixed both hatches in the open position. The air which flowed into the cabin was humid and had a slight metallic scent to it. Mostly, it did not smell anything like stale human sweat. It smelled wonderful.

We all pulled ourselves outside and breathed deeply of the foreign air.

"No one more than ten meters from the airlock," Captain Brighton ordered, as he saw us spreading out to enjoy our newfound capaciousness more fully. "Ms. Chowdhury, retrieve our weapons from the locker, if you please. Pistols only, I think. No need for the extra weight of the rifles."

"Mr. Long, I want you to make repairs to the outer hull where the micropuncture occurred, and inspect the rest of the hull for damage. Begin at once, because our time here will be as short as we can manage."

"Food should be our first priority, I'd think, not a leak that's already plugged. If you mean to leave here without letting us rest and regain our strength, I'm opposed. Sir," he added that last after a pause that made it clear that it was given grudgingly.

Long could see that his calculated insult was causing the captain's anger to rise, but he seemed not to care. Long matched Captain Brighton glare for glare. The situation looked to me as if it were about to come to blows. Steve Long was big, strong, and quick with his hands. If there was any of our group who were a match for Captain Brighton physically, it would be either Long or Mackey. At least, that would be the case if you don't include Sheli Chowdhury, anyway. She could have reduced the three of them to unconsciousness without breaking a sweat.

"Mr. Long," the captain began with a tight jaw, "it is not my habit, nor my inclination, to explain my reasons for the orders I give. I certainly will not explain them to any man who displays such insubordination. I will, however, give you a choice. You will either follow my orders or I will put you off my ship. In which case, you will have all the time you desire to rest and regain your strength."

I moved to get between the two men. Tempers had flared, but they were both reasonable men, and I was sure I could convince them both to avoid any drastic action if I moved quickly. I addressed both of them with a measured, calming tone, "Now wait, both of y—"

"Stand down, Ward!" the captain bellowed. Everyone in our party flinched. I don't know which was more surprising to me, being cut off or that, for the first time in my hearing, Captain Brighton had failed to precede my name with its usual honorific. Even in private conversations he had always called me Doctor Ward.

Dangerous eyes blazed their fury, and I was supremely grateful that they were not aimed at me; at least not directly. "Yessir," I said quickly, and retreated back from between the two men. I could see that the captain fully intended to stand firm in his promise to Long. Steve would receive neither more information, nor any other option but to answer until he had made his decision.

In my mind I tried to will Steve to see reason and accept Captain Brighton's authority. Perhaps he was more fearless than sensible, or perhaps he felt the captain had been spouting empty threats. Whatever the case, he did not seem ready to submit, and I feared for his safety. Clearly, he did not see the same things in the captain's face and stance that I did. The Captain would be neither dissuaded nor disobeyed. He was immovable as stone.

"I'll admit you've the right to give whatever orders you want, Captain," and this last word was almost spit out, as if it had a foul taste, "but I'll not turn my own brain off while you do. If your orders don't make sense, or look like they're going to kill the lot of us, then I'm going to question them until I'm hoarse, if I have to."

Neither of the two men made any move to approach the other, but they still eyed one another as if sizing up an opponent for no holds barred combat. As the two stood eyeing one another, out of the wilderness on the other side of *Vanguard* came a hideous shriek. It was an odd mix of tearing fabric and stone grating on stone. It was answered by a clearly terrified squeal. And then, just as quickly, everything was returned to its previous silence.

All eyes were drawn back to the unfolding tableau before us as Captain Brighton spoke again. "Well, Long, I am tired of waiting. You have your choices, though perhaps they are a little clearer now, and those are your only options. You will obey my orders in all things, or I will leave you alone on this planet to fend for yourself. What is it to be?"

"Do you think I am going to stop thinking because you throw a little fear and intimidation at me? Well, it won't work! I am not afraid of anything on this planet."

Long looked around him then, gauging what support he might have, and found none. As he turned from face to face, he stopped abruptly as he saw Sheli Chowdhury. She had two pistols tucked in her belt, and another in each of her hands. She didn't glare at him, or appear to threaten him in any way. In fact, I think it was the emotionlessness of her gaze that stopped him short. She simply watched him pitilessly, like a snake evaluating its next meal.

He gulped, and turned back to the captain.

Guilt at his actions seemed finally to have hit him. His bluster and bravado had leaked out of him like a punctured waterpouch. His position was indefensible, and he now realized it. Essentially, the captain had outmaneuvered him, so that he had no viable options but to submit himself to the captain's direction.

I couldn't bring myself to pity him, though. What options had Captain Brighton had? If one person felt that orders were negotiable, what was to keep the next person in line? Clearly, it was in the best interest of our whole group to maintain draconian discipline until the crisis had past.

"Sorry, Captain," Long was saying now, "I let my emotions get away from me. I'll do as ordered, and it won't happen again."

"See to it, then," Captain Brighton said, as a dismissal.

The tension of the last few minutes eased away, and our group began to mill about again. Some headed back in *Vanguard*, remembering the predator's snarl earlier.

Chowdhury was moving past me to turn over the weapons to Captain Brighton. I tapped her elbow to get her attention.

"You wouldn't have let the captain leave Long here, would you?"

She tilted her head quizzically, and pondered the question for a moment.

"No," she finally said, and a breath of relief left me. "I would have done him the mercy of shooting him first." She turned and continued over to where Captain Brighton stood.

A cold shiver ran the full length of my spine. *That is one scary person*, I thought, neither for the first nor the last time.

CHIEF WARRANT OFFICER 2 STEPHEN A. LONG

Excerpted from his testimony,
Warner Naval Board of Inquiry
25 July

Brighton had given me an assignment to make repairs to *Vanguard*, though I thought the task unnecessary. I suggested to the captain that there might be other duties more pressing, but he disagreed, so I set about completing the task. It was still morning on the planet, though the ship's clock showed early afternoon. I was glad that the punctures to repair were on the off side of the ship, where there was still some shade. It looked like it was going to be a hot day.

Brighton had other orders to hand out. Johnson was to remain with half the crew to guard the ship. Those assigned this duty were myself, Williams, Queneau, George, Mitchell, Paul, Delacoeur, and Smith. I thought at the time that this was a poor division of labor. Brighton left only four weapons, a pistol and three rifles, and took the other three pistols with him. If there was something to guard against, and there was, what were unarmed crewmen going to do, throw rocks? If I had been in charge, I would have taken more people with me to help carry the power cells.

His exact orders to Johnson were to complete the repairs as quickly as possible, locate the water source we had seen on the way in, refuel the *Vanguard*, and then to keep everyone inside ready to take off.

With his decrees issued, Brighton left, headed roughly westward. I dismissed them from my mind and focused on patching *Vanguard*'s skin. Johnson poked her head around the corner to let me know that she was leaving Paul to stand watch, and the rest of the crew were going to find a place to relocate the ship where she could refill her fuel tanks. I acknowledged the information, and got back to work.

Patching the holes was not a problem. Finding the [edited phrase] things was a pain in the [edited phrase], though. If I hadn't known the general area to look in, I would have taken all day to find it. Because of that, I made sure to pay even closer attention to my inspection of the rest of the ship. I found two other micropunctures which had not penetrated into the cabin area. I sealed these also and then reentered *Vanguard*.

Claire Paul remained outside, so I had the place to myself. I took advantage of the space this afforded me to catch some sack time. I sat in the pilot's seat, which, along with the copilot's slot, had the only padding on the ship. Everything else that resembled a cushion had been thrown off the ship back on A3. Brighton tended to hog it for himself, but there was no one around to keep me out of it.

I had settled in, and was just dozing off, when Paul came rushing in shouting. "There's something out there!" I could see that I was not going to get any sleep with a [edited phrase] hysterical woman yapping in my ear, so I sat up and asked, "What's out there?" So she says, "Well, it's a … um, a … a something!"

I could see where this was going, I was the only guy around, so I was nominated to 'check it out,' the same as strange noises in the dark or a spider on the wall. I took it about that seriously, too. I knew I wouldn't get any [edited phrase] rest until I went out to see.

When I poked my head out, I didn't hear anything, nor did I see anything other than what had been there the whole time. I stepped out and took a slow walk all the way around the *Vanguard*. Nothing. So I went back inside and told Paul that she must have been seeing things.

Yeah, she took that idea [edited phrase] well.

There was nothing else to do, so we both went out to look. "There!" she pointed out immediately. I didn't see anything … and then I did. The leaves on a low bush shook without any wind.

"Back inside," I said at once. She did as instructed.

The first thing we needed to do was make sure that we were safe, which wasn't hard. Once inside, all we had to do was close the hatch and we were protected from whatever was out there. I didn't seal the hatch right away, because I wanted to keep a lookout to judge the situation. Instead, I leaned against the wall just inside the outer hatch, where I could seal it at a moment's notice.

That item handled, the next was to figure out how to warn Johnson and the others of what was out there, before they walked right into it. That one was more difficult to figure out. I thought about it while I was watching the tree line. We didn't have any kind of short-range communications gear, which would have made things much easier.

While I was gathering wool, whatever was out there was just plain gathering. I still couldn't see them, but I could see glimpses of motion that indicated they were there. Whatever they were, they seemed content to hide in the shadows, for now at least. Still, their numbers were increasing. It was looking less and less likely that Johnson and the others could walk back to the ship without getting their [edited phrase] chewed off.

I turned back to Paul. "You a pilot?" I asked her.

"No. Why?"

"Because if we wait for the others to come back, they have to walk through all those [edited phrase] beasties out there. I think it would be better to go pick them up from wherever they are instead."

She nodded that she understood.

"All right, then, I'll pilot, and you get on the scanners and find out where they are for me."

I was about to seal up the hatch when she replied, "It won't work."

"Why not? I can pilot an assault shuttle, I can pilot this." *If everyone is going to tell me to do everything, the least they could do is accept that I can do what I say I can,* I thought.

"No, I mean the scanners won't work without someone to generate power for them."

"[Edited phrase]," I said, then repeated myself for emphasis. "We need to power the control net just to fly. [Edited phrase]. How could I forget that?"

"I thought we had to run the generators to have air to breathe, too," Claire brought up next.

"No," I replied. "We need to run the generators to power the oxygen scrubbers, but there's a good hour's worth of air in the cabin, as long as it's just the two of us in here."

"Oh," was all she said.

"All right, this is what we'll have to do. You run the generator and I'll fly the ship. We'll put down again near the water supply they went out to find, and we'll hope they aren't [edited phrase] and can see us land."

So that's what we did. I closed and sealed the hatch, Claire sat at the generator, back on the floor, legs in the air, while I sat in the pilot's seat that was oriented correctly for the gravity of the planet.

I had told Claire that I could pilot the ship, and I really had not expected any problems with it. I was a rated pilot for anything up to the size of assault shuttle, and I had more than a hundred hours logged. But I had again failed to take into account the way *Vanguard's* systems had been reconfigured.

Everything I had piloted used a gravitic drive, and our ship was using a reaction drive instead. Not only was the physical method of propulsion different, but I had to use a completely different set of controls to fly the ship than I was used to.

So I played it safe and made sure I had everything clear in my head before I raised ship. And even then I took things as slow and easy as I could while I felt my way around how the ship reacted. It was not nearly as easy as I had assumed it would have been. The working of the controls was not nearly as straightforward as a gravitic drive ship would have been. For instance, to set your relative altitude you would normally unlock, set the value, and lock it back in. With *Vanguard*, there were nineteen analog throttles, corresponding to the exterior thrusters. In order to move any particular direction, you had to identify which thruster pointed that way, and increase its output.

Needless to say, this was not a [edited phrase] easy task, and it took some getting used to. A lot of [edited phrase] getting used to, actually. So I took my time, got her up in the air, and started looking for that river that was supposed to be nearby. I couldn't see it. I couldn't see anything worthwhile. *Vanguard* doesn't have a [edited phrase] downward view.

I started out from the landing site heading roughly northeast. That was the direction Johnson and the others were headed the last time I saw them. I set the lower thrusters to just offset the pull of gravity, just high enough to clear the trees, and used the rear thrusters to move forward at a crawling pace. It was only a matter of a few minutes before I saw the break in the trees. As I came over it, I could see … nothing. Why the [edited phrase] wasn't there a way to look below us? I finally tried adding some altitude and "bouncing" the rear of the ship up so that I could look down. This also involved adding thrust to the forward retro nozzles to keep from dropping meters at a time with every bounce.

I neglected to warn Claire about the bouncing thing. She let me know how she felt about that, too.

Anyway, I could see that it was indeed a river, and further that there was a rocky bed that would have been more river at a wetter time of year, but would do nicely just then as a parking slip. I took a good last look, and then glided slowly to the proper location. I gently eased back on the downward throttles, until we landed with a loud and heavy thump. I had thought I was coming down gently, anyway.

Claire let me know how she felt about the jarring end to our flight, too. I didn't think it was that bad. Of course, I had the only padding.

"Oh, pipe down," I told her. "You're still walking - it's a good landing."

My words were lighthearted, but it suddenly hit me what a terrible risk I had taken with *Vanguard*. The survey launch represented our lifeline. As the old saying goes, we were sitting at the corner of no and where, and *Vanguard* was our ticket out. If I had damaged something beyond our capability to repair, we would all be stranded on this [edited phrase] rock for the rest of our likely short lives. Even if someone came looking, why would they think to look here?

I was hoping that we could put the ship back, and Brighton would never hear about me flying it. The way he would always overreact to everything, he'd have been likely to leave me behind, just to spite me, whether my actions were appropriate or not.

I glanced at the clock as I moved aft to the hatch. 1820. Planetary time was just coming into the hottest part of the day.

Claire beat me to the hatch, and she was unsealing the outer door when I got there. I jumped to the ground right behind her and immediately heard, "Move, move, move!"

Johnson came vaulting over a bleached log at the high water mark. Her long black ponytail flying as she twisted in the air and landed on her knees facing the trees, pistol braced on the log. She was squeezing bursts of energy off, and puffs of smoke appeared here and there in the dense foliage of the forest. The rest of the group was sprinting toward *Vanguard* as fast as their legs would pump. Unbelievably, Delacoeur was actually in the lead.

Johnson had the only gun, so there was no way for me to help cover their retreat. There would not be time enough to retrieve the rifle in the ship. Then I remembered my previous words. I picked up a few smooth river rocks, about fist-sized, and hefted them into the bushes. Yeah, that was [edited phrase] effective. I hit where I meant to, but I couldn't even see anything to throw at, just vague motion in the shadows.

Johnson's shots must have scared them off, because they never came out of the woods. She hopped up as the last person passed her and backpedaled toward the ship while covering with her pistol. Delacoeur reached the ship then, puffing and wheezing, and collapsed into the main cabin.

Williams jumped in next, followed by Kara George, and Queneau, then Smith and Mitchell. Paul climbed back in and I jumped in behind her. I scrunched to the side and grabbed the hatch, pulling it closed and sealing it as soon as Johnson came through.

She collapsed to the deck and looked up at me. "Was I ever glad to see

Vanguard fly over." She flashed me a big smile. "How did you know we were in trouble?"

"I didn't," I said. "We had company of our own, and it sent Claire over there into a tizzy. Nothing else would do but to come find you."

"[Edited phrase]," Claire said, then repeated herself for emphasis. Kara's eyebrows tried to climb up into her hairline, but Johnson just let out a big belly laugh.

When she quieted down she wiped water from her eyes. "Steve," she said to me, still with a big smile, "you are a bad, bad influence on these young, impressionable crewmen."

"Now, you know that it's a warrant's duty to teach sailors how to swear. It's a required skill. Navy equipment only works right with someone there to kick it and swear at it."

"True, and what warrant officer is there that works right without an officer there to kick him and swear at him?" she shot right back.

"Oh," I riposted. "Perhaps I should fly this ship back where it was and wait for you to come and kick me into action?"

Not to be outdone, she shot right back, "No, that's Captain Brighton's specialty."

Well, that [edited phrase] shut me up. I was not very comfortable imagining the captain kicking and cursing at me. Johnson, sensing the sudden shift in the mood, stood up and quickly had everyone's attention.

"Smith, Mitchell, I want you on the generators. Williams, you keep watch out the cockpit. Queneau, break out one of those heavy rifles and watch the hatch and shout out anything Williams sees. No sense conserving their charge for future need if these nasty things get to us first. Long, you're with me."

Everyone moved to comply with her orders. Johnson and I moved around Queneau to get out of the ship and back into the oppressive heat. The ell-tee had her pistol out before her boots clicked on the rocks. "All right, Steve, I'll watch your back, and you run the line out to the river to fill the tanks."

[Edited phrase], she knew how to make a guy nervous. Now, I still had not actually seen anything in the woods, but everyone else had clearly been running from something. I was willing to bet that they all agreed that running was a good idea at the time. The ship was only about twenty-five meters from the tree line. It wasn't hard to imagine how quickly whatever was out there could cover that distance. Even more, I knew that the … whatevers were close by. If Johnson had scared them off, how long would they stay scared?

Johnson must have seen my hesitation, or the nervous glances I was sending toward the shadows below the trees. She said to me in her sweetest voice, "Now, Chief, don't tell me that there is something on this planet you are afraid of, after all."

"What do you mean?" I asked her. I really didn't remember having used the exact words she was referring to.

"You know exactly what I mean. You told Captain Brighton that he couldn't intimidate you into obedience. You said that staying here would be just fine, and that you weren't afraid of anything on this planet."

"Well, yeah. It wouldn't be my first choice, but I could get by here just fine," I told her.

"Steve, do you know why we're not staying on this planet to rest?"

The question seemed to come out of left field, but I didn't really need to think about it long. "Yes. We're not staying here because High Lord Mucky Muck Brighton ordered us not to. He intends to get back to civilization no matter who has to die to get him there."

Her mouth popped open. Her jaw worked, but no sound came out, like she was a fish out of water. "You're an idiot, Long. I can't find any other reason to explain it. Your mind clearly does not work the way it is supposed to."

"Now hold on—" I started in. She cut me off before I could explain why I felt that way.

"No, you hold on. We are not staying here because there is nothing on this miserable planet that a human being can digest. As far as I know, you are the only one who did not know that long before we hit dirt. Certainly everyone with ears and a working brain did."

She didn't really yell at me, but she was clearly angry. I was a little disappointed in her. I had always had more respect for Lt. Johnson than most officers I had known. She was not the kind of officer to lord her authority over others, the way most tended to do. I had thought that she held me at a similar level of respect, but it appeared that I was wrong in that belief.

"Then why didn't Brighton just tell me that instead of staging that [edited phrase] staredown! If he had just explained—"

Again she cut me off. "Why should he have to explain anything to you!" She was yelling now. "You looked the captain in the eye and you told him to his face that you would do whatever he asked you to do in order to get through this situation. But when the captain gives you an order, instead of doing it, or even asking courteously for more information, you tell the captain that he's wrong, and that you know better! What did you expect, that he would trip over himself rushing to bow down at your feet?" She took a deep breath and her voice went back to its normal level. "You *are* an idiot, Long. And if you ever do anything like that again, don't expect me to step in or try to minimize your punishment, because it won't happen. If Captain Brighton decides to hang you, I'll tie the knot for him. Now get that line run out so we can refuel and get out of here."

"Yes, Ma'am," I said, and threw in a salute. She'd been hanging around Brighton too much, and it seemed to be the kind of frippery she would expect now. *So much for respect*, I thought.

She returned the salute, then stormed off, taking up a position roughly halfway between the *Vanguard* and the trees. I don't know if she was trying to get closer to the threat to keep a better watch, or if she just wanted to get away from me.

I unlocked the compartment that contained the pump line and unfolded it on the ground. The [edited phrase] thing wasn't long enough. I threw it on the ground in disgust and walked over to the front of the ship, where Williams could see me. I gave her the two thumbs up motion that was sign language for "raise ship," and waited.

Twenty seconds later, the hatch popped open and Clémence stuck her head out. "Lieutenant Johnson, Ms. Williams sends her regards and requests permission to raise ship, per Chief Long's request."

Oh [edited phrase], I thought. *It's spreading everywhere. If we have to go through this [edited phrase] every time we need to do anything, we might as well curl up and die right now. [Edited phrase] military protocol!*

Johnson looked back at me with reproach and said, "My compliments, and permission granted." Like I need to check with an officer just to move the ship fifteen meters? [Edited phrase] that idea. Most inefficient thing I'd ever heard.

I waited long enough for word to get back to Williams then repeated the sign. I guided her over the required distance with a few more signs, and then gave the "power down" sign and moved back to the fuel port. I connected the draw line to the pump and dropped the other end into the water of the river. I went back to the ship and closed the power switch. Nothing happened. [Edited phrase]. Maybe Johnson was right; maybe I was an idiot. The power was disconnected after the last time we used the pump to avoid losses due to leakage current.

I walked around to the hatch and climbed back in past Queneau. I glared at her on my way by and silently dared her to try to make me request permission to come aboard. I retrieved the tool kit and went back out into the heat. It had to have been forty degrees at least. I pulled my shirt off and went to work.

The power connections were definitely not located with an eye to easy access. [Edited phrase] ship designers. Back on A3, Alcaraz had done the disconnecting. He had skinnier fingers to work in the confined enclosure, and it had still taken him about an hour. I managed to do the job in half again as long, and I was a sweaty, dirty mess by then. I closed the circuit again, and this time I was rewarded with a rhythmic hum as the pump drew water into the storage tank.

While the pump was working, I decided to clean myself up a little. I got my hands wet and tried to scrub the dirt off of my arms. It was slow going so I changed my angle of attack. I walked out about waist-deep and fell in. [Edited phrase] that water was cold! It felt wonderful. Cleaning up then was much easier. I dipped and rinsed a number of times before I thought to wonder whether there was anything analogous to a crocodile around.

I decided I didn't much care. If something came and killed me, they'd have to find someone else to do all the grunt work for them.

By the time I did walk back to the ship I was shivering. Now the hot day seemed as wonderful as the cold water had a few minutes before. I switched off the pump and coiled up the line, placing it back in its sealed compartment. Then I went and undid the power connections. After I finished I washed again quickly and returned to the ship. Walking back to the other side of the ship, I called out, "Job's done, Lieutenant."

"Thank you, Long," she said as she trotted back to the *Vanguard*. "Now let's get … Why are you all wet?"

I stiffened. "Nobody ordered me not to clean up." I was going to explain further, then decided to leave it at that.

She looked concerned. "You didn't drink any, did you?"

"No, Ma'am," I smiled. "What, you think I'm an idiot?"

She smiled herself. "I heard something like that somewhere, but the source escapes me at the moment." She handed me the pistol. "You're on guard duty, Mister."

She walked up to the hatch, popped it open, and stuck her head inside. "You all stink!" she pronounced loudly. "All of you, outside, double-time."

Fifteen minutes later, everyone was smiling as they came back out of the water. There had not been any of what I would call frolicking in the water.

No one had energy for that. At the same time it would be hard to overstate the emotional lift we got from simply being clean again. Even Delacoeur smiled, which was a first.

Surprisingly, there had not been any sign of wildlife since everyone had come out of the woods and into the open, not that I was complaining. In the back of my mind, I kept waiting for the creatures that had been after them to reappear. It was just one of those times where you keep waiting for the other shoe to drop and it never does.

Once we got back inside, Delacoeur and George caught generator duty, Mitchell manned the sensor station, and Johnson took the helm. We headed back to our original landing site, then, when we saw that the other group had not yet returned, continued on in the same direction we had seen Brighton and his minions go.

Mitchell tried to isolate their location from the scanners but couldn't do it. Their sensitivity to detecting lifesigns was minimal. It wasn't that it wouldn't pick up the energy patterns. They were everywhere. We just couldn't tell which ones were human. Eventually, Johnson decided to go back to the original location and wait. That was where Brighton would expect us to be, so we would have to just wait for him to show up.

Johnson landed the ship, and then remained in the cockpit, watching the trees around the clearing we were in. Before long, there was movement detectable in the scrub brush. Eventually, some of the braver ones wandered out where they could be seen. That was the first look I had at the animals that had pursued the rest of the party earlier.

They were hard to really make out clearly because the animals continued to stay at the edge of the clearing, keeping to the shadows. They were low-slung, with short legs and dark coloring. They reminded me of crocodiles enough that I revisited my decision to have taken a bath. Oh, well. It was worth it not to have to smell myself anymore.

The ship's clock read twenty to twenty-two, which made it late afternoon or early evening outside. The hottest part of the day had past. Smith asked Johnson for permission to open the hatch to the outside air so that we could stop turning the generator wheels.

The ell-tee agreed to that. She sent Smith up to the cockpit to watch there. She moved to the open hatch and sat with her legs dangling outside, rifle across her lap.

I had been staying awake because I had been due to take a turn at the generators at 2200, but with the door propped open and the generators still, I figured it was a good time to hit the sack. I stretched out on the floor, and was amazed at how good it felt to really stretch out. Being down on the planet, the floor was again the floor, and it was much larger than the wall we had been using for one. We also had only half of our usual amount of people to fit in the available space.

Sleep was not in the plan for the evening, however. Instead, I got to listen to Kara George and Claire Paul gossip. The two of them were taking advantage of the fact that Brighton was away to avoid his bizarre edict not to talk about our former ship. As if avoiding the reality of what happened could change it.

They had been part of a large circle of friends on *Pathfinder*, and they had to talk about each one of them; what they might be doing, why they had chosen to stay, who might have been the unlucky soul killed in the lifeboat, yadda, yadda, yadda. On and on like that. I wasn't sure the hatch would let in enough oxygen at the rate they were using it up.

I tried to shut the sound out and sleep, but it was no [edited phrase] use. I finally gave up and moved over next to Johnson. She was no longer sitting as she had been. Evening had arrived, and the sky had quickly darkened. The animals outside were getting bolder in approaching the ship. She had stood up to free the hatch to close quickly, if necessary. I could tell by the way she stood and the way she was scanning the woods in the direction the others had gone that she was getting more and more concerned for them.

"How long did Brighton expect it would take him to get back?" I asked.

"Four hours," she said. The clipped response told me that she had moved beyond concern to worry, and probably was headed to panic next. Her next words proved me wrong though. She was worried, yes, no doubt about that. But she was still in control, still acting rationally and calmly.

"Steve, with fewer people in the cabin, the generators would produce enough power that there would be some left over, right?"

"Yes," I agreed.

"Can you get to the power connections for the landing lights without going outside?"

"Yes," I answered. "You planning on going for a midnight joyride?"

"No," she answered seriously, "but our people are out in unfamiliar woods and it will be dark soon. I think we need to light a candle in the window for them. I mean, what if they got lost and they're out there wandering around?"

"Ell-tee, they took Chowdhury with them, remember? Can you seriously imagine her losing her way, no matter what kind of unfamiliar terrain you dropped her in?" I reassured her.

She chuckled, indicating my success. "When you put it that way, no, I can't quite picture it."

"Still a good idea, ma'am. I'll get to work on it."

While not exactly easy to get to, these connections proved to be much easier to access than my last job. I had been the one who disconnected it, so I knew exactly where to go and what to do. It took me less than fifteen minutes to complete, but that was enough time for it to become completely dark outside.

Johnson had shut the hatch, and Smith and Williams had begun operating the generators. I didn't reconnect the control line, but it was a simple matter to turn them on from the local access. When the switch was thrown, all the belly and side lights lit up like Founding Day. There was a hideous shriek from outside and the sound of running animals scattering away from the ship.

"Well, Lieutenant," I told her, "sounds like we did better than light a beacon. Sounds like we cleared a [edited phrase] landing zone."

"Yeah," she agreed. "But what's going to clear a path for them to get to it?"

"Chowdhury," I answered at once. "She won't even have to draw her side-arm. She could just glare at them and they'd move out of the way for her."

My humor had less success this time. Not even a smile. "I hope you're right, Steve. I hope you're right."

25–26 July

Once again we were moving through the jungle. It was good to be out of the ship. The enforced confinement was not good for anyone. To be able to be moving and exercising our muscles was a great thrill for me. If I had had to sit and listen to some of those Pollyannas in the ship for very much longer I wouldn't be responsible for the results.

Captain had moved out front again as we made our way down the trail. There was no sense in reminding him that one of my duties was to protect him. He didn't seem hesitant this time as he had on the first planet. He moved as if everything was familiar and he knew just where he was going. I moved out onto the left flank where at least I would have a chance to get a shot off if he got into trouble.

He was moving and watching as if he was expecting trouble, too. Every twenty or thirty steps he would stop and sniff the air almost as if he was following the scent of some animal. This was something new.

Where the previous planet had been dense jungle, this area seemed to be forested in a lighter manner. The soil was lighter in color and the trees grew farther apart. The game trail that we were following led up a steep hill. The trees continued to thin as we moved up the slope.

The temperature still felt like we were in a jungle. The humidity was much lower, but as we struggled against the slope, all of us were soon soaked in sweat.

As we reached the top of the first summit, Captain called a rest. Fujinami and Ward threw themselves down and closed their eyes. O'Neill, Alcaraz and Roberts sat down more slowly, but were obviously just as happy for the break. Mackey, of course, didn't even seem winded, and he wandered around the perimeter looking at the flora. Captain was surveying the terrain. He called me over as he moved farther away from the group.

"I need to update you. I think the DaGaman's may be following us. Their goal, I believe is to capture *Vanguard*. If they are successful, I don't think they plan to leave witnesses."

"Do you think they are in league with *Pathfinder*?"

"I don't believe so. They wouldn't need *Vanguard* if they had *Pathfinder*.

In any case, be ready for anything. We must move quickly and get back into space."

"Aye-aye, sir," I responded and moved back out to my covering position at the top of the ridge.

The trail ahead moved back down the other side of the hill that we had just climbed and then disappeared into a grey forest at the far side of the hill. Off in the distance I could see the line of cliffs containing the cave that was our destination. As I patrolled the perimeter, I began to be aware of the distinctive smell of Fleet "stinkpots." No one who had ever had anything to do with the odorous, noxious, overpowering smell-producing cylinders would ever mistake the odor when they came across it, no matter how many years had passed since the last occurrence. Now I understood the captain's preoccupation with smelling for the trail. I don't know why he was taking big lungfuls of air if he was expecting stinkpots. Small sniffs have always been good enough for me.

Captain got everyone up and moving. The sun was closer to going down and it looked like sunset was coming much more quickly than anyone had thought.

We started moving closer to the smell. Great.

The others started to notice the smell as we moved down the hill. The muscles that had felt so good earlier as I stretched them with the climb up the hill were starting to protest as they slowed my descent from the summit. I watched faces between scanning the brush trying to take my mind off my protesting legs. While the confused look on Ensign Hayes' face was entertaining to watch, it wasn't enough of a distraction. It looked as if he was debating whether it was worth the risk of the Captain's reprimand to ask what the smell was. He was really struggling. I was betting that he wouldn't be able to contain himself for more than 200 meters.

"Captain, what is that smell?" he finally asked. He still had 170 meters to go.

"Stinkpots, Ensign." I loved it when Captain did that. The whole, 'answer the question but don't answer the question,' thing. Now Hayes was going to have to take another 100 meters to get his nerve up again. This was fun.

"They were designed by Fleet to use as a non-lethal deterrent to wildlife. They seem to be effective." Mackey expanded on Captain's explanation with his normal deadpan delivery. Killjoy.

"After sixteen years?" His incredulity overcame his restraint.

"Yes, Ensign," Captain replied. "Do not get any on you if you expect to ride home with me."

We were working our way through a lower section of the trail. Small streams and puddles worked their way across the trail and we had to be careful of our footing. The captain was still leading the way with his pistol out, no matter how many times I had tried to take the point from him.

Currently, I was again out on the left flank where the jungle seemed to be the thickest. Hayes was directly opposite me with the last of our pistols. We went across several hillocks that were drier than the rest of the trail before we started to climb again.

Everyone was breathing very hard, and all conversation had come to a stop before we finally got to the cave at about 1600 by the sun angle, but I knew that the ship's chrono was a few hours ahead of the planetary time. It had taken nearly six hours to reach the cave from the ship. Most of the group seemed to be at the end of their capabilities just getting one foot in front of the other. The sun was still up, but I didn't think that we had enough daylight left to get back to the ship. I looked at the captain. He was obviously trying to make the same decision.

"We need to move quickly. I want everything that is usable to be stacked here at the entrance to the cave so we can decide what to take back. I would like to get back to the ship if we can. It is not altogether safe to be out in this area after dark."

The people moved as if stung. Batteries, water, food packs, everything was moved forward. Brighton looked at me and nodded outside. I nodded back and moved to the cave entrance to watch for whatever it was that had him so worried. It was too early for the DaGamans.

Captain did a second sorting as things were moved up. Just as on the previous planets, much of the food was spoiled. In the end, we got eight batteries, four water bladders, and only six food packages. Everyone grabbed a battery and at least one other item. Brighton came up and traded my battery for his pistol and started out down the trail back to the ship. I finally got to move out on point. With both pistols and only lightly encumbered, I felt much better.

We were loaded and out of the cave within a half hour of entering it. If we had some sort of dangerous animals to deal with, I would rather stay in the cave for the night. It was a much more defensible position but Captain knew that. If he wanted us to move then there was a reason and I wouldn't argue. He did grab one of those noxious stinkpots and threw it in with his load. I hoped that it would help enough to be worth the smell.

Feeling the captain's urgency, I set a quick pace. Most of our return trip would be downhill which would take less energy than the trip up, but most of the group was at the end of their endurance. Tim O'Neill moved over next to Fujinami at our first rest break and pulled the extra food packs from his stack to lighten his load. Mackey did the same with Ward, Roberts and Alcaraz. Fujinami, especially, had been really struggling. He had tripped twice and had gone down the second time. He said that he was all right, but the tightness around his eyes showed the determination and concentration that he had to exert just to keep up with the group.

I put the most heavily loaded members of the party in the middle of the group and we started out again. I moved over to Roberts and gave her the second pistol. I had seen her marks from the academy, and she was a fair shot. Not as good as Hayes, but she had kept her cool and not panicked during the skirmish on A3.

As we reached the lowlands in the middle of our trek, I could tell that most were at the end of their strength. The light was almost gone. We climbed a large hillock so we were out of the water, and from there we had a good field of vision in all directions. There were trees here for shelter but not so dense that they cut off our visibility. We also had a nice clearing for a camp.

I signaled to Captain and he nodded.

"All right," I called, "we aren't going to make it all the way back, and this looks like the best spot for a camp that we have found so far, so let's stop here."

There were looks and noises of relief from all of the party. While you can steel yourself to accomplish a task, it is a welcome relief when you get to stop.

"Alcaraz, get that stinkpot into the center of the clearing then start moving all of the supplies to the center around it. Mackey, take Ensign Roberts' sidearm and patrol back along our trail. Don't get out of sight of camp."

"Aye-aye, ma'am," rang back from each of them as they moved off to take care of their tasks.

"Hayes, take Ward, O'Neill and Fujinami and get some wood for a fire and see if you can get one going. You stay alert with your sidearm. Let them collect the wood." Sometimes with ensigns you need to be very specific with your instructions. Half an hour later all of the groups were back and Hayes had managed a creditable fire. Apparently, he was paying attention on A3. Would wonders never cease?

Brighton opened one ration bag and tossed it to Mackey. Mackey pulled out the contents and we all shared three tubes of "Chicken a la King." I couldn't personally find any chicken and the king seemed more like a joker. What is chicken a la king, anyway?

I resumed my patrol of the perimeter. Brighton never asked for anyone to take guard duty, but he always left those things to me. The others seemed to be taking turns with the other two pistols. There were only three blankets in the supplies that we carried and we had been using those as slings to help transport the supplies. Soon everyone was curled up and snoozing. I went over and nudged Alcaraz with my foot and when he opened his eyes, I motioned him to a spot closer to the fire in the center of the clearing. Just in case.

I continued my circuit around the perimeter. It was good exercise and I knew from experience that it would keep my muscles from aching quite so much in the morning.

Soon, even the other watchers had dozed in their places. I took note of where the pistols were. Hayes still had his in his hand and he was asleep sitting up with his back against the batteries. Alcaraz had the other. He was on the opposite side of the supply stack. That should give us fairly good covering fire if we ran into trouble.

Maybe we would get lucky and the stinkpots would do their job. Our luck had been so good lately, after all.

Right.

27 July

"They have to be there somewhere," Lt. Vasconcellos said after Cpl. Udorra reported an unsuccessful scan for the third time.

"We have three mass readings that could possibly be the ship but there are absolutely no energy signatures involved with any of the three.

"Can we get a visual on any of them?"

"Negative. The cloud cover is very heavy over each of those sites. It seems to be fairly universal over most of the planet."

"Is there any way to firm up those readings? Any way to determine which is the ship? I really don't want to go down chasing rocks."

"I'm working on it, sir," she said mildly, carefully not showing him the expression that would indicate her true feelings about officers who watch their charges too closely and slow down the work. "No luck, Lieutenant. There is no way to resolve any differences between any of the three readings. Not with this equipment, sir," she said finally.

"Okay," he said, turning to his Marines. Ten anonymous faceplates looked back at him as his unit relaxed as much as possible in the minimum armor required to use the drop capsules. Heavy battle armor would have been the best for the pods but Vasconcellos wanted to be able to move fast. Light armor was more than sufficient against unarmored foes. "We don't have enough people to hit all three of these sites simultaneously so we will drop units on these first two sites that are close enough together to mutually support each other. The shuttle will fly a circle above us and be ready to support either unit at need. If neither group finds the ship, we will recombine and hit the third site together," he said as he scanned the body language of his team. "Any questions?"

When none were forthcoming, he continued, "Sgt. Olavo, you are in command of second platoon. Don't get overconfident. Brighton is a sadistic cull who would like nothing better than to lead you into another ambush. We'll drop the pods in stealth mode but these Warners are very capable and they won't be surprised by us no matter what we do, so be extra careful. Cpl. Romero, you will stay on board with third platoon and be ready to support either group as needed. Olavo, call in as soon as you have confirmation of their location and the shuttle will drop third to help and then work back to pick us up for additional support."

"Yes, sir," came Olavo's disembodied confirmation over the speaker of the helmet, which Vasconcellos held cradled in the crook of his left arm. Romero contented himself with a curt nod.

"Okay, let's go."

With that order, the designated Marines backed into the drop capsules that lined both walls of the cargo bay while their fellows watched. After placing their backs securely against the rear padding they touched the buttons that closed the capsules and deployed the cushioning foam within its confines. The capsules on the port bulkhead dropped in sequence and thirty seconds later those on the starboard side followed them through the floor. Both formations dropped from space in a high speed descent that left multiple diverging trails smoking through the atmosphere.

Once they were on the ground, Lt. Vasconcellos had no time to think about his comrades two hundred kilometers away to the east. First platoon landed just in front of the planetary terminator as the light was fading from the local jungle.

Vasconcellos keyed his radio with his chin. "Team one, on the ground and moving out."

The drop computer had chosen a small clearing about six clicks to the west of the mass reading that could be *Vanguard*. As darkness fell around them they took off down a well worn game trail that the group of inexperienced city dwellers had no reason to distrust.

Vasconcellos moved as carefully as possible as his team hurried down the trail.

"Emergency call from team two, moving to support," came the strident call in his earpiece that caused him to jump. He gave an embarrassed head shake as the others turned at the sudden movement. He motioned with his assault rifle to keep moving, knowing that they could not see his blushing features through the facemask of his helmet.

"Report," he called to the shuttle when they did not follow up their previous message.

"We dropped Team Three to support and are returning to your position. There is a clearing just past the target on the rise above. That will be our LZ."

"Roger. We are about a click short of the target. We'll be there."

They slowed as they approached the target clearing. They had to cross a small pocket of water to reach the edge of the trees.

The group emerged from the cover of the trees into a clearing. At the far end, nestled into the trees at the face of a rock cliff, was an old Forsner probe. It was overgrown and rusted and had obviously been there for a long time.

"Command, confirm this site is negative," Vasconcellos called over the vocom.

"Roger, team one, negative contact at your site. Shuttle is two minutes out."

"Roger," the lieutenant replied. "Let's make tracks, team. We've got to be on top of that rise in 90 seconds."

The shuttle dropped right on schedule and the team loaded quickly. The shuttle lifted from the surface forty seconds after touching down.

"Status," he called as the shuttle clawed for altitude.

"No contact since the drop," responded the copilot as the pilot applied herself to the task of plotting a ballistic trajectory to their next landing site.

The shuttle set down seventeen minutes later on a small hill that was completely surrounded by a shallow stagnant swamp. The locator showed that they were less than four hundred meters from the combined teams. The sound of weapon's fire greeted them as the shuttle door dropped for their exit.

"Deploy in formation gamma," Vasconcellos yelled as he moved out the door. "Let's hustle."

They had not moved two hundred meters before they were met by the returning team. Four raiders were slung over their companion's shoulders while the remaining troopers formed a rearguard that fired blindly into the brush.

Vasconcellos' troops took up firing positions as the other two teams interpenetrated with their position and kept moving towards the shuttle. They fired at any movement and continued to fall back behind their comrades.

Vasconcellos was the last one onto the shuttle and called for the pilot to lift off as he slammed the hatch closure.

"Was it the Warners?" he called to Sgt. Olavo who was being tended by a medic.

"No, sir. It was a bunch of the Devil's own crocodiles."

23 July

Cold dew dripped off the broad grey-green leaves above me and landed on my nose, providing my wake up call. The night remained dark and still all about me. My muscles were stiff and sore from a combination of the previous day's exertions and the overnight chill. I stretched and rose, then moved a short distance out of the clearing to take care of morning business. This was yet another day without a bowel movement; one more thing on my list of health concerns. It seemed that my body was so desperate for fuel, that it was converting everything available to it, and there was nothing left over.

When I returned to the clearing, I noticed for the first time that Sheli Chowdhury was walking slowly about our encampment peering outward against threats. I did not remember Brighton assigning her this duty. Perhaps he hadn't. While the stinkpots seemed to have proven effective at keeping predators away, Sheli is not one to leave us unprotected against any potential threat. She nodded a greeting in my direction. I bade her good morning, but did not approach her or attempt any greater communication.

Our fire had burned down to coals but was still providing some warmth. I headed there instead. We still had a bit of a pile of fuel near the fire, and I was about to begin adding it in the hopes of providing more heat and comfort for those more fortunate souls who were still sleeping.

Before I could do so, however, Sheli stopped her circuit of our campsite and looked over my head at the direction I had slipped off to relieve myself. She remained silent, listening for a repeat of whatever sound had caught her attention. I heard nothing.

She jerked her head to stare out at the predawn gloom in two other directions and then started shouting.

"Everybody up! Up now!"

"Gather in the center by the fire. Pull everything in where we can defend it," she continued. The command in her voice roused everyone, though some were slow to come fully awake. Captain Brighton was not one of these, of course. He immediately made sure that the other two armed personnel, Jordan and Roberto, were up and moving into supporting positions.

Since I was not armed, I hurried to complete her directive to gather everyone and everything into a central location. I still had no clue what Sheli had heard or what threat she feared, but I trusted her to know what she was about. Sore muscles, the cold, even the pervasive fatigue we all felt were ignored as adrenal glands fed our haste. We frantically gathered all our stores to one side of the fire pit and then stood around it. We all peered nervously at the forest, imagining all sorts of beasts that might be out there. In less than two minutes, the task was completed, and we were all abruptly cast adrift again. Too much nervous energy with no outlet.

We all stood there straining to hear what was stalking us. Finally, a low growl was discernable from the direction that Sheli was facing.

"Don't waste power shooting at sounds," the security head directed the other two. "Wait until you've got a visible target."

I looked around at our surroundings and was not impressed. The majority of our group was all gathered in one place, with our spoil in the middle. Chowdhury and the other two with pistols were a pace or two outside our tight circle, facing out. The fire along one side gave us some protection against an assault from that quarter.

That still left too much ground to be adequately covered by three armed people. What we needed was some kind of barrier around us to keep the night creatures safely on the other side. The problem being that we did not have suitable materials for building such a protection. The power cells could be stacked, but to extend them around our group would leave them only about a meter high.

The fire was some protection, but even that, now that I was evaluating, likely would not serve us too well, since it would not take too much of a leap to clear it. If it were to stop an incursion, it would have to be much higher, and we did not have enough wood left from what was gathered to fuel such a blaze.

Fuel…I had it. Frantically, I dug into the medical packs we had harvested from the supply cache. One, two, … nine bottles in all of antiseptic fluid; mainly composed of isopropyl alcohol. I opened one and hurried out to pour a line around our group, in my haste forgetting to inform anyone of my plan.

"Doctor Ward! Where do you think you're going?" Captain Brighton was just as courteous as ever, even while in our current emotion-charged setting.

"I'm sorry, sir." I replaced the lid on the bottle and backtracked to report first to the captain. I sketched out my idea to try to start a fire around us as a defensive blockade. He quickly overrode me with several objections.

"Firstly, Doctor, if you go out there to pour out that fluid you will be dangerously exposed. Secondly, a fire here could quickly get out of hand and become an even greater danger. Lastly, we don't have enough fuel to completely encircle us, and if we did, the fuel wouldn't burn for more than a few minutes.

"I think you are on the right track, though. Do you have bandaging materials in those medical supplies?"

I answered him in the affirmative, and he directed that the rest of us put together some torches which might be used to help defend our camp. It was a brilliant idea, and made much better use of the materials available for the purpose I had envisioned.

I gathered everyone that was not armed around me and explained to those who had not overheard. Jens distributed some long sticks from our collection of firewood. Jherri retrieved the bandages from the kit and began to pass them out. Unfortunately, the predators weren't willing to give us enough time to properly prepare.

Grey shapes, nearly the same color as the foliage surrounding the small clearing we occupied, emerged into the open from several places almost concurrently. The three who carried weapons were having difficulty tracking all the threats in their assigned area of responsibility. The creatures had broad heads and broad bodies, carried low to the ground. Advancing slowly, as they were, they brought to mind alligators, though they had no tails and their snouts were not elongated. The heads resembled more closely a bat's: large black eyes, turned up noses, and with ears that pointed upward and swiveled. They did not appear to have fur or feathers for covering, and their skin was not shiny; rather a flat, light-consuming grey.

I was the first to get my torch put together, possibly because I was familiar enough with the materials to be able to complete it without taking my eyes off the approaching menace. The others were constantly looking back and forth between the task at hand and the reason for it. After pouring the alcohol slowly, with all my nerves urging haste, and letting it soak in, I held it down to contact the brightest of the remaining coals. It sprang to life with a "whoosh" sound that was followed immediately by the pop of pistol fire.

At first, Chowdhury was the only one shooting, more certain of her accuracy than the others. It was a matter of a few seconds before the beasts had come near enough that all three were picking targets and dispatching them.

The other creatures were not dissuaded by the deaths of their companions, as I had been hoping they would. If anything, it pushed them toward us with greater speed. The pistols accounted for perhaps eight deaths before they closed with us.

At that point, I lost track of everything which was happening outside of my immediate area. I had Ensign Hayes to my left and Derrick Mackey to my right. Derrick never did get his torch finished, but he may have been more effective because of it. With my torch, the best I could do was poke the flame toward any bat-gator that came within reach, holding it at bay until Jordan's gaze swept back my way and he could shoot it.

Derrick, on the other hand, was able to employ his branch, twice as long as the one I had selected, as an offensive weapon, taking massive swings at the heads of any nearby threat.

For their part, the creatures showed unexpected quickness. We had all felt we had the measure of their speed from seeing their advance. Apparently, they could not run too fast, but they could dodge and change directions unpredictably, making them difficult targets, both for the guns and the other weapons we had fashioned.

I had one of them more or less contained, awaiting Jordan's attention, when one dodged away from Derrick and came at me from that side. I pulled the torch back to fend off this new threat, which allowed the beast in front of me to lunge toward me. I swung the flaming instrument back to the fore, and that was enough of an opening to allow the flanking creature to slip inside my guard. It clawed and bit my right calf and I screamed in pain.

The torch came flying back and caught the beast in mid-torso. It disengaged itself, at least long enough for aid to come. My scream at least had the benefit of catching Jordan's attention. He accounted for the animal in front of me, which otherwise would have likely taken out my throat, as I had collapsed to my knees, and brought that vulnerable spot within the creature's reach. Derrick accounted for the other, which I was not able to get at again for it had backed up directly behind me, and turning while on my knees with one injured leg was more than I was able to manage.

Once the immediate difficulty was handled, I scanned our area for new threats, and found none. Looking about me, I saw that there were no more of the beasts to be driven off. All of them lay unmoving in a rough circle around our group. Silence filled the clearing while all of our party strained to detect any further danger beyond our visibility.

With no immediate menace evident, I collapsed to the ground in pain.

"Derrick, will you get the medkit?" I managed to gasp through the waves of agony. He ran to comply, and I examined the wound.

Wounds, it turned out. Both teeth and claws had savaged my leg. The animal's teeth were not long, but it had sunk them in and yanked and shook; the result of which was that the muscle was badly torn and bleeding profusely.

Derrick returned in a moment and I set to work on myself. Fortunately, the kit was well-stocked with the items I needed most just then. I applied coagulant first, to stop the bleeding before I passed out. Numbspray came next, then stitches where the wound was still bleeding. Finally, I bandaged the leg, and made cutoffs out of my pants, the lower right leg of them, which were essentially useless now.

When I finished, I was exhausted. The leftover adrenaline had kept me going long enough to see to my own injuries, but I could feel that letdown that indicated its absence. I wanted nothing more than to lie back down and not move for a week.

I was not the only one injured in the attack, though I was my only patient. Jens was clawed across the back of his left shoulder. Jherri's was a similar wound, three parallel slashes, hers located on the left hip and upper thigh.

Captain Brighton and Sheli Chowdhury had dressed their wounds while I was occupied with my own. I was glad to see it, for I doubt that I could have done anything for either of them if I had to. I lay back down and trembled for some time with the aftereffects of the encounter and my injuries.

As I rested on the ground, waiting for some of my strength to return, the captain and Sheli were discussing how we were going to transport our supplies back to *Vanguard*. Eventually, both of them had to admit that there was no way to accomplish it. We had all been carrying as much as we could handle before. Now, Jherri and I would not be able to carry anything, and Jens probably would not either, though I expected that he would try.

Captain Brighton cast his eyes around the clearing, searching for some solution to present itself. After looking this way and that, a grin slowly emerged through his ruddy beard. "If Mohammad can't go to the mountain … " I heard him say.

He directed the able-bodied of the crew to again relocate our collection of power cells over to one edge of the clearing, and then set us on the rough trail back to the launch.

I managed to get to my foot, but quickly realized that balancing on only one was not one of my hidden talents. Derrick gave me the long stick he had used to brain the bat-gators which allowed me to hop forward using it for support. It was a horrible exertion. It took everything I had to cross the clearing. I didn't know how I would make it all the way back.

The real sun (not its tiny partner) was just coming up when I entered the woods, and most of the party was well ahead of me. Jherri seemed to be moving well, if a bit stiffly. There were still two or three that were hanging back to make sure I was coming along okay. Derrick and Jens, for certain, and…

It was odd how the world lost its color, and suddenly turned black and white and grey…

When I regained consciousness, I was back inside *Vanguard*, and we were moving.

"Welcome back," Elle said to me, noticing my eyes open once again.

"What happened?" I asked. She pushed me back down on the decking when I tried to sit up. She didn't have to push very hard, I noticed.

"You passed out. Lost too much blood, and your constitution isn't what it once was."

"No one's is," I said, my head safely back on the deck.

"Except Captain Brighton. He carried you all the way back to *Vanguard*."

I said nothing; what could I have said? In my head, I knew that it was not my fault, that I had done everything in my power to pull my own weight. Still, I felt like I had let people down, that I had added to the captain's burdens, quite literally. Elle and I shared a look of understanding, and I felt no need to speak. There was no condemnation in her eyes, only concern for me.

Seeing that, the fist squeezing my heart eased a little and I released the breath I hadn't realized I was holding. "What's happening?" I asked her, to move the conversation in a new direction.

"When Captain Brighton and the rest of you returned, we were enormously relieved. We had been so worried when you weren't back by nightfall, not knowing if you had gotten lost, or injured, or killed, or what. I think Lt. Johnson would have sent out a search party if you had been gone another hour.

"So we loaded everyone inside and Lt. Johnson flew *Vanguard* back to the clearing where you were attacked. We quickly loaded up the supplies left there, watching the forest around us all the time—"

"I don't think they would attack in the daylight," I interrupted.

She tilted her head slightly in that way she always did when her curiosity was aroused. "Why do you say that?"

"Large eyes would tend to indicate a nocturnal nature. The bright light in an open clearing, out from under the forest's shade would probably be painful to them."

She smiled. I smiled back; I couldn't help it. "Well, doctor, your mind seems to have recovered from passing out just fine."

"I don't think my leg is going to recover with equal speed," I said a bit morosely. It was hurting quite a bit; a lot, actually. The numbspray had worn off, as had the pain medication I had given myself. I was about to ask her if she would get me my medical bag when Captain Brighton warned us to prepare for landing.

The landing was as smooth and easy as if it had been done on computer control. The captain climbed out of the pilot's compartment and announced that we would have lunch before departing back to the cache site. It was almost an hour before our normal mealtime by the ship's clock, though still early morning outside on the planet.

I was pleased to see that the captain added a piece of the jerky and part of the extra supplies we had acquired to each person's portion, both on a personal and professional level. Personally, I was hungry, and the effort and energy I had expended needed to be replaced. Without it, I knew my body would not be able to heal the torn muscles in my leg. Professionally, of course, I recognized that all of us were in the same desperate need for fuel. While no one else had the same level of injury, our bodies could not continue to exert themselves endlessly without resupplying. Everyone has a limit to their strength, and I feared that many of us were approaching ours.

After the brief meal was completed, Captain Brighton again divided us into two groups, one to accompany him to retrieve the supplies and one to remain with the ship. The latter group was comprised of Lt. Johnson and the three of us who had been injured.

Weakened as I was, I was willing to leave that onerous task to others, recognizing my own limitations. Still, I felt somewhat guilty that the rest of the crew would have to do more because I was unable to contribute. I knew that this would only get worse, since stronger members of the crew would also need to take my place operating the generators.

After the others had departed, Fyonna propped the airlock hatches open and took up station outside, repeating a casual circuit about our craft and eyeing the distant trees.

After a while, I was able to sit up without dizziness. My first action upon doing so was to renew my pain medication. I asked the two others in the cabin if either of them needed me to check their bandages, or needed a painkiller. Both of them declined, assuring me that they were all right for the moment.

With no tasks requiring our attention, Jens and I slipped into a comfortable conversation about our recent experiences. I asked him how he came to be wounded so high on his body from such short-legged creatures. I made no headway in receiving a serious answer from him. I suspect that it involved some carelessness on his part that he desired not to admit. Eventually, I gave up, guessing that he would tell me when he was ready to do so.

Jherri Roberts sat clear on the other side of the cabin from the two of us, her dark brown eyes attentive. I tried to draw her into our conversation a few times, but never received anything but polite two- or three- word responses. I realized, as I tried to think of what topics she might be interested in discussing, that I knew next to nothing about her. I had never actually seen her as a patient; somehow her exams and medical needs must have always turned up while Dr. Johnson had the watch.

To look at her now, she seemed painfully shy, though she had not ever seemed that way before. Perhaps she was just more comfortable in larger groups, or perhaps I was reading more into the situation than was there. It could easily have been explained by her discomfort arising from her recent injuries.

Ms. Roberts was spared too much close confinement with Jens and me by the efficient return of the raiding party. Captain Brighton had relocated us at the base of the hill where the supplies had been deposited. The party was able to take advantage of the direct route and had returned several hours before nightfall.

Batteries were installed and locked into place by several of the men, while everyone else gathered outside. They had encountered no difficulties, other than the physical strain of climbing up and down the hill yet again.

Space beckoned, and we did not keep it waiting long. Having already determined that there was nothing native to the planet that would be of any help, there was no point in delaying our departure. *Vanguard* was sealed up, and at 2058, ship's time, we lifted off, directing our ship to our final stop along the way.

Lt. Johnson had her station in the pilot's seat. Second watch was manning the duty stations, and just like that we were back to our well-worn routine.

Brighton asked for all our attention, so that he could address us.

When he stood before us, he seemed hesitant to speak, which was a unique experience, and more than a little disquieting. All eyes fixed on him, waiting for what was sure to be bad news.

"Jump points are tricky," he finally began. This seemed to be neither bad nor news to me, so I was sure there was more to it. Again, he hesitated, not as if he were undecided on what to do, but as if seeking the best way to explain what he had decided.

"I believe that we have a very good chance of successfully jumping out of this system and making our way back to Earth. Most of the original supplies left on B2 were still there, because the terraforming team had to temporarily abandon the project before it was completed. I know that three of you will likely disagree with me, but we actually owe those beasts our thanks. Had the terraforming project not run into problems requiring them to abort, there probably would not have been enough batteries remaining for us to jump clear of this system.

"However, there are still some possibilities that I cannot leave us unprepared for.

"First, there is the possibility that we will not be able to collect enough Turin cells at our final depot to jump, or that we will not be able to isolate the jump point precisely enough to take advantage of it. In either of these cases, we will be stranded in this system until help can arrive from Earth.

"Second, there is the possibility that we will successfully jump to the Gemmill system, but find it has been abandoned by the Portales Family. If this is so, we may or may not be able to scavenge the wherewithal to survive.

"At any rate, we cannot put all our hopes on one set of circumstances when we cannot determine beforehand if those circumstances will prevail. We must leave ourselves as many options as possible, for as long as possible. Therefore, we will need to have a margin of safety in our food supply, in case it becomes necessary to survive on it longer than we had originally anticipated."

Now it sounded bad.

"And how are we going to find a reserve of food?" Steve Long asked, with a tone that indicated he already knew the answer.

"Effective at 0800 tomorrow, we will reduce our rations to two meals per day."

Silence hung in the air for all of two seconds.

"Well," said Derrick jovially, "it's not as if you're asking us to give up very much, after all. What's 40 or 50 calories, more or less?"

And that was that. With a little bit of humor, Derrick Mackey had headed off any possible objections. I'm sure that everyone still had their reservations, but no one would give them a voice now.

The captain smiled, evidently relieved that there would not be the grumbling and complaining he had prepared himself to face. He climbed back up the makeshift ladder to the pilot's compartment and took his accustomed seat from Elle.

Mackey grinned as she climbed down and he slid over to make room for her to sit next to me. I smiled a thank you to him without Elle noticing. I had become very fond of her during our time together, and I sensed that she felt the same. Apparently, this had also been noticed by others of the crew.

I suppose that this should not be surprising. Our enforced closeness left no room for secrets or private conversations, after all. There really is no need to gossip when any conversation you may have had was within the hearing of everyone else on the ship.

More than anything, I wished to have another non-private conversation with her, but the combination of the injury and the pain medication left me with little in the way of energy to carry on such a dialog.

Instead, I leaned against her and fell asleep again.

27–28 July

Queneau was humming a song when I awoke. My head and leg hurt so much I nearly yelled at her to shut up. Fortunately, I managed to contain my outburst by simply gritting my teeth. She was among the youngest of the crew, who tended to have a greater reserve of both energy and optimism. Even if I had yelled at her, it would not have been a permanent solution. The humming was just an unconscious outward sign of the positive outlook she continued to have.

I would have to admit that my own optimism had taken a crashing dive of late.

I think I still had the same surety that Captain Brighton would see *Vanguard* home, but I was much less sure that I would still be numbered among the crew by then. That is always the problem with a doctor who treats himself. He can't lie to himself, at least not convincingly. I knew how badly my leg was torn up, and I knew that I did not have the strength to heal it properly. The longer it took to heal, the more likely it was that it never would. In order to really get better, I needed to believe that I would. Yet knowing that was the case, I still knew how unlikely it was, and so I had no foundation on which to lay my faith. It made me feel … lost, I guess, or losing myself. Perhaps it just made me feel cranky. I wished Clémence would stop that bouncing little ditty. It was going to get stuck in my head for the rest of the day, I was sure.

I carefully maneuvered myself backward a bit to allow the wall, what used to be the ceiling, to prop me up in a seated position. A quick inspection demonstrated that the bandaging on my leg would need to be changed already. Bandages were something else in limited supply just then, but I could see that it would not wait. Who could tell what sort of germs I'd been exposed to now that I'd been doused with bat-gator saliva?

I pulled myself up to a standing position, with the intent of crossing the small space to the storage bin which contained the medical supplies. On one foot, I was not sure I could thread my way through the cramped area. Tim saw my hesitation and came to my rescue. He waved me back into my seat.

After reseating myself, Tim passed the medkit over and I extracted the materials I needed. I took a discrete look at each of the faces nearby as I worked, trying to judge how each of them felt about our current situation. Perhaps it was my own dark mood, but I could not believe how cheerful and positive most people were.

Clémence, of course, had unshakeable faith in Captain Brighton, so it was inevitable that she would feel that all was well and truly under control. Jens simply was not capable of a foul mood, so he should hardly be used as an emotional barometer. Captain Brighton himself exuded confidence by the bucketload, but who could tell with him what he actually felt and what he merely wanted to portray? He was always an extremely difficult man to read.

Apart from these three, whom I would expect to be affirmative in even the direst of situations, the general feeling was still a positive one. Steve Long had something of a glower, and Kieran seemed aggrieved, but otherwise the crew was upbeat. There were still several side conversations going on and even a few chuckles now and then.

I sealed the last tab on my new bandage, returned the unused supplies to the medical kit, and handed it back over to Tim to put back in the storage locker for me.

Now that my full attention was on the people surrounding me, I could see that not everyone was as positive as I had first thought. Several, who I had thought were sleeping, were simply lying on the floor, silent and motionless, doing exactly as I thought they ought. A chill ran down my spine. They looked dead already; emaciated and still.

Weakened, lethargic, positive. As contradictory as it is to say so, that was the state of our crew.

The other injured were doing as well as could be expected, from what I had seen. Jens seemed to be moving comfortably enough, which was a good sign. Roberts was still sleeping, lying on her uninjured side, so I couldn't say for sure how she was feeling. I had not had any opportunity to change her dressing, so I could not even confirm that it was healing properly. She seemed to always take care of that herself while I was sleeping.

A few of my shipmates had complained to me earlier that they were getting sores from laying on the hard flooring, and those I had been able to attend to. At least I treated the symptoms, but I had no remedy for them. Everything that might have provided any padding was long since discarded as nonessential.

Experience has taught me many things over the years, but this is one thing I will never forget; the sheer capacity to endure which is wrapped up in the human organism. I previously had no inkling of how much a body could take from fate's hand and still struggle on.

Had my opinion been asked prior to this mandated case study, I would have estimated our survival to have ended about a week or so ago, given the conditions of need and exertion which we had endured.

Fortunately, no one had asked my opinion, and I had not shared my assessment with anyone else. As things stood at this point, I would give most everyone a 3 in 4 chance of living long enough to reach the jump point Captain Brighton had identified as our goal. For myself, I projected no better than one chance in five.

Time continued on, and shortly it was time for breakfast. Captain Brighton had been piloting from the helm station, and directed Fyonna to again take up that task. He further ordered a piece of the dried fruit be added to everyone's normal piece of arbar. Perhaps he knew we needed the extra boost, or perhaps he was trying to take the sting out of our newly-reduced rations. Whatever the case, the energy from the additional nourishment, if such a term was not overstating the case, was most welcome.

There was one incident, which happened about that time which highlighted how Captain Brighton was undercutting his own efforts to inspire confidence among the rest of us. As I have noted previously, it was his habit to put forth more effort than any of the rest of us. It had also become his habit not to descend from the cockpit except to sleep, which he seemed to be doing less and less frequently, or to operate the generator. The captain had been piloting *Vanguard* now for close to 16 hours, since shortly after we had lifted from Antoc-B2. The last time he slept was the previous night until 3 or 4, when Sheli roused us all.

That meant that he had been awake for the previous 28 or 29 hours.

I would like to say that I thought that should excuse a certain amount of surliness on the part of the captain. I didn't think so at the time, probably because of my own surliness. Since then, I have softened my condemnation. At the time, I felt that the captain had no one to blame but himself for his lack of sleep. There were two other capable pilots who could have taken over for him at any time. He had himself set up the watch rotation to have one of the pilots available in each, intending 8-hour shifts at the helm. Since then, I have come to understand that this was simply part of Captain Brighton's character, that he would require the utmost of himself before asking special duties of anyone else.

The incident itself came as a direct result of the captain's sleeplessness, in two ways. Elle had seen that the captain was driving himself too hard. She climbed partway up the makeshift ladder and asked the captain if he would like for her to take over piloting for him.

He snapped back angrily, "Is there something wrong with the way I'm handling this craft, Ms. Williams? Do you think you are a better pilot than me? Think you can do a better job?"

Her response was meek and yet unabashed. "I don't think there is a finer pilot in any fleet I've ever heard of, sir. I only thought that you might like a chance to sleep, since you've been awake so long."

Captain Brighton turned in his seat to look at Elle, and it was clear that her words had made him ashamed of his outburst. "My apologies, Ms. Williams. You did nothing to deserve such treatment from me. I will remain at this station until after we complete turnover at 1100 hours. At that time, I will turn the conn over to Ms. Johnson for the remainder of her watch."

"Yes, sir," she said, and returned to her seat.

She sat down next to me, and apparently wasn't quite done trying to take care of the rest of us.

"How are you feeling, Leon?"

"Well enough," I lied airily. It was the attempt at appearing indifferent which gave me away. She knew I was lying by the fact that I was not taking it seriously. She looked at me with equal parts reproof and disbelief.

I found that I could no longer dissemble to her. "Okay, it hurts…a lot."

"And how long since you took anything for the pain," she pressed.

I stared at her for a moment and took in both the firm set of her jaw and the tender concern in her blue eyes. I didn't even try to lie this time.

"I took something a little after we raised from B2."

"You should take some now. The pain will slow your healing."

I met her eyes, and allowed the first genuine smile in more than a day. "Yes, Doctor."

She smiled too, at that.

I did take something for the pain, though only about half of a normal dose. I would need to stretch the supply as long as I could, and there was no telling how many others could wind up needing it also. Elle had decided to rest, after watching to make sure I took my medicine.

When her eyes were no longer on me, my melancholy returned full force. My love for Elle had grown slowly during our travails, though I had never spoken those words aloud to her. Such a declaration needed to be done privately, and no opportunity for such had yet presented itself. I sensed that she returned at least my interest, though I couldn't guess if she had feelings any deeper than that. Before my injury, I had been making tentative plans to pursue a relationship with her, after this was all over. Now, that might not happen, and I was consumed by sadness to think of my loss.

It was silly, I know, to grieve the loss of something you didn't have yet, but who ever claimed that emotions were rational things?

The drowsiness brought on by the medication soon overcame me, and I again slept.

Excited voices roused me. There was quite a commotion in progress. At least, as much commotion as our limited space and energy allowed. The ship's clock showed just less than three hours left in third watch. When I was informed the animation the crew was demonstrating was in response to the announcement to prepare for re-entry, I felt the sudden return of my previous hopeful spirits. Captain Brighton had mentioned, during our long journey back from the supply depot on B2, that B3 was a very different sort of place. We should find food which humans could consume there, as well as a generally pleasant climate.

I remembered also that the captain had told the officers, some time ago, that this world was very dangerous to land on, because it possessed a very strong magnetic field around it.

Turbulence bounced our craft this way and that, unpredictably. We slid and bounced along with it. We had no proper straps available, only rubber medical tubing we had affixed to the wall. It worked fine for holding one in place in zero g, but was not strong enough to overcome the forces we faced here. Many tried to use them, but they readily broke free of their mountings. Other than those working the generators, no one had anything to hold onto.

Lt. Johnson was in the pilot's seat, with Captain Brighton in the copilot's place. Both were attempting to predict and counter the forces arrayed against us. I wondered then if Captain Brighton had had any sleep, before guiltily realizing that I had been unconscious for about fourteen hours, giving the captain ample opportunity to have slept well without my ever knowing.

Countergravity field engines, and the inertial compensators that accompany them, would have been most welcome at that point. Had we been able to use *Vanguard*'s main engines, we likely would not have even noticed the minor jostling to be felt within the field. As it was, in order to conserve the batteries that represented our main power source, we were beset by all the worst of Newtonian physics, reacting to all the action going on outside during re-entry.

As our ship banked, turned, and shook, those of us on the floor slid and bumped against each other. The ship, of course, had been re-oriented. The thrusters were mostly disengaged, providing only attitude and directional corrections. Downward was once again toward the floor, which offered us a little more room. There were still no seats; those had been discarded back on A3 to lighten our craft; so the extra room generally meant only that we had built up more speed before slamming into some other object, or person.

I tried my best to protect my injured leg, but I was not wholly successful. Once I had rolled over to the mounting brackets that had once held the seats and currently functioned as our "ladder," I took advantage of it to steady myself and tuck my knees into my chest. Remaining relatively motionless kept me from running into things, but gave everyone else one more thing to run into.

After Kieran flew into me I managed to turn the other way and brace myself against the wall with my good leg. There were no further impacts after that.

The tossing and tumbling seemed to go on for far longer than I would have expected. I knew, only because Elle had explained it to me, that we were using the atmosphere to somehow slow us down. This allowed us to cover the required distances somewhat faster. Since we did not have to arrive at the planet with no velocity, our average speed was somewhat higher.

Captain Brighton, shoulders taut and hunched in concentration, was the same unchanging force we had come to rely on. Even though he had lashed out at Elle only a short time ago, by my reckoning, it was comforting to me, and to the others, to see that stalwart officer in command, and dealing with each problem and variance as they arose.

"Overheating is a real possibility here," he said then, over his shoulder. "Put as much as you can into the generators to keep the cabin cool."

I hadn't even noticed the heat, being too busy dodging my crewmates. Now that he pointed it out, I felt the ambient temperature had gone up five or ten degrees. Sheli and Roberto Alcaraz were working on the generators, and they put forth additional effort for a short time, but they could not maintain the accelerated pace for long.

It turned out to be enough.

The temperature continued to rise for a time, at least another 5 degrees, probably well above 40. The heat was uncomfortable, but not yet unbearable, when our speed slowed enough that our ride became calm and smooth. Within five more minutes, we were on the ground.

Balmy air flooded into the ship as Fyonna chocked the airlocks in the open position. An unmistakable salty scent could be detected, along with the sound of waves breaking on a rocky beach.

Captain Brighton, Johnson, and Chowdhury immediately went out and began looking around the vicinity. Steve, Derrick, and Elle, along with the three ensigns, were not far behind. Clémence staggered out on unsteady legs, but under her own power. Alcaraz simply sat at the generator for a few minutes gathering his strength before he, too, walked out on shaky legs. Smith and O'Neill were the next to make it out. They had to lean against the wall all the way out, and once out, I suspect they crawled, though I couldn't see them to be certain.

The other five of us: Kara, Claire, Kieran, Jens, and I, stayed put, not because we weren't just as anxious to get outside, but because we didn't have the energy to move ourselves.

Within a few moments, Derrick poked his head back in *Vanguard*. Seeing us all lying motionless, he apologized several times and quickly picked the largest of us, Kieran, to assist in getting out in the open. Others saw this and came back to lend a hand also. Sheli practically carried Claire out. Johnson helped George get to her feet and moving. Two of the ensigns, Mitchell and Hayes, helped Jens and I out of the craft, up a gentle slope and settled us in a grassy spot.

I was glad to be done moving. It wasn't just the pain of bouncing my leg while hopping. The exertion, what would normally have been such a minor thing, had left me sweaty and shaking.

I didn't like the look of Jens, either. His skin was pallid, and his breathing was very shallow. As if my scrutiny had wakened him, he opened his eyes and looked at me.

"Don't worry about me, Leon. A good night's sleep in the open sea air will put me right back in shape. You'll see."

I couldn't help grinning at the idiot. He sounded completely serious when he said it.

I lay back down in the soft grass, which was an odd color. Not that I cared much at the time. Energy seemed to seep into me as if I had become a solar collector. After a time, I felt revitalized to some extent. Not enough to want to move, mind you. But at least a more positive outlook on things was definitely in the offing.

Maybe I wouldn't die, after all.

28 July

Lt. Johnson was really getting an incredible feel for *Vanguard*, or the shaking and bouncing we endured as we screamed down through Antoc-B3's atmosphere might have been even worse. Hopefully, there was nothing broken on the ship. My faith in Lt. Johnson was renewed as she settled *Vanguard* down softly and I heard Captain say, "Right on target, XO. I couldn't have done better myself, truly."

Jos must've heard too, as he let out a slow whistle. I nodded at him as he brushed his fingernails on his chest emphasizing what I was thinking. That kind of praise was about as high as it got from Captain.

The hatch hissed a little as it was opened, and the crew began to disembark. Major Chowdhury was first, of course, especially after what we had run into previously. No one would attempt to get off without letting her get in front, not that anyone would ever get the chance.

As we all got off *Vanguard*, I could see that Lt. Johnson had landed us squarely between the ocean, which sounded great, and what was left of the camp that Brighton had targeted. Jos and I helped some of the weaker among us out of the ship, as did a few others.

Captain briefly spoke with Major Chowdhury and Lt. Johnson and then Lt. Johnson announced assignments. Captain and Chowdhury would be taking Long and O'Neill inland to explore. Lt. Johnson and her group would be going down to the seashore to try to gather food. Ensign Roberts would be accompanying her, as would Smith.

Mitchell would have a small group to search the surrounding jungle, closer to the camp, for anything edible. He would have Mackey and Claire Paul to assist him. I saw Chowdhury give one of the guns to Mitchell as Johnson announced that I would have a small group to search the old overgrown, weathered camp.

Lt. Ward would remain here near *Vanguard* with others who were still a little too weak or injured to go traipsing, and Warrant Williams would remain with them to keep watch on the ship. Chowdhury gave her the fourth pistol. I thought briefly that it was good that we would leave them with a chaperone. Chowdhury came over and handed me the assault rifle that matched the one slung over her shoulder.

"You will have to cover *Vanguard*. If anything happens, you get back here with this. Is that clear, Ensign?" she demanded.

"Yes, Ma'am. Crystal clear," I answered, coming to full attention.

"If you pull the trigger, I expect you to hit exactly what you aim at," she continued. "You put a hole in *Vanguard* and you will walk home."

She looked more edgy than normal, almost as if some sixth sense had been triggered. This made me determined to keep my wits (what I had left of them) about me today. She moved on quickly, forming up with Captain Brighton, moving swiftly to take point.

I assumed that Lt. Johnson had one of the pistols, although I didn't know for sure. It was possible that Captain Brighton had it. I knew with absolute certainty that Chowdhury had a rifle.

The landing area was a clear field of a heavy grass, somewhat prototypical of open areas near to seashores. It was open enough that I would have a nearly unobstructed view of *Vanguard* the entire time I was up at the camp. I am sure this had been obvious to Captain and Major Chowdhury.

I formed up my group, which, besides me, consisted of Clémence Queneau and Roberto Alcaraz. I told Dr. Ward that if he needed us for anything, to just yell for us, and we would come back as soon as we could. If it was urgent, he should have Elle scream, since I could probably hear that better over the sound of the surf. He smiled at that, and Elle gave me a look that said I was useless. I grinned anyway.

I made sure that my group all had their water, and packs in case we found something useful we wanted to bring back down to *Vanguard*, and we set off toward the camp. Clémence started softly singing something (it must have been in French, but I didn't recognize the song). None of us made any move to stop her.

Arriving at the camp's central grounds, I could see that the slight rise we had come up did indeed give us a fine view of the entire field around *Vanguard* and Dr. Ward. This made me feel a little better about things. Not that I expected to have to go running back to their aid, but it eased my mind knowing I would see anything or anyone approaching them long before they could get to them. Providing I wasn't inside a structure, I mentally amended, looking back at the buildings and the task at hand.

The camp was clearly run down. Even in a mild environment, facilities didn't last forever. These had been placed between an encroaching jungle and the seashore. Not exactly a mild environment. There was debris, and vine and plant growth everywhere, but it appeared from the outside that most of the structures were intact.

I advised Clémence to stand outside the first one we came to, and to keep an eye on us, and on *Vanguard* as we entered to check it out. Mostly, there was nothing inside. A lot of debris, a few scattered animal bones, and some stray materials that could possibly have been left behind by the original team. The second building we checked was the same.

As we came up on the third building, Roberto spotted a sign that said "Commissary." That was promising. We again had Clémence wait outside for us, and entered the kitchen. There was a lot of equipment in this one. Apparently, nobody had thought to gut this facility before leaving B3. We scoured it pretty thoroughly and managed to determine that every powered device had failed, due to the lack of battery cells. All of them were completely empty in here.

We did, however find a functional liquid fuel stove. Some sort of butane or similar derivative powered it. We grabbed it, even knowing that while we might use it for a few days here, Captain would probably not want it aboard. Actual flame coming from this fuel source might create some fumes on *Vanguard* we wouldn't be able to scrub. I didn't know. I would let Captain decide. Cooking was cooking, though, and anything that worked, even here, seemed good to me. In addition to the stove, the commissary also contained four large cooking pots, and a few other cooking utensils.

Two hours into our search we found the building that housed the Turin cells we needed. These we carried immediately back to *Vanguard* before resuming our search.

The only other discoveries that my group managed in our three hour search of the compound were a long coil of cord that would work for straps, a fully sealed battlefield medical kit, the single unit kind, and a rusty toolbox. I was sure that the med-kit would come in handy for Dr. Ward, and so we packed it out with us.

We had checked every building here, and I was confident we had gone through every room in them. This was all we were going to get here. I rounded everyone up and headed back over to *Vanguard*, aware that Jos' group was heading back in, too.

We made it back over to the ship well ahead of Jos, and showed our meager finds to Dr. Ward. He in no way thought it a slight thing when we showed the sealed medkit to him.

"This may yet prove a saving blessing, Ensign," he said to me with his voice low, as he cracked the seals and began a slow inventory.

At this point, Jos and Mackcy walked up. They had found three different kinds of nuts that Jens had determined were safe, two grain-like plants that he wanted to test, and a coconut-looking fruit or vegetable a little bigger than a fist. They had brought back a fair amount of all of them, and Jos said he knew where they could find more of the grain if it proved to be useful.

I helped their group unload what they had gathered, and showed them the things we had gotten. By the time we had accomplished this, Lt. Johnson's group was arriving from the seashore with a large amount of shellfish, sort of similar to oysters, as well as some mussels and a few other things. Apparently, Smith had found a whole large tide-pool filled with the creatures, and had gathered up every single one of them.

I got Mackey to help me get the outdoor stove going, and Delacoeur (a bit recovered at the thought of food) and Smith began boiling them. We didn't have much in the way of spices, but we would be having nuts and cooked shellfish tonight. As soon as I could, I went back over to talk with Lt. Ward to see how the others were doing.

"They are slowly dying, just like all of us are," Dr. Ward said softly to me, more dejected than I had seen him before.

I looked at him for a minute to see if there was more to his statement forthcoming, but apparently that was all he had to say, as he had closed his eyes and was leaning back against *Vanguard*.

"The food will help, though," I said, trying to lift Ward's spirits. "We just need to get enough nourishment in us all, and we will be a lot better off. You are doing fine, Doctor. No one asks more of you than what you can give."

"We had all better take it slow on how much we eat at one time. Our bodies have slowed their metabolisms down a lot, and too much food would do far more harm than good," he said, deflecting the subject away from himself.

"I know. We have migrated once again into almost starvation mode. I should have thought of it," I replied.

"Almost?" Ward said with upturned eyebrows.

I laughed. I had to. Dr. Ward was starting to sound defeated. He looked at me funny for a minute and finally laughed a little, too.

"Ah, to be young and invincible again, Ensign. What a treat that would be," he said, smiling.

"Not so sure about the invincible anymore, sir. And I am not feeling as young as I did a few weeks ago," I replied back with a smile.

Dr. Ward smiled and so did Jens. He didn't open his eyes, though.

"No, I don't suppose any of us feel as young as we did a few weeks ago," Dr. Ward replied softly while turning away.

Captain and his group arrived back just as the food preparations had finished. Mackey said grace for us, and we dished out and ate a very filling meal. There was some celebration, after I informed Captain that we had found the needed batteries, and that *Vanguard* had a full complement now. Everyone was happy. We even had dessert. It turned out the coconut things were some sort of melon, and very tasty.

I would be awakened to take the third security watch, but we turned in that night more content than we had been in a long time.

29–30 July

Captain had promised me that doing my duty would be enough, and so far, he was right.

It had been hard trying to understand what my new duties were. After five years as a senior grade lieutenant, I had been pretty comfortable with what was included in my scope of responsibility. Becoming helm officer had added to that, but the list of duties was clearly spelled out for me when I took on the job. Currently, though, I had entered the nebulous station of second-in-command. It was a world of difference from the duties and responsibilities I was used to.

I had not expected it either. Sheli Chowdhury outranked me. Having not thought about the fact that she was a jarhead, and thus outside the chain of command on a ship, I had assumed that she would take the second spot, and welcome to it, until Captain Brighton first addressed me as 'XO.' My heart had missed several beats. And just like that, I had a new load of worries to take care of, with no one to teach me how to do it.

Of the two people who had the knowledge, one was the captain. I couldn't go to him for help because I knew enough to know that my primary duty was to lighten his load, take care of the mundane, everyday things that always come up so that the captain could lead. The other was Chowdhury.

My problem there was that I was not sure how she would react to being pestered with questions. What if I made her mad? She really was not someone I wanted angry at me, and asking for guidance in doing the job that put me in a position of authority over her could potentially make that worse. Not to mention that asking advice of those "junior" to you did not inspire confidence. Still, I had decided recently that my options were limited to one. I needed information, and there was only one source available to me. I was hoping that now that we were dirtside again, maybe I might find an opportunity to talk it over with her. At least I hoped she felt like talking. She intimidated me sometimes.

Everyone was awake while I passed out breakfast, so it was not necessary to take leftover ration bar pieces back to the ship. Most finished off their meal and went straight to sleep, though. Among those who stayed awake, Hayes and Mitchell asked permission to continue exploring and looking for food. We really were lucky in the ensigns we had with us. They were top-notch in my book, all of them. It pleased me to see them take the initiative, and not wait for someone to tell them what needed doing. Roberts, Mackey, Williams, Alcaraz and Smith soon followed suit. I decided to join them to make four teams of two, counting the two ensigns. Hayes and Mitchell were already gone, Hayes packing one of the two rifles. Chowdhury issued the rest of us one weapon per team, keeping the other rifle for herself. Smith and I accepted our pistol and headed south along the nearby beach.

We had been walking maybe fifteen minutes when Rick asked for a break. I readily agreed. We didn't have any assigned distance to cover, after all, we just wanted a look around to see what was out there. He no sooner sat down on the damp sand than he started making those 'I'm going to be sick' sounds. I backed off a few steps.

He managed to keep everything down, but he clearly wasn't feeling well. I don't know if it was too much dinner last night or something else. In either case, I was glad to see him keep all of the calories inside. When he was ready, we started back to the ship, which was still visible to us on a grassy rise to the right of the gentle waves of the sea.

Food was waiting for us when we got back to camp. Mitchell had fashioned a three-pronged spear with barbs on it when he had seen fish swimming in the stream that flowed into the ocean north of camp. It had been well-made, and well-designed for the purpose of fishing. Unfortunately, it would never catch any fish now because the barbs had broken off when Mitchell swung it like a club to take down a seabird he had startled out of the grass right in front of him. Still, food was food, and I certainly wasn't about to complain.

Ward had checked the bird and had named it safe to eat. Long had started a fire also. Smith must have been feeling better, because he volunteered to clean the bird and cook it. Watching him eviscerate the creature was enough to make my gorge rise, but Rick didn't seem to have any difficulties. After it was cleaned, he skewered it on three sticks and set it over the fire to cook.

Finding a way to divide it up eighteen ways was another challenge. The captain had an idea in that regard. He told me to close my eyes and call out a name at random when prompted. The captain took the cooked meat and sliced off pieces of roughly equal size and each time asking me, "Who gets this piece?" Ward got the first portion, and I got the seventh, but I don't remember how they broke down beyond that. When I had my eyes open again I saw that Mackey had received a larger portion from the breast, which he was trading to Kieran for his smaller back piece. Kieran slicked it right up. Ward saw the same thing, and it prompted him to trade portions with Kara George, who still had him concerned. The sugar water he had given her before was all used up, so there was nothing left to compensate for the rapid metabolisms among us.

After our mid-meal snack was consumed, Captain passed out an assignment to those fit enough to again hunt and gather whatever food could be had here. After Hayes' and Mitchell's earlier success, they both went off with big sticks looking for unlucky birds that might cross their path. Captain Brighton went out with Williams, Paul, and Queneau; Roberts and Chowdhury teamed up to look for edible plants. Long paired up with Smith, and I went out with Mackey. The others were not in a fit condition to be sent out, so they remained close by the ship and tended the fire.

Derrick and I found something soft and squishy in a tidepool on the beach to the south. I'm not sure whether it was plant or animal, but we lugged it back to Ward to have him check to make sure it wouldn't kill us to eat it. He assured me that it wouldn't. Not quite, but still not particularly helpful to our stomachs. It would likely be painful to digest. He said we weren't that desperate yet. I agreed.

While I was back at camp, Hayes and Mitchell returned, carrying yet another bird. This one was of a different breed, much bigger than the first one. Smith wasn't back in camp to clean this one, and I didn't know what to do. I did know that I wasn't hungry enough to gut the bird Jordan was holding, so I ordered Jordan to see to it. Rank does have some privileges. While cleaning the bird, Jordan discovered three fish in its belly. More food for all of us. Every bit of protein was a blessing for us. Heaven knows we needed it in the worst way.

Our accustomed ship's time was offset from the local day here, so it was about 1500 on the 29th when we all turned in to get some rest. Chowdhury set a watch roster, which included me during the middle stretch, and we all turned in.

The next day, the hunters definitely outdid the gatherers again. The three ensigns came back into camp carrying three birds, Hayes having collected two and Roberts none, which Mitchell had to needle her about every few minutes. Smith had them cooked up for us at the lunch meal. They tasted like chicken, but everyone always says that. They really did, though, which surprised me. I mean, this was a completely different planet, and terraforming can only go so far, so why were there even birds here? It was beyond my education to answer that one. I would leave that to exozoologists and theologians to debate.

Doctor Ward pointed out some preventative tips that it looked like we might need here. Claire had gotten the beginnings of a sunburn the day before, and so Leon lectured all of us on what we could do to be more careful. He also suggested wearing an extra shirt or cloth over our heads to protect them from the heat. He said that dipping them in water and letting it evaporate would help to avoid negative effects from too much sun.

Chowdhury immediately took to wearing a red cloth on her head, recognizing good advice when she heard it. I thought it made her look like a pirate. It didn't make her look any less scary, so I chose to keep the pirate comments to myself.

MASTER CHIEF PETTY OFFICER DERRICK MACKEY

From his journal

30 July

I woke up the next morning as Antoc-B was coming up over the beach. Many had slept down on the beach as I had but others were up by *Vanguard* in a clearing a few hundred meters to the north. As I looked around, I could see many of the others were already awake. Lieutenant Johnson and Major Chowdhury were walking along the beach standing guard. Major Chowdhury never seemed to sleep dirtside, as if she had taken it upon herself to guard the crew whenever we were on the ground. I was glad that she had been vigilant on the first planet where soldiers masquerading as terraformers had tried to ambush us as well as with the predators on our last planet. Regardless of her caution, however, there was no evidence that there were any enemies on this planet or any dangerous predators.

Well, I guess her job is to anticipate, not wait for evidence of a problem. She was a great help to all of the officers, especially the young ensigns.

Jherri Roberts emerged from her blankets and made her way down the beach to where Johnson and Chowdhury were talking. Soon they all went in different directions, probably looking for more food.

By then, the rest of the camp was making the attempt to rise. Jens Fujinami stood shakily for a few moments, but then laid back down clutching his stomach. It appeared that he had been exhausted by the attempt. Many of the rest found similar difficulties. A few simply crawled back into their blankets.

Johnson made her way over to the camp and called for Smith to help her gather 'oysters.' Others were headed inland to gather fruits and berries.

I didn't feel up to a long walk yet, so I returned up the trail to the clearing that held the ship itself. *Vanguard* had been through a lot for us, so far. I decided to give her a look over and inspect for any damage. It would be much simpler to fix here on the surface than at any time after we lifted off. Long was there doing much the same thing. The waves on the beach and the quiet kind of lulled me into a relaxing mood. I was making a slow, easy inspection. Not really paying much attention until I put my hand on the aft number two thruster. The whole unit turned at my touch. The thruster unit is mounted to the fuselage by six large hex bolts and there were only two still in place. One of the remaining bolts was loosened to the last three threads. The mounting holes were oblonged and might turn out to be unusable.

I called Long over and he began to shake his head immediately.

"That explains it," he said.

"What's that?" I asked.

"Well, after we started re-entry, I could feel a vibration through the hull. I thought that it might be something on the skin that was banging but this was probably it."

"It has to have been slack for some time for all of the bolts to have worked loose," I added.

"Yeah, probably. I'll see what I can do with it. It won't be stable the way it is."

We worked on the assembly until Smith yelled for everyone to come for lunch.

Lunch turned out to be a stew. That was probably the easiest way to put all of the various ingredients together for everyone to be able to have some.

I sat in a corner of the beach away from everyone and watched the ocean. I said grace over my food and thanked the Lord for the bounty that we had received today. I had said those words many times in my life, but never had I felt them as strongly as I did right then. The stew was very thin with pieces of 'oysters' and jerky and I even got a chunk of ration bar in one bite. Smith had added just a bit of sea water, both for seasoning and to replenish our salt. It was one of the greatest meals that I had ever had.

After finishing my lunch, I resumed work on the ship. Long and I were able to reseat the thruster but we could not locate anything that we could use as a substitute for the missing bolts. In the end we took one bolt from each of the other three thrusters so that each assembly was only missing a single bolt and then we re-torqued the bolts on all of the rear thruster assemblies.

Both of us went down to the water's edge and washed. The position of Antoc-B was indicating mid-afternoon, so I decided to take a walk into the woods rather than lay around in the sun, which was Long's occupation of choice after washing.

Smith was just finishing up his cleanup and wanted to get away from camp for a while, so he asked to accompany me. That was great, because it probably wasn't a good idea for me to wander off alone, anyway.

"This is my idea of a planet to settle on, unlike B2," said Smith.

"I'm tired of referring to these planets by their numbers. I'm going to name them."

"Shouldn't we let the captain do that?" Smith asked.

"No, Captain Brighton is a great officer, but he would go to his grave still calling them B2, A3 or whatever. He has no poetry in his soul," I said. "Meaning no disrespect to him, you understand. It's just the way he is."

"Well, what are you going to name them?" Smith said, leaning in.

"Yes, I'd be interested to know that, too," came a voice out of the jungle in front of us. Lt. Johnson and Major Chowdhury came out of the vegetation carrying several 'coco-melons' in their hands. These were the best fruit that we had found so far on the planet. They were very juicy, and very tasty.

"I don't know, maybe coco-melon," I said, motioning to their burden.

"That doesn't seem very poetic either," said Johnson.

"Maybe not…how about La Paz?" I said as we reached the summit of the cliffs above our ship. The vista stretched out all around us and the breeze was cool and clean.

"The Peace," murmured Chowdhury. "I don't think we'll be able to enjoy that particular sentiment for some time yet."

We all settled ourselves on a fallen log that ran parallel to the cliff, about four meters from the edge. The officers laid down their fruit and sat quietly with us, each of us absorbed in our own thoughts. After a few minutes, Long emerged from the jungle and made his way over to where we were sitting.

"Then we could name A3, 'Drew's Rest,'" said Chowdhury without any prelude.

A pall came over the group at the reminder of the loss. Chowdhury got up and moved back down the trail after collecting her coco-melons.

Smith seemed more and more uncomfortable around the group and he finally got up and said, "I've got to go get dinner started." He moved off down the trail after Chowdhury.

"This whole thing should be called 'Brighton's Folly,' if you ask me," mumbled Long.

"We've talked about that, Long," Johnson said with a warning tone.

"Well, you have to admit he's the strictest…cuss…in the Fleet. That's what got him into this situation in the first place- and landed us here along with him."

"Captain Brighton might have a tendency to micro-manage, and expect perfection in everything, but that is not necessarily a negative. It's just his personality and he happens to be the best Captain that I have ever had the opportunity to serve with," she said with a note of finality. "Let's go gather some shellfish for dinner." Somehow it didn't come across as a request.

"There is no one that I would rather have with us in these circumstances," I added with feeling. "Brighton was made for situations like this."

Long looked up at me as we all got to our feet. He shook his head slightly but he said nothing.

I walked down toward the seashore with the XO, and saw that the group that had been down there was coming back up the beach toward us. We found another of the small tide pools, and began gathering up the various mussels and other shellfish that we had been collecting for meals.

Soon enough, the other group reached us. It appeared that they were in a good enough mood. I could hear the strains of laughter as they moved closer, and saw that Ensigns Hayes and Mitchell were happily arguing back and forth about something. Those two would always be giving each other a hard time, but they were probably best of friends, and still somewhat adolescent, so that made sense.

They indeed had reason to be in a good mood. We were eating well here, and tonight would be better, since Mitchell had added a slight boost to tonight's menu.

Dinner was mostly more of the same. Shellfish, jerky, and ration bars, but with the addition of two fish that were caught by Mitchell and pronounced edible by Dr. Ward. It was even very filling. The coco-melons were a welcome dessert. At times, it was hard to believe how much we were all rejuvenating, just through eating and being in the sun.

The conversation at dinner turned to the exploration that had been done that day. Alcaraz, Roberts and George had come across tracks of some kind of animal, but they couldn't identify them as even being similar to anything that they had seen before.

Lt. Johnson asked Smith a question which evoked strange looks from those near them, and prompted Smith into motion after a nod. Smith was headed over to *Vanguard*, with Ms. Johnson not too far behind. I wondered what it was about, but just then the Captain came into my view and I realized we hadn't told him about the work on *Vanguard* from earlier today.

I reported on the work that Long and I had done that morning and asked the Captain if he would care to inspect the work before it was too dark to see.

"No, I'm sure that the work is up to your usual standards, Master Chief," he said in a distracted way, without even looking up.

I could tell that the Captain was preoccupied, lost in his thoughts, so I nodded and moved up the slope toward the ship, where a small group had gathered.

Ricardo had come back from *Vanguard* and he and Lt. Johnson were talking. Ms. Johnson had his razor, and was just sitting down with him holding his mirror up for her. The other three people and I crowded in to see what she was doing.

"Are you cutting off your hair?" I asked, as it dawned on me what she intended. She lifted up the razor while looking in the mirror that Smith held steady.

"Yes, Bosun, I am. It's too bothersome, and I am tired of taking care of it. Especially in zero g," she said. I hadn't considered that aspect. My own close-cropped hair had not caused me any problems, and I simply had not looked at it from her perspective until it was pointed out to me.

"Oh," was all I got out.

We all sat and watched while she neatly sliced her long hair off, leaving it much shorter, but very neatly done. Just looking at her perform the task, you would have thought she had done it before. I doubted, though, that Ms. Johnson had ever had short hair before, let alone cut it herself with a man's old fashioned straight razor. She probably would have preferred to have made her first attempt without everyone coming over to see the show. If it bothered her, though, she never gave any indication.

Soon after she had finished, our little group broke up and I wandered back to the dinner area, after telling Lt. Johnson that I thought her hair looked very good. She smiled and said thank you.

When I got back down to the main group, I saw that the captain was still sitting where he had been when I had moved off. Most folks had risen and were mingling in quiet conversations. Captain Brighton hadn't joined in, however. I saw Major Chowdhury hovering around him and realized why no one else had bothered him there. She may be a little mean-spirited at times, but there was no denying how effective a security officer she was.

Captain Brighton stood and started moving up the trail toward the ship, almost like he was looking far in the distance and had noticed something he wanted to investigate. When he reached the trailhead he turned and said,

"Everyone sleeps in the clearing or in the ship tonight. Major Chowdhury, please arrange for two people to be on watch at all times." He then turned and moved off to the ship.

"Aye-aye, sir." Chowdhury replied.

After a few moments, we all gathered up our belongings and moved up the dark trail in his wake. He was asleep on the floor of the ship when we got into camp.

31 July - 1 August

When I awoke, the pilot's chronometer showed 1257 hours, 31 July. It was hard to match the stated time with Antoc-B just starting to rise above the trees to the east of the camp.

I had again put Johnson in charge of the scrounging parties and she took her chosen crew and moved off into the jungle without further questions. For the rest, the most urgent demands of hunger had been assuaged by our food of the last few days but many were beyond a quick recovery.

While it was not evident by their energy levels who might have stolen the jerky from the storage area, I had not let go of that problem. To steal at any time was despicable, but to take food from your comrades in this situation could be considered attempted murder. The guilty one would not profit from it, if I could help it.

I was very pleased with the performance of Lt. Johnson. No doubt, she was suffering the effects of hunger as much as any of the rest, but she never complained, even in private. She was energetic and scrupulous in following through on any orders or directions. With the exception of her long dark hair which she had chopped short with Smith's razor the night before, she seemed to make no allowances for the conditions. She was still properly dressed in the black and crimson of her navy uniform, and she never faulted in either courtesy or form of address. This had become her ritual. She would not give in even one centimeter. If she happened to die on this mission, death would find her properly doing her duty. I knew that I could leave the food gathering in her hands and not need to worry about it again.

I chuckled slightly to myself as the quiet words of Chief Miller came back to me from my first command. "There are many things that only you can do as captain," he had said. "Delegate everything else, so that you can concentrate on those." At the time, I felt that he was wrong. As captain, I needed to oversee everything, because I was responsible for everything. This had been the hardest lesson for me to learn, and I had a tendency to slip into old patterns of behavior if I was not careful. I generally felt that if I could do it, then I should do it, because it wasn't fair to ask others to do things that I could do myself. I found, over time, that there were two problems with this pattern of thought. First, I spent all my time busy, but not accomplishing a percentage of everything that needed to be done. Secondly, my junior officers never developed the ability to solve small problems, and thus were overwhelmed by larger problems when they came along.

At that thought, I began to feel that maybe I had been pushing too many items onto Lt. Johnson, and maybe I needed to spread it out to the ensigns and give them more responsibilities. Roberts, Hayes and Mitchell seemed level-headed and able.

As I made my way out of the ship, I decided that there would be no further assignments for the morning. I would let those who remained gather some of their lost strength. Smith was over near the commissary building, working with the salvaged field-stove. It appeared that he had all three of the burners functional now. There were pots of what I assumed to be water boiling away on all three of them. Smith, at least, seemed happy to be back amid familiar duties. There were two or three others that were busy with self-assigned tasks, but the others were content to remain in their chosen beds until they were forced out by order or biological need. Mackey was sitting near Smith's stoves with his back against a tree. He wore neither shirt nor shoes, and he had what appeared to be a fishing net spread out across his lap. He looked to be repairing some tears with electrical wire. The only other movement in the camp was Jens Fujinami as he walked in my direction. He was pulling a tattered backpack he must have found in the abandoned camp over his shoulders as he moved. His strength was still low, as he was not moving with his usual energy, but the smile on his face was no less dim for all of his hardships. He carried a walking stick that was taller than he was and he had sharpened the upper end to use as a spear. He reached back and pulled his shoulder-length blond hair out of his collar and straightened his burden on his shoulders as he came even with me.

"Good morning, sir," he said with a new bounce in his step. "Great day for exploring. Have you seen the samples I brought in last night, sir? Truly spectacular. There is one leaf that I want to examine at length. It is truly unique and could be the key to understanding many questions that I have had about this system. There seems to be a direct correlation between the two planets and there shouldn't be if you see what I mean." The whole monologue was spoken rapidly and apparently without taking a breath. This last comment was thrown over his shoulder as he disappeared around a corner in the path and was lost from view.

Johnson and her four chosen food gatherers returned about mid-morning. Though fewer people had gone out this morning, they had actually returned with more supplies.

O'Neill, Hayes, Mitchell and Alcaraz quickly went to work with Delacoeur and Smith cleaning fish and separating out what needed to be cooked immediately and what could be set aside for later. Johnson left them to their work and came over to where I was sitting in the shade to report.

"There seems to be ample food and supplies here in the near vicinity, sir. What are our plans?" From her manner it was impossible to tell which answer would please her more, that we were staying or that we would leave immediately.

"I think that we need to recover our strength a little before leaving, but we don't have much time to waste," I said.

"Yes, sir."

"Lieutenant," I called as she started to turn away. "Have Smith and Delacoeur put the remaining jerky into our lunch stew. There is no sense in leaving it for the thief."

"Aye-aye, sir."

"And inform the crew that I will address them after the meal."

"Aye-aye, Captain."

After everyone had completed their lunch, they moved in ones and twos to the entry of the launch where I had been seated to finish my stew. I gave them enough time to assemble. Hayes and Alcaraz grabbed a fallen log and pulled it over for several to sit on. I waited until everyone had settled themselves. There was remarkably little jostling or fidgeting. No one had the energy to spare, apparently.

"I think we are all grateful to be out of *Vanguard* today," I said. "Unfortunately, we will not be able to stay as long as any of us would like. We need to be underway in a little under three days from now, and there are a number of things that need to be done between now and then."

"Rescue is not going to come for us. If we remain here, as I'm sure many of you are thinking, we will remain here for years on this planet with no guarantee of any eventual rescue. The only other option would be to leave a part of the crew here and then continue on with a smaller group that could make the passage with less hardship. I will not do that to any crew member. If *Vanguard* were lost, you would be marooned here for the rest of your lives, in all probability," I said, as I surveyed the faces of my diminished command. "The only acceptable option is to continue as before.

If we are moving on, then we must go quickly before *Pathfinder* is able to get underway. We will stock as much food as we can prepare in the next three days and then we will depart." I looked at Ensign Roberts. "That will be your assignment, Ensign. Take a crew of four, plus Smith. Concentrate on fish that we can smoke and fresh fruit. Check with Dr. Ward for which will be the best for us. I want as much as you can get by 0600 ship's time on the fourth, stowed into the storage locker. Prepare a list of what you were able to gather and supply that to Lt. Johnson." Both officers nodded their understanding and I could see Ensign Roberts begin to survey the group as she silently began selecting her gatherers.

"Aye-aye, sir," she said, her head continuing to move.

"Ensign Hayes, your job is to pull everything out of the cabin of *Vanguard* and do three things. First, and most importantly, check the entire inner cabin for any damage. We have the supplies and the access to correct those problems now and we may not have either at a later time. Second, clean everything. We cannot allow serious illness, and a thorough cleaning will help reduce that risk. I believe I saw some cleaning supplies in one of the structures, but use whatever you can find. Last, we need to reduce our weight, so anything that is not absolutely necessary does not go back in. Do you understand?"

"Yes, sir"

"You can have everyone except Long, O'Neill, Delacoeur, Ward and whoever Ms. Roberts takes."

"Aye-aye, sir."

"Before we disperse, I want you all to know that we will lift off at 1450 ship's time on the fourth. That will be about three hours after local dawn.

"Mr. Long, Mr. O'Neill, Ensign Mitchell, Ms. Chowdhury, you are with me. The rest of you are dismissed."

I waited for my chosen crew to move toward the front where I stood. The other crew began to move off with their officers. Alcaraz, Smith, Williams, Fujinami, and Mackey with Roberts, good choices I thought, and the rest with Hayes. I motioned to my small group to follow me toward the tail of *Vanguard*. When we arrived at the faulty nozzle, I motioned to it and said, "After Mackey reported on your repairs last night, I decided to check the alignment of all of the nozzles. This nozzle is still slightly misaligned. We need to pull the assembly and repair it. Ms. Chowdhury," I said, motioning to the dense forest behind me, a few meters from where we all stood. "We are out of sight of the rest of the crew here. Please supply an overwatch for us so we can work without worrying about what may be coming out of the forest."

"Aye-aye, sir" she said.

The work proceeded quickly with very little complaint. Long made several mumbled comments which I carefully ignored. I could not continue to do so indefinitely, but the penalties would be so severe if I took official notice that it could damage his career. Normally, there are several layers between NCO's and the captain. Grumbling could be absorbed at lower levels. An experienced XO would see the problem and deal with it outside of official channels. Lt. Johnson was too busy learning her basic duties to look at those peripheral duties. *Or maybe not*, I thought as I reconsidered a meaningful look that I had noticed between Johnson and Long a few days before. I would leave it in her hands until I could no longer do so.

We soon finished with the realignment and I dismissed the workers to their personal pursuits.

For me, the rest of the afternoon was spent exploring the area around the camp. I was able to bring in several baskets full of the yellow-green fruit that tasted vaguely like dried pears. Finally, I decided that I needed to get away from camp. The junior officers were doing a fine job of performing their tasks and I desperately needed to get away and be alone. I had seen a trail that led to the top of the overlooking cliff, so I headed through the trees in that direction. It was an hour's hike to the top, but the view was worth it. Ever since I was a small child I loved to watch the sea. I don't know how long I had been standing there watching the spray before I noticed Johnson and Mitchell twenty meters ahead. They were also standing and staring out to sea, apparently oblivious to my presence as well.

I made my way over and said, "It seems that the more we explore the galaxy, the more we find of Earth."

"I don't know, sir. I've seen plenty of things that are truly strange and bizarre," Johnson replied without taking her eyes off of the surf. "This does feel good, though."

"Yes, it does."

"Do we really need to get back into the boat so soon?" Mitchell asked with longing in his voice.

"Yes, Ensign. You know the choices that we have had to make. If we are going to be able to get out of this system in time to do anything about the pirates, then we must leave on the schedule we have in place."

"I just wish there were more time to explore is all, Captain."

"Well, Ensign, we will be back, and maybe there will be time to explore then."

"Yes, sir."

"I'll tell you this, though. The difficulties are just beginning and we have a long way yet to go," I said. I turned and started back down the hill. For some reason, the sight didn't excite me any more.

1–2 August

Life on B3 was much more pleasant than we had experienced in some time. We were consuming quite a bit more than we had been while in space. Our normal portion of a food bar continued, and was supplemented by what we were able to forage from the land here. Initially, I limited how much each should eat, to avoid dangerous consequences to our systems, which were used to a much sparser quantity. Within a few meals, though, I was able to relax the restrictions, and the crew began to regain their vigor.

Jens, especially, looked so improved it was hard to envision his condition when we first arrived on this planet. He had told me that he would be fine after a good night's sleep, and he had exaggerated only a little. After his second night here, he was as animated and energetic as ever. He still appeared thinner than was healthy, but the feeling that he was hovering around death's door was long dispelled.

Captain Brighton had commented on the change. "You look infinitely improved, Mr. Fujinami. I don't mind admitting that I had been concerned for you. When we arrived here, it looked to me like you had one foot in the grave, yet now … I can't describe the difference."

"No early death for me, Captain. I'm sure that's what Teach and his bunch had in mind for us, but I mean to live long enough to see them face justice. And I'm stubborn enough to do it, just to spite them!"

"I have no doubt of that, Mr. Fujinami, no doubt at all," he said with a rare chuckle.

He paused for a moment, weighing out his words before he spoke them. "When we return to Earth, and I can address The Board, I plan to ask for a ship so that I can bring them back in myself. For me, it is a personal matter." He eyed both of us for a moment, then continued. "Not the way you are probably thinking. Yes, I feel betrayed by a man I once considered a friend, but that isn't the personal part. It would be enough for me simply to know that he had been caught and made to pay for his crime.

"No, for me, it is a personal matter to retrieve *Pathfinder*. She was entrusted to me, and she was my … she *is* my responsibility until I have been properly relieved of it," he said, with iron in his tone.

It looked like he had more he wanted to add, but he did not. Perhaps he had said more than he had intended. It was certainly more open than he had ever been within my hearing. Instead, he nodded to both of us and moved downslope toward the beach.

That had been the day before. By this time, the first of August, I was actually contributing again. Tim O'Neill and Derrick Mackey had helped me construct a sort of combination splint and removable cast for my leg. By immobilizing my ankle, I did not need to flex my calf muscle, and thus was able to walk about, after a fashion. A very slow, painful, wearying fashion.

Still, I was grateful for what mobility I had, and even more thankful that I could again share in the responsibilities which had been distributed by the captain. At the time, Jens and I were working to identify and collect anything edible, both for immediate use, and possibly to be stored for use on the ship.

Jens was not showing any impatience at the slower pace I was forced to maintain. Instead, he was ranging out to every side as we went, looking at all the plants, taking samples, performing simple tests. In fact, slow as I was moving, there were several times where I had to wait for him to be ready to move on.

Little was gained from our foray that day, at least in adding to our stores. I suppose you might take Edison's view; we had learned of several dozen places wherein not to look for food. Our one success was in identifying a small pod which had edible seeds. The pods were a dark green, but the seeds were a light grey color, somewhere in size between a sunflower seed and a pea, and very hard. It would not do to eat them raw, but they would make a welcome addition to our habitual stew, if boiled sufficiently.

We gathered all that we could find in the meadow where the patch was located, which amounted to about a kilo and a half. A search of nearby clearings yielded no more of the small beans, so we headed back to camp a little early. We knew that our contribution would need the extra cooking time. We thought that perhaps we could do a little foraging near camp after we deposited our collection into the pot.

It was not too long before other parties began to return. Long and his group had brought back a sizable quantity of some shellfish. These had been obtained from an area of rocky outcroppings to the northwest of us.

Chowdhury's group returned bearing every portable container in our possession, except the stewpot, full of fresh water. They carried little in the way of food, but they had restocked our supply of fresh water from the nearby river.

Instead of adding their food to the communal pot, Sheli came over to where Jens and I were resting in the shade. It seemed that the area they had explored had not contained anything which had already been identified as safe to consume, and so they had brought samples of what was available, instead. Jens went immediately to work in testing the items which had been procured.

Johnson's group was the last to arrive prior to the appointed time for dinner. They carried with them the carcasses of two birds along with three eggs. Our stew that evening would wind up with quite a variety of flavors, indeed. Delacoeur and Smith set to work at once to prepare the birds for the pot.

Elle Williams was among that group, and she came and sat next to me while we waited for the meal to be completed.

"Look at the way everyone is hovering around the cookpot," I commented to her.

"You can hardly blame them. As hard as pedaling the generator is, we're using up more energy now than we had been on the ship," she replied.

"Oh, no, I don't mean it in a negative way. I'm pleased to see that their hunger is back. Their bodies are functioning normally once again. I don't know if you noticed last week, and even beginning the week before, most of us were not getting hungry at all. That's a bad sign, one I'm relieved to see ending."

Dinner was served not long after that, and Lieutenant Johnson had a few items of business to discuss.

"If I could have your attention. The captain and I have been discussing our situation, and we have a change in assignments to announce.

"First, Ensign Hayes has completed his assigned task well ahead of schedule," both exchanging nods of acknowledgement, "and his team is ready to be reassigned to other duties. Second, Ensign Roberts' team has been doing more searching for food than storing, because we have been eating most everything we collect. Third, we have all been expending too much energy gathering the extra food. The plan was to allow our bodies to regain strength while we are here. While we have more energy from the extra food, we are burning it all up just as quickly, and we're not really replenishing what we have lost.

"So, from now on, everyone will be assigned to gather food, but for no more than six hours per day. Additional duties may be assigned around camp, such as preparing meals or storing food for the next leg of our journey, but for no more than two hours. I and the other officers will be setting up a rotation for everyone to fit these new parameters. We expect everyone to rest while not on duty."

She might have worded it as an expectation, but the tone of voice made it clear that it was an order, and everyone received it as such. There was some discussion afterward, various strategies promoted as to how to be the most efficient at gathering food, and most everyone participated to a greater or lesser extent.

When the discussion concluded, Johnson had assigned a group, including Elle, to go back to the nesting area they had discovered earlier to see if they could collect more of the birds which lived there. They were on their way immediately.

I would have to wait a while longer to find a little private time with Elle.

As ordered, I returned to my accustomed place and lay down to rest. The exertions of earlier that day made falling asleep a duty gratefully accomplished.

I awoke to the minor commotion which accompanied the return of the foraging party. What commotion there was centered on the fact that they had returned all but empty-handed. They had brought back none of the birds, and only three eggs. These eggs were more than twice the size of a chicken egg, but that still would not be much when split eighteen ways.

Sheli was explaining to Lt. Johnson that it had been a good idea, but the timing was poor. When the group had arrived, the birds were still very active and alert. They had been impossible to sneak up on (and if Sheli could not sneak up on one, then impossible was the correct word to use), and they could easily hover or circle out of reach for hours.

Eventually, she had decided to leave, bearing in mind the recent injunction to limit our time out gathering, and to recommend sending another group back after dark when the birds would be settling down for the night.

"There are hundreds of birds with their nests right on the rocks just above the high tide line. I would bet the next group could easily get 50 or 60 birds," Tim added.

"All right then, Ensign Hayes, you have the next rotation. Take Derrick, Kieran, and Clémence with you. Wait about an hour before you leave. That should still give you plenty of time to settle in before the sun goes down."

With an hour to wait, most went back to resting, but I walked stiffly over to Lt. Johnson. I was glad that Captain Brighton had assigned her responsibility for collecting food. I am not sure I would have had the courage to make my next request if I had to stand before the captain himself.

"Lieutenant, could I have a word?"

"Yes, Leon, what is it?"

"I'd like your permission to accompany Ensign Hayes."

I could see that she was marshalling her objections, so I jumped back in before she could voice them. "I understand why you and the captain have not given me any duty assignments, and I appreciate you allowing my leg to heal when there clearly is a need for every hand to pitch in. But I think in this case, it might do more harm in the long run. With the lack of food, everyone's bodies are scavenging energy from their own tissues. If I don't use my leg at all, my body is going to decide that it doesn't really need those muscles and they will be absorbed.

"So if I need to exercise my leg anyway, I would prefer to contribute what I can. I may not be fast enough to catch and kill any birds myself, but I can help to carry them back."

She stood pondering my request for a few moments, then said, "But by exercising your leg, you're not allowing it to heal, are you?"

"No, but I don't think it could heal right now in any case. Not without some food to turn into building material. If we can catch two or three birds per person, that protein would help a lot."

"All right, I'll inform Jordan. Plan to leave in half an hour instead, so you don't push yourself too hard getting there before dark."

"Yes, ma'am."

The five of us departed according to the revised schedule. Within a few minutes it was clear why we needed the extra time. Kieran became impatient and decided to go on ahead at a normal pace. Jordan went with him, probably to avoid anyone going off alone. Sheli and Captain Brighton had both stressed the need to stick together. It seemed like common sense to me, but I had spent more time outdoors while growing up than most in our group could claim.

Derrick and Clémence seemed content to keep to my sedate pace. When the other two were out of hearing range Clémence brought up the topic which we had assiduously avoided previously.

"Have you two thought about Teach taking over the ship?"

I wasn't sure how to answer the question. Certainly, I had thought about it; many dozens of times. Still, Captain Brighton had declared the topic not open to discussion, quite angrily, in fact. Queneau was usually quite obedient, and it seemed out of place for her to want to talk about it.

Still, it was a topic of great interest to all of us, for obvious reasons. Initially, it had been difficult to avoid the subject. Over time, though, it had simply become habitual to avoid talking about the events which led to our current struggle.

I chuckled. "It's hard not to think of it, even if the captain does not want it discussed." I thought that perhaps a gentle reminder would close the matter, but it did not. I felt that I had made my token effort to forestall the dialogue, and so joined in then with a clear conscience.

"I know I'm not supposed to bring it up, but there is one question I have that's driving me crazy. How could the captain know who was on the lifeboat before it blew up?"

"By deductive reasoning, and by keeping his eyes open and his brain working," Derrick said.

"What do you mean?" Clémence asked.

"Well, take it step by step. The lifeboats had already been launched before Teach and his pack of thieves began rounding all of us up. You all saw how he reacted when McIntire told him that the lifeboats were gone." Not all of us had. That had happened while I was back in the medbay, but he continued anyway.

"I don't think Teach planned to put us in *Vanguard* to begin with. I think he was going to dump us in the lifeboats. It was only after he heard the lifeboats were gone that he started loading us in the survey launch. So, clearly, Teach was not the one who launched the lifeboats. That means that Captain Brighton launched them, probably to force Teach to give us *Vanguard*, and a chance to get home.

"Now you want to know how Captain Brighton could know there's no one on the other lifeboats we saw, and only one person in the one that exploded. I think I can answer that one. You may not know this, but Captain Brighton has almost total recall. When Johnson reported that someone was in that lifeboat, I'm sure he thought the same thing all the rest of us did, 'Who could that be?' Unlike us, though, he can remember everyone he had seen since the lifeboats launched, even a brief glimpse. I would bet that the captain knows who died in that explosion because he can account for everyone else after the lifeboats had been launched."

"So who was it?" Queneau queried.

"I don't know," Derrick replied. "I know I didn't see everyone. Captain Brighton would have seen those who had come to take the bridge, and I was not there. Nor were either of you."

"True," I said. "But I can account for who was there from a conversation I had with Elle. I bet the three of us together could account for most of the crew."

It took us quite a while to organize a list. Almost every person would be discounted as quickly as their name was mentioned. After ten minutes of racking our brains, we were still short of the total ship's company by three.

"Beacham," Derrick called out in the midst of our silence. "He was one of them on the radio after they launched us."

"That's right," confirmed Clémence, "and Goodwin was the other one. I had forgotten about the radio because I never actually saw them."

"I can't believe I forgot. I've never been so close to wishing harm on another person in my life," Derrick berated himself.

"That leaves only one person," I stated. "Neil Lamont, the astrogation officer."

"So what was Lamont doing in one of the lifeboats when it launched?" Clémence pondered aloud.

That question made everyone stop. It was several minutes before anyone spoke again.

Finally Derrick's subdued voice asked, "What if the facts that the lifeboat blew up and Lamont was on it are related?"

"What do you mean?" I asked.

"What if we were supposed to be the ones in those lifeboats, and they were set to explode to get us out of the picture?"

It was a chilling thought, but not as incredible as I would have liked.

"So how does that put Lamont on one of the lifeboats?" Clémence asked.

"I think Teach must have planned to kill all of us from the beginning," I said, beginning to follow Mackey's logic. "He must have thought the only way he could be safe was to have no witnesses to his crime."

"He couldn't share that part of the plan with everyone following him, for he needed every hand that he could convince to stay in order to operate *Pathfinder*, and not everyone would want to kill us. So he rigged the lifeboats to explode after they had left the area. All of those aboard *Pathfinder* would believe us still alive, though marooned on an isolated planet, but we would all be dead, along with any evidence of what had really happened.

"Now, when we had all been collected, Teach discovered that the lifeboats were gone, and he had to alter his plan on the fly. Those following him expected that we were to be put off the ship, for that was what he had told them to gain their complicity. He had no other option, then, but to place us all in *Vanguard*.

"Teach knew that the captain had been in this system before, and that he would be familiar enough with it to find a jump point back home, which he could not allow. So he took away a sufficient amount of our power and food to leave us no option but to remain on the nearest habitable planet."

"You still haven't answered my question, Leon," Queneau reminded me.

"It makes sense that Lamont would have been caught in one of the life-boats when they launched," I continued.

"How so?" she asked.

"Well, assuming that everything we've deduced is correct, Teach would have had to have someone he could confide in to rig the lifeboats to explode. If he didn't want the crew in general to know about it, then he would have to assign one of the senior officers that task. So he sends the AO to do the dirty work. He can't have him set the explosive charges too early because it might be discovered. So, when Teach is ready to make his move, he starts things off by sending his trusted lieutenant to take care of the witnesses. Lamont was thereby in the act of sabotaging the lifeboats, when the unplanned launch caught him at it."

When I had first heard that someone had died in the lifeboat explosion, I had been sick to my stomach. I suddenly found that I was no longer ill at the thought of Neil Lamont being blasted into tiny pieces. In fact, the poetic justice of the whole thing brought a smile to my face.

Mackey evidently had different thoughts on the matter, as demonstrated by his next words.

"I liked Lt. Lamont," the big bosun said, very quietly. "He could be short with his subordinates from time to time, but I never would have suspected him of this kind of thing."

"Is there anyone you know whom you don't like?" I asked him. He turned red and looked at his shoes as we walked along the wet sand of the beach.

"Please don't take that as a rebuke, Derrick, because I did not intend it as such. You are, without a doubt, the most gentle and trusting individual I have had the pleasure of meeting. And I think that your amiable nature has been invaluable in maintaining the morale of our group.

"Your positive outlook, and Clémence's trust and confidence in the captain are what has kept a lot of us going."

Clémence chimed in, "I am confident in Captain Brighton. And I am certain that Teach will hang for his piracy. The Captain (you could hear the capital C in the way she said "Captain") is determined to see justice done, and I do not think there is any power in this universe which would be able to stop him."

The power and conviction in her words again left us with nothing to say for several minutes. I broke the silence by moving the conversation in a new direction.

"Derrick, don't take this amiss, but you're a devout Christian, aren't you?"

"Yes," he said simply, with neither arrogance nor apology.

"Do you believe that God can forgive Teach for what he has done?"

"Yes," he repeated, equally simply.

"And have you forgiven him?" I pressed.

The answer was not so simple this time. I could see by his face in the receding sunlight that he was struggling to determine his own feelings about the man. The pause stretched on until we had passed around a 20-meter-tall rock that was part of the headland and we could see our destination.

His voice, when it came, was quiet and full of remorse.

"No, I have not."

---

4 August

Commander Agostinho was so far beyond annoyed with *Vanguard*'s ability to keep away from them that she had taken her frustration out on her crew and Marines more than once. They all gave a wide berth if they saw her, and no one asked her anything. She knew it was not good for morale, and in the long term it would not serve to have her staff and crew think of her as a tyrant, but just now, she didn't really care. The only one who seemed not to be bothered by it was Lt. Vasconcellos. His comment before landing on B2 had been that he felt their luck was about to change.

Yeah, had it ever. It went from bad to worse. If there were such a thing as good luck, or good fortune, it was eluding them. They had experienced nothing but problems and disappointments in capturing the technology they wanted. When *Vanguard* had first appeared, and changed their plans, she had assumed that it was a boon; how much more wrong could she have been?

Vanguard had cost them several Marines on their first encounter, an assault shuttle with her crew and Marine contingent on their second, and several more Marines on the last planet. Captain Brighton had managed to elude them and escape at every turn. She had vastly underestimated his capability, and potentially that of *Vanguard* as well. This time though, would have to be different.

Agostinho had brought *Oeiras* with all the Marines at the base. A full contingent of eighteen (including the four from base security) battle armored Marines was behind her in the deployment bay. They had opted for the light combat armor, leaving them mobile enough for planetary movement, but still offering more protection in case they came across native problems like those cursed komodos. They would also hold out well against the very minimal weaponry of the crew of *Vanguard*. Lt. Vasconcellos wanted this confrontation more than she did, she believed. Good Marines didn't take well to losing men without achieving their objectives.

They had seen *Vanguard* headed for B3 when they had left B2 for the base to get the wounded some treatment. As they came into closer range of

By now, there was only one possible sensor reading that could be *Vanguard*. For the first time, they would be able to get the drop on these people.

"Vasconcellos, come up here," the commander said into the com. She wasn't exactly sure what this Brighton was up to, but she was becoming aware that based on her own resources, the DaGamans weren't going to have any more chances at them.

The shuttle cockpit hatch slid open and an armored Vasconcellos, minus his helmet, came through the opening.

"What have we got ma'am?" he asked without preamble. His face was pulled taught, almost as if he was oozing frustration and anger.

She understood that sentiment. "There is only one spot on the entire planet with the readings that could be *Vanguard*, Lieutenant. It has to be them. Here is the map of the terrain there, where do you want us to set down, and how do you want to run this?"

The Marine reviewed the surroundings and surveyed the layout for about three minutes before speaking again. "There, mark that as drop zone alpha. I will split the unit into three squads. I will take the main squad straight in from here, along this ridge until we cross over to their side. Sgt. Carmo will take the second fire-team over and flank from the left, using this other ridge to shield them until they can cut through this pass to the valley. His team will try to cut off anyone outside from *Vanguard*, and try to secure the perimeter around her. Lt. Cinquini will take the third fire-team over to the right and flush anyone there back into the valley. He will hold this high ground to offer supporting fire.

"They've been planetside long enough they're likely to be scattered. Even if they are concentrated around *Vanguard*, they only have a few blast pistols, and our armor will protect us sufficiently to get in on them," he said in explanation of his plan once he had made up his mind, still looking intently at the data.

After a moment he continued, "Worst case, I will have some heavy ammo that I will be packing with us that should be able to blow out their drives before or just as they take off if they try to escape us again." After Vasconcellos finished speaking, he turned and looked back at her.

It sounded like the best option considering the location. In keeping with their poor luck so far, the position where *Vanguard* sat was actually fairly defensible, it looked like they had chosen an open area which allowed good visibility all the way around.

"All right, pass your plan around; I am uploading these screens to the

vids in the back. Go over it with them and let me know of any adjustments you make as you continue thinking this over. We will be hitting your
drop zone in about an hour and a half. You have that long to make sure
this works," she said, trying to sound ominous in her pronouncement. The
Marine simply saluted and walked back through the hatch. She doubted
that he thought much about the way anyone talked to him. He was mad
at himself, and those in *Vanguard*, and nothing else mattered to him other
than bringing them to heel.

3–4 August

Everyone was gathered around the fire waiting when the hunters arrived. Hayes and his group had managed to bring down thirty-nine birds before the remainder took flight and circled out of reach. With their return, the camp took on a festive mood. The birds were soon cleaned and roasted. With two birds each, everyone was filled and happy. Captain slowly stood and everyone quieted.

"The ship lifts at 1450 on the dot which is about three hours after the local dawn," Captain said, looking at all of us, "see that all of your tasks are taken care of before that time." Reluctantly, people began to make their way to their beds and I followed, climbing into the spot that I had prepared by digging a shallow hole in the sand and stacking it full of coco-melon leaves. I closed my eyes and listened to the murmured conversations around me. Most were positive and supportive of the captain but some were not. Only one was truly firm in his disagreement. Long, of course, had a better solution and was walking between the small groups that were clustered around the fire and the cook pot letting every one know how he would run things. I filed that away as a project for tomorrow and drifted off to sleep.

I awoke the next morning several hours before sunrise. The fire was just a pile of glowing coals but the sky was beginning to lighten enough for me to see Mitchell, Queneau and Smith on guard duty several meters outside of the clearing. Mitchell, holding one of the heavy rifles to his chest, nodded to me as I moved off down the trail. I'm sure he thought I was headed out for a quick trip to take care of the morning necessities but I had bigger plans. Once I had taken care of those same necessities, I kept moving up the trail towards the ship and into the camp beyond. Ensign Hayes and his crew of scavengers had piled everything that they had collected at the head of the trail near the ship. I sorted through the pile and pulled out what I needed. Hayes had described everything that he had found and he had been particularly pleased with his find of one centimeter nylon cord that he wanted to use to make straps for acceleration and deceleration. I had another use for it this morning. I ran it through my hands and checked the length to make sure that there was enough for my plan. Part of a security officer's 'unofficial' duties include heading off possible troublemakers before they become a problem or nuisance to the captain or the crew. This was my purpose today.

I arrived back at camp just as the sky was truly lightening and the rest of the crew was starting to move around.

I sat with my back to a coco-melon tree and ran the cord through my hands while I waited for my prey. I didn't have long to wait, as Steve Long soon climbed out of his chosen sleeping spot and staggered out towards the surrounding brush. I let him get a few meters ahead of me and then made my way into the tree line behind him. I had planned my lesson through most of the night and had everything prepared for him. It shouldn't do any permanent damage but it should get the message across that he needed to get on Captain's side and pull his own weight.

Everything went as planned until the sound of pistol and blaster fire spun me from my observation. I left Long and rushed towards the sounds.

I slowed as I got closer to the ship. From my slight elevation I could see that Captain had a group of the crew under cover by our camp and was returning fire. Mitchell had another group, with two pistols and his captured rifle, nearer to the beach. They were doing their best with almost no cover. The attackers were between both groups and the ship. I was the only one in a position to break them out of the blockade and allow them to get back to the ship.

I could see six attackers in light attack armor directly in front of me on the trail. For some reason, they were staying close together instead of spreading out to surround the groups. They must have others out trying to flank those on the beach. None of our groups were in immediate danger. I sat for a few moments to make sure there would be no surprises. I saw movement on the far ridge behind Mitchell and others moving up the path to the beach. If we didn't move quickly, we would be surrounded and the captain and Mitchell's groups were already cut off from the ship.

I started to move towards the attackers on the trail. My pistol had a nearly full charge but it was of limited use against even the light armor that these raiders were wearing. I moved silently to follow one of the raiders who had separated himself from the main group and was headed up the trail towards the ship. I drew my knife with my left hand and closed the distance rapidly. Light attack armor is designed for planetary uses against armed resistance and it is quite effective at deflecting even armor piercing rounds.

It is not as effective against the energy weapons that the captain, Mitchell and Smith carried and it is very ineffective against an Elite Marine if you let them get in close. I grabbed the right edge of the visor ridge with my right hand and gave a sharp jerk. If you pull hard enough on this area of the helmet, it spins in the seal and disengages the coupling that holds it to the breastplate. If it is done correctly, it also breaks the occupant's neck. I jammed my knife in from the left and pulled back towards myself just in case his neck hadn't broken. I let him fall and grabbed his heavy pulse rifle. That weapon had enough power to punch though the light armor with a single shot. I flipped it up and looked at the charge meter on the under side and saw that it still had almost a half charge. He had been using it on its lowest setting to preserve power. I ratcheted the power setting up and moved back to my spot overlooking the trail. My first duty was to protect the ship.

Several other raiders had moved out in the time that I had been gone. There were only two troopers holding the center of the trail. I held my fire until I had located all of the other troopers to ensure that I didn't get myself caught in a crossfire. The group on the ridge was firing on Mitchell's position. I could make out at least four raiders in that group. The unit on the beach behind the captain jumped up and began to move around the bluff. Once they cleared the small rock face they would be directly behind the captain and his small group and they would be trapped in the crossfire. I opened fire and hit the first two troopers to move. At this range, I wasn't sure of the shots but I doubted that they would be getting up again. I saw a large raider stand briefly to look in my direction. He had his helmet off and I recognized him as the one that Roberts had nailed with the rock at A3. That answered a lot of questions. I squeezed off a shot but he was already dropping down and it went harmlessly over his head.

Maybe the waiting had gotten to everybody because two troopers on my right made a charge towards the captain's position from the front, trusting their armor to protect them long enough to get in among the crew and kill them. Only the captain's energy pistol stood between them and their objective as Mitchell was engaged with the group on the ridge and could not break cover to support the main party. Captain stood, turned slightly sideways behind a large tree as if on the dueling field, and calmly began a measured rate of fire. Each shot hit the closest attacker in the center of his faceshield. It would take several shots to burn through the transparency but the captain maintained his fire. The trooper kept running through the brush, obviously believing himself safe in his armor. *What an idiot*, I thought.

I continued my fire on the group on the beach to keep them pinned in place as any shots at the charging raiders would be blocked by the foliage. The raider's shots were going wild as they thundered down on their objective. They were firing to keep heads down rather than firing at targets. Several hit the tree that the captain was using for partial protection but his fire never wavered. When they were about twenty meters from their objective they finally came into the open so that I had a clear shot. I shifted my target and just as I depressed the firing stud Jens Fujinami lifted himself out of the underbrush and jammed his long sharpened walking stick into the joint under my targets' armpit. The improvised spear went in cleanly and lifted the target off of his feet. Unfortunately, this caused my shot to miss. The raider went down in the brush and was hidden from my vantage point. I turned my attention to the captain's target in time to see him go down ten meters short of his objective. Smoke was rising from the ruined faceplate. *Who lets someone shoot you that many times in the same spot without ducking? Idiot.* He must have been an ensign.

Fujinami's target was trying to rise as I shot him cleanly through the back of the head. I shot the two raiders that were on the trail and then I quickly shifted my fire back to the group on the beach.

Seeing that the trail was clear, the captain yelled for everyone to make their way to the ship. He led the way back up the trail as I had cleared the two remaining obstacles from the middle of the path. I saw Hayes and Ward of all people grab the fallen rifles as they stepped over the dead raiders on their way back to the ship. There was still at least one raider from the main party unaccounted for so I scanned the area as the group made their way up the hill towards me. As the captain passed below me he yelled that he intended to raise ship as soon as he had everyone on board.

"Hayes," the captain yelled. "Circle around and support Mitchell and his group until they are clear."

"Aye-aye, sir!" Hayes yelled and moved off at a trot. The idiot was grinning.

"Mackey," the captain called, tossing Ward's rifle to the large man, "go and help Mr. Fujinami to the ship."

"Aye-aye, sir." He moved off with the same speed that the ensign had shown but without any trace of a grin on his dour face.

"Chowdhury," he said, turning his attention up to me, "bring up the rear and make sure everyone is on board before you enter."

"Aye-aye, sir," I said, thinking of WO Long still lying on the ground.

"I'll be right behind you." I moved as far back up the hill as I could get and still cover all of the groups. As soon as they were near the ship I snapped off a few more rounds at the group on the beach. There were still at least three people down there including Rockhead.

I sprinted to the spot where I had left Long. "Run for the ship," I called as I saw that he was already moving in that direction.

As he sprinted down the trail, I moved back to my overwatch position. No one was visible on the beach. Mitchell and Hayes were just moving out of sight near the ship. A cluster of trees hid them momentarily and then they reemerged and entered the ship through the opened airlock. It looked like the others were already inside the ship. I watched Long sprint down the trail and follow them in. No one else was in sight so I took off to the ship myself. I moved as quietly as I could and still move quickly.

I was almost to the ship when I rounded a corner and found Rockhead and one of his friends blocking the trail. Luckily for me, they were moving towards the ship and had their backs to me. They spun quickly at my sounds and I snapped off a couple of quick shots as I dove behind the nearest tree. I didn't have a chance to aim so I just pointed at center mass and squeezed off my rounds. Rockhead was very quick and jumped almost as soon as I did, but his partner was not as good. He took a blast in the center of his chest, flew over backwards and was still. Rockhead disappeared into the brush on the opposite side of the trail from me and from the noises I guessed that he hadn't escaped totally unscathed. He wouldn't be moving very quickly wearing the rocket pack that I had seen on his back. By the time that I worked my way around to his position, he was gone. But he left me a gift of the rocket pack. I collected my bounty and moved off to the ship, carefully staying in the brush and off of the trail in case Rockhead was watching.

As I jumped through the airlock hatch I quickly checked for Long, Mitchell, Hayes and Mackey to account for each group. I knew that Mackey would not be inside if there were crewmen still outside.

"All clear, Captain. Lift ship!" I yelled, and grabbed for the nearest hand hold.

The engines rumbled almost immediately and we began our ascent.

After lift-off, Brighton had dropped our acceleration down to 1 g and started us on the last leg of our journey.

The captain soon turned over the piloting duties to Fyonna and began mapping the gravitation readings in as much detail as possible.

From my position, I could hear the conversation in the cockpit as long as there was no great disturbance near me. I shook my head as I remembered Fujinami telling me that the ensigns had taken to calling the cockpit 'Brighton's office.' That thought made me search for the diminutive exobiologist. He was not in the ship. I touched Mackey's arm and he opened his eyes and looked at me. He just shook his head to the question in my eyes.

"He was dead when I got to him," he said in a hushed voice.

Somehow, it came as more of a blow than I would have believed. I had lost friends in combat many times before. It is never easy but this was especially hard. Jens Fujinami was easily the most gentle, alive man that I had ever met. It did not feel real. The cabin was very quiet as everyone dealt with the loss in their own way.

Mapping the system seemed to take a lot of the captain's attention. He seemed to relax with a task to concentrate on. Despite the many changes and disruptions of the past few days, we quickly slipped back into our old routines.

Captain Brighton continued to come down for his shifts on the generator even though I don't think anyone expected him to. He never failed to complete his full shift.

I had just finished my shift on the generator, and came back to my spot and laid down when I heard Captain Brighton yell from the cockpit for Lt. Johnson to come forward. She made her way up the ladder. Captain Brighton yelled to prepare for zero g and soon I heard the rumbling of the thrusters stop completely.

Soon both Fyonna and Brighton came down to the cabin.

"One of the thrusters is *seriously* misaligned and we are not able to hold a stable course," he said. "We will have to go out and fix it."

The crew was very loud in blaming Warrant Long for the repairs that he made on the planet. Steve looked at me and never said a word in his defense. The captain told them to keep their comments to themselves and help to solve the problem.

"I will go out and take care of the thruster," he said calmly and quietly.

The crew, unfortunately, didn't take it that well. And I can't say that I blamed them very much.

4–5 August

"Captain, I'll go. We can't afford to lose you," said Tim O'Neill as the captain continued to don the hardsuit and prepared to go out and repair the thrusters. We hadn't been aloft very long before Captain had noticed the misalignment problem.

"No, O'Neill. You are in no condition to be outside the ship," said Captain with the air of finality.

I admired O'Neill's attitude, but he was the last one who should be going out. Of the three or four people qualified to do the job, I trusted Brighton the most. Of course, I trust Brighton without question, always. O'Neill was having trouble just holding his position next to Captain and helping him dress in the zero g. His face was pale and he was sweating and breathing hard in the cool atmosphere of the cabin. Long looked healthy enough, but I wasn't sure enough about his attitude adjustment. Besides, he needed to rewire the second generator into the ship's systems to enable us to use the airlock. The pumps and other airlock systems would not operate without power. Mackey was another possibility, but while he seemed willing and fairly capable, it was far outside his area of expertise.

"Captain, you're right that O'Neill is not up to it, but he is correct that you are invaluable to the crew. Let me take care of it. Please, sir," Mackey said pleadingly.

He could have saved his breath. Once Brighton decides on the best course of action, he has looked at all of the options and chosen the one with the greatest chance of getting the results that he is after. I listened to the conversation with half of my attention. The rest was focused on the weaponry that I had appropriated from Rockhead.

"How much time do you have EV, Bosun?" Captain asked simply. "I happen to know that you have never been out of a ship in a suit. The Marine unit from the planet may be along at any moment and we don't have the time for you to acquire the necessary skills. I appreciate, as well as any of you, the risk that I am taking, but it is the best solution. There are a few things that you are all unaware of," he said raising his voice and addressing the whole crew. "You know that there is a Marine unit of the DaGama Family operating in this system. They posed as terraformers on A3 and returned to attack us on B3 with the goal of taking *Vanguard*. If they are successful, none of us will get home. Some of you may have guessed their identity already. If they are tracking this ship, then they may be here before we can finish repairs. We must make repairs as quickly as possible."

Captain completed suiting and waited with his helmet in hand while Long made the final connections on generator two and then turned to the XO.

"Lt. Johnson, the plan and courses are recorded in the log. You will proceed as you see fit as commanding officer should anything unfortunate happen while I am out," he said, as if he were leaving his office for a few minutes to run to the store. "Keep in mind that you must not allow this ship to be boarded and *any* of us is expendable to ensure that does not happen."

"Aye-aye, sir."

With that, he gave a slight jump and set himself moving for the inner hatch. Alcaraz peddled his generator harder to produce the power to open the inner hatch. Queneau maintained a steady pace on the other generator to his left.

As the inner door closed and sealed, Lt. Johnson held onto a rail with her left hand and pressed the cycle button with her right. She continued to watch as Captain snapped on his safety line and made his way gingerly aft to examine the thruster units.

The quiet of the cabin was unbroken. Many withering looks were aimed at Long, who seemed either not to notice or not to care, though his gaze turned toward me many times. The Captain quickly became lost to view and the tenseness in the cabin ratcheted up another notch. I continued to make modifications to the rockets within the weapons pack. And I waited.

I glanced at the forward chrono. It read 1850, 4 August. I prepared for a long wait. Everyone else seemed to settle in and get comfortable as well.

The inevitable small talk started up. In whispers at first and gradually louder. Many brutal comments were leveled at Long. As always, Long seemed impervious to any criticism.

I remained silent. It served no purpose. Johnson apparently agreed because she called a halt to the comments.

Finally, I pushed off from the cabin wall very gently and stopped myself with one of the seat mountings. I retrieved my jacket from where I had tied it onto the bracket. With only one generator on environmental systems, the cabin was starting to chill. I donned my jacket and, hooking a foot through the bracket, continued to wait.

The quiet waiting resumed. It seemed like forever, but since the suit only had air for 4.5 hours, we had to be within that limit. I glanced at the chrono again, for the fourth time in the last five minutes, as I had vowed that I would not do. It read 2203. Brighton only had about seventy minutes of air left. Maybe a little less if he had been exerting himself. I tried to relax. Captain wouldn't push the limit, I told myself. Truthfully though, I wasn't convinced. I caught Fyonna Johnson's attention. She looked worried and tense. This was truly being thrown into the deep end. Once she was looking in my direction, I said, "With your permission, I would like to suit up and stand by within the hatch in case I'm needed."

"Permission granted."

I was halfway into the suit when the outer hatch started to cycle. Mackey had taken over on the second generator and he also increased his speed slightly when it closed and the pumps engaged and started to equalize the pressure in the airlock to the pressure inside the ship. By the time the hatch was ready to open, I had removed and stowed my suit.

The slight burst of air that accompanied the opening of the inner hatch was even colder than the air inside the cabin. Captain immediately began to strip off the hardsuit as Johnson and Hayes held onto either shoulder to give him some leverage.

As soon as he had his helmet off, he handed it to Williams and said, "Well, it should hold for a while. It wasn't number two after all, it was number four. One of the bolts was missing. We must have had some sort of extra vibration on lift-off. They should all be tight now."

The loudest of Long's critics seemed to look abashed that he hadn't been responsible after all. Long continued to ignore everyone.

"Ensign Mitchell, assist Mackey and Long in restoring the second generator to the environmental systems."

"Aye-aye, sir."

"Everyone else, find a spot on the 'floor,'" he said, pointing at the rear bulkhead. I'm going to give everyone five minutes to get settled and then we will burn at 1/8 g for five minutes to put some weight on everything. At that point, we will resume our 1 g burn. Let me know about any issues before that time."

A chorus of accepting affirmations followed.

I found a place on the back wall moments before the slight acceleration kicked in. This was meant to let any loose objects settle to the bulkhead without becoming missiles. It also allowed us to settle gradually instead of being slammed to the deck.

After nearly six days of being on the planet and having room to stretch and move at will, it was exceptionally hard to constrain ourselves back into our small patch of bulkhead. I noticed Tim O'Neill curl himself into a ball and slide as far into the corner as he could get. It seemed that the larger individuals were even more careful about violating the personal space of others.

In time, our normal weight returned as the Captain went to our standard acceleration. It barely registered as I fell asleep.

The next morning it was obvious that many of the crew were in bad shape. O'Neill had not moved in his corner and could barely be roused for the morning 'meal.' George, Ward and Queneau were not much better. All four were content to lay in their chosen spots and sleep. Others were making the same choice more often.

I had hoped that everybody would gain more strength from our days on the planet. The more plentiful food and the ability to move and exercise muscles had helped me a lot. However, after only about two days back aboard ship, bodies were starting to shut down again.

Captain came down the ladder with the rations. Many looked up but most were too absorbed in their own agonies to pay attention.

"I have an announcement," he said in a voice that showed more strain than I had seen in him since before the last planetfall.

"After a review of our rations and flight plan, and in view of the physical condition of many of you, I have decided that we will triple the ration for the next two meals."

This was welcome news. My strength had just started returning after our long ordeal up to B3 and now after two days on short rations, I had lost back all of my gain and then some. Most were excited about the news, but I also saw the gamble that Captain was taking. He was betting everything that *Vanguard* would be able to make the jump at the jump point. If we couldn't pull that off, there wasn't enough food left for any other options. For the first time, I saw Captain throw the dice on a single plan with no fallback position. I felt a chill that had nothing to do with the overworked environmental system.

Everyone eagerly took their share and ate. Mackey and Long were taking their shift on the generators. Everyone had shifts more often now to accommodate those who could not manage their share. The shifts had been shortened to thirty minutes because that was all that most could manage. Mackey, Long, Hayes, Roberts, Mitchell and I were probably taking the majority of the turns, because we enjoyed the best health of the group. Captain still took his usual turn but he had taken to staying more and more in the copilot's chair even when not on duty. I think that even his strength was beginning to run out. I also think he was staying there so no one would see him struggle.

The dinner meal came eventually, and the tedium of the day continued. Johnson asked me to carry the shares to the cockpit for Williams, who had the duty, and Brighton, who had not come down yet. I took the six small portions and climbed the ladder to the pilot's area.

That task done, I returned to my area in the corner farthest from the generators. I watched O'Neill holding his rations loosely, too weak to eat them. Queneau and Ward weren't much better.

"Hayes, help Queneau with her dinner. Mitchell, you help Ward. Roberts, you take Kara," I said. They all jumped up as if I had goosed them. *Ensigns*, I thought.

I moved over to help O'Neill. I broke his rations into smaller pieces and placed one on his tongue. That didn't help either.

"Johnson, could you get me some water, please," I asked.

When it arrived, I broke his rations into it and got them to dissolve finally. Working little by little, with his head in my lap, I got him to drink a little over half of the small cup. After that, I couldn't get any more down him.

I laid him down with my jacket for a pillow and returned to my corner.

"Five minutes to turnover," The captain yelled. Everyone was busy strapping in as best they could.

I tended to O'Neill and strapped myself down.

The weightlessness, movement, weight sequence of turnover is never fun. In the shape we were in now, I just hoped I wasn't wearing someone else's dinner when it was over.

The rest of the journey was uneventful until we neared the area of the JP. Most of the crew slept as much as possible. Long sat sullenly in the corner as far as he could get from me. That was fine, I didn't need him as a friend, I only needed him to stay out of the way and let Captain get us home. I sat in the corner near O'Neill and worked on my gift for Rockhead. It kept my hands busy and my mind off of other things. I was of two minds on the configuration that I wanted. I made my decision and went to work.

There was still a possibility that we would have to fight our way to the JP. If so, I had made the wrong choice.

As we neared the jump point I had Long reconnect generator two to the forward airlock and moved my bundle inside.

When Captain announced twenty seconds to jump, I climbed the ladder and vented the airlock to space. My bundle tumbled out and continued away.

5 August

Vasconcellos' jaw ached from clenching his jaw hard enough to pulverize stone. The more time passed without any sign of *Vanguard*, the more his rage built. His right shoulder and left cheek ached again as well; the shoulder from his tumble down a hill as he dove to avoid fire from that dark-haired Warner Marine, and the cheek from the second degree burn from his lack of complete success in that goal. He wasn't sure how long ago he had taken something for the pain, but whatever relief it had offered was once again dissipated.

Part of the frustration came from the looks that Commander Agostinho gave him every now and then. They were condemning looks, and to Vasconcellos' mind, they were justified. Four attempts they had made to take *Vanguard*, and four unmitigated disasters had resulted.

Three of them were his fault. Not from poor planning, but he had not managed to execute the plans, or adapt quickly enough when the situation turned to muck. *Vanguard* had slipped out of his grasp again. And the only thing he could do about it was grind his molars and fume.

A day and a half they had been trying to pick up the trail and Vasconcellos had not slept more than a quarter hour in that time. Most of the other officers were relatively fresh, which was good. Vasconcellos justified his not taking a break to himself by noting that he did not actually have a station to man on the bridge, even though he recognized it as a thin premise.

He simply could not rest until he remedied the situation and that was...

"Energy contact bearing 182 by 2.1! High readings," Sgt. Carmo sang out from his post. That revelation was followed immediately with, "Contact lost."

Vasconcellos was suddenly hovering behind the sensor station, leaning in to wrest data from the console but he was a fraction of a second too late to see anything at all.

"Helm, set course to intercept. Scan, what do you have for me?" Agostinho demanded.

"I can't tell from this range, but either a jump gate just opened in the middle of nowhere or *Vanguard* has suffered a complete engine flareout."

"Active scan, last known bearing. Let's find out which it is." Her voice sounded more resigned than anxious.

There was no mistaking the excitement in Carmo's voice. "I've got a signal return! She's still out there!"

Agostinho showed signs of new life herself now. "Well, finally some good luck for a change. They can't run away from us now!"

Quiet, happy conversations started in the bridge and soon spread throughout the ship. Relief and a certain amount of gloating were shared amongst the crew and Marines for several minutes, but eventually everyone's duties took them back to what they had been about before the discovery.

An hour of closing the distance to their goal made Carmo certain enough of his readings that he finally spoke up again.

"Ma'am, there's something wrong with the signal I'm getting back from *Vanguard*."

"What is it, Bonifacio?"

"It's … well, it's too small. Even if we were catching them exactly edge on, we should be seeing a better return than this. Maybe … um, maybe it's not *Vanguard* after all."

The sergeant's hesitation was reasonable considering the potential explosion his commander was likely to display. As it turned out, she didn't have the energy for it and simply deflated deeper into her seat.

"Well, if it's not *Vanguard*, what is it?"

"Still too far away to tell. That's actually what tipped me off. If it was a ship, we should have been able to pick it up visually by now."

"Show me what you can see," she ordered.

The main display screen switched from its default astrogation setting to present nothing but black void with occasional random pinpoints of light.

"Can you magnify?"

"This is at maximum, ma'am."

Silence returned to the bridge as most everyone tried their best to make out what they were looking at. Gradually, a minute part of the darkness turned grayish in the light of distant Antoc-B. Little by little it could be made out into a boxlike shape.

"What is that?"

"That is a GA-4, ma'am. *My* GA-4," Vasconcellos instructed with dreadful gravity.

"Veer off!" Agostinho yelled desperately.

Chowdhury had tried to set her cobbled together proximity switch to activate right at the limits of visual detection. Given the inherent difficulties in forcing components into behavior outside of their design, it is understandable that she was off by ten seconds. Given those difficulties it was a wonder that the switch worked at all, but function it did.

The switch closed and the firing circuit lit off all four of the ground to air missiles in the launch package. All four emerged with their eyes open and took only two or three tenths of a second to detect and target *Oeiras*.

Agostinho barely had time to swear.

5–8 August

Excitement reigned in the cabin as we all realized that the difficult portion of our journey had come to an end. Our jump had been successful and we had arrived in the Gerrix system. Several faces could be seen with tears running unabashedly down their cheeks. I took a deep breath and mentally pulled out my list of tasks for this section of the journey.

Looking at the battery indicator it was obvious that we had more power left over than I had believed would be the case.

"Alcaraz, we need the long-range communications reconnected."

"Ensign Roberts," I called. "Take Mr. Long and reconnect the Gravitas drive."

"Ensign Hayes, discontinue cranking the generators and reconnect all functions back to battery power. We have enough power left for all of our needs. See if you can assist Alcaraz with the LR-comm unit."

This pronouncement was met with a renewed buzzing of excitement throughout the cabin.

Both officers, as well as Alcaraz and Long, moved stiffly to these final duties as others made way for them or moved to help as needed. I had thought to include O'Neill in this last assignment but his condition had worsened and finally plummeted, as if his massive body had finally reached the end of its endurance and had shut down. I could not see him from my spot in the copilot's seat, but I was aware that he had not moved in quite some time. Bosun Mackey and the ensigns were diligent in checking all of the invalids on a regular basis, so for me it was a situation where no news was indeed good news.

Treaties had been in place for decades between the Warner Family and the Portales Combine who controlled this system but I was still unsure of our welcome. While Portales had been a firm ally of the Warner Family for many years, things had grown strained over the last decade. All of the treaties were still in force, but we had been increasingly competing for the same resources and planets and we had each gone our own way to an extent. Understanding and help might be in short supply.

At this point, since we now had our more efficient Gravitas engines running, we had the time lag down to about seven minutes. Lt. Johnson was able to negotiate our landing and conveyed enough of our situation to get a response from Medical. Dr. Ward joined us and detailed the needs of the various crewmen to the medical staff on the surface.

Finally, there was nothing left to do but pilot the ship and relax. I reached up and shut off the receiver. I needed to think without interruptions. I started to ask Lt. Johnson to go aft and leave me to my thoughts but she had earned the right to sit in the pilot's chair and I would not take it away from her, even temporarily.

I closed my eyes and began to make a list of the things that would be our most urgent needs once we were on the surface.

Someone's snoring caused me to open my eyes. I could not identify the guilty party but it did not seem to be important enough to pursue. It had seemed very close though.

Sweat was rolling down my face and soaking my uniform tunic as I sat in the copilot's seat and watched Lt. Johnson pilot *Vanguard* toward our planetfall on Gemmill, the only habitable planet in this system. The ever-present chill of the compartment had been replaced by a normal setting as the environmental systems came back online on battery power. We no longer needed the reduced levels that were all that our diminishing physical endeavors could maintain with our generator. While the additional heat was nice and would improve our comfort in the long run, our bodies had not had time to adjust to the change. It was also hoped that the full environmental unit could do something with the growing miasma created by seventeen sweating bodies in close quarters, but I was not personally very hopeful in that regard.

Our planetfall, when it came, was anti-climactic. After numerous unpowered descents, our computer controlled, anti-grav descent was ridiculously easy. I no longer trusted my own hands on the controls because of weakness and a slight uncontrollable tremor, so I instructed Lt. Johnson to take us down. Her face shone with pride and I felt guilty that she had misunderstood my reasons. I said nothing, however. She truly deserved this moment, no matter how I had arrived at the decision.

She showed that my faith was not misplaced by setting us down without the slightest bump directly in the center of the landing platform at Gemmill's main spaceport.

Medical needs came first. Captain Farel of the Portales Combine Navy was on hand with what appeared to be the entire medical detachment of the Navy Base when the hatch opened on the side of *Vanguard*. The hot, dry desert air swirled into our home and began to replace the overused atmosphere within. The heat was another challenge to our newly adapted bodies. Ricardo Smith, who was leaning on the wall near the hatch began to wobble and would have gone down if not for the quick reactions of Ensign Hayes, who was standing next to him. Hayes caught him around the shoulders and gently laid him on the deck at his feet. His body effectively blocked the exit, but such was the respect for our diminutive cook that no one complained nor moved. Dr. Ward hobbled to his side as quickly as his own injuries allowed, and the Portales medical team moved in from outside. Ward pushed their helping hands aside in one of the only exhibitions of pique that I had ever seen from our cheerful doctor. He finally allowed their help when he had satisfied himself that there was nothing life-threatening involved. It was then that I noticed O'Neill. His shrunken frame was curled up in the corner and he had not moved in the general milling toward the exit.

"Dr. Ward," I said quietly, not wanting to upset the crew. "Could you check on O'Neill?" Ward never moved. He had not heard my soft question, but Major Chowdhury had. She turned and saw the once burly electronics technician and let out a muffled moan. She moved hesitantly to his side as if afraid of what she would find. She reached down and put a finger to the side of his neck as the Portales crew lifted Smith onto an anti-grav stretcher and moved him to the waiting ambulance. Ward followed him out but no one else moved through the now open hatch. They were all waiting for Major Chowdhury's pronouncement.

"He's alive, sir. I can feel a faint pulse, but his chest is barely moving. We need to get him out of here to where help is available," Chowdhury said.

Hayes reacted most quickly, again. Finding hidden reservoirs of strength, he jumped out of the hatch and grabbed one of the medical personnel, a petite young doctor who couldn't be more than a year out of med school, and physically propelled her into the hatch. The startled medic took one look at the patient and began to work as if she were used to being thrown around. Seeing this healthy, active young medic made me reevaluate our own condition. We were truly a sorry lot indeed. Starvation was evident on some faces and the marks of prolonged depravation on all of the rest. All of these effects were magnified now that we had healthy bodies to compare ourselves to.

I felt an overwhelming, crushing sorrow. Wrapped around that sorrow was the burning fury that demanded justice for the wrongs that we had been made to endure. I looked to where Hayes had sat down on the dusty concrete and was crying uncontrollably. He was receiving several disapproving glances from the Portales personnel until Mackey, Mitchell and Alcaraz moved between them, creating a wall to shield him from prying eyes. They were all still protecting each other when they could not even protect themselves. I closed my eyes on the sudden sting that was evidently brought on by the aridness that now filled our small cabin.

I came to myself to find that I was alone on the ship except for Lt. Johnson and the petite young doctor, Dr. Aruch.

"They are all on their way, sir," Lt. Johnson said.

"Where have they gone, Lieutenant?" I asked, feeling slightly disjointed.

The doctor moved forward and bent down to where I had seated myself and said, "They will all have at least a short stay in the infirmary, Captain. There is not enough space there for them to remain, however, so the most able will be moved out to other accommodations. Captain Allen, the System Governor, has authorized everyone to stay at his home as long as necessary."

As she spoke she had taken my arm in her hand and was slowly lifting me to a standing position. Close up, I realized that she was not as young as I had previously believed. Her boundless energy made her seem much younger, though I guessed that she was still a little younger than I was myself. She was certainly younger than I felt at that moment. It was all that I could do to move myself out of the hatch and into the waiting ground vehicle. I had a curious reluctance to leave *Vanguard* unattended. I stopped just outside the hatch and ignored the gentle, insistent tug on my arm. After Johnson had stepped out into the bright sun, she reached up, released the small access panel on the side and keyed the hatch closed and secured it with the keypad.

"*Vanguard* is secured, sir," she said in a firm voice that I could not have matched.

With that, we climbed into the vehicle for the short trip to the infirmary. Somehow, I fell asleep before we arrived.

EPILOGUE—COSINA

19 August

I stood in the shadows of the huge observation blister overlooking the great Warner Space Museum. There are a multitude of exhibits and ships to be seen both within the blister and outside the panoramic windows before me. One of the exhibits is my own ship *Courser*, where I had spent twenty-three years of my life. Even she cannot pull my attention from the scene below me. *Courser* is not why I am here today. None of these lesser trivialities can even tempt me nor hold my attention. Instead, my whole attention is focused on the group that has assembled in front of me. A tall, solitary figure had occupied the view port in front of the museum's newest addition as I entered. A dark, black clad figure stood protectively behind him and slightly to one side. The Marine had rarely left his side since *Vanguard* had docked two days ago. He was quickly joined by over a dozen people. They had come in ones and twos. Some were in uniform, others in civilian clothes. One appeared to have escaped from a local hospital. He towed an IV drip bottle on a float cushion above his head and he was dressed in those ubiquitous hospital garments that are usually referred to as 'scrubs' for some unknown reason, but one pant leg was cut away to make room for the heavy bandages on his leg.

Regardless of their mode of dress, all seemed tired and haggard. Most sported large dark circles under their eyes like bruises.

I had come to know each of these men and women in the course of my duties as chairman of the committee investigating what was coming to be called the "The *Pathfinder* Mutiny." I don't personally believe this to be a mutiny at all, but rather a carefully planned and executed theft of an extremely valuable asset. Captain Brighton was correct to refer to it as piracy. He never used the word mutiny, even if it was put forth by others.

Nearly twenty years had passed since the last time that I had the opportunity to have then Ensign Brighton under my command. However, I was still very conversant with his progress and career. I had carefully watched and tried to guide his career for several years, and now I was both saddened and elated that he had finally come into his own as an officer. He had always had the skill and knowledge to become an exceptional commander but he never fully trusted his instincts and consequently rarely inspired the loyalty of the officers under his command. He spent so much time overthinking his decisions that they had an air of stiffness when they came out. This same stiffness was evident in his relations with his officers and crew as he never seemed to know the proper way to relate to them.

The assembled group was much different in appearance than the group that had jumped back into the Sol system on 17 August. The last few days had finally begun to erase the effects of their hardship that even their short respite on Gerrix had not. Maybe they had not truly believed they were done with their ordeal until they were completely home.

Whatever the reasons, they were truly on the mend now.

I stood in the background and watched the impromptu reunion. For a long moment, no one said anything. It was as if being in familiar company was enough for all of them.

Since their return, they had been the subjects of all kinds of rumor, speculation and even several feature articles in the faxes once the story had gotten out. They had been run ragged with requests for information, both from official sources and newsmongers of various types and reputations.

Brighton had not helped the situation by walking directly through the customs officials and presenting himself at WSN headquarters and demanding his right to a full court of inquiry into the loss of WSN *Pathfinder* and, despite being weak and trembling from stress and fatigue, had stood there in front of Admiral Graves until the court was appointed, despite the Admiral's rather pointed 'recommendations' that he let the matter sit for a few days until he could recover his strength.

The days following their arrival had been consumed by the statements and questioning of the survivors of this ordeal.

Admiral Graves had been very pale as he read the committee's final report—which had been completed in record time- on the events that transpired between the theft of *Pathfinder* and the return of our valiant crewmen.

After approving all of the recommendations of the court, his only comment had been, "Blazes, Conrad, that has to be the single greatest feat of astrogation that I have ever heard of. He deserves much more than you have recommended here," indicating the official recommendations of the court.

"Nevertheless, that is all that he has asked for and all that he will accept," I had responded, secretly agreeing with the CNO.

My thoughts cleared as Captain Brighton began to speak. At first he continued to stare out the viewport while a crew of workmen busily attached securing cables to *Vanguard* and moved her into a position of honor between my own *Courser* and Admiral Overman's *Fury*. *Vanguard* was to become one of only three ship's names to be perpetually commissioned in WSN service so that they would always retain this pinnacle of honor that they had achieved. *Courser*, *Fury*, and now *Vanguard* would forever be listed as active duty ships of the line.

I took a few steps forward so that I could hear the words that he was speaking to his crew.

"…so with your new rank, Lt. Commander Johnson, you will take command of the destroyer *Yargus* and accompany me back to Antoc. I have convinced Fleet that *Pathfinder* has no way to leave that system quickly and if we can respond before they make repairs, then we will be able to recover the ship."

"Will you be returning on another ship?" she asked with a note of sorrow in her voice.

"I have been given overall command of the squadron consisting of *Yargus* and the light cruiser *Dagger*," he replied, not quite answering the question. I knew that he had argued for several hours trying to convince Admiral Graves to allow him to have *Yargus* as his flagship so he wouldn't be separated from his crew. Apparently, he was still not ready to surrender his fight. That was all right. He just may find that he had won this round.

"Due to the nature of your last experience in the Antoc system, you are all due as much leave time as you feel necessary before returning to duty," he said, turning to address the assembled group at last.

"We will, however, depart at 1900 hours tomorrow. Any who wish to accompany us back there to see justice done will need to report for duty aboard *Yargus* by 1600. I have the permission of the Board to accept any of you into the crew who reports aboard by that time. I won't ask anyone to come with us. You have all done enough. I am very proud of all of you." This last was delivered almost as a whisper.

The hospital case stepped forward and I was surprised to see tears rolling unashamedly down his cheeks. "I won't be able to come, sir. I'd give anything to sail with you again, but I won't be released in time and well…" he looked back at the tall blonde woman on his arm and shrugged. "You understand, don't you, sir?"

"Indeed, Doctor. You have other duties to attend to. We will take care of everything else for you."

The doctor stood as straight as possible considering his bandages and delivered his best parade ground salute. "Thank you, sir," he said simply, but I could tell that he was referring to more than just these words.

"Beg pardon, sir, but would it be possible to accompany you on *Dagger*? Meaning no disrespect to Commander Johnson," asked a large, stocky man in the front.

"That won't be necessary, Master Chief Mackey," I said, finally emerging from the background where I had been unnoticed by either captain or crew.

"There have been some changes in the plans since I last had the opportunity to speak with your captain." I turned to look at the man in question. "If I may?" I asked motioning to the crew at large.

"By all means, sir."

"Captain Andrus and several of his crew have taken ill aboard *Dagger* and her XO is a Lieutenant not yet ready for command. Consequently, we have had to shuffle commands among the officers available in-system in order to make our departure schedule. As soon as her new captain reports aboard, *Dagger* will be ready to get underway."

"With respect, sir, I don't see how that will change the situation," Mackey replied with a slightly confused scowl on his dour face.

"Oh yes, I forgot to mention that, didn't I?" I said with a grin. "Lt. Commander Johnson has been assigned as *Dagger*'s new captain and she will be Commodore Brighton's new flag captain. Lieutenant Ramirez will be promoted to command *Yargus*. Any officers or crewmen that wish to accompany Commodore Brighton will need to report aboard *Dagger* before the appointed time. Major Chowdhury, if you are willing to waive your leave time, you are requested to report aboard to take command of the Marine contingent on *Dagger*. Does that clear things up for you, Master Chief?"

I turned and walked away amid the joyous shouts and cheers of a happy crew.